THE
JENNIFER
MORGUE

CHARLES
STROSS

orbit

www.orbitbooks.net

ORBIT

First published in the United States in 2006 by Golden Gryphon Press
First published in Great Britain in 2007 by Orbit
This paperback edition published in 2013 by Orbit

3 5 7 9 11 12 10 8 6 4 2

A CIP catalogue record for this book
is available from the British Library.

ISBN 978-0-356-50238-0

Typeset in Garamond by M Rules
Printed and bound by Clays Ltd, St Ives plc

Papers used by Orbit are from well-managed forests
and other responsible sources.

MIX
Paper from
responsible sources
FSC
www.fsc.org   FSC® C104740

Orbit
An imprint of
Little, Brown Book Group
100 Victoria Embankment
London EC4Y 0DY

An Hachette UK Company
www.hachette.co.uk

www.orbitbooks.net

For Andrew, Lorna, and James

ACKNOWLEDGMENTS

No book gets written in a vacuum, and this one is no exception. I'd like to thank my editors, Marty Halpern at Golden Gryphon and Ginjer Buchanan at Ace, and my agent Caitlin Blasdell, all of whom helped make this book possible. I'd also like to thank my hundreds of test readers — in no particular order: Simon Bradshaw, Dan Ritter, Nicholas Whyte, Elizabeth Bear, Brooks Moses, Mike Scott, Jack Foy, Luna Black, Harry Payne, Andreas Black, Marcus Rowland, Ken MacLeod, Peter Hollo, Andrew Wilson, Stefan Pearson, Gavin Inglis, Jack Deighton, John Scalzi, Anthony Quirke, Jane McKie, Hannu Rajaniemi, Andrew Ferguson, Martin Page, Robert Sneddon, and Steve Stirling. I'd also like to thank Hugh Hancock, who valiantly helped me MST3K my way through the Bond canon.

CONTENTS

CONTENTS

PROLOGUE:

JENNIFER

August 25, 1975
165°W, 30°N

The guys from the "A" and "B" crews have been sitting on their collective ass for five weeks, out in the middle of nowhere. They're not alone; there's the ship's crew, from the captain on down to the lowliest assistant cook, and the CIA spooks. But the other guys have at least got something to do. The ship's crew has a vessel to run: an unholy huge behemoth, 66,000 tons of deep-ocean exploratory mining ship, 400 million bucks and seven years in the building. The CIA dudes are keeping a wary eye on the Russian trawler that's stooging around on the horizon. And as for the Texan wildcat drilling guys, for the past couple of days they've been working ceaselessly on the stabilized platform, bolting one sixty-foot steel pipe after another onto the top of the drill string and lowering it into the depths of the Pacific Ocean. But the "A" and "B" teams have been sitting on their hands for weeks with nothing to do but oil and service the enormous mechanism floating in the moon pool at the heart of the ship, then twiddle their thumbs nervously for eighty hours as the drill lowers it into the crushing darkness.

And now that Clementine is nearly on target, there's a storm coming.

"Fucking weather," complains Milgram.

"Language." Duke is a tight-ass. "How bad can it get?"

Milgram brandishes his paper, the latest chart to come out of the weather office on C deck where Stan and Gilmer hunch over their green-glowing radar displays and the telex from San Diego. "Force nine predicted within forty-eight hours, probability sixty percent and rising. We can't take that, Duke. We go over force six, the impellers can't keep us on station. We'll lose the string."

The kid, Steve, crowds close. "Anyone told Spook City yet?" The guys from Langley hang out in a trailer on E deck with a locked vault-type door. Everyone calls it Spook City.

"Nah." Duke doesn't sound too concerned. "Firstly, it hasn't happened yet. Secondly, we're only forty fathoms up from zero." He snaps his fingers at the curious heads that have turned in his direction from their camera stations: "Look to it, *guys!* We've got a job to do!"

Clementine – the vast, submersible grab at the end of the drill string – weighs around 3,000 tons and is more than 200 feet long. It's a huge steel derrick, painted gray to resist the corrosive effects of miles of seawater. At a distance it resembles a skeletal lobster, because of the five steel legs protruding from either flank. Or maybe it's more like a giant mantrap, lowered into the icy stillness of Davy Jones's locker to grab whatever it can from the sea floor.

Duke runs the engineering office from his throne in the center of the room. One wall is covered in instruments; the other is a long stretch of windows overlooking the moon pool at the heart of the ship. A door at one side of the window wall provides access to a steel-mesh catwalk fifty feet above the pool.

Here in the office the noise of the hydraulic stabilizers

isn't quite deafening; there's a loud mechanical whine and a vibration they feel through the soles of their boots, but the skull-rattling throbbing is damped to a survivable level. The drilling tower above their heads lowers the endless string of pipes into the center of the pool at a steady six feet per minute, day in and day out. Steve tries not to look out the window at the pipes because the effect is hypnotic: they've been sliding smoothly into the depths for many hours now, lowering the grab toward the bottom of the ocean.

The ship is much bigger than the grab that dangles beneath it on the end of three miles of steel pipe, but it's at the grab's mercy. Three miles of pipe makes for a prodigious pendulum, and as the grab sinks slowly through the deep-ocean currents, the ship has to maneuver frantically to stay on top of it in the six-foot swells. Exotic domes on top of the vessel's bridge suck down transmissions from the Navy's *Transit* positioning satellites, feeding them to the automatic Station Keeping System that controls the ship's bow and stern thrusters, and the cylindrical surge compensators that the derrick rests on. Like a swan, it looks peaceful on the surface but under the waterline there's a hive of frantic activity. Everything – the entire 400-megabuck investment, ten years of Company black operations – depends on what happens in the next few hours. When they reach the bottom.

Steve turns back to his TV screen. It's another miracle of technology. The barge has cameras and floodlights, vacuum tubes designed to function in the abyssal depths. But his camera is flaking out, static hash marching up the screen in periodic waves: the pressure, tons per square inch, is damaging the waterproof cables that carry power and signal. "This is shit," he complains. "We're never going to spot it – if . . ."

He trails off. Good-time Norm at the next desk is standing up, pointing at something on his screen. There's a whoop from the other side of the room. He squints at his screen and between the lines of static he sees a rectilinear outline. "Holy—"

The public address system crackles overhead: "Clementine crew. K-129 on screens two and five, range approximately fifty feet, bearing two-two-five. Standby, fine thruster control."

It's official – they've found what they're looking for.

The atmosphere in Spook City is tense but triumphant. "We're there," announces Cooper. He smirks at the hatchet-faced Brit in the crumpled suit, who is smoking an unfiltered Camel in clear violation of shipboard fire regulations. "We did it!"

"We'll see," mutters the Brit. He stubs the cigarette out and shakes his head. "Getting there is only half the struggle."

Nettled, Murph glares at him. "What's your problem?" he demands.

"You're messing with something below 1,000 meters, in strict contravention of Article Four," says the Brit. "I'm here as a neutral observer in accordance with Section Two—"

"Fuck you and your neutral status, you're just sore because you guys don't have the balls to stand on your waiver rights—"

Cooper gets between them before things can escalate again. "Cool it. Murph, how about checking with the bridge again to see if there's been any sign of the commies taking an interest? They'll twig when they see we've stopped lowering the string. James—" He pauses. Grimaces slightly. The Brit's alias is transparent and, to a Company man, borderline insulting: Cooper wonders, not for the first time, *Why the fuck does he call himself that?* "—let's go take a hike down to the moon pool and see what they've found."

"Suits me." The Brit stands up, unfolding like a stick-insect inside his badly fitting gray suit. His cheek twitches but his expression stays frozen. "After you."

They leave the office and Cooper locks the door behind him. The Hughes GMDI ship may be enormous — it's bigger than a Marine Corps assault carrier, larger than an Iowa-class battleship — but its companionways and corridors are a cramped, gray maze, punctuated by color-coded pipes and ducts conveniently located at shin-scraping and head-banging height. It doesn't roll in the swells but it rocks, weirdly, held solidly on station by the SKS thrusters (a new technology that accounts for a goodly chunk of the cost of the ship). Down six flights of steps there's another passage and a bulkhead: then Cooper sees the dogged-back hatch leading out into the moon pool at the level of the fifty-foot catwalk. As usual it takes his breath away. The moon pool is just under 200 feet long and 75 feet wide, a stillness of black water surrounded by the gantries and cranes required for servicing the barge. The giant docking legs are fully extended below the waterline at either end of the pool. The drill string pierces the heart of the chamber like a black steel spear tying it to the ocean floor. The automatic roughneck and the string handling systems have fallen silent, the deafening clatter and roar of the drill system shut down now that the grab has reached its target. Soon, if all goes well, the derrick above them will begin hauling up the string, laboriously unbolting the hundreds of pipe segments and stacking them on the deck of the ship, until finally Clementine — also known as the HMB-1 "mining barge" — rumbles to the surface of the pool in a flurry of cold water, clutching its treasure beneath it. But for now the moon pool is a peaceful haven, its surface marred only by shallow, oily ripples.

The engineering office is a hive of activity in contrast to the view outside the windows, and nobody notices Cooper and the British spook as they slip inside and look over the operations controller's shoulder at his screens. "Left ten, up six," someone calls. "Looks like a hatch," says someone else.

Strange gray outlines swim on the screen. "Get me a bit more light on that . . ."

Everyone falls silent for a while. "That's not good," says one of the engineers, a wiry guy from New Mexico who Cooper vaguely remembers is called Norm. The big TV screen in the middle is showing a flat surface emerging from a gray morass of abyssal mud. A rectangular opening with rounded edges gapes in it – a hatch? – and there's something white protruding from a cylinder lying across it. The cylinder looks like a sleeve. Suddenly Cooper realizes what he's looking at: an open hatch in the sail of a submarine, the skeletonized remains of a sailor lying half-in and half-out of it.

"Poor bastards probably tried to swim for it when they realized the torpedo room was flooded," says a voice from the back of the room. Cooper looks around. It's Davis, somehow still managing to look like a Navy officer even though he's wearing a civilian suit. "That's probably what saved the pressure hull – the escape hatch was already open and the boat was fully flooded before it passed through its crush depth."

Cooper shivers, staring at the screen. *Consider Phlebas,* he thinks, wracking his brain for the rest of the poem.

"Okay, so what about the impact damage?" That's Duke, typically businesslike: "I need to know if we can make this work."

More activity. Camera viewpoints swivel crazily, taking in the length of the Golf-II-class submarine. The water at this depth is mostly clear and the barge floodlights illuminate the wreck mercilessly, from the blown hatch in the sail to the great gash in the side of the torpedo room. The submarine lies on its side as if resting, and there's little obvious damage to Cooper's untrained eye. A bigger hatch gapes open in front of the sail. "What's that?" he asks, pointing.

The kid, Steve, follows his finger. "Looks like the number

two missile tube is open," he says. The Golf-II class is a boomer, a ballistic missile submarine – an early one, diesel-electric. It had carried only three nuclear missiles, and had to surface before firing. "Hope they didn't roll while they were sinking: if they lost the bird it could have landed anywhere."

"Anywhere—" Cooper blinks.

"Okay, let's get her lined up!" hollers Duke, evidently completing his assessment of the situation. "We've got bad weather coming, so let's haul!"

For the next half-hour the control room is a madhouse, engineers and dive-control officers hunched over their consoles and mumbling into microphones. Nobody's ever done this before – maneuvered a 3,000-ton grab into position above a sunken submarine three miles below the surface, with a storm coming. The sailors on the Soviet spy trawler on the horizon probably have their controllers back in Moscow convinced that they've been drinking the antifreeze again, with their tale of exotic, capitalist hypertechnology stealing their sunken boomer.

The tension in the control room is rising. Cooper watches over Steve's shoulder as the kid twiddles his joystick, demonstrating an occult ability to swing cameras to bear on the huge mechanical grabs, allowing their operators to extend them and position them close to the hull. Finally it's time. "Stand by to blow pressure cylinders," Duke announces. "Blow them now."

Ten pressure cylinders bolted to the grab vent silvery streams of bubbles: pistons slide home, propelled by a three-mile column of seawater, drawing the huge clamps tight around the hull of the submarine. They bite into the mud, stirring up a gray cloud that obscures everything for a while. Gauges slowly rotate, showing the position of the jaws. "Okay on even two through six, odd one through seven. Got a partial on nine and eight, nothing on ten."

The atmosphere is electric. Seven clamps have locked tight around the hull of the submarine: two are loose and one appears to have failed. Duke looks at Cooper. "Your call."

"Can you lift it?" asks Cooper.

"I think so." Duke's face is somber. "We'll see once we've got it off the mud."

"Let's check upstairs," Cooper suggests, and Duke nods. The captain can say "yes" or "no" and make it stick – it's his ship they'll be endangering if they make a wrong call.

Five minutes later they've got their answer. "Do it," says the skipper, in a tone that brooks no argument. "It's what we're here for." He's on the bridge because the impending bad weather and the proximity of other ships – a second Russian trawler has just shown up – demands his presence, but there's no mistaking his urgency.

"Okay, you heard the man."

Five minutes later a faint vibration shakes the surface of the moon pool. Clementine has blown its ballast, scattering a thousand tons of lead shot across the sea floor around the submarine. The cameras show nothing but a gray haze for a while. Then the drill string visible through the control room window begins to move, slowly inching upward. "Thrusters to full," Duke snaps. The string begins to retract faster and faster, dripping water as it rises from the icy depths. "Give me a strain gauge report."

The strain gauges on the giant grabs are reading green across the board: each arm is supporting nearly 500 tons of submarine, not to mention the water it contains. There's a loud mechanical whine from outside, and a sinking feeling, and the vibration Cooper can feel through the soles of his Oxford brogues has increased alarmingly – the *Explorer's* drill crew is running the machines at full power now that the grab has increased in weight. The ship, gaining thousands of tons in a matter of seconds, squats deeper in the Pacific swell.

"Satisfied now?" asks Cooper, turning to grin at the Brit, who for his part looks as if he's waiting for something, staring at one screen intently.

"Well?"

"We've got a little time to go," says the hatchet-faced foreigner.

"A little . . .?"

"Until we learn whether or not you've gotten away with it."

"What are you smoking, man? Of course we've gotten away with it!" Murph has materialized from the upper decks like a Boston-Irish ghost, taking out his low-level resentment on the Brit (who is sufficiently public-school English to make a suitable whipping boy for Bloody Sunday, not to mention being a government employee to boot). "Look! Submarine! Submersible grab! Coming up at six feet per minute! After the break, film at eleven!" His tone is scathing. "What do you think the commies are going to do to stop us, start World War Three? They don't even goddamn know what we're doing down here – they don't even know where their sub went down to within 200 miles!"

"It's not the commies I'm worried about," says the Brit. He glances at Cooper. "How about *you?*"

Cooper shakes his head reluctantly. "I still think we're going to make it. The sub's intact, undamaged, and we've got it—"

"Oh shit," says Steve.

He points the central camera in the grab's navigation cluster down at the sea floor, a vast gray-brown expanse stirred into slow whorls of foggy motion by the dropping of the ballast and the departure of the submarine. It should be slowly settling back into bland desert-dunes of mud by now. But something's moving down there, writhing against the current with unnatural speed.

Cooper stares at the screen. "What's that?"

"May I remind you of Article Four of the treaty?" says the Brit. "No establishment of permanent or temporary structures below a depth of one kilometer beneath mean sea level, on pain of termination. No removal of structures from the abyssal plain, on pain of ditto. We're trespassing: legally they can do as they please."

"But we're only picking up the trash——"

"They may not see it that way."

Fine fronds, a darker shade against the gray, are rising from the muddy haze not far from the last resting place of the K-129. The fronds ripple and waver like giant kelp, but are thicker and more purposeful. They bring to mind the blind, questing trunk of an elephant exploring the interior of a puzzle box. There's something disturbing about the way they squirt from vents in the sea floor, rising in pulses, as if they're more liquid than solid.

"Damn," Cooper says softly. He punches his open left hand. "Damn!"

"Language," chides Duke. "Barry, how fast can we crank this rig? Steve, see if you can get a fix on those things. I want to peg their ascent rate."

Barry shakes his head emphatically. "The drill platform can't take any more, boss. We're up to force four outside already, and we're carrying too much weight. We can maybe go up to ten feet per minute, but if we try to go much above that we risk shearing the string and losing Clementine."

Cooper shudders. The grab will still surface if the drill string breaks, but it could broach just about anywhere. And *anywhere* includes right under the ship's keel, which is not built to survive being rammed by 3,000 tons of metal hurtling out of the depths at twenty knots.

"We can't risk it," Duke decides. "Keep hauling at current ascent rate."

They watch in silence for the next hour as the grab rises toward the surface, its precious, stolen cargo still intact in its arms.

The questing fronds surge up from the depths, growing toward the lens of the under-slung camera as the engineers and spooks watch anxiously. The grab is already 400 feet above the sea floor, but instead of a flat muddy desert below, the abyssal plain has sprouted an angry forest of grasping tentacles. They're extending fast, reaching toward the stolen submarine above them.

"Hold steady," says Duke. "Damn, I said hold steady!"

The ship shudders, and the vibration in the deck has risen to a tooth-rattling grumble and a shriek of over-stressed metal. The air in the control room stinks of hot oil. Up on the drilling deck the wildcats are shearing bolt-heads and throwing sixty-foot pipe segments on the stack rather than taking time to position them — a sure sign of desperation, for the pipe segments are machined from a special alloy at a cost of $60,000 apiece. They're hauling in the drill string almost twice as fast as they paid it out, and the moon pool is foaming and bubbling, a steady cascade of water dropping from the chilly metal tubes to rain back down onto its surface. But it's anyone's guess whether they'll get the grab up to the surface before the questing tentacles catch it.

"Article Four," the Brit says tensely.

"Bastard." Cooper glares at the screen. "It's ours."

"They appear to disagree. Want to argue with them?"

"A couple of depth charges . . ." Cooper stares at the drill string longingly.

"They'd fuck you, boy," the other man says harshly. "Don't think it hasn't been thought of. There are enough methane hydrates down in that mud to burp the granddaddy of all gas bubbles under our keel and drag us down like a gnat in a toad's mouth."

"I know that." Cooper shakes his head. *So much work!* It's outrageous, an insult to the senses, like watching a moon shot explode on the launch pad. "But. Those bastards." He punches his palm again. "It should be ours!"

"We've had dealings with them before that didn't go so badly. Witch's Hole, the treaty zone at Dunwich. You could have asked us." The British agent crosses his arms tensely. "You could have asked your Office of Naval Intelligence, too. But no, you had to go and get creative."

"The fuck. You'd just have told us not to bother. This way——"

"This way you learn your own lesson."

"The fuck."

The grab was 3,000 feet below sea level and still rising when the tentacles finally caught up with it.

The rest, as they say, is history.

IF YOU WORK FOR THE LAUNDRY LONG ENOUGH, eventually you get used to the petty insults, the paper clip audits, the disgusting canteen coffee, and the endless, unavoidable bureaucracy. Your aesthetic senses become dulled, and you go blind to the decaying pea-green paint and the vomit-beige fabric partitions between office cubicles. But the big indignities never fail to surprise, and they're the ones that can get you killed.

I've been working for the Laundry for about five years now, and periodically I become blasé in my cynicism, sure that I've seen it all – which is usually the signal for them to throw something at me that's degrading, humiliating, or dangerous – if not all three at once.

"You want me to drive a *what?*" I squeak at the woman behind the car rental desk.

"Sir, your ticket has been issued by your employer, it says here und here—" She's a brunette: tall, thin, helpful, and very German in that schoolmarmish way that makes you instinctively check to see if your fly's undone. "The, ah, Smart Fortwo coupé. With the, the kompressor. It is a perfectly good car. Unless you would like for the upgrade to pay?"

Upgrade. To a Mercedes S190, for, oh, about two hundred

euros a day. An absolute no-brainer – if it wasn't at my own expense.

"How do I get to Darmstadt from here?" I ask, trying to salvage the situation. "Preferably alive?" (Bloody Facilities. Bloody budget airlines that never fly where you want to go. Bloody weather. Bloody liaison meetings in Germany. Bloody "cheapest hire" policy.)

She menaces me with her perfect dentistry again. "If it was me I'd take the ICE train. But your ticket—" she points at it helpfully "—is non-refundable. Now please to face the camera for the biometrics?"

Fifteen minutes later I'm hunched over the steering wheel of a two-seater that looks like something you'd find in your corn flakes packet. The Smart is insanely cute and compact, does about seventy miles to a gallon, and is the ideal second car for nipping about town but I'm not nipping about town. I'm going flat out at maybe a hundred and fifty kilometers per hour on the autobahn while some joker is shooting at me from behind with a cannon that fires Porsches and Mercedes. Meanwhile, I'm stuck driving something that handles like a turbocharged baby buggy. I've got my fog lights on in a vain attempt to deter the other road users from turning me into a hood ornament, but the jet wash every time another executive panzer overtakes me keeps threatening to roll me right over onto my roof. And that's before you factor in the deranged Serbian truck drivers driven mad with joy by exposure to a motorway that hasn't been cluster-bombed and then resurfaced by the lowest bidder.

In between moments of blood-curdling terror I spend my time swearing under my breath. This is all Angleton's fault. He's the one who sent me to this stupid joint-liaison committee meeting, so he bears the brunt of it. His hypothetical and distinctly mythological ancestry is followed in descending order by the stupid weather, Mo's stupid training schedule, and then anything else that I can think of to curse. It keeps the tiny corner of my mind that isn't focused on my immediate survival occupied — and that's a very tiny corner, because when you're sentenced to drive a Smart car on a road where everything else has a speed best described by its mach number, you tend to pay attention.

There's an unexpected lull in the traffic about two-thirds of the way to Darmstadt, and I make the mistake of breathing a sigh of relief. The respite is short-lived. One moment I'm driving along a seemingly empty road, bouncing from side to side on the Smart's town-car suspension as the hairdryer-sized engine howls its guts out beneath my buttocks, and the next instant the dashboard in front of me lights up like a flashbulb.

I twitch spasmodically, jerking my head up so hard I nearly dent the thin plastic roof. Behind me the eyes of Hell are open, two blinding beacons like the landing lights on an off-course 747. Whoever they are, they're standing on their brakes so hard they must be smoking. There's a roar, and then a squat, red Audi sports coupe pulls out and squeezes past my flank close enough to touch, its blonde female driver gesticulating angrily at me. At least I think she's blonde and female. It's hard to tell because everything is gray, my heart is trying to exit through my rib cage, and I'm frantically wrestling with the steering wheel to keep the roller skate from toppling over. A fraction of a second later she's gone, pulling back into the slow lane ahead of me to light off her afterburners. I swear I see red sparks shooting out of her two huge exhaust tubes as she vanishes into the distance, taking about ten years of my life with her.

"You stupid fucking bitch!" I yell, thumping the steering wheel until the Smart wobbles alarmingly and, heart in mouth, I tentatively lift off the accelerator and let my speed drift back down to a mere 140 or so. "Stupid fucking Audi-driving Barbie girl, brains of a chocolate mousse——"

I spot a road sign saying DARMSTADT 20KM just as something – a low-flying *Luftwaffe* Starfighter, maybe – makes a strafing run on my left. Ten infinitely long minutes later I arrive at the slip road for Darmstadt sandwiched between two eighteen-wheelers, my buttocks soaking in a puddle of cold sweat and all my hair standing on end. Next time, I resolve, I'm going to take the train and damn the expense.

Darmstadt is one of those German towns that, having been landscaped by Allied heavy bombers, rezoned by the Red Army, and rebuilt by the Marshall Plan, demonstrates perfectly that (a) sometimes it's better to lose a war than to win one, and (b) some of the worst crimes against humanity are committed by architecture students. These days what's left of the '50s austerity concrete has a rusticated air and a patina of moss, and the worst excesses of '60s Neo-Brutalism have been replaced by glass and brightly painted steel that clashes horribly with what's left of the old Rhenish ginger-bread. It could be Anytown EU, more modern and less decrepit than its US equivalent, but somehow it looks bash-ful and self-effacing. The one luxury Facilities did pay for is an in-car navigation system (the better to stop me wasting Laundry time by getting lost en route), so once I get off the Death Race track I drive on autopilot, sweaty and limp with animalistic relief at having survived. And then I find myself in a hotel parking bay between a Toyota and a bright red Audi TT.

"The fuck." I thump the steering wheel again, more angry than terrified now that I'm not in imminent danger of death. I peer at it – yup, it's the same model car, and the same color. I can't be certain it's the same one (my nemesis was going so fast I couldn't read her number plate because of the Doppler shift) but I wouldn't bet against it: it's a small world. I shake my head and squeeze out of the Smart, pick up my bags, and slouch towards reception.

Once you've seen one international hotel, you've seen them all. The romance of travel tends to fade fast after the first time you find yourself stranded at an airport with a suitcase full of dirty underwear two hours after the last train left. Ditto the luxury of the business hotel experience on your fourth overseas meeting of the month. I check in as fast and as painlessly as possible (aided by another of those frighteningly helpful German babes, albeit this time with slightly worse English) then beam myself up to the sixth floor of the Ramada Treff Page Hotel. Then I hunt through the endless and slightly claustrophobic maze of air-conditioned corridors until I find my room.

I dump my duffle bag, grab my toilet kit and a change of clothes, and duck into the bathroom to wash away the stink of terror. In the mirror, my reflection winks at me and points at a new white hair until I menace him with a tube of toothpaste. I'm only twenty-eight: I'm too young to die and too old to drive fast.

I blame Angleton. This is all his fault. He set me on this path exactly two days after the board approved my promotion to SSO, which is about the lowest grade to carry any significant managerial responsibilities. "Bob," he said, fixing me with a terrifyingly avuncular smile, "I think it's about time you got out of the office a bit more. Saw the world, got to grips with the more mundane aspects of the business, that sort of thing. So you can start by standing in for Andy Newstrom on a couple of low-priority, joint-liaison meetings. What do you say?"

"Great," I said enthusiastically. "Where do I start?"

Well okay, I should really blame myself, but Angleton's a more convenient target — he's very hard to say "no" to, and more importantly, he's eight hundred miles away. It's easier to blame him than to kick the back of my own head.

Back in the bedroom I pull my tablet PC out of my luggage and plug it in, jack it into the broadband socket, poke my way through the tedious pay-to-register website, and bring up the VPN connection back to the office. Then I download an active ward and leave it running as a screen saver. It looks like a weird geometric pattern endlessly morphing and cycling through a color palette until it ends up in a retina-eating stereoisogram, and it's perfectly safe to sneak a brief glance at it, but if an intruder looks at it for too long it'll Pwnz0r their brain. I drape a pair of sweaty boxer shorts across it before I go out, just in case room service calls. When it comes to detecting burglars, hairs glued to door frames are passé.

Down at the concierge desk I check for messages. "Letter for Herr Howard? Please to sign here." I spot the inevitable Starbucks stand in a corner so I amble over to it, inspecting the envelope as I go. It's made of expensive cream paper, very thick and heavy, and when I stare at it closely I see fine gold threads woven into it. They've used an italic font and a laser printer to address it, which cheapens the effect. I slit it open with my Swiss Army cybertool as I wait for one of the overworked Turkish baristas to get round to serving me. The card inside is equally heavy, but hand-written:

Bob,

  Meet me in the Laguna Bar at 6 p.m. or as soon as you arrive, if later.

  Ramona

"Um," I mutter. *What the fuck?*

I'm here to take part in the monthly joint-liaison meeting with our EU partner agencies. It's held under the auspices of the EU Joint Intergovernmental Framework on Cosmological Incursions which is governed by the Common Defense provisions of the Second Treaty of Nice. (You haven't heard of this particular EU treaty because it's secret by mutual agreement, none of the signatories wanting to start a mass panic.) Despite the classified nature of the event it's really pretty boring: we're here to swap departmental gossip about our mutual areas of interest and what's been going on lately, update each other on new procedural measures and paperwork hoops we need to jump through to requisition useful information from our respective front-desk operations, and generally make nice. With only a decade to go until the omega conjunction – the period of greatest risk during NIGHTMARE GREEN, when the stars are right – everyone in Europe is busy oiling the gears and wheels of our occult defense machinery. Nobody wants their neighbors to succumb to a flux of green, gibbering brain-eaters, after all: it tends to lower real estate values. After the meeting I'm supposed to take the minutes home and brief Angleton, Boris, Rutherford, and anyone else in my reporting chain, then circulate the minutes to other departments. *Sic transit gloria spook.*

Anyway, I'm expecting an agenda and directions to a meeting room, not a bar invite from a mysterious Ramona. I rack my brains: *Who do I know who's called Ramona? Wasn't there a song . . .? Joey Ramone . . . no.* I fold the envelope and stuff it in my back pocket. *Sounds like a porn spammer's alias.* I break out of the slowly shuffling coffee queue just in time to annoy the furiously mustachioed counter dude. *Where the hell is the Laguna Bar?*

I spot a number of dark, glass-partitioned areas clustered around the atrium in front of the check-in desk. They're the usual hotel squeeze joints, overpriced restaurants, and 24-hour shops selling whatever you forgot to pack yesterday morning at four o'dark. I hunt around until I spot the word *LAGUNA* picked out in teensy gold Fraktur Gothic to one side of a darkened doorway, in an evident attempt to confuse the unwary.

I peek round the partition. It's a bar, expensively tricked out in that retro-seventies style with too much polished Italian marble and sub-Bauhaus chrome furniture. At this time of evening it's nearly empty (although maybe the fact that they charge six euros for a beer has something to do with it). I check my phone: it's 6:15. *Damn.* I head for the bar, glancing around hopefully in case the mysterious Ramona's wearing a cardboard sign saying: I'M RAMONA – TRY ME. So much for subtle spy-work.

"*Ein Weissbier, bitte,*" I ask, exhausting about sixty percent of my total German vocabulary.

"Sure thing, man." The bartender turns to grab a bottle.

"I'm Ramona," a female voice with a vaguely East Coast accent murmurs quietly in my left ear. "Don't turn around." And something hard pokes me in the ribs.

"Is that the aerial of your mobile phone, or are you displeased to see me?" It probably is a phone, but I do as she says: in this kind of situation it doesn't do to take chances.

"Shut up, wise guy." A slim hand reaches discreetly under my left arm and paws at my chest. The bartender is taking an awfully long time to find that bottle. "Hey, what is this Scheiss?"

"You found the shoulder holster? Careful, that's my Bluetooth GPS receiver in there. And that pocket's where I keep the noise-canceling headphones for my iPod – hey, watch out, they're expensive! – and the spare batteries for my PDA, and—"

Ramona lets go of my fishing jacket and a moment later the stubby object disappears from the small of my back. The bartender swings round, beaming and clutching a weird-looking glass in one hand and a bottle with a culturally stereotyped label in the other. "Dude, will this do? It's a really good Weizenbock . . ."

"Bob!" trills Ramona, stepping sideways until I can finally see her. "Make mine a dry gin and tonic, ice, but hold the fruit," she tells the barman, smiling like sunrise over the Swiss Alps. I glance at her sidelong and try not to gape.

We're in supermodel territory here – or maybe she's Uma Thurman's stunt double. She's almost five centimeters taller than me, blonde, and she's got cheekbones Mo would kill for. The rest of her isn't bad, either. She has the kind of figure that most models dream about—if indeed that isn't what she does for a living when she isn't sticking guns in civil servants' backs—and whatever the label on her strapless silk gown says, it probably costs more than I earn in a year before you add in the jewelry dripping from her in incandescent waves. Real physical perfection isn't something a guy like me gets to see up close and personal very often, and it's something to marvel at – then run away from, before it hypnotizes you like a snake staring into the eyes of something small, furry, and edible.

She's beautiful but deadly, and right now she has one slim hand in her black patent-leather evening bag: judging from the slight tension at the corners of her eyes I'll bet hard money she's holding a small, pearl-handled automatic pistol just out of sight.

One of my wards bites me on the back of my wrist and I realize what's come over me: it's a glamour. I feel a sudden pang of something like homesickness for Mo, who at least comes from my own planet, even if she insists on practicing the violin at all hours.

"Fancy meeting you here like this, darling!" Ramona adds, almost as an afterthought.

"How unexpected," I agree, taking a step sideways and reaching for the glass and bottle. The bartender, dazzled by her smile, is already reaching for a shot glass. I manage an experimental grin. Ramona reminds me of a certain ex-girlfriend (okay, she reminds me of Mhari: I admit it, try not to wince, and move on) done up to the nines and in full-on predator mode. As I get used to the impact of her glamour I begin to get an edgy feeling I've seen her before. "Is that your red Audi in the car park?"

She turns the full force of her smile on me. "What if it is?"

Glub glub . . . chink. Ice cubes sloshing into gin. "That'll be sixteen euros, man."

"Put it on my room tab," I say automatically. I slide the card over. "If it is, you nearly rubbed me out on the A45."

"I nearly—" She looks puzzled for a moment. Then even more puzzled. "Was it you in that ridiculous little tin can?"

"If my office would pay for an Audi TT I'd drive one, too." I feel a stab of malicious glee at her visible disquiet. "Who do you think I am? And who are you, and what do you want?"

The bartender drifts away to the other end of the bar, still smiling blissfully under her influence. I blink back little warning flickers of migraine-like distortion as I look at her. *That's got to be at least a level three glamour she's wearing*, I tell myself, and shiver. My ward isn't powerful enough to break through it so I can see her as she really is, but at least I can tell I'm being spoofed.

"I'm Ramona Random. You can call me Ramona." She takes a chug of the G&T, then stares down her nose at me with those disquietingly clear eyes, like an aristocratic Eloi considering a shambling, half-blind Morlock who's somehow made it to the surface. I take a preliminary sip of my beer, waiting for her to continue. "Do you want to fuck me?"

I spray beer through my nostrils. "You have got to be kidding!" It's more tactful than *I'd rather bed a king snake* and sounds less pathetic than *my girlfriend would kill me*, but the instant I come out with it I know it's a gut reaction, and true: *What's under that glamour?* Nothing I'd want to meet in bed, I'll bet.

"Good," says Ramona, closing the door very firmly on that line of speculation, much to my relief. She nods, a falling lock of flax-colored hair momentarily concealing her face: "Every guy I've ever slept with died less than twenty-four hours later." It must be my expression, because a moment later she adds, defensively: "It's just a coincidence! I didn't kill them. Well, most of them."

I realize I'm trying to hide behind my beer glass, and force myself to straighten up. "I'm very glad to hear it," I say, a little too rapidly.

"I was just checking because we're supposed to be working together. And it would be real unfortunate if you slept with me and died, because then we couldn't do that."

"Really? How interesting. And what exactly is it you think I do?"

She puts her glass down and removes her hand from her bag. It's déjà vu all over again: instead of a gun she's holding a three-year-old Palm Pilot. It's inferior tech, and I feel a momentary flash of smugness at knowing I've got the drop on her in at least one important department. She flips the protective cover open and glances at the screen. "I think you work for Capital Laundry Services," she says matter-of-factly. "Nominally you're a senior scientific officer in the Department of Internal Logistics. You're tasked with representing your department in various joint committees and with setting policy on IT acquisitions. But you really work for Angleton, don't you? So they must see something in you that I—" her suddenly jaundiced gaze takes in my jeans, somewhat elderly tee shirt, and fishing vest stuffed with geek toys "—don't."

I try not to wilt too visibly. *Okay, she's a player.* That makes things easier – and harder, in a way. I swallow a mouthful of beer successfully this time. "So why don't you tell me who you are?"

"I just did. I'm Ramona and I'm not going to sleep with you."

"Fine, Ramona-and-I'm-not-going-to-sleep-with-you. What are you? I mean, are you human? I can't tell, what with that glamour you're wearing, and that kind of thing makes me nervous."

Sapphire eyes stare at me. "Keep guessing, monkey-boy."

Oh, for fuck's sake— "Okay, I mean, who do you work for?"

"The Black Chamber. And I always wear this body on business. We've got a dress code, you know."

The Black Chamber? My stomach lurches. I've had one run-in with those guys, near the outset of my professional career, and everything I've learned since has taught me I was damned lucky to survive. "Who are you here to kill?"

She makes a faint moue of distaste. "I'm supposed to be working *with you.* I wasn't sent here to kill anyone."

We're going in circles again. "Fine. You're going to work with me but you don't want to sleep with me in case I drop dead, *Curse of the Mummy* and all that. You're tooled up to vamp some poor bastard, but it's not me, and you seem to know who I am. Why don't you just cut the crap and explain what you're doing here, why the hell you're so jumpy, and what's going on?"

"You really don't know?" She stares at me. "I was told you'd been briefed."

"Briefed?" I stare right back at her. "You've got to be kidding! I'm here for a committee meeting, not a live-action role-playing game."

"Huh!" For a moment she looks puzzled. "You *are* here to attend the next session of the joint-liaison committee on cosmological incursions, aren't you?"

I nod, very slightly. The Auditors don't usually ask you what you *didn't* say, they're more interested in what you *did* say, and who you said it to.[1] "You're not on my briefing sheet."

"I see." Ramona nods thoughtfully, then relaxes slightly. "Sounds like a regular fuck-up, then. Like I said, I was told we're going to be working together on a joint activity, starting with this meeting. For the purposes of this session I'm an accredited delegate, by the way."

"You—" I bite my tongue, trying to imagine her in a committee room going over the seventy-six-page agenda. "You're a *what?*"

"I've got observer status. Tomorrow I'll show you my ward," she adds. (That clinches it. The wards are handed out to those of us who're assigned to the joint committee.) "You can show me yours. I'm sure you'll be briefed before that – afterward we'll have a lot more to talk about."

"Just what—" I swallow "—are we supposed to be working on?"

She smiles. "Baccarat." She finishes her G&T and stands up with a swish of silk: "I'll be seeing you later, Robert. Until tonight . . ."

I buy another beer to calm my rattled nerves and hunker down in a carnivorous leather sofa at the far side of the bar. When I'm sure the bartender isn't watching me I pull out my Treo, run a highly specialized program, and dial an office extension in London. The phone rings four times, then the voice mail picks it up. "Boss? Got a headache. A Black Chamber operative called Ramona showed up. She claims that we're supposed to be working together. What the hell's

---

[1] Blabbing secrets to beautiful femme fatale agents is frowned upon, especially when they're not necessarily human.

going on? I need to know." I hang up without bothering to wait for a reply. Angleton will be in around six o'clock London time, and then I'll get my answer. I sigh, which draws a dirty look from a pair of overdressed chancers at the next table. I guess they think I'm lowering the tone of the bar. A sense of acute loneliness comes crashing down. *What am I doing here?*

The superficial answer is that I'm here on Laundry business. That's Capital Laundry Services to anyone who rings the front doorbell or cold-calls the switchboard, even though we haven't operated out of the old offices above the Chinese laundry in Soho since the end of the Second World War. The Laundry has a long memory. I work for the Laundry because they gave me a choice between doing so . . . or not working for anyone, ever again. With 20/20 hindsight I can't say I blame them. Some people you just do not want to leave outside the tent pissing in, and in my early twenties, self-confident and naïve, I was about as safe to leave lying around unsupervised as half a ton of sweating gelignite. These days I'm a trained computational demonologist, that species of occult practitioner who really can summon spirits from the vasty deep: or at least whatever corner of our local Calabi-Yau manifold they howl and gibber in, insane on the brane. And I'm a lot safer to have around these days — at least I know what precautions to use and what safety standards to obey: so call me a bunker full of smart bombs.

Most Laundry work consists of tediously bureaucratic form-filling and paper-pushing. About three years ago I got bored and asked if I could be assigned to active service. This was a mistake I've been regretting ever since, because it tends to go hand-in-hand with things like being roused out of bed at four in the morning to go count the concrete cows in Milton Keynes, which sounds like a lot more fun than it actually is; especially when it leads to people shooting at you and lots more complicated forms to fill in and hearings in front of the Audit Committee. (About whom the less said the better.)

But on the other hand, if I hadn't switched to active service status I wouldn't have met Mo, Dr. Dominique O'Brien – except she hates the Dominique bit – and from this remove I can barely imagine what life would be like without her. At least, without her in principle. She's been on one training course or another for months on end lately, doing something hush-hush that she can't tell me about. This latest course has kept her down at the secure facility in Dunwich Village for four weeks now, and two weeks before *that* I had to go to the last liaison meeting, and frankly, I'm pining. I mentioned this to Pinky at the pub last week, and he snorted and accused me of carrying on like I was already married. I suppose he's right: I'm not used to having somebody wonderful and sane in my life, and I guess I'm a bit clingy. Maybe I should talk about it with Mo, but the subject of marriage is a bit touchy and I'm reluctant to raise it – her previous matrimonial experience wasn't a happy one.

I'm about halfway down my beer and thinking about calling Mo – if she's off work right now we could chat – when my phone rings. I glance at it and freeze: it's Angleton. I key the cone of silence then answer: "Bob here."

"Bob." Angleton's voice is papery-thin and cold, and the data compression inflicted by the telephone network and the security tunnel adds a hollow echo to it. "I got your message. This Ramona person, I want you to describe her."

"I can't. She was wearing a glamour, level three at least— it nearly sent me cross-eyed. But she knows who I am and what I'm here for."

"All right, Bob, that's about what I expected. Now this is

what I want you to do." Angleton pauses. I lick my suddenly dry lips. "I want you to finish your drink and go back to your room. However, rather than entering, I want you to proceed down the corridor to the next room along on the same side, one number up. Your support team should be checked in there already. They'll continue the briefing once you're in the secure suite. Do not enter your room for the time being. Do you understand?"

"I think so." I nod. "You've got a little surprise job lined up for me. Is that it?"

"Yes," says Angleton, and hangs up abruptly.

I put my beer down, then stand up and glance round. I thought I was here for a routine committee meeting, but suddenly I find I'm standing on shifting sands, in possibly hostile territory. The middle-aged swingers glance disinterestedly at me, but my wards aren't tingling: they're just who they appear to be. *Right. Go directly to bed, do not eat supper, do not collect* . . . I shake my head and get moving.

To get to the elevator bank from the bar requires crossing an expanse of carpet overlooked by two levels of balconies – normally I wouldn't even notice it but after Angleton's little surprise the skin on the back of my neck crawls, and I clutch my Treo and my lucky charm bracelet twitchily as I sidle across it. There aren't many people about, if you discount the queue of tired business travelers checking in at the desk, and I make it to the lift bank without the scent of violets or the tickling sense of recognition that usually prefigures a lethal manifestation. I hit the "up" button on the nearest elevator and the doors open to admit me.

There is a theory that all chain hotels are participants in a conspiracy to convince the international traveler that there is only one hotel on the planet, and it's just like the one in their own home town. Personally, I don't believe it: it seems much more plausible that rather than actually going somewhere I have, in fact, been abducted and doped to the gills by aliens, implanted with false and bewildering memories of humiliating security probes and tedious travel, and checked in to a peculiarly expensive padded cell to recover. It's certainly an equally consistent explanation for the sense of disorientation and malaise I suffer from in these places; besides which, malevolent aliens are easier to swallow than the idea that other people actually *want* to live that way.

Elevators are an integral part of the alien abduction experience. I figure the polished fake-marble floor and mirror-tiled ceiling with indirect lighting conspire to generate a hypnotic sense of security in the abductees, so I pinch myself and force myself to stay alert. The lift is just beginning to accelerate upwards when my phone vibrates, so I glance at the screen, read the warning message, and drop to the floor.

The lift rattles as it rises towards the sixth floor. My guts lighten: *we're slowing!* The entropy detector wired into my phone's aerial is lighting up the screen with a grisly red warning icon. Some really heavy shit is going on upstairs, and the closer we get to my floor the stronger it is. "Fuck fuck fuck," I mumble, punching up a basic countermeasure screen. I'm not carrying: this is supposed to be friendly territory, and whatever's lighting up the upper levels of the Ramada Treff Page Hotel is — I briefly flash back to another hotel in Amsterdam, a howling wind sucking into the void where a wall should be—

Clunk. The door slides open and I realize at the same instant that I should have leapt for the lift control panel and the emergency stop button. "Shit," I add — the traditional last word — just as the flashing red dial on my phone screen whisks counterclockwise and turns green: green for safety, green for normal, green to show that the reality excursion has left the building.

"*Zum Teufel!*"

I glance up stupidly at a pair of feet encased in bullet-proof-looking, brown leather hiking boots, then further up at the corduroy trousers and beige jacket of an elderly German tourist. "Trying to get a signal," I mutter, and scramble out of the lift on all fours, feeling extremely stupid.

I tiptoe along the beige-carpeted corridor to my room, racking my brains for an explanation. This whole set-up stinks like a week-old haddock: What's going on? Ramona, whoever the hell she is — I'd put hard money on her being mixed in with it. And that entropy blip was big. But it's gone now. *Someone gating in?* I wonder. *Or a proximal invocation?* I pause in front of my door and hold my hand above the door handle for a few seconds.

The handle is cold. Not just metal-at-ambient cold, but frigid and smoking-liquid-nitrogen cold.

"Oops," I say very quietly, and keep on walking down the corridor until I arrive at the next room door. Then I pull out my phone and speed-dial Angleton.

"Bob, Sitrep."

I lick my lips. "I'm still alive. While I was in the elevator my tertiary proximity alarm redlined then dropped back. I got to my room and the door handle feels like it's measuring room temperature in single-digit Kelvins. I'm now outside the adjacent door. I figure it's a hit and unless you tell me otherwise I'm calling a Code Blue."

"This isn't the Code Blue you're here to deal with." Angleton sounds dryly amused, which is pretty much what I expect from him. "But you might want to make a note that your activation key is double-oh-seven. Just in case you need it later."

"You what?" I glare at the phone in disbelief, then punch the number into the keypad. "Jesus, Angleton, someday let me explain this concept called password security to you, I'm not meant to be able to hack my own action locks and start shooting on a whim—"

"But you didn't, did you?" He sounds even more amused as my phone beeps twice and makes a metallic clicking noise. "You may not have time to ask when the shit hits the fan. That's why I kept it simple. Now give me a Sitrep," he adds crisply.

"I'm going live." I frantically punch a couple of buttons and invisible moths flutter up and down my spine; when they fade away the corridor looks darker, somehow, and more threatening. "Half-live. My terminal is active." I fumble around in my pocket and pull out a small webcam, click it into place in the expansion slot on top of my phone. Now my phone has got two cameras.

"Okay, SCORPION STARE loaded. I'm armed. What can I expect?"

There's a buzzing noise from the door lock next to me and the green LED flashes. "Hopefully nothing right now, but . . . open the door and go inside. Your backup team should be in place to give you your briefing, unless something's gone very wrong in the last five minutes."

"Jesus, Angleton."

"That *is* my name. You shouldn't swear so much: the walls have ears." He still sounds amused, the omniscient bastard. I don't know how he does it – I'm not cleared for that shit – but I always have a feeling that he can see over my shoulder. "Go inside. That's an order."

I take a deep breath, raise my phone, and open the door.

"Hiya, Bob!" Pinky looks up from the battered instrument case, his hands hovering over a compact computer keyboard. He's wearing a fetching batik sarong, a bushy handlebar moustache, and not much else: I'm not going to give him the pleasure of knowing just how much this disturbs me, or how relieved I am to see him.

"Where's Brains?" I ask, closing the door behind me and exhaling slowly.

"In the closet. Don't worry, he'll be coming out soon enough." Pinky points a digit at the row of storage doors fronting the wall adjacent to my room. "Angleton sent us. He said you'd need briefing."

"Am I the only person here who doesn't know what's going on?"

"Probably." He grins. "Nothing to worry about, ol' buddy." He glances at my Treo. "Would you mind not pointing that thing at me?"

"Oh, sorry." I lower it hastily and eject the second camera that turns it into a SCORPION STARE terminal, a basilisk device capable of blowing apart chunks of organic matter within visual range by convincing them that some of their carbon nuclei are made of silicon. "Are you going to tell me what's happening?"

"Sure." He sounds unconcerned. "You're being destiny-entangled with a new partner, and we're here to make sure she doesn't accidentally kill and eat you before the ritual is complete."

"I'm being *what?*" I hate it when I squeak.

"She's from the Black Chamber. You're supposed to be working together on something big, and the old man wants you to be able to draw on her abilities when you need help."

"What do you mean *draw on her?* Like I'm a trainee tattooist now?" I've got a horrible feeling I know what he's talking about, and I don't like it one little bit: but it would explain why Angleton sent Pinky and Brains to be my backup team. They're old housemates, and the bastard thinks they'll make me feel more comfortable.

The closet door opens and Brains steps out. Unlike Pinky he's decently dressed, for leather club values of decency.

"Don't get overexcited, Bob," he says, winking at me: "I was just drilling holes in the walls."

"Holes——"

"To observe her. She's confined to the pentacle on your bedroom carpet; you don't need to worry about her getting loose and stealing your soul before we complete the circuit. Hold still or this won't work."

"Who's in what pentacle in my bedroom?" I take a step back towards the door but he's approaching me, clutching a sterile needle.

"Your new partner. Here, hold out a hand, this won't hurt a bit——"

"Ouch!" I step backwards and bounce off the wall, and Brains manages to get his drop of blood while I'm wincing.

"Great, that'll let us complete the destiny lock. You know you're a lucky man? At least, I suppose you're lucky – if you're that way inclined——"

"Who is she, dammit?"

"Your new partner? She's a changeling sent by the Black Chamber. Name of Ramona. And she is stacked, if that sort of thing matters to you." He pulls an amused face, oh so tolerant of my heterosexual ways.

"But I didn't——"

A toilet flushes, then the bathroom door opens and Boris steps out. And that's when I know I'm in deep shit, because Boris is not my normal line manager: Boris is the guy they send out when something has gone terribly wrong in the field and stuff needs to be cleaned up by any means necessary. Boris acts like a cut-rate extra in a Cold War spy thriller – right down to the hokey fake accent and the shaven bullethead – although he's about as English as I am. The speech thing is a leftover from a cerebral infarction, courtesy of a field invocation that went pear-shaped.

"Bob." He doesn't smile. "Welcome to Darmstadt. You

come for joint-liaison framework. You are attending meeting tomorrow as planned: but are also being cleared for AZORIAN BLUE HADES as of now. Are here to brief, introduce you to support team, and make sure you bond with your, your, *associate*. Without to be eated."

"Eaten?" I ask. I must look a trifle tense because even Boris manages to pull an apologetic expression from somewhere. "What is this job, exactly? I didn't volunteer for a field mission—"

"Know you do not. We are truly sorry to put this on you," says Boris, running a hand over his bald head in a gesture that gives the lie to the sentiment, "but not having time for histrionics." He glances at Brains and gives a tiny nod. "First am giving briefing to you, then must complete destiny-entanglement protocol with entity next door. After that—" he checks his watch "—are being up to you, but estimating are only seven days to save Western civilization."

"What?" I know what my ears just heard but I'm not sure I believe them.

He stares at me grimly, then nods. "If is up to me, are not be relying on you. But time running out and is short on alternatives."

"Oh Jesus." I sit down on the sole available chair. "I'm not going to like this, am I?"

"*Nyet*. Pinky, the DVD please. It is being time to expand Robert's horizons . . ."

2: GOING DOWN TO DUNWICH

The river of time may wait for no man, but sometimes extreme stress causes it to run shallow. Cast the fly back four weeks and see what you catch, reeling in the month-old memories . . .

IT'S LATE ON A RAINY SATURDAY MORNING IN February, and Mo and I are drinking the remains of the breakfast coffee while talking about holidays. Or rather, she's talking about holidays while I'm nose-deep in a big, fat book, reacquainting myself with the classics. To tell the truth, each interruption breaks my concentration, so I'm barely paying attention. Besides, I'm not really keen on the idea of forking out money for two weeks in self-catering accommodations somewhere hot. We're supposed to be saving up the deposit for a mortgage, after all.

"How about Crete?" she asks from the kitchen table, drawing a careful red circle around three column-inches of newsprint.

"Won't you burn?" (Mo's got classic redhead skin and freckles.)

"We in the developed world have this advanced technology

called sunblock. You may have heard of it." Mo glares at me. "You're not paying attention, are you?"

I sigh and put the book down. *Damn it, why now?* Just as I'm getting to Tanenbaum's masterful and witty takedown of the OSI protocol stack . . . "Guilty as charged."

"Why not?" She leans forwards, arms crossed, staring at me intently.

"Good book," I admit.

"Oh. Well that makes it all right," she snorts. "You can always take it to the beach, but you'll be kicking yourself if we wait too long and the cheap packages are all over-booked and we're left with choosing between the dregs of the Club 18-30 stuff, or paying through the nose, or one of us gets sent on detached duty again because we didn't notify HR of our vacation plans in time. Right?"

"I'm sorry. I guess I'm just not that enthusiastic right now."

"Yes, well, I just paid my Christmas credit card bill, too, love. Face it, by May we're both going to be needing a vacation, and they'll be twice as expensive if you leave booking it too late."

I look Mo in the eyes and realize she's got me metaphorically surrounded. She's older than I am – at least, a couple of years older – and more responsible, and as for what she sees in me . . . well. If there's one disadvantage to living with her it's that she's got a tendency to *organize* me. "But. Crete?"

"Crete, Island of. Home of the high Minoan civilization, probably collapsed due to rapid climactic change or the explosion of the volcano on Thera – Santorini – depending who you read. Loads of glorious frescos and palace ruins, wonderful beaches, and moussaka to die for. Grilled octopus, too: I know all about your thing for eating food with tentacles. If we aim for late May we'll beat the sunbathing masses.

I was thinking we should book some side tours – I'm reading up on the archaeology – and a self-catering apartment, where we can chill for two weeks, soak up some sun before the temperature goes into the high thirties and everything bakes . . . How does that sound to you? I can practice the fiddle while you burn."

"It sounds—" I stop. "Hang on. What's the archaeology thing about?"

"Judith's had me reading up on the history of the littoral civilizations lately," she says. "I thought it'd be nice to take a look." Judith is deputy head of aquatic affairs at work. She spends about half her time out at the Laundry training facility in Dunwich and the other half up at Loch Ness.

"Ah." I hunt around for a scrap of kitchen roll to use as a bookmark. "So this is work, really."

"No, it's not!" Mo closes the newspaper section then picks it up and begins to shake the pages into order. She won't stop until she's got them perfectly aligned and smooth enough to sell all over again: it's one of her nervous tics. "I'm just curious. I've been reading so much about the Minoans and the precedent case law behind the human/Deep One treaties that it just caught my interest. Besides which, I last went on holiday to Greece about twenty years ago, on a school trip. It's about time to go back there, and I thought it'd be a nice place to relax. Sun, sex, and squid, with a side order of archaeology."

I know when I'm defeated, but I'm not completely stupid: it's time to change the subject. "What's Judith got you working on, anyway?" I ask. "I didn't think she had any call for your approach to, well . . . whatever." (It's best not to mention specifics: the house we share is subsidized accommodation, provided by the Laundry for employees like us – otherwise there's no way we could honestly afford to live in Central London on two civil service salaries – and the flip-side of this arrangement is that if we start discussing state secrets the walls grow ears.)

"Judith's got problems you aren't briefed on." She picks up her coffee mug, peers into it, and pulls a face. "I'm beginning to find out about them and I don't like them."

"You are?"

"I'm going down to Dunwich next week," she says suddenly. "I'll be there quite some time."

"You're what?"

I must sound shocked because she puts the mug down, stands up, and holds out her arms: "Oh, Bob!"

I stand up, too. We hug. "What's going on?"

"Training course," she says tightly

"*Another* bloody training course? What are they doing, putting you through a postgraduate degree in Cloak and Dagger Studies?" I ask. The only training course I did at Dunwich was in field operations technique. Dunwich is where the Laundry keeps a lot of its secrets, hidden behind diverted roads and forbidding hedges, in a village evacuated by the War Department back during the 1940s and never returned to its civilian owners. Unlike Rome, no roads lead to Dunwich: to get there you need a GPS receiver, four-wheel drive, and a security talisman.

"Something like that. Angleton's asked me to take on some additional duties, but I don't think I can talk about them just yet. Let's say, it's at least as interesting as the more obscure branches of music theory I've been working on." She tenses against me, then hugs me tighter. "Listen, nobody can complain about me telling you I'm going, so . . . ask Judith, okay? If you really think you need to know. It's just a compartmentalization thing. I'll have my mobile and my violin, we can talk evenings. I'll try to make it back home for weekends."

"Weekends plural? Just how long is this course supposed

to take?" I'm curious, as well as a bit annoyed. "When did they tell you about it?"

"They told me about this particular one yesterday. And I don't know how long it runs for – Judith says it comes up irregularly, they're at the mercy of certain specialist staff. At least four weeks, possibly more."

"Specialist staff. Would this specialist staff happen to have, say, pallid skin? And gill slits?"

"Yes, that's it. That's it exactly." She relaxes and takes a step back. "You've met them."

"Sort of." I shiver.

"I'm not happy about this," she says. "I told them I needed more notice. I mean, before they spring things like this special training regime on me."

I figure it's time to change the subject. "Crete. You figure you'll be out of the course by then?"

"Yes, for sure." She nods. "That's why I'll need to get away from it all, with you."

"So that's what this Crete thing is all about. Judith wants to drop you headfirst into Dunwich for three months and you need somewhere to go to decompress afterwards."

"That's about the size of it."

"Ah, shit." I pick up my book again, then my coffee cup. "Hey, this coffee's cold."

"I'll fix a fresh jug." Mo carries the cafetière over to the sink and starts rinsing the grounds out. "Sometimes I hate this job," she adds in a singsong, "and sometimes this job hates me . . ."

The name of the job is mathematics. Or maybe metamathematics. Or occult physics. And she wouldn't be in this job if she hadn't met me (although, on second thoughts, if she hadn't met me she'd be dead, so I think we'll call it even on that score and move swiftly on).

Look, if I come right out and say, "Magic exists," you'll probably dismiss me as a whack job. But in fact you'd be – well, I say you'd be – mistaken. And because my employers agree with me, and they're the government, you're outvoted.[2]

We've tried to cover it up as best we can. Our predecessors did their best to edit it out of the history books and public consciousness – the Mass Observation projects of the 1930s were rather more than the simple social science exercises they were presented as to the public – and since then we've devoted ourselves to the task of capping the bubbling cauldron of the occult beneath a hermetic lid of state secrecy. So if you think I'm a whack job it's partly my fault, isn't it? Mine, and the organization I work for – known to its inmates as the Laundry – and our opposite numbers in other countries.

The trouble is, the type of magic we deal with has nothing to do with rabbits and top hats, fairies at the bottom of the garden, and wishes that come true. The truth is, we live in a multiverse – a sheath of loosely interconnected universes, so loosely interconnected that they're actually leaky at the level of the quantum foam substrate of space-time. There's only one common realm among the universes, and that's the platonic realm of mathematics. We can solve theorems and cast hand-puppet shadows on the walls of our cave. What most folks (including most mathematicians and computer scientists – which amounts to the same thing) don't know is that in overlapping parallel versions of the cave other beings – for utterly unhuman values of "beings" – can also sometimes see the shadows, and cast shadows right back at us.

Back before about 1942, communication with other realms was pretty hit and miss. Unfortunately, Alan Turing

---

[2] Not to mention outgunned.

partially systematized it — which later led to his unfortunate "suicide" and a subsequent policy reversal to the effect that it was better to have eminent logicians inside the tent pissing out, rather than outside pissing in. The Laundry is that subdivision of the Second World War-era Special Operations Executive that exists to protect the United Kingdom from the scum of the multiverse. And, trust me on this, there are beings out there who even Jerry Springer wouldn't invite on his show.

The Laundry collects computer scientists who accidentally discover the elements of computational demonology, in much the same way Stalin used to collect jokes about himself.[3] About six years ago I nearly landscaped Wolverhampton, not to mention most of Birmingham and the Midlands, while experimenting with a really neat, new rendering algorithm that just might have accidentally summoned up the entity known to the clueful as "fuck, it's Nyarlathotep! Run!" (and to everyone else as "Fuck, run!").[4]

In Mo's case . . . she's a philosopher by training. Philosophers in the know are even more dangerous than computer scientists: they tend to become existential magnets for weird shit. Mo came to the Laundry's attention when she attracted some even-weirder-than-normal attention from a monster that thought our planet looked good and would be crunchy with ketchup. How we ended up living together is another story, albeit not an unhappy one. But the fact is, like me, she works for the Laundry now. In fact, she once told me the way she manages to feel safe these days is by being as dangerous as possible. And though I may bitch and moan about it when the Human Resources fairy decides to split us

---

[3] He had two Gulags full.
[4] Except the Black Chamber, who would say, "You're late — we're going to dock your pay."

up for months on end, when you get down to it, if you work for a secret government agency, they can do that. And they've usually got good reasons for doing it, too. Which is one of the things I hate about my life . . .

. . . and another thing I hate is Microsoft PowerPoint, which brings me back to the present.

PowerPoint is symptomatic of a certain type of bureaucratic environment: one typified by interminable presentations with lots of fussy little bullet-points and flashy dissolves and soundtracks masked into the background, to try to convince the audience that the goon behind the computer has something significant to say. It's the tool of choice for pointy-headed idiots with expensive suits and skinny laptops who desperately want to look as if they're in command of the job, with all the facts at their fiddling fingertips, even if Rome is burning in the background. Nothing stands for content-free corporate bullshit quite like PowerPoint. And that's just scratching the surface . . .

I'm sorry. Maybe you think I'm being unjustifiably harsh — a presentation graphics program is just a piece of standard office software, after all — but my experience with PowerPoint is, shall we say, nonstandard. Besides, you've probably never had a guy with a shoulder holster and a field ops team backing him up drag you into a stakeout and whip out a laptop, to show you a presentation that begins with a slide stating: THIS BRIEFING WILL SELF-DESTRUCT IN FIFTEEN SECONDS. It's usually a sign that things have gone wronger than a very wrong thing indeed, and you are expected to make them go right again, or something doubleplus ungood is going to happen.

Double-plus ungood indeed.

"Destiny-entanglement protocol," I mutter, as Pinky fusses around behind me and turns the fat-assed recliner I'm sitting in to face the wardrobe while Boris pokes at his laptop. As protocols go, I've got to admit it's a new one on me. "Would you mind explaining—hey, what's that duct tape for?"

"Sorry, Bob, try not to move, okay? It's just a precaution."

"Just a—" I reach up with my left hand to give my nose a preemptive scratch while he's busy taping my right arm to the chair. "What's the failure rate on this procedure, and should I have updated my life insurance first?"

"Relax. Is no failure rate." Boris finally gets his laptop to admit that its keyboard exists, and spins it round so I can see the screen. The usual security glyph flickers into view (I think that particular effect is called wheel, eight spokes) and bites me on the bridge of my nose. It's visual cortex hackery to seal my lips. "Failure not an option," repeats Boris.

The screen wheels again, and – morphs into a video of Angleton. "Hello, Bob," he begins. He's sitting behind his desk like an outtake from *Mission: Impossible,* which would be a whole lot more plausible if the desk wasn't a cramped, green metal thing with a contraption on top of it that looks like the bastard offspring of a microfiche reader by way of a 1950s mainframe computer terminal. "Sorry about the video briefing, but I had to be in two places at once, and you lost."

I catch Boris's eye and he pauses the presentation. "How the hell can you call this confidential?" I complain. "It's a video! If it fell into the wrong hands—"

Boris glances at Brains. "Tell him."

Brains pulls a gadget out of his goodie bag. "Andy shot it on one of these," he explains. "Solid-state camcorder, runs on MMC cards. Encrypted, and we stuffed a bunch of footage up front to make it look like amateur dramatics. That and the geas field will make anyone who steals it think they've stumbled over the next *Blair Witch Project* – cute, huh?"

I sigh. If he was a dog he'd be wagging his tail hard

enough to dent the furniture. "Okay, roll it." I try to ignore whatever Pinky is doing on the carpet around my feet with a conductive pencil, a ruler, and a breakout box.

Angleton leans alarmingly towards the camera viewpoint, looming to fill the screen. "I'm sure you've heard of TLA Systems Corporation, Bob, if for no other reason than your complaints about their license management server on the departmental network reached the ears of the Audit committee last July, and I was forced to take preemptive action to divert them from mounting a full-scale investigation."

Gulp. The *Auditors* noticed? That wasn't my idea – no wonder Andy seemed pissed off with me. When I'm not running around pretending to be Secret Agent Man and attending committee meetings in Darmstadt, my job's pretty boring: network management is one component of it, and when I saw that blasted license manager trying to dial out to the public internet to complain about Facilities running too many copies of the TLA monitoring client, I cc'd everyone I could think of on the memo—

"TLA, as you know – Bob, pay attention at the back, there – was founded in 1979 by Ellis Billington and his partner Ritchie Martin. Ritchie was the software guy, Ellis the front man, which is why these days Ellis has a net worth of seventeen billion US dollars and Ritchie lives in a hippie commune in Oregon and refuses to deal with any unit of time he can't schedule on a sundial."

Angleton's sallow visage is replaced (no dissolve, this time) by a photograph of Billington, in the usual stuffed-suit pose adopted by CEOs hoping to impress the *Wall Street Journal*. His smile reveals enough teeth to intimidate a megalodon and he's in such good condition for a sixty-something executive that he's probably got a portrait squirreled away in a high-security facility in New Mexico that gives people nightmares when they look at it.

"TLA originally competed in the relational database market with Ingres, Oracle, and the other seven dwarves, but rapidly discovered a lucrative sideline in federal systems— specifically the GTO[5] market."

Lots of government departments in the '90s tried to save money by ordering their IT folks to buy only commercial, off-the-shelf software, or COTS. Which is to say, they finally got a clue that it's cheaper to buy a word processor off the shelf than to pay a defense contractor to write one. After their initial expressions of shock and horror, the trough-guzzling, platinum-wrench defense contractors responded by making GTO editions – ostensibly commercial versions of their platinum-plated, government-oriented products, available to anyone who wanted to buy them – $500,000 word processors with MILSPEC encryption and a suite of handy document templates for rules of engagement, declarations of war, and issuing COTS contracts to defense contractors.

"TLA grew rapidly and among other things acquired Moonstone Metatechnology, who you may know of as one of the primary civilian contractors to the Black Chamber."

Whoops. Now he's definitely got my attention. The presentation cuts back to Angleton's drawn-to-the-point-of-mummification face. He looks serious.

"Billington is from California. His parents are known to have been involved in the Order of the Silver Star at one point, although Billington himself claims to be Methodist. Whatever the truth, he has a stratospheric security clearance and his corporation designs scary things for an assortment of spooky departments. I'd reference CRYSTAL CENTURY if you were in London, but you can look it up later. For now, you can take it from me that Billington is a player."

[5] Gran Turismo Omologato

Now he throws in a fancy fade-to-right to show a rather old, grainy photograph of a ship . . . an oil-drilling ship? A tanker? Something like that. Whatever it is, it's big and there's something that looks like an oil rig amidships. (I like that word, "amidships." It makes me sound as if I know what I'm talking about. I am to seagoing vessels pretty much what your grandmother is to Windows Vista.)

"This ship is the *Hughes Glomar Explorer*. Built for Summa Corporation – owned by Howard Hughes – for the CIA in the early 1970s, its official mission was to recover a sunken Soviet nuclear missile submarine from the floor of the Pacific Ocean. It was mated with this—" another screen dissolve, to something that looks like a stainless steel woodlouse adrift at sea "—the HMB-1, Hughes Mining Barge, built by, you'll be interested to know, Lockheed Missiles and Space."

I lean forwards, barely noticing the duct tape holding my wrists and ankles against the chair. "That's really neat," I say admiringly. "Didn't I see it in a Discovery Channel documentary?"

Angleton clears his throat. "If you've quite finished?" (*How does he do that?* I ask myself.) "Operation JENNIFER, the first attempt at recovering the submarine, was a partial success. I was there as a junior liaison under the reciprocal monitoring provisions of the Benthic Treaty. The CIA staff was . . . overly optimistic. To their credit, the Black Chamber refused to be drawn in, and to *their* credit, the other Signatory Party didn't use more than the minimum force necessary to prevent the recovery. When Seymour Hersh and Jack Anderson broke the story in the *Los Angeles Times* several months later, the CIA gave up, the *Glomar Explorer* was formally designated property of the US government and mothballed, a discreet veil was drawn over the fate of the HMB-1 – it was officially 'scrapped' – and we thought that was that."

Pinky has finished drawing a pentacle around my chair, and he finally signals that he's got it wired up to the isochronous signal generator – two thumbs up at Boris. Boris shuts the laptop lid with a click and sticks it under his arm. "Is time for entanglement," he tells me, "briefing will continue after."

"Whoa! What has she—" I nod at the far wall, beyond which the sleeping beauty lies "—got to do with this?" I glance at the laptop.

Boris harrumphs. "If had spend your time on briefing, would understand," he grumbles. "Brains, Pinky, stations."

'Yo. Good luck, Bob." Pinky pats me on the shoulder as he scuttles past the end of the beds to a small ward he's already set up on the carpet in front of the TV set. "It'll be all right – you'll see." Brains and Boris are already in their safety cells.

"What if someone's in the hall outside?" I call.

"The door's locked. And I put the DO NOT DISTURB sign out," Brains replies. "Stations, everyone?" He pulls out a black control box and twists a knob set on its face. I force myself to settle back in the chair; and in the other room, beyond the two spy-holes drilled through the back of the wardrobe, a very special light comes on and washes over the trapped entity in the pentacle.

When you go summoning extra-dimensional entities, there are certain precautions you should be sure to take.

For starters, you can forget garlic, bibles, and candles: they don't work. Instead, you need to start with serious electrical insulation to stop them from blowing your brains out through your ears. Once you've got yourself grounded you also need to pay attention to the existence of special optical high-bandwidth channels that demons may attempt to use to download themselves into your nervous system – they're called "eyeballs." Timesharing your hypothalamus with alien brain-eaters is not recommended if you wish to live long enough to claim your index-linked, state-earnings-related pension; it's about on a par with tap dancing on the London Underground's third rail in terms of health and safety. So you need to ensure you're optically isolated as well. *Do not stare into laser cavity with remaining eye*, as the safety notice puts it.

Most demons are as dumb as a sack full of hammers. This does not mean they're safe to mess with, any more than a C++ compiler is "safe" in the hands of an enthusiastic computer science undergrad. Some people can mess up anything, and computational demonology adds a new and unwelcome meaning to terms like "memory leak" and "debugger."

Now, I have severe misgivings about what Boris, Pinky, and Brains propose to do to me. (And I am *really* pissed at Angleton for telling them to do it.) However, they're more than passingly competent and they've certainly not skimped on the safety aspects. The entity that calls itself Ramona Random – hell, that might even be her real name, back when she was human, before the Black Chamber rebuilt her into the occult equivalent of a guided missile – is properly secured in the next room. Sitting in the bedroom closet – in front of the two holes Brains has drilled in the wall – is a tripod with a laser, a beam splitter, and a thermostatically controlled box containing a tissue culture grown from something that really ought not to exist, all wired up to a circuit board that looks like M. C. Escher designed it after taking too much LSD.

"Everyone clear?" calls Brains.

"Clear." Boris.

"Clear." Pinky.

"Totally unclear!" Me.

"Thank you, Bob. Pinky, how's our remote terminal?"

Pinky looks at a small, cheap television screen hooked up to a short-range receiver. "Drooling slightly. I think she's asleep."

"Okay. Lights." A diode on the back of the circuit board begins to flash, and I notice out of the corner of my eye that Brains is controlling it with a television remote. *That's smart of him*, I think, right before he punches the next button. "Blood."

Something begins to drip from the box, sizzling where it touches a wired junction on the circuit, which suddenly flares with silver light. I try to look away but it sucks my eyes in, like a bubble of boiling mercury that expands to fill the entire world. Then it's like my blind spot is expanding, creeping up on the back of my head.

"Symbolic link established."

There's an incredibly strong stink of violets, and a horde of ants crawl the length of my spine before holing up in the pit of my stomach to build a nest.

Hello, Bob. The voice caresses my ears like the velvet fuzz on a week-dead aubergine, sultry and somehow rotten to the core. It's Ramona's voice. My stomach heaves. I can't see anything but the swirling pit of light, and the violets are decaying into something unspeakable. **Can you hear me?**

I hear you. I bite my tongue, tasting the sound of steel guitars. Synesthesia, I note distantly. I've read about this sort of thing: if the situation wasn't so dangerous it would be fascinating. Meanwhile my right arm is straining against the duct tape without me willing it to move. I try to make it stop and it won't. **Leave my arm alone, damn you!**

I'm already damned, she says flippantly, but the muscles in my arm stop twitching and jumping.

Then I realize I haven't been moving my lips, and more

importantly, Ramona hasn't been speaking aloud. **How do we control this?** I ask.

The will becomes the act: if you want me to hear, I hear you.

Oh. The light show is beginning to slow down, with reality bleeding back in through the edges, and my head feels like someone's rammed a railroad spike through my skull right behind my left eye. **I feel sick.**

Don't do that, Bob! She sounds — feels? — disturbed.

Okay. *Try not to think of invisible pink elephants*, I think grimly, my skin crawling as the implications set in. I've just been rendered uncontrollably telepathic with a woman — or something woman-shaped — from the Black Chamber, and I'm such a dork my first reaction wasn't to run like fuck. Why'd Angleton do a thing like that? Hey, isn't this asking for a really *gigantic* security breach — at least, if both of us survive the experience? *How am I going to keep Ramona out of my head——?*

Hey, stop blaming me! Somehow I can tell she's irritated by my line of thought. **My head hurts, too.**

So why didn't you run away? I let slip before I manage to clamp a lid down on the thought.

They didn't give me the option. A metallic, bitter taste fills my mouth. **I'm not entirely human. Constitutional rights don't apply to non-humans. All I can say is, those bastards better hope I never get loose from this geas . . .** I feel like spitting, then I realize the glands full of warmth at the back of her throat aren't salivary ducts.

"Bob."

I blink in confusion. It's Brains. He looms over me, out of his grounded pentacle. "Can you hear me?"

"Yuh, yeah." I try to swallow, feeling the sensation of venom sacs throbbing urgently inside my cheeks begin to fade. I shudder. There's a trailing wisp of wistfulness from

Ramona, and a malicious giggle: she doesn't have fangs, she just has a really good somatic imagination. **Let me get my head together,** I tell her, and then try to do the invisible pink elephant thing in her general direction.

"How do you feel?" asks Brains. He sounds curious.

"How the fuck do you think *you'd* feel?" I snarl. "Jesus fuck, give me ibuprofen or give me a straight razor. My head is killing me." Then I realize something else. "And cut me loose from here. Someone's got to go next door and release Ramona, and I don't think any of you guys want to get within spitting range of her without a chair, a whip, and a can of pepper spray."

I remember the shape of her anger at her employers and shiver again. Working with Ramona is going to be like riding sidesaddle on a black mamba. And that's *before* I get to tell Mo, "Honey, they partnered me with a demon."

3: TANGLED UP IN GRUE

THEY WAIT FOR THE IBUPROFEN TO START WORKING before they untie me from the chair, which is extremely prudent of them.

"Right," I say, leaning against the back of the chair and breathing deeply. "Boris, what the fuck is this about?"

"It is to be stopping her from killing you." Boris glowers at me. He's annoyed about something, which makes two of us. "And to be creating an untappable communication, for mission which you have not be briefed on because—" He gestures at the laptop and I realize why he's so irritated: they weren't joking when they said the briefing would self-destruct. "Here are your ticket for flight, is open for next available seat. Will continue the briefing in Saint Martin." He shoves a booklet of flight vouchers at me.

"Where?" I nearly drop them.

"They're sending us to the Caribbean!" It's Pinky. He's almost turning handstands. "Sun! Sand! And skullduggery! And we've got great toys to play with!" Brains is methodically packing up the entanglement rig, which breaks down into a big rolling suitcase. He seems amused by something.

I try to catch Boris's eye: Boris is staring at Pinky in either deep fascination, pity, or something in between. "Where in the Caribbean?" I ask.

Boris shakes himself. "Is joint operation," he explains. "Is European territory, joint Franco-Dutch government – they ask us to operate in there. But Caribbean is American sea. So Black Chamber send Ramona to be working with you."

I wince. "Tell me you're joking."

Another voice interrupts, inaudible to everyone else: **Hey, Bob! I'm still stuck here. A girl could get bored waiting.** I have a feeling that a bored Ramona would be a very bad girl indeed, in a your-life-insurance-policy-just-expired kind of way.

"Am not joking. This is joint operation. Lots of shit to spread all round." He carefully picks up his dead laptop and drops it into an open briefcase. "Go to committee meeting tomorrow, take memos, then go to airport and fly out. Can file liaison report later, after save the universe."

"Uh-huh. First I better go unlock Ramona from that containment you stuck her in." **I'm coming,** I send her way. "How trustworthy is she, really?"

Boris smiles thinly. "How trustworthy is rattlesnake?"

I excuse myself and stagger out into the corridor, my head still throbbing and the world crinkling slightly at the edges. I guess I now know what that spike of entropy change was. I pause at the door to my room but the handle is no longer dewed with liquid nitrogen, and is merely cold to the touch.

Ramona is sitting in an armchair opposite the wall with the holes in it. She smiles at me, but the expression doesn't reach her eyes. **Bob. Get me out of this.**

This is the pentacle someone has stenciled on the carpet around her chair and plugged into a compact, blue, noise generator. It's still running – Brains didn't hook it up to his remote. **Give me a moment.** I sit down on the bed opposite her, kick off my trainers, and rub my head. **If I let you go, what are you going to do?**

Her smile broadens. **Well, personally——** she glances at the door **——nothing much.** I get a momentary flicker of unpleasantness involving extremely sharp knives and gouts of arterial blood, then she clamps down on it, with an almost regretful edge, and I realize she's just daydreaming about someone else, someone a very long way away. **Honest.**

Second question. Who's your real target?

Are you going to let me go once we get through this game of twenty questions? Or do you have something else in mind? She crosses her legs, watching me alertly. *Every guy I've ever slept with died less than twenty-four hours later*, I recall. **I wasn't joking,** she adds, defensively.

I didn't think you were. I just want to know who your real target is.

She sniffs. **Ellis Billington. What's your problem?**

I'm not sure. Bear with me for one last test?

What? She half stands as I get off the bed, but the constraining field prohibits her from reaching me: **Hey! Ow! You bastard!**

It brings tears to my eyes. I clutch my right foot and wait for the pain to subside from where I kicked the bed-base. Ramona is bent over, hugging her foot as well. **Okay,** I mumble, then kneel down and switch off the signal generator. I don't particularly want to switch it off – I feel a hell of a lot safer with Ramona trapped inside a pentacle; the idea of setting her free makes my skin crawl – but the flip side of the entanglement is fairly clear: not only can we talk without being overheard, there are other (and drastically less pleasant) side effects.

You're not a masochist, are you? she asks tightly as she hobbles towards the bathroom.

No——

Good. She slams the door shut. A few seconds later I clutch at my crotch in horror as I feel the unmistakable sensation of a full bladder emptying. It takes me seconds to realize it's not mine. My fingers are dry.

Bitch! Two can play at that game.

It's your fault for keeping me waiting for ages.

I breathe deeply. **Look. I didn't ask for this—**

Me neither!

—so why don't we call it a truce?

Silence, punctuated by a sharp sense of impatience. **Took you long enough, monkey-boy.**

What's with the monkey-boy business? I complain.

What's with the abhuman-bloodsucking-demon-whore imagery? she responds acidly. **Try to keep your gibbering religious bigotry out of my head and I'll leave your bladder alone. Deal?**

Deal — hey! How the hell am I a gibbering religious bigot? I'm an atheist!

Yeah, and the horse you rode in on is a member of the College of Cardinals. I hear the toilet flush through the door, a sudden reminder that we're not actually talking. **You may not believe in God but you still believe in Hell. And you think it's where people like me belong.**

But isn't that where you come from . . .?

The door opens. Her glamour's as strong as ever: she looks like she just stepped out of a cocktail party to powder her nose. **We can go over it some other time, Bob. You can just call room service if you want to eat, I have to make more elaborate arrangements. See you tomorrow.** With that, she picks up her evening bag from the bedside table and departs in a snit.

"Mo?"

"Hi! Where are — hold on a moment — Bob? You still there? I was about to jump in the bath. How's it going?"

Gulp. "About a ton of horse manure just landed on me. Have you seen Angleton this week?"

"No, they've billeted me in the Monkfish Motel again and it's really dull – you know what the night life in Dunwich is like. So what's Angleton up to now?"

"I, uh, well, I got here – Darmstadt – to find—" I double-check my phone to confirm we're in secure mode "—new orders waiting for me, care of Boris and the two mad mice. Almost got run off the autobahn on the way in and, well—"

"Car accident?"

"Sort of. Anyway, I'm being shunted off on a side trip instead of coming home. So I won't be back for the weekend."

"Shit."

"My thoughts exactly."

"Where are they sending you?"

"To Saint Martin, in the Caribbean."

"The—"

"And it gets worse."

"Do I want to hear this, love?"

"Probably not."

Pause. "Okay. I'm sitting down."

"It's a joint operation. They've inflicted a minder from the Black Chamber on me."

"But – Bob! That's crazy! It just doesn't happen! Nobody even knows what the Black Chamber is really called! 'No Such Agency' meets 'Destroy Before Reading.' Are you telling me . . .?"

"I haven't been fully briefed. But I figure it's going to be extremely ungood, for, like, Amsterdam values of ungood." I shudder. Our little weekend trip to Amsterdam involved more trouble than you can shake a shitty stick at. "I guess you know the Chamber specializes in taking the HUM out of HUMINT? Golems and remote viewing and so forth, never send a human agent to do a job a zombie can do? Anyway, the minder they've sent me is, you know, existentially challenged. They've sicced a demon on me."

"Jesus, Bob."

"Yeah, well, *He* isn't answering the phone."

"I can't believe it. The bastards."

"Listen, I've got a feeling there's more to this than meets the eye and I need someone watching my back who isn't just looking for a good spot to sink their fangs into. Can you do some discreet digging when you get back to the office? Ask Andy, perhaps? This is under Angleton, by the way."

"Angleton." Mo's voice goes flat and cold, and the hair on the back of my neck rises. She blames Angleton for a lot of things, and it could turn very ugly if she decides to let it all hang out. "I should have guessed. It's about time that bastard faced the music."

"Don't go after him!" I say urgently. "You're not meant to know this. Remember, all you know is I've been sent off somewhere to do a job."

"But you want me to keep my ear to the ground and listen for oncoming train wrecks."

"That's about the size of it. I'm missing you."

"Love you, too." A pause. "What is it about this spook that's got you so upset?"

Whoops. I'm no good at hiding things from her, am I? "For starters she's crazier than a legful of ferrets. She's seriously bad magic, wearing a perpetual glamour – level three, if I'm any judge of such things. The only thing keeping her on track is the geas that ate Montana. She's not a free actor. Actress."

"Uh-huh. What else?"

I lick my lips. "Boris, um, applied some sort of destiny-entanglement protocol to us. I didn't run away fast enough."

"Destiny – *what?* Entanglement? What's that?"

I take a deep breath. "I'm not sure, but I'd appreciate it if you could find out and tell me. Because whatever it is, it's scaring me."

It's still early in the evening, but my encounter with Ramona has shaken me, and I don't much want to run into Pinky and Brains again (if they haven't already packed up and left: there's quite a lot of banging coming from next door). I decide to hole up in my room and lick my wounded dignity, so I order up a cardboard cheeseburger from room service, have a long soak under the shower, watch an infinitely forgettable movie on cable, and turn in for the night.

I don't usually remember my dreams because they're mostly surreal and/or incomprehensible – two-headed camels stealing my hovercraft, bat-winged squid gods explaining why I ought to accept job offers from Microsoft, that sort of thing – so what makes this one stand out is its sheer gritty realism. Dreaming that I'm me is fine. So is dreaming that I'm an employee of a vast software multinational, damned and enslaved by an ancient evil. But dreaming that I'm an overweight fifty-something German sales executive from an engineering firm in Dusseldorf is so far off the map that if I wasn't asleep I'd pinch myself.

I'm at a regional sales convention and I've been drinking and living large. I like these conferences: I can get away from Hilda and cut loose, party like a young thing again. The awards dinner is over and I split off with a couple of younger fellows I know vaguely, which is how we end up in the casino. I don't usually gamble much but I'm on a winning streak at the wheel, and all the ladies love a winning streak; between the brandy, the Cohiba panatelas, and the babe who's attached herself to my shoulder – a call girl, natürlich but classy – I'm having the time of my life. She leans against me and suggests I might cash in my winnings, and this strikes me as a good idea. After all, if I keep gambling, my streak will end sooner or later, won't it? Let it pay for her tonight.

We're in the lift, heading up to my room on the fourteenth floor, and she's nuzzling up against me. I haven't felt smooth flesh like this in . . . too long. Hilda was never like that and since the kids the only side of her body she's shown me is the sharp edge of her tongue: serves her right if I enjoy myself once in a while. The babe's got her arms around me inside my jacket and I can feel her body through her dress. Wow. This has been a day to remember! We cuddle some more and I lead her to my room, tiptoeing – she's giggling quietly, telling me not to make a noise, not to disturb the neighbors – and I get the door open and she tells me to go wait in the bathroom while she gets ready. *How much does she want?* I ask. She shakes her head and says, *Two hundred but only if I'm happy*. Well, how can I refuse an offer like that?

In the bathroom I take my shoes off, remove my jacket and tie – *enough*. She calls to say she's ready, and I open the door. She's lying on the bed, in a provocative position that still allows her to see me. She's taken off her dress: smooth, stocking-clad thighs and a waterfall of pure corn-silk hair, blue eyes like ice diamonds that I can fall into and drown. My heart is pounding as if I've run a marathon, or I'm about to have a heart attack. She's smiling at me, hungry, needy; I take a step forwards. My back is clammy with cold sweat and my crotch feels like a steel bar, painfully erect. I need her like I've never needed a woman before. Another step. Another. She smiles and kneels on the carpet in front of me, opening her mouth to take me in. I dread her touch, even though I blindly crave it. *Tap-dancing on the third rail*, I think fuzzily, trying to force my paralyzed ribs to take a racking breath of air as she reaches out to touch me.

"Uh – uh!"

I open my eyes. It's dark in the hotel room, my heart's

hammering, and I'm lying in a puddle of cold sweat with an erection like a lump of wood and a ghastly sense of horror squatting on my chest. "Uh!" All I can do is grunt feebly. I flail for a bit, then shove the clammy sheet away from me. I'm erect – and it's not like waking from an erotic dream, it's more like someone's using a farmyard device to milk me. "Ugh." I begin to sit up, meaning to go to the bathroom and towel my back off, and right then I come.

It's weird, and wonderful, like no orgasm I've ever had before. It seems to go on and on forever, scratching the unscratchable itch inside me with an intensity that rapidly becomes unbearable. There's something about it that feels terminal – not repeatable, an endpoint in someone's life. When it begins to subside I whimper slightly and reach for my crotch. Surprise: I'm still erect – and my skin is dry.

That wasn't me, I realize, disturbed. *That was Ramona –* I clutch my prick protectively.

Distant laughter. **Go on, jerk yourself off.** There's a warm glow of satisfaction in her stomach. **You know you really want to, don't you?** she thinks, licking her lips and sending me the taste of semen. Then I feel her reach over and pull the sheets up over the dead businessman's face.

I manage to reach the bathroom and lift the toilet lid before I throw up. My stomach knots and tries to climb my throat. *Every guy I've ever slept with died less than twenty-four hours later,* she said, and now I know why. She's right about one thing: despite the sudden gag reflex I'm still sprouting a woody. Despite everything, despite the dread, despite the almost furtive guilt I feel, I *really* enjoyed whatever it is Ramona just did. And now I feel inexplicably guilty on account of Mo, because I wasn't looking for an adventure on the side – and I feel really dirty as well, because I found it exciting.

The overspill from what Ramona was doing turned me on

in my sleep, but the reason I'm throwing up now is that what she was doing wasn't sex: she was feeding on the guy's mind, and he died, and it gave her an orgasm, and I got off on it. I want to scrub my brains out with a wire brush, and I want to crawl into a deep hole in the ground, and I want to do it all over again . . . because I'm entangled with her, I hope, but the alternative is worse: there are some things I don't want to find out about myself, and a secret taste for hot, kinky demon sex is one of them.

I really hope Mo finds out that this entanglement thing is reversible. Because if it isn't, the next time she and I go to bed together—

Let's not think about that right now.

I spend an uneasy night tossing and turning between damp sheets despite the dream catcher screensaver I leave running on my tablet PC. By dawn I've just about worried myself into a mild nervous breakdown: if it's not trying to avoid thinking about invisible pink elephants (subtype: man-eaters), it's what Angleton's got in mind for me in Saint Martin. I don't even know where the place is on a map. Meanwhile, the committee meeting is another unwelcome distraction. How am I supposed to represent my organization when I'm terrified of falling asleep?

I somehow manage to fumble my way into my suit – an uncomfortable imposition required for overseas junkets – then shamble downstairs to the dining room for breakfast. Coffee, I need coffee. And a copy of the *Independent*, imported from London on an overnight flight. The restaurant is a model of German efficiency and the staff mostly leave me alone, for which I'm grateful.

I'm just about feeling human again by a quarter to nine, the meeting's optimistically scheduled to start in another fifteen minutes, but at a guess half the delegates will still be working on their breakfasts. So I wander over to the lobby where there's free WiFi, to see if there are any messages for me, and that's when I run into Franz.

"Bob? Is that you?"

I blink stupidly. "Franz?"

"Bob!" We do the handshake thing, feinting around our centers of gravity with briefcases held out to either side, like a pair of nervous chickens sizing each other up in a farmyard. I haven't seen Franz in a suit before, and he hasn't seen me in one either. I met him on a training seminar about six months ago when he was over from Den Haag. He's very tall and very Dutch, which means his accent is a lot more BBC-perfect than mine. "Fancy meeting you here."

"I guess you must be on the joint-session list?"

"I'll show you mine if you show me yours," he jokes. "I was just looking for a postcard before I go upstairs . . . will you wait?"

"Sure." I relax slightly. "Have you done one of these before?"

"No." He spins the rack idly, looking at the picturesque gingerbread castles one by one. "Have you?"

"I've done one, period. Shouldn't talk about it outside class, but what the hell."

Franz finds a postcard showing a beaming buxom German barmaid clutching a pair of highly suggestive jugs. "I'll have this one." He attracts the attention of the nearest sales clerk and rattles something off in what sounds to me like flawless German. My tablet finishes checking for mail, bins the spam, and dings at me to put it away. I rub my head and glance at Franz enviously. I bet he wouldn't have any problems with Ramona: he's scarily bright, good-natured, incisive, handsome, cultured, and all-round competent. Not to mention being able to out-drink me and charm the socks off everyone who meets him. He's clearly on his way up the ladder of the AIVD's occult counterintelligence division, and he'll make deputy director while I'm still polishing Angleton's filing cabinet.

"Ready?" he asks.

"Guess so."

We head for the lift to the conference room. It's on the fourth floor. Lest you think this is an altogether too casual approach to confidential business, the hotel is security certified and our hosts have block-booked the adjacent rooms and the suites immediately above and below. It's not as if we're going to be discussing matters of national security, either.

Franz and I are early. There's a coffee urn and cups in place on the sideboard, an LCD projector and screen next to the boardroom table, and comfortable leather-lined swivel chairs to fall asleep in. I claim one corner of the table, opposite the windows with their daydream-friendly view of downtown Darmstadt, and plunk my tablet down on the leather place mat beside the hotel notepad. "Coffee?" asks Franz.

"Yes, please. Milk, no sugar." I pick up the agenda and carry it over.

"What's the routine?" he asks. He actually sounds interested.

"Well. We show each other our authorizations first. Then the chair orders the doors sealed." I wave at the far end of the suite: "Rest room's through there. Chair this time is—" I riffle the sheets "—Italy, which means Anna, unless she's ill and they send a replacement. She'll keep things tight, I think. Then we get down to business."

"I see. And the minutes . . .?"

"Everyone who's got a presentation is supposed to bring copies on CD-ROM. The host organization[6] provides a secretarial service, that's the GSA's job this time."

---

[6] The Geheime Sicherheit Abteilung to their mothers, although everyone else calls them the Faust Force.

Franz's brow wrinkles. "Excuse me for saying, but this sounds as if the meeting itself is . . . unnecessary? We could take it to email."

I shrug. "Yup. But then we wouldn't get to do the real business, over coffee and biscuits."

His expression clears. "Ah, now I see——"

The door opens. "*Ciao*, guys!" It's Anna, short and bubbly and (I suspect) a little hung-over, judging from her eyes. "Oh, my head. Where is everybody? Let us keep this short, shall we?"

She makes a beeline for the coffee pot. "Tell Andrew he is a naughty, naughty man," she chides me.

"What's he done now?" I ask, steeling myself.

"He got my birthday wrong!" Flashing eyes, toothy grin. "A, what is it, a fencepost error."

"Oh, uh, yeah, I'll do that." I shrug. I'm still uncomfortable in this type of situation. Most of the people here were grades above me until six months ago, and half of them still are, I'm very much the junior delegate and Andy – who used to be one of my managers – is the guy into whose boots I've stepped. "Last time I saw him he was kind of busy. Overworked dealing with fallout from——" I clear my throat.

"Oh, say no more." She pats me on the arm and moves on to say hello to the other delegates who're letting themselves in. We ought to have a full house of security management types from Spain, Brussels, and parts east within NATO, but for some reason attendance today looks unusually light.

Delegates are beginning to arrive, so I head back towards my seat. "Who's that?" Franz asks me quietly, with a nod at the door. I glance round and do a double-take: it's Ramona. She's almost unrecognizable in a business suit with her hair up, but being this close to her still makes the skin crawl in the small of my back.

"That's, um, Ms. Random. An observer. We're privileged

to have her here." My cheek twitches and Franz stares at me from behind his rimless spectacles.

"I see. I was unaware that we had that type of guest present." I get the feeling he sees a whole lot more than I told him, but there's not a lot I can say.

Hello, darling, slept well? she asks. I start: then I realize she's still on the other side of the room, coolly pouring herself a cup of coffee and smiling at Anna.

No thanks to you, I think at her.

I hear a rude noise. **A girl's got to eat sometime.**

Yes, but midnight snacking— Invisible pink elephants. Think of invisible pink elephants, Bob. Think of invisible pink throbbing elephants in the night – no, cancel the throbbing—

I sit down dizzily. "Is something wrong?" asks Franz.

"Supper disagreed with me," I say weakly. Ramona's supper, that is: *pâté de gros ingénieur.* "I'll be okay if I sit down." A hot flush is trying to follow the shivers up and down my spine. I glance at her across the room and she looks back at me, blank-faced.

People are heading towards the table, apparently following my lead. To my annoyance Ramona oozes into the chair next to me then stares sharply at Anna's end of the table.

"*Ciao* everybody. I see a lot of vacant seats and new faces today! This meeting will now commence. Badges on the table, please." Anna looks up and down the table pointedly as clusters of conversation die down.

I reach into my pocket and slide my Laundry warrant card onto the table. Everyone else is doing likewise with their own accreditation: the air twists and prickles with the bindings. "Excusez-moi." François leans across the table towards Ramona: "You have credentials?"

Ramona just looks at him. "No. As a matter of policy my

organization does not issue identification papers." Heads turn and eyes narrow around the table.

I clear my throat. "I can vouch for her," I hear myself saying. "Ramona Random—" words slide seamlessly into my mind "—Overseas Operations Directorate, based out of Arkham." **Thanks,** I tell her silently, **now get out of my head.** "Here by direct invitation of my own department, full observer status under Clause Four of the Benthic Treaty."

Ramona smiles thinly. There's a low buzz of surprised conversation. "Quiet!" calls Anna. "I'd like to welcome our . . . today's observer here." She looks slightly flustered. "If you could contrive some form of identification in future, that would be helpful, but—" she looks at me hopefully "—I'm sure Robert's superiors will cover this time."

I manage to nod. I can't cover it on my authority, but this is Angleton's bloody fault, after all, and he actually gets to talk to Mahogany Row. Let *them* sort it out.

"Fine!" She claps her hands together. "Then, to business! First item, attendees, I believe we have taken care of. Let the doors be locked. Second item, travel expense claims in pursuit of joint investigation warrants on overseas territory, at the request of non-issuing governments. Arbitration of expense allocation among participating member states – traditionally this has been carried out on an ad hoc basis, but since the Austrian civil service strike last year the urgency of formalizing arrangements has become apparent . . ."

The next hour passes uneventfully. It's basically bureaucratic legwork, to ensure that none of the European partner agencies tread on each other's toes when operating on each other's soil. Proposals to allow agents of charter countries to claim expenses for mopping up after another member's business are agreed upon and bounced up to the next level of management for approval. Suggestions for standardizing the various forms of ID we use are proposed, and eventually shot down because they serve very different purposes and some of them come with powers which are considered alarming, illegal, or immoral in different jurisdictions. I take notes on my tablet, briefly consider a game of Minesweeper before deciding it's not worth the risk of exposure, and finally settle down to the grim business of not falling asleep and embarrassing myself in public.

Glancing around the table I realize things are pretty much the same all round. Anyone who isn't actively talking or jotting notes is twiddling their thumbs, gazing out the window, staring at the other delegates, or quietly drooling over their complementary notepad. *Ah, the joy of high-level negotiations.* I glance at Ramona and see she's one of the doodlers. She's inscribing something black and scary on her notepad: geometric lines and arcs, repeated patterns that sink into one another in a self-similar way. Then she glances sidelong at me, and very deliberately slides a blank sheet of paper across her pad.

I shake myself; must stay focused. We're up to item four on the agenda, drilling down into issues of software resource management and a proposal to jointly license an auditing and license management system being developed by a subsidiary of – TLA Systems

I sit bolt upright. Sophie from Berlin is soporifically talking us through the procurement process Faust Force has come up with, a painfully politically correct concoction of open market tenders and sealed bidding processes intended to evaluate competing proposals and then roll out a best-of-breed system for common deployment. "Excuse me," I say, when she pauses for breath, "this is all very well, but what can you tell us about the winning bid? I assume the process has already been approved," I add hastily, before she can explain that this is all very important background detail.

"Ah, but this is necessary to understand the process-oriented quality infrastructure, Robert." She looks down her nose at me over her bifocals and brandishes a scarily thick sheaf of papers. "I have here the fully documented procurement analysis for the system!" The only inflection in her voice is on the last word, making a sort of semantic hiccup out of it. She sounds like a badly programmed speech synthesizer.

"Yes, but what does it *do*?" Ramona butts in, leaning forwards. It's the first thing she's said since I introduced her, and suddenly she's the focus of attention again. "I'm sorry if this is all understood by everybody present, but . . ." she trails off.

Sophie pauses for a few seconds, like a robot receiving new instructions. "If you will with me bear, I shall explain it. The contractors have a presentation prepared, to be played after lunch." *Oops*, I think, visions of the usual postprandial siesta torture running through my head. Dim the lights, turn the heating up, then get some bastard in a suit to stand up and drone through a PowerPoint presentation — have I said how much I hate PowerPoint? — while you try to stay awake. Then I blink and notice Ramona's sidelong glance. *Oops again*. What's going on?

Lunch arrives mercifully soon, in the form of a trolley, parked outside the conference suite door, laden with sandwiches and slices of ham. Sophie accepts the enforced pause with relatively good grace, and we all stand up and head for the buffet, except Ramona. While I'm stuffing my face on tuna and cucumber I catch Franz looking concerned. "Are you hungry?" he asks her quietly.

Ramona smiles at him, turning on the charm. "I'm on a special diet."

"Oh, I'm so sorry."

She beams up at him: "That's all right, I had a heavy meal last night."

Don't, I warn her silently, and she flashes a scowl at me.

You're no fun, monkey-boy.

Eventually we go back to the table. Anna fidgets with the remote control to the blinds until she figures out how to block off the early afternoon sunlight. "Very good!" she says approvingly. "Sophie, if you will continue?"

"*Danke*." Sophie fidgets with her laptop and the projector cable. "Ah, *gut*. Here we go, very soon . . ."

There is something about PowerPoint presentations that sends people to sleep. It's particularly effective after lunch, and Sophie doesn't have the personal presence to get past the soothing wash of pastel colors and flashy dissolves and actually make us pay attention. I lean back and watch, tiredly. TLA GmBH is a subsidiary of TLA Systems Corporation, of Ellis Billington. They're the guys who do for the Black Chamber what QinetiQ does – or used to do – for the UK's Ministry of Defense. This integrated system we're watching a promo video for is basically just a tarted-up-for-export – meaning, it speaks Spanish, French, and German technobabble – version of a big custom program they wrote for Ramona's faceless employers. *So what's Ramona doing here?* I wonder. *They must already know all this. Wake up, Bob!* I've got a stomach full of tuna mayo and smoked salmon on rye, and it feels like it weighs a quarter of a ton. The sunlight slanting through the half-drawn blinds warms the back of my hands where they lie limply on the tabletop. Asset-management software is so not my favorite afternoon topic of conversation. *Bob, pay attention at the back! Ramona shouldn't be here,* I think fuzzily. *Why is she here? Is it something to do with Billington's software?*

*Bob! Pay attention right now!**

I jolt upright in my seat as if someone's stuck a cattle prod up my rear. The sharp censorious voice in my head is Ramona's. I glance along the table but everybody else is nodding or dozing or snoozing m tune to Sophie's repetitive cadence – except Ramona, who catches my eye. She's alert, ready and waiting for something.

What's going on? I ask her.

We're at slide twenty-four, she tells me. **Whatever happens next, it happens between numbers twenty-six and twenty-eight.**

What . . . ?

We're not omniscient, Bob. We just caught wind of – aha, twenty-five coming up.

I glance at the end of the table. Sophie stands next to the projector and her laptop, swaying slightly like a puppet in the grip of an invisible force. ". . . The four-year rolling balance of assets represents a best-of-breed optimization for control of procurement processes and the additional neural network intermediated Bayesian maintenance workload prediction module will allow you to control your inventory of hosts and project a stable cash flow . . ." My guts clench. A whole lot of things suddenly come clear: *The bastards are trying to brainwash the committee!*

It's PowerPoint, of course. A hypnotic slide into a bulleted list of total cost of ownership savings and a pie chart with a neat lime-green slice taken out of it – *ooh look, it's three dimensional*; it's also a bar graph with the height of the slices denoting some other parameter – and a pale background of yellow lines on white that looks a little like the TLA logo we began the slide show with: an eye floating in a tetrahedral Escher paradox, and a diagram a little bit like whatever Ramona was sketching on her notepad – I grab my tablet PC and poke the power button, trying to keep my hands from shaking.

Screen saver. *Screen saver.* I eject the pen and hastily hit on the control panel to bring up the screen saver. The dream catcher routine I had running last night is all I can think of right now.

I set it running then slide the tablet face-up, with the hypnotic blur of purple lines cycling across it, on the conference table so that it lies directly between me and the projection screen.

Good move, monkey-boy.

Franz is leaning back in his chair beside me. His eyes are closed and there's a fine thread of spittle dangling from one side of his mouth. François is face-down on the mat, snoring, and Anna is frozen, glassy-eyed, at the foot of the table, her open eyes fixed unseeing on the projector screen. I take care not to look at it directly.

What's it meant to be doing? I ask Ramona.

That's what we're here to find out. Nobody who's been in one of these sales sessions before has come out in any state to tell us.

What? You mean they were killed?

No, they just insisted on buying TLA products. Oh, and they'd had their souls eaten.

What would you know about that?

They don't taste the same. Shut up and get ready to yank the projector cable when I give the word, okay?

Sophie hits the mouse button again and the light in the room changes subtly, signaling a dissolve from one frame to another. Her voice mutates, morphs and deepens, taking on a vaguely familiar cadence. "Today, we celebrate the first glorious anniversary of the Information Purification Directives. We have created, for the first time in all history, a garden of pure ideology. Where each worker may bloom secure from the pests of any contradictory and confusing truths . . ."

The dream catcher in front of me is going crazy. **I've seen that before. It's the Apple 1984 ad, the one they commissioned Ridley Scott to direct for the launch of the Macintosh computer. The most expensive ad in the entire history of selling beige boxes to puzzled posers. What the hell are they doing with *that*?**

Law of contagion. Ramona sounds tense. **Very strong imagery of conformity versus mold-breaking, concealing conformity disguised *as* mold-breaking. Ever wondered why Mac users are so glassy-eyed about their boxes? This is slide twenty-six; okay, we've got about ten seconds to go . . .**

I briefly debate standing up right there and yanking the power cable. I've seen the original ad so many times I don't need to look at the screen to follow it; it's famous throughout the computer industry. "Our Unification of Thoughts is more powerful a weapon than any fleet or army on Earth. We are one people, with one will, one resolve, one cause. Our enemies shall talk themselves to death and we will bury them with their own confusion. We shall prevail!"

Seconds to go. The female runner races towards the huge screen in front of the arena, clutching a sledge hammer, poised to hurl it through Big Brother's face – and I know exactly what's going to happen, what those shards of glass are going to morph into with the next dissolve as I take my tablet by both sides (careful to keep my hands from touching the toughened glass screen cover) and pick it up, flipping it over as the crescendo builds towards what would be, in the real advertisement, the announcement of a revolutionary new type of computer—

Ready—

The light flickers and something that feels like an out-of-control truck punches into the screen of the tablet PC as I hold it between my face and the projection screen. It's not a physical force, but it might as well be from the acrid smoke spewing from the vents under my fingertips and the way the battery compartment begins to glow.

Go!

I drop the PC, cover my eyes with one hand, and dive for where the back of the projector used to be. I flop on my belly halfway across the table, flailing around until I catch a bunch of wires and yank hard, pulling and tearing at them, too frightened to open my eyes and see which ones I've got hold of. Someone is screaming and someone else is crying behind me, emitting incoherent moans like an animal in pain. Then someone punches me in the ribs.

I open my eyes. The projector's out and Ramona is sitting on top of Sophie from the Faust Force, or the thing that's animating Sophie's body, methodically whacking her head on the floor. Then I realize that the pain in my side is Ramona's: Sophie is fighting back. I roll over and find myself facing Anna. Her face hangs like a loose mask and her eyes glow faintly in the twilight that the almost-closed blinds allow into the room. I scrabble desperately, grab the edge of the table, and pull myself over it into her lap. She grabs for my head but whatever's inside her isn't very good at controlling a human body and I roll again, drop arse-first onto the floor (my coccyx will tell me about it tomorrow), and scramble to my feet.

The previously orderly meeting is dissolving into the kind of carnage that can only ensue when most of the members of an international joint-liaison committee turn into brain-eating zombies. Luckily they're not Sam Raimi zombies, they're just midlevel bureaucrats whose cerebral cortices have been abruptly wiped in the presence of a Dho-Na summoning geometry (in this case, embedded in the dissolve between two PowerPoint slides), allowing some random extradimensional gibberers to move in. Half of them can't even stand up, and those who can aren't very effective yet.

Have you got her? I ask Ramona, working my way past Anna (who is currently keeping François occupied by chewing on his left hand) and nearly tripping over the wreckage of my tablet PC.

She's fighting back! A stray, booted foot lashes out at

me and now I succeed in falling over, on top of Sophie as luck would have it. Sophie looks up at me with blank eyes and makes a keening noise like a cat that wants to break a furry critter's neck.

Well fucking *do* something! I yell.

Okay. Sophie jerks underneath me and tries to sink her teeth into my arm. But Ramona's ready with a spring-loaded syringe and nails her right through the shoulder. **You'll need to open the wards so we can get out.**

I'm going to— *Oh, right. Ramona's a guest.* I lurch upright and lunge for the blotter in front of Anna's seat, grab at her gavel, and rap it on the table. "As the last quorate member standing I hereby unanimously promote myself to Chair and declare this session closed." Five heads, their eyes swimming with luminous green worms, turn to face me. "School's out." I race for the door, piling into Ramona as I yank the handle open. **Got her?**

Yes. Grab her other arm and move!

Sophie is kicking and writhing wordlessly but Ramona and I drag her through the doorway and I yank it shut behind us. The latch clicks, and Sophie goes limp.

Hey. I look sideways. **What's—**

Ramona lets go of her other arm and I stagger. **Well isn't that a surprise,** she comments, looking down at Sophie, who sprawls on the hotel carpet in front of the door. **She's dead, Jim.**

Bob, I correct automatically. **What do you mean, she's dead?**

Poison-pill programming, I think.

I lean against the wall, dizzy and nauseated. **We've got to go back! The others are still in there. Can we break it? The control link, I mean. If it's just a transient over-ride—**

Ramona winces and stares at me. **Will you stop that?**

It's not a transient and there's nothing we can do for them.**

But she's dead! We've got to do something! And they're—

They're dead, too. Ramona stares at me in obvious concern. **Did you hit your head or something? No, I'd have felt that. You're squeamish, aren't you?**

We could have saved them! You knew what was going to happen! You could have warned us! If you hadn't been so fucking curious to know what was buried in the presentation – shit, why didn't you just snarf a copy and edit it yourself? This isn't the first time it's happened, is it?

She lets me rant for a minute or so, until I run down. **Bob, Bob. This is the first time this has happened. At least, the first time anyone's gotten out of one of these presentations alive.**

Jesus. Then why do you keep having them? I realize I'm waving my arms around but I'm too upset to stop. I have a terrible feeling that if I'd just given in to my first impulse to yank the cord on the projector— **It's murder! Letting it go ahead like that—**

We don't. My – department – doesn't. TLA is selling hard outside the US, Bob. They sell in places like Malaysia or Kazakhstan or Peru, and in places that aren't quite on the map, if you follow me. We've heard rumors about this. We've seen some of the . . . fallout. But this is the first time we've gotten in on the ground floor. Sophie Frank was fingered by your people, if you must know. Your Andy Newstrom raised the flag. She's been behaving oddly for the past couple of months. You were sent because, unlike Newstrom, you're trained for this category of operation. But nobody else took the warnings sufficiently seriously – except for your department, and mine.

But what about the others?

She stares at me grimly. **Blame Ellis Billington, Bob. Remember, if he wasn't into the hard sell, this wouldn't have happened.**

Then she turns and stalks away, leaving me alone and shaking in the corridor, with a corpse and a locked conference room full of middle-management zombies to explain.

4: YOU'RE IN THE JET SET NOW

MY CHECKOUT IS EVER SO SLIGHTLY DELAYED. I spend about eight hours at the nearest police station being questioned by one GSA desk pilot after another. At first I think they're going to arrest me – shoot the messenger is a well-known parlor game in spook circles – but after a few fraught hours there's a change in the tone of the interrogation. Someone higher up has obviously got a handle on events and is smoothing my path. "It is best for you to leave the country tomorrow," says Gerhardt from Frankfurt, not smiling. "Later we will have questions, but not now." He shakes his head. "If you should happen to see Ms. Random, please explain that we have questions for her also." A taciturn cop drives me back to the hotel, where a GSA cleaning team has replaced the conference room door with a blank stretch of brand-new wall. I walk past it without quite losing my shit, then retreat to my shielded bedroom and spend a sleepless night trying to second guess myself. But not only is the past another country, it's one that doesn't issue visas; and so, first thing in the morning, I head downstairs to collect the hire car.

A tech support nightmare is waiting for me down in the

garage. Pinky is goose-stepping around with a clipboard, trying to look officious while Brains is elbow-deep in the trunk with a circuit tester and a roll of gaffer tape.

"What. The. Fuck?" I manage to say, then lean against a concrete pillar.

"We've been modifying this Smart car for you!" Pinky says excitedly. "You need to know how to use all its special features."

I rub my eyes in disbelief. "Listen guys, I've been attacked by brain-eating zombies and I'm due on a flight to Saint Martin tonight. This isn't the right time to show me your toys. I just want to get home—"

"Impossible," Brains mutters around a mouthful of oily bolts that look suspiciously as if they've just come out of the engine manifold.

"Angleton told us not to let you go until you'd finished your briefing!" Pinky exclaims.

There's no escape. "Okay." I yawn. "You just put those bolts back and I'll be going."

"Look in the boot, here. What our American friends would call the trunk. Careful, mind that pipe! Good. Now pay attention, Bob. We've added a Bluetooth host under the driver's seat, and a repurposed personal video player running Linux. Peripheral screens at all five cardinal points, five grams of graveyard dust mixed with oil of Bergamot and tongue of newt in the cigarette lighter socket, and a fully connected Dee-Hamilton circuit glued to the underside of the body shell. As long as the ignition is running, you're safe from possession attempts. If you need to dispose of a zombie in the passenger seat, just punch in the lighter button and wait for the magic smoke. You've got a mobile phone, yes? With Bluetooth and a Java sandbox? Great, I'll email you an applet – run it, pair your phone with the car's hub, and all you have to do is dial 6-6-6 and the car will come to you, wherever you are. There's another applet to remotely trigger all the car's countermeasures, just in case someone's sneaked a surprise into it."

I shake my head, but it won't stop spinning. "Zombie smoke in the lighter socket, Dee-Hamilton circuit in the body shell, and the car comes when I summon it. Okay. Hey, what's—"

He slaps my hand as I reach for the boxy lump fastened to the gearshift with duct tape. "Don't touch that button, Bob!"

"Why? What happens if I touch that button, Pinky?"

"The car ejects!"

"Don't you mean, the passenger seat ejects?" I ask sarcastically. I've had just about enough of this nonsense.

"No, Bob, you've been watching too many movies. The *car* ejects." He reaches across the back of my seat and pats the fat pipe occupying the center of the luggage area.

I swallow. "Isn't that a little . . . dangerous?"

"Where you're going you'll need all the help you can get." He frowns at me. "The tube contains a rocket motor and a cable spool bolted to the chassis. The airbags in the wheel hubs blow when the accelerometer figures you've hit apogee, if you haven't already used them in amphibious pursuit mode. Whatever you do don't push that button while you're in a tunnel or under cover." I glance up at the concrete roof of the car park and shudder. "The airbags are securely fastened, if you land on water you can just drive away." He notices my fixed, skeptical stare and pats the rocket tube. "It's perfectly safe – they've been using these on helicopter gunships for nearly five years!"

"Jesus." I close my eyes and lean back. "It's still a fucking Smart car. Range Rovers carry them as lifeboats. Couldn't you get me an Aston Martin or something?"

"What makes you think we'd give you an Aston Martin, even if we could afford one? Anyway, Angleton says to remind you that it's on lease from one of our private sector partners. Don't bend it, or you'll answer to the Chrysler Corporation. You've already exceeded our consumables budget, totalling that Compaq in the meeting – there's a new one waiting for you in the case in the boot, by the way. This is serious business: you're representing the Laundry in front of the Black Chamber and some very big defense contractors, old school tie and all that."

"I went to North Harrow Comprehensive," I say wearily, "they didn't trust us with neckties, not after the upper fifth tried to lynch Brian the Spod."

"Oh. Well." Pinky pulls out a thick envelope. "Your itinerary once you arrive at Juliana Airport. There's a decent tailor in the Marina shopping center and we've faxed your measurements through. Um. Do you dress to the left, or . . .?"

I open my eyes and stare at him until he wilts. "Eight dead." I hold up the requisite number of fingers. "In twenty-four hours. And I have to drive up the fucking autobahn in this pile of shit—"

"No, you don't," says Brains, finally straightening up and wiping his hands on a rag. "We've got to crate up the Smart if we're going to freight it to Maho Beach tomorrow – you're riding with us." He gestures at a shiny black Mercedes van parked opposite. "Feel better?"

Wow – I'm not going to be strafed with BMWs again. Miracles do sometimes happen, even in Laundry service. I nod. "Let's get going."

I sleep most of the way to Frankfurt. We're late getting to the airport – no surprise in light of preceding events – but Pinky and Brains prestidigitate some sort of official ID out of their warrant cards and drive us through two chain-link barriers and past a police checkpoint and onto the apron, hand me a briefcase, then drop me at the foot of the steps of an air bridge. It's latched onto a Lufthansa airbus bound for Paris's Charles de Gaulle and a quick transfer. "Schnell!" urges a harried-looking flight attendant. "You are the last. Come this way."

One and a half hours and a VIP transfer later, I'm in business class aboard an Air France A300 bound for Princess Juliana International Airport. The compartment is half-empty. "Please fasten your seatbelts and pay attention to the preflight briefing." I close my eyes while they close the doors behind me. Then someone shakes my shoulder: it's a flight attendant. "Mr. Howard? I have a message to tell you that there's WiFi access on this flight. You are to call your office as soon as we are airborne at cruising altitude and the seatbelt light goes off."

I nod, speechless. WiFi? On a thirty-year-old tourist truck like this? "Bon voyage!" She stands up and marches to the back of the cabin. "Call if you need anything."

I doze through the usual preflight, waking briefly as the engine note rises to a thunderous roar and we pile down the runway. I feel unnaturally tired, as if drained of life, and I've got a strange sense that somebody else is sleeping in the empty seat beside me, close enough to rest their head on my shoulder — but the next seat over is empty. *Overspill from Ramona?* Then my eyes close again.

It must be the cabin pressure, the stress of the last couple of days, or drugs in the after-takeoff champagne, because I find myself having the strangest dream. I'm back in the conference suite in Darmstadt, and the blinds are down, but instead of a room full of zombies I'm sitting across the table from Angleton. He looks half-mummified at the best of times, until you see his eyes: they're diamond-blue and as sharp as a dentist's drill. Right now they're the only part of him I can see at all, because he's engulfed in the shadows cast by an old-fashioned slide projector lighting up the wall behind him. The overall effect is very sinister. I look over my shoulder, wondering where Ramona's gotten to, but she's not there.

"Pay *attention*, Bob. Since you had the bad grace to take so long during my previous briefing that it self-erased before you completed it, I've sent you another." I open my mouth to tell him he's full of shit, but the words won't emerge. *An Auditor ward*, I think, choking on my tongue and beginning to panic, but right then my larynx relaxes and I'm able to close my jaw. Angleton smiles sepulchrally. "There's a good fellow."

I try to say *blow me*, but it comes out as "brief me" instead. It seems I'm allowed to speak, so long as I stay on topic.

"Certainly. I have explained the history of the *Glomar Explorer*, and Operations JENNIFER and AZORIAN. What I did not explain – this goes no further than your dreams, and the inside of your own eyeballs, especially when Ramona is awake – was that JENNIFER and AZORIAN were cover stories. Dry runs, practical experiments, if you like. To retrieve artifacts from the oceanic floor, in the zones ceded by humanity to BLUE HADES – the Deep Ones – in perpetuity under the terms of the Benthic Treaties and the Agreement of the Azores."

Angleton pauses to take a drink from a glass of ice water beside his blotter. Then he flicks the slide advance button on the projector. *Click-clack.*

"This is a map of the world we live in," Angleton explains. "And these pink zones are those that humans are allowed to roam in. Our reservation, if you like. The arid air-swept continents and the painfully bright low-pressure top waters of the oceans. About thirty-four percent of the Earth's surface area. The rest, the territory of the Deep Ones, we are permitted to sail above, but that is all. Attempts to settle the deep ocean would be resisted in such a manner that our species would not survive long enough to regret them."

I lick my lips. "How? I mean, do they have nuclear weapons or something?"

"Worse than that." He doesn't smile. "This—" *click-clack* "—is Cumbre Vieja, on the island of La Palma. It is one of seventy-three volcanoes or mountains located in deep water – most of the others are submerged guyots rather than climbable peaks – that BLUE HADES have prepared. Three-quarters of humanity live within 200 miles of a sea coast. If they ever lose their patience with us, the Deep Ones can trigger undersea landslides. Cumbre Vieja alone is poised to deposit 500 billion tons of rock on the floor of the North Atlantic, generating a tsunami that will be twenty meters high by the time it makes landfall in New York. Make that more like fifty meters by the time it hits Southampton. If we provoke them they can wreak more destruction than an all-out nuclear war. And they have occupied this planet since long before our hominid ancestors discovered fire."

"But we've got a deterrent, surely . . .?"

No." Angleton's expression is implacable. "Water absorbs the energy of a nuclear explosion far more effectively than air. You get a powerful pressure wave, but no significant heat or radiation damage: the shock wave is great for crushing submarines, but much less effective against undersea organisms at ambient pressure. We could hurt them, but nothing like as badly as they could hurt us. And as for the rest of it—" he gestures at the screen "—they could have wiped us out before we discovered them, if they were so inclined. They have access to technologies and tools we can barely begin to imagine. They are the Deep Ones, BLUE HADES, a branch of an ancient and powerful alien civilization. Some of us suspect the threat of the super-tsunami is a distraction. It's like an infantryman pointing his bayonet-tipped assault rifle at a headhunter, who sees only a blade on a stick. Don't even think about threatening them, we exist because they bear us no innate ill will, but we have at least the power to change that much if we act rashly."

"Then what the hell was JENNIFER about?"

Click-clack. "A misplaced attempt to end the Cold War prematurely, by acquiring a weapon truly hellish in its potential. The precise nature of which you have no need to know right now, in case you were thinking of asking."

I'm looking down on a gloomy gray scene. It takes me a few seconds to realize that it's a deep-ocean mudscape. Scattered across the layered silt are small irregular objects, some of them round, some of them long. A couple more seconds and my brain acknowledges that what my eyes are seeing is a watery field of skulls and femurs and ribs. I've got an idea that not all of them are entirely human.

"The Caribbean sea hides many secrets. This field of silt covers a deep layer rich in methane hydrates. When some force destabilizes the deposits they bubble up from the depths – like the carbon dioxide discharge from the stagnant waters of Lake Nyos in the Cameroon. But unlike Lake Nyos, the gas isn't confined by terrain so it dissipates after it surfaces. It's not an asphyxiation threat, but if you're on a ship that's caught above a hydrate release, then the sea under your keel turns to gas and you're going straight down to Davy Jones's locker." Angleton clears his throat. "BLUE HADES have some way of replenishing these deposits and triggering releases. They use them to keep us interfering hominids away from things that don't concern us, such as the settlement at Witch's Hole in the North Sea . . . and the depths of the Bermuda Triangle."

I swallow. "What's down there?"

"Some of the deepest oceanic trenches on Earth. And some of the largest BLUE HADES installations we're aware of."

Angleton looks as if he's bitten into a lemon expecting an orange. "That isn't saying much – most of their sites are known to us only from neutrino mapping and seismology. The portion of the biosphere we understand is limited to the surface waters and continental land masses, boy. Below a thousand fathoms of water, let alone below the Mohorovičić Discontinuity, it's a whole different ball game."

"The Moho-what?"

"The underside of the continental plates we live on – below the discontinuity lies the upper mantle. Didn't you study geography at school?"

"Uh . . ." I spent most of my school geography lessons snoozing, doodling imaginary continents in the backs of exercise books, or trying to work up the courage to pass a message to Lizzie Graham in the next row. Now it looks like those missed lessons are about to come back and bite me. "Moving swiftly on, let me see if I've got this straight. Ellis Billington has purchased a CIA spy ship designed for probing BLUE HADES territory. He's got a high enough security clearance to be aware what it's capable of, and his people are trying to suborn various intelligence organizations, like in Darmstadt. He's playing some kind of endgame and you don't like the smell and neither does the Black Chamber, which explains me and Ramona. Am I right so far?"

Angleton nods minutely. "I should remind you that Billington is extraordinarily rich and has fingers in a surprising number of pies. For example, by way of his current wife – his third – he owns a cosmetics and haute couture empire; in addition to IT corporations he owns shipping, aviation, and banking interests. Your assignment – and Ramona's – is to get close to Billington. Ideally you should contrive to get yourself invited aboard his yacht, the *Mabuse*, while Ramona remains in touch with your backup team and the local head of station. Your technical backups are Pinky and Brains, your muscle backup is Boris, and you're to liaise with our Caribbean station chief, Jack Griffin. Officially, he's your superior officer and you'll be under his orders when it comes to nonoperational matters but you're to report directly to me, not to him. Unofficially, Griffin is out to pasture — take anything he says with a pinch of salt. Your job is to get close to Billington, remain in touch with us, and be ready to act if and when we decide to take him down."

I manage not to groan. "Why does it have to be me aboard the yacht — why not Ramona? I think she'd be a whole lot better at the field ops thing. Or the station chief guy? Come to think of it, why aren't the AIVD doing this? It's their territory—"

"They invited us in; all I can say for now is, we have specialist expertise in this area that they lack. And it has to be you, not Ramona. Firstly, you're an autonome, a native of this continuum: they can't trap you in a Dho-Nha curve or bind you to a summoning grid. And secondly, it's got to be you because those are the rules of Billington's game." Angleton's expression is frightening. "He's a player, Bob. He knows exactly what he's doing and how to work around our strengths. He stays away from continental land masses, uses games of chance to determine his actions, sleeps inside a Faraday cage aboard a ship with a silver-plated keel. He's playing us to a script. I'm not at liberty to tell you what it is, but it has to be you, not Ramona, not anyone else."

"Do we have any idea what he's planning? You said something about weapons—"

Angleton fixes me with a steely gaze. "Pay attention, Bob. The presentation is about to commence." And this time I can't stifle the groan, because it's another of his bloody slideshows, and if you thought PowerPoint was pants, you haven't suffered through an hour of Angleton monologuing over a hot slide projector.

SLIDE 1: Photograph of three men wearing suits with the exaggerated lapels and wide ties of the mid-1970s. They're standing in front of some sort of indistinct building-like structure, possibly prefabricated. All three wear badges clipped to their breast pockets.

"The one on the left is me: you don't need to know who the other two are. This photograph was taken in 1974 while I was assigned to Operation AZORIAN as our liaison – officially from MI6 as an observer, but you know the drill. The building I'm standing in front of is . . ."

SLIDE 2: A photograph taken looking aft along the deck of a huge sea-going vessel. To the left, there's a gigantic structure like an oil drilling rig, with racks of pipes stacked in front of it. Directly ahead, at the stern, is the structure glimpsed in the previous slide—a mobile office, jacked up off the deck, its roofline bristling with antennae. Behind it, a satellite dish looms before the superstructure of the ship.

"We're aboard the *Hughes Glomar Explorer* on its unsuccessful voyage to raise the sunken Soviet Golf-II-class ballistic missile submarine K-129. Announced as Operation JENNIFER, this was leaked to the press by someone acting on unofficial orders from the director of ONI – the usual goddamn turf war – and Watergated to hell by mid-1975. I said Operation JENNIFER was unsuccessful. Officially, the CIA only retrieved the front ten meters or so of the sub because the rear section broke off. In reality . . ."

SLIDE 3: Grainy black-and-white photographs, evidently taken from TV screens: a long cylindrical structure grasped in the claws of an enormous grab. From below, thin streamers rise up towards it.

"BLUE HADES took exception to the intrusion into their territory and chose to exercise their salvage rights under Article Five, Clause Four of the Benthic Treaty. Hence the tentacles. Now . . ."

SLIDE 1 (Repeat): This time the man in the middle is circled with a red highlighter.

"This fellow in the middle is Ellis Billington, as he looked thirty years ago. Ellis was brilliant but not well socialized back then. He was attached to the 'B' team as an observer, tasked with examining the circuitry of the cipher machine they hoped to recover from the sub's control room. I didn't pay much attention to him at the time, which was a mistake. He already had his security clearance, and after the JENNIFER debacle he moved to San Jose and set up a small electronics and software business."

SLIDE 4: A crude-looking circuit board. Rather than fiberglass, it appears to be made of plywood that has been exposed to seawater for too long, and has consequently warped. Sockets for vacuum tubes stud its surface, one of them occupied by the broken base of a component; numerous diodes and resistors connect it to an odd, stellate design in gold that covers most of the surface of the board.

"This board was taken from a GRU-issued Model 60 oneiromantic convolution engine found aboard the K-129. As you can see, it spent rather longer in the water than was good for it. Ellis reverse-engineered the basic schematic and pieced together the false vacuum topology that the valves disintermediated. Incidentally, these aren't your normal vacuum tubes – isotope imbalances in the thorium-doped glass sleeves suggest that they were evacuated by exposure in a primitive wake-shield facility, possibly aboard a model-three *Sputnik* satellite similar to the one first orbited in 1960. That would have given them a starting pressure about six orders of magnitude cleaner than anything available on Earth at the time, at a price per tube of about two million rubles, which suggests that someone in the GRU's scientific directorate *really* wanted a good signal, if that wasn't already obvious. We now know that they'd clearly cracked the Dee-

Turing Thesis by this point and were well into modified
Enochian metagrammar analysis. Anyway, young Billington
concluded that the Mod-60 OCE, NATO code 'Gravedust,'
was intended to allow communication with the dead.
Recently dead, anyway."

SLIDE 5: An open coffin containing a long-dead body.
The corpse is partially mummified, the eyelids sunken into
the empty sockets and the jaw agape with lips retracted.

"We're not sure exactly what a Gravedust system was
doing aboard the K-129. According to one theory that was
remarkably popular with our friends at ONI around the
time, it had something to do with the former Soviet Union's
postmortem second strike command-and-control system, to
allow the submarine's political officer to ask for instructions
from the Politburo after a successful decapitation stroke.
They were very keen on maintaining the correct chain of
command back then. There's just one problem with that
theory: it's rubbish. According to our own analysis after the
event – I should add, the Black Chamber was remarkably
reluctant to part with the Gravedust schemata, we finally got
it out of them by remote viewing – Billington underestimated the backreach of the Gravedust interrogator by a
factor of at least a thousand. We were told that it would only
allow callbacks to the recently dead, within the past million
seconds. In actual fact, you could call up Tutankhamun himself on this rig. Our best guess is that the Soviets were
planning on talking to something that had been dead for a
very long time indeed, somewhere under the ocean."

SLIDE 6: A Russian submarine, moored alongside a pier.
In the distance, snow-capped mountains loom above the far
shore of a waterway.

"The K-129 was rather an elderly boat at the time she
sank. In fact, a few years later the Soviets retired the last of
the Golf-II class – except for one of the K-129's sister ships,

which was retained for covert operations duty. As a ballistic missile boat it had a large hold that could be repurposed for other payloads, and as a diesel-electric it could run quietly in littoral waters. Diesel-electrics are still popular for that reason: when running on battery juice they're even quieter than a nuke boat, which has to keep the reactor coolant pumps running at all times. Without the rear section – including the missile room – we could only theorize that K-129 had already been converted to infiltration duty. However . . ."

SLIDE 7: A blurry gray landscape photographed from above. A structure, clearly artificial, occupies the middle of the image: a cylindrical artifact not unlike a submarine, but missing a conning tower and equipped with a strange, roughly surfaced conical endcap. Its hull is clearly damaged, not crumpled but burst open as if from some great internal pressure. Nevertheless, it is still recognizable as an artificial structure.

"We believe this was the real target of K-129's abortive operation. It's located on the floor of the Pacific, approximately 600 nautical miles southwest of Hawaii and, by no coincidence at all, on the K-129's course prior to the unfortunate onboard explosion that resulted in the submarine's loss with all hands."

SLIDE 8: Not a photograph but a false-color synthetic relief image of the floor of the Pacific basin, southwest of Hawaii. The image is contoured to represent depth, and colored to convey some other attribute. Virulent red spots dot the depths – except for a single, much shallower one.

"Graviweak neutrino imaging spectroscopes carried aboard the SPAN-2 Earth resources satellite are a good way of pinpointing BLUE HADES colonies. For obvious reasons, BLUE HADES do not make extensive use of electricity for their domestic and presumed industrial processes; Monsieur

Volt and Herr Ampère are not your friends when you live under five kilometers of saltwater. Instead, BLUE HADES appear to control inaccessible condensed matter states by varying the fine-structure constant and tunneling photinos – super-symmetrical photon analogs that possess mass – between nodes where they want to do things. One side effect of this is neutrino emissions at a very characteristic spectrum, unlike anything we get from the sun or from our own nuclear reactors. This is a density scan for the zone around the K-129 and Hawaii. As you can see, that isolated shallow point – near where the K-129 went down – is rather strong. There's an active power source in there, and it's not connected to the rest of the BLUE HADES grid as far as we can tell. The site is classified JENNIFER MORGUE, incidentally, and is known as Site One."

SLIDE 9: A rock face, evidently inside a mine, is illuminated by spotlights. Workers in overalls and hard hats surround it, and are evidently working on something – possibly a fossil – with small hand-tools.

"As you can see, this is not a BLUE HADES specimen. It's some other palaeosophont. This photograph was taken in 1985 in the deep mine at Longannet in Fife, right on our doorstep. Longannet – and indeed the rest of the British deep-mining industry – was shut down some time ago, officially for economic reasons. However, you would be right to conclude that the presence of nightmares like this was a contributing factor. This is in fact a DEEP SEVEN cadaver, and appears to have undergone some sort of postmortem vitrification process, or perhaps a hibernation from which it failed to emerge, approximately seven million years ago. We believe that DEEP SEVEN were responsible for the JENNIFER MORGUE machines and the neutrino anomaly in the previous slide. We know very little about DEEP SEVEN except that they appear to be polymorphous, occupy areas of the upper crust near the polar regions, and BLUE HADES are terrified of them."

SLIDE 10: A close-up of the cylindrical structure from Slide 7. Intricate traceries of inlaid calligraphy – or perhaps circuit diagrams – cover the walls of the machine, disturbing in their non-linearity. At one edge of the picture the conical top is visible, and in close-up the details become apparent: a conical spike with a cutting edge spiraling around it.

"This is our closest photograph of JENNIFER MORGUE Site One. It presents a clear hazard to this day: K-129 was lost inspecting it, as were several ROVs sent by the US Office of Naval Intelligence. It was the secondary target for Operation AZORIAN/JENNIFER before that project was Watergated. It's a rather recalcitrant target because there seems to be some sort of defense field around it, possibly acoustic—anything entering within a two-hundred-and-six-meter radius stops working. (If you look near the top right of this photograph you'll see the wreckage of a previous visitor.) Our current theory is that it is either a DEEP SEVEN artifact or a BLUE HADES system designed to prevent incursions by DEEP SEVEN. We presume the Soviets were trying to make contact with DEEP SEVEN by way of the Gravedust system on the K-129 – and failed, catastrophically."

SLIDE 11: A similar-looking photograph of another machine, this time looking less badly damaged. The photograph is taken from much closer range, and though one curved side has a jagged hole in it, the hull is otherwise intact.

"This is a similar artifact, located near the north end of the Puerto Rico Trench, about four kilometers down on a limestone plateau. JENNIFER MORGUE Site Two appears to be damaged, but the same exclusion field is still in place and operational. Initial exploratory investigation with an ROV discovered . . ."

SLIDE 12: A very dim, grainy view through the jagged hole in the side of the artifact. There appears to be a rectangular structure within. Odd curved objects surround it, some of which recall the shape of internal organs.

"This structure appears to contain – or even consist of – vitrified or otherwise preserved DEEP SEVEN remnants. You'll note the similarity of this structure to some sort of cockpit: we believe it to be a deep-crustal or high-mantle boring machine, possibly making it the DEEP SEVEN equivalent of a tank or a space suit. We're not sure quite what it's doing here, but we are now extremely intrigued by Ellis Billington's interest in it. He's purchased the *Explorer*, heavily modified it, and, using it as a host, has been conducting sea trials with a remotely operated vehicle. Our intel on Billington's activities is alarmingly deficient, but we believe he intends to raise and possibly activate the DEEP SEVEN artifact. His expertise in Gravedust systems suggests that he may try to retrieve information from the dead DEEP SEVEN aboard it, and the direction of his operation suggests that he has some idea of what it's doing there.

"I do not intend, at this point, to get into a lengthy discussion of the consequences of annoying the Chthonians – excuse me, DEEP SEVEN – or of getting involved in a geopolitical pissing match between DEEP SEVEN and BLUE HADES. Suffice to say, preserving the collective neutrality of the human species is a high priority for this department, and you should take that as your primary point of reference in the days ahead.

"But in summary, your mission is to get close to Billington and find out what the hell he's planning on doing with JENNIFER MORGUE Site Two. Then tell us, so we can work out what action we need to take to stop him pissing off BLUE HADES or DEEP SEVEN. If he wakes the ancient sleeping horrors I am going to have to brief the private secretary and the Joint Intelligence Oversight Committee so that they can explain CASE NIGHTMARE GREEN to the COBRA Committee, chaired by the Prime Minister, and I expect that will make them extremely unhappy. Britain is relying on you, Bob, so try not to make your usual hash of things."

Angleton fades out, to be replaced by a more normal dream sleep, punctuated by vague echoes of thrashing around restlessly in a huge hotel bed. I wake up eventually, to discover that the in-flight movie is over and we're in the middle of nowhere in particular. The airbus bores on through the clear Atlantic skies, ghosting high above the sunken treasure galleons of the Spanish Main. I stretch in place, try to massage the crick out of the side of my neck, and yawn. Then I wake up my laptop. Almost immediately the Skype window starts flashing for attention. *You have voice mail*, it says.

Voice mail? Hell, yes – in this Brave New World there's no escape from the internet, even at 40,000 feet. I yawn again and plug in my headset, trying to shake off the influence of Ramona's distantly sensed repose. I glance at the screen. It's Mo, and she's on Skype, too, so I place a call.

"Bob?" Her voice crackles a little – the signal is being bounced via satellite to the plane and the latency is scary.

"Mo, I'm on a plane. Are you in the Village?"

"I'm in the Village, Bob – checking out tomorrow. Listen, you asked me a question yesterday. I've been doing some poking around and this destiny-entanglement stuff is really ugly. Have they already done it to you? If not, run like hell. You'll start to share dreams, there's telepathy going with it, but worse, there's reality leakage, too. You end up taking up aspects of your entanglement partner, and vice versa. If they're killed you're likely to drop dead on the spot; if it lasts more than a couple of weeks it goes beyond sharing thoughts, you could end up merging with them permanently. The good news is, the entanglement can be broken by a fairly simple ritual. The bad news is, it takes both parties cooperating to do it. Do you have any way out of it?"

"Too late. They ran it yesterday—"

"Shit. Love, how long is it going to take you to realize that if they ask you to do them a special favor you need to run like—"

"Mo."

"Bob?"

"I know—" My throat closes up and I stop talking for a moment. "I love you."

"Yes." Her voice is faint at the end of the internet connection. "I love you, too—"

This is too painful to hear. "She's asleep."

"She?"

"The demon." I glance round, but there's nobody in the row in front of me and I'm directly in front of the partition between business and cattle class. "Ramona. Black Chamber operative. I don't—" This is too unpleasant: I start trying to figure out another way of approaching the subject.

"Has she hurt you?" Mo's tone is chilly enough to freeze my ear.

"No." Not yet. "I don't want you to go near her, Mo. It's not her fault. She's as much a victim of this as—"

"Bullshit, love. I want you to tell her, from me, that if she even *thinks* about messing with you I'll break every bone in her body—"

"Mo! Stop it!" I lower my tone of voice. "Don't even think about it. You don't want to get involved in this. Just don't. Wait 'til it's all over and we'll go on holiday together and get away from it all."

A pause. I tense up inside, desperately hoping for the best. Finally: "It's your judgment call and I can't stop you.

But I'm warning you, don't let them fuck with you. You know how they use people, what they did to me, right? Don't let them do it to you, too." A sigh. "So why did they send you?"

I swallow. "Angleton says he needs me to get inside an operation and I think he wants an unblockable communications channel back to the field controller. Did you ask him what it's about—"

"Not yet I haven't. Hang in there, love. I'm finishing up here and I've got to go back to London tomorrow: I'll drag everything out of Angleton before sunset. Where is he sending you? Who's your backup?"

"I'm on my way to the Princess Juliana Airport on Saint Martin, staying in the Sky Tower at Maho Bay. He's sent Boris, Pinky, and Brains to look after—" I suddenly realize where this is leading. Quick on the uptake I ain't. "Listen, don't bother trying to—"

"I'll be on the next flight out, I just have to touch base long enough to mug Harry the Holiday Piggy Bank. It'll be a cold day in Hell before I'm trusting your skin to their—"

"Don't!" I can see it already, horrible visions welling up out of the twisted depths of my subconscious. Does Mo realize what my being entangled with Ramona means? I hate to think what she'll do if she figures it out and Ramona's on the same continent. Mo is a very tactical person. Tactile, too — passionate, fiery, and capable of thinking outside the box — but if you show her an obstacle, she has a disturbing tendency to punch right through it. That's how she ended up in the Laundry, after all: making an end run round the Black Chamber, straight into our organization's lap. I love her dearly, but the thought of her turning up at my hotel room and me trying not to touch her while I'm in this embarrassing bind with Ramona scares the shit out of me. It's not exactly your normal sordid extramarital affair, is it? It's not as if I'm actually sleeping with Ramona and it's not as if I'm married to Mo, either. But it's got all the same potential to explode in my face – and that's before you factor in the little extra details like Ramona being the corporeal manifestation of a demonic entity from beyond space-time and Mo being a powerful sorceress.

"You're breaking up. Hang in there! See you the day after tomorrow!" She buzzes, then the connection drops.

I stare at the screen for a moment. Then I dry-swallow and press the SERVICE button for the flight attendant. "I need a drink," I say, "vodka and orange on the rocks." Then some instinct makes me add: "Shaken." Just like me.

I spend a good chunk of the rest of the flight determinedly trying to get drunk. I know you're not supposed to do that sort of thing when flying in a pressurized cabin—you get dehydrated, the hangover's worse—but I don't give a shit. Somewhere near Iceland Ramona wakes up and snarls at me for polluting her cerebral cortex with cocktail fallout, but either I manage to barricade her out or she decides to give me the day off for bad behavior. I play a drunken round of Quake on my Treo, then bore myself back to sleep by reading a memorandum discussing my responsibility for processing equipment depreciation and write-off claims pursuant to field-expedient containment operations. I don't want to be on the receiving end of a visit from the Auditors over a misfiled form PT-411/E, but the blasted thing seems to be protected by a stupefaction field, and every time I look at it my eyelids slam shut like protective blast barriers.

I wake up half an hour before landing with a throbbing forehead and a tongue that tastes like a mouse died on it. The huge gleaming expanse of Maho Beach is walled with hotels: the sea is improbably blue, like an accident in a chemistry lab. The heat beats down on me like a giant oven as I stagger down the steps onto the concrete next to the terminal building. Half the passengers are crumblies; the rest are surf Nazis and dive geeks, like extras auditioning for an episode of *Baywatch*. A strike force of hangover faeries is diving and weaving around me on pocket jet-packs when they're not practicing polo on my scalp with rubber mallets. It's two in the afternoon here, about six o'clock in Darmstadt, and I've been in transit for nearly twelve hours: the business suit I'm wearing from the meeting in the Ramada feels oddly stiff, as if it's hardening into an exoskeleton. I feel, not to put too fine a point on it, like shit; so when I come out of baggage claim I'm deeply relieved to see a crusty old buffer holding up a piece of cardboard upon which is scrawled: HOWARD – CAPITAL LAUNDRY SERVICES.

I head over towards him. "Hi. I'm Bob. You are . . .?"

He looks me up and down like I'm something he's just peeled off the underside of his shoe. I do a double-take. He's about fifty, very British in a late-imperial, gin-pickled kind of way – in his lightweight tropical suit, regimental tie, and waxwork mustache he looks like he's just stepped out of a Merchant-Ivory movie. "Mr. Howard. Your warrant card, please."

"Oh." I fumble with my pocket for a while until I find the thing, then wave it vaguely in his direction. His cheek twitches.

"That'll do. I'm Griffin. Follow me." He turns and strides towards the exit. "You're late."

I'm late? But I only just got here! I hurry after him, trying not to lurch into any walls. "Where are we going?" I ask.

"To the hotel." I follow him outside and he waves an arm peremptorily. An old but well-kept Jaguar XJ6 pulls up and the driver jumps out to open the door. "Get in." I almost fall into the seat, but manage to cushion my briefcase just in time to save the laptop. Griffin shoves the door shut on me then gets into the front passenger seat and raps the dash-board: "To the Sky Tower! Chop-chop."

I can't help it: my eyes slide closed. It's been a long day and my snatch of sleep aboard the airbus wasn't exactly refreshing. My head's spinning as the Jag pulls out onto a freshly resurfaced road. It's oppressively hot, even with the air conditioning running flat-out, and I just can't seem to stay awake. Seemingly seconds later we pull up in front of a large concrete box and someone opens the door for me. "Come on, get out, get out!" I blink, and force myself to stand up.

"Where are we?" I ask.

"The Sky Tower Hotel; I've booked you in and swept the room. Your team will be working out of a rented villa when they arrive – that's in hand, too. Come on." Griffin leads me past reception, past a stand staffed by Barbies giving away free cosmetic samples, into an elevator, and down another anonymous hotel-space passage decorated randomly with cane furniture. We end up in some corporate decorator's vision of a tropical hotel room, all anonymous five-star fur-niture plus a French door opening onto a balcony exploding with potted greenery. A ceiling fan spins lazily, failing to make any impression on the heat. "Sit down. No, not there, here." I sit, suppress a yawn, and try to force myself to look at him. Either he's frowning or he's worried. "When are they due, by the way?" he asks.

"Aren't they here yet?" I ask. "Say, shouldn't you show me *your* warrant card?"

"Bah." His mustache twitches, but he reaches into his jacket pocket and pulls out a thing that anyone who isn't expecting a warrant card will see as a driving license or a passport. There's a faint smell of sulfur in the air. "You don't know."

"Know what?"

He peers at me sharply, then apparently makes his mind

up. "They're late," he mutters. "Bloody cock-up." Louder: "Gin and tonic, or whisky soda?"

My head's still throbbing. "Have you got a glass of water?" I ask hopefully.

"Bah," he says again, then walks over to the minibar and opens it. He pulls out two bottles and two glasses. Into one of them he pours a double-finger of clear spirits; the other he puts down next to the tonic water. "Help yourself," he says grudgingly.

This isn't what I'm expecting from a station chief. To tell the truth, I'm not sure what I should be expecting: but antique Jaguars, regimental ties, and gin-tippling in midafternoon isn't it. "Have you been told why I'm here?" I ask tentatively.

He roars so loudly I nearly jump out of my skin. "Of course I have, boy! What do you think I am, another of your goddamn paper-pushing Whitehall pen-pimps?" He glares at me ferociously. "God help you, and God help both of us because nobody back home is going to. Bloody hell, what a mess."

"Mess?" I try to sound as if I know what he's talking about, but there's a quivery edge to my voice and I'm feeling fuzzy about the edges from jet lag.

"Look at you." He looks me up and down with evident contempt — or mild disdain, which is worse — in his voice. "You're a mess. You're wearing trainers and a two-guinea suit, for God's sake you look like a hippie on a job interview, you don't know where your fucking backup team has gotten to, and you're supposed to get into Billington's hip pocket!" He sounds like Angleton's cynical kid brother. I know I mustn't let him get to me, but this is just too much.

"Before you go on, you ought to know that I've been up for about thirty hours. I woke up in Germany and I've already crossed six time zones and had a roomful of flesh-eating zombies try to chow down on my brain." I gulp the glass of water. "I'm not in the mood for this shit."

"You're not in the mood?" He laughs like a fox barking. "Then you can just go to bed without your dinner, boy. You're not in London anymore and I'm not going to put up with temper tantrums from undisciplined wet-behind-the-ears amateurs." He puts his glass down. "Listen, let's get one thing absolutely clear: this is my turf. You do not fly in, shit all over the place, squawk loudly, and fly out again, leaving me to pick up the wreckage. While you're here, you do exactly as I say. This isn't a committee exercise, this is the Dutch Antilles and I'm not going to let you fuck up my station."

"Eh?" I shake my head. "Who said anything about . . .?"

"You didn't have to," he says with heavy and sarcastic emphasis. "You turn up six hours behind a FLASH notice from some dog-fucker in Islington who says you're to have the run of the site facilities and I'm to render all necessary et cetera. If you get the opposition stirred up you'll be dead in a gutter within six hours and I'll get landed with the paperwork. This isn't Camden Market and I'm not the bloody hotel concierge. I'm the Laundry point man for the Caribbean, and if you put a step wrong on my patch you can bring all the hounds of Hell down on our collective neck, boy, so you're not going to *do* that. While you're working on my station, if you want to fart you ask me for permission first. Otherwise I'll rip you a new sphincter. For your own good. Got that?"

"I guess." I do a double-take. "What's the opposition presence like, hereabouts?" I ask. Actually I want to say, *What is this "opposition" you speak of, strange person?* — but I figure it'll just make him shout at me again.

Griffin stares at me in disbelief. "Are you trying to tell me they haven't briefed you about the opposition?"

I shake my head.

"What a mess. This is the Caribbean: Who do you think the opposition are? Tourists! Wander around, drop in on the casinos and clubs, and what do you see? You see tourists. Half of 'em are Yanks, and maybe half of those are plants. Okay, not half, maybe one in a hundred thousand. But you see, we're about 200 miles from Cuba here, which means they're always trying to sneak assets into the generalissimo's territory. And you wouldn't want to mess with the smugglers, either. We've got money laundering, we've got the main drug pipeline into Miami via Cuba, and we've got police headaches coming out of our ears before we add the fucking opposition trying to use us as a staging post for their crazy-ass vodoun pranks." He shakes his head then stares at me. "So you've got to keep one eye peeled for the tourists. If the oppo send an assassin to polish your button they'll be disguised as a tourist, you mark my words. Are you *sure* they didn't brief you?"

"Um." I do my best to consider my next words carefully, but it's difficult when your head feels like it's stuffed with cotton wool: "You are talking about the Black Chamber when you use the term 'opposition,' aren't you? I mean, you're not really trying to tell me that the tourists are all part of some conspiracy——"

"Who the hell else would I be talking about?" He stares at me in disbelief, chugs the rest of his glass back, and thumps it down on the side table.

"Okay, then I've been briefed," I say tiredly. "Listen, I really need to get settled in and catch up on my briefing papers. I don't think they're going to assassinate me, my boss has arranged an, uh, accommodation." I manage to stand up without falling on the ceiling, but my feet aren't responding too well to commands from mission control. "Can we continue this tomorrow?"

"Bloody hell." He looks down his nose at me, his expression unreadable. "An accommodation. All right, we'll continue this tomorrow. You'd better be right, kid, because if you guessed wrong they'll eat your liver and lights while you're still screaming." He pauses in the doorway. "Don't call me, I'll call you."

5: HIGH SOCIETY

THE NEXT HOUR PASSES IN A HAZE OF EXHAUSTION. I lock the door behind Griffin and somehow manage to make it to the bed before I collapse face-first into the deep pile of oblivion. Only strange dreams trouble me – strange because I seem to be dressing up in women's clothing, not because my brain's being eaten by zombies.

An indeterminate time later I'm summoned back to wakefulness by a persistent banging on my door, and a warmly sarcastic voice at the back of my head: **Get up, monkey-boy!**

"Go 'way," I moan, clutching the pillow like a life preserver. I want to sleep so badly I can taste it, but Ramona's not leaving me alone.

"Open the door or I'll start singing, monkey-boy. You wouldn't like that."

"Singing?" I roll over. I'm still wearing my shoes, I realize. And I'm still wearing this fucking suit. I didn't even take it off for the flight – I must be turning into a manager or something. I have a sudden urge to wash compulsively. At least the tie's snaked off to wherever the horrid things live when they're not throttling their victims.

"I'll start with D:Ream. *'Things can only get better'*—"

"*Aaaugh!*" I flail around for a moment, and manage to fall

off the bed. That wakes me up enough to sit up. "Okay, just hold it right there . . .

I stumble over to the entrance and open the door. It's Ramona, and for the second time since I arrived here I experience the sense of existential angst that afflicts chewing gum cling-ons on the shoe sole of a higher order. Her supermodel-perfect brow wrinkles as she looks me up and down. "You need a shower."

"Tell me about it." I yawn hugely. She's dressed up to the nines in a slinky, black strapless gown, with a fortune in diamonds plugged into her ear lobes and wrapped around her throat. Her hairdo looks like it cost more than my last month's salary. "What's *up?* Planning on dining out?"

"Reconnaissance in force." She steps into the room, shoves the door shut behind her, and locks it. "Tell me about Griffin. What did he say?" she demands.

I yawn again. "Let me freshen up while we talk." *Pinky said something about a toilet kit in my briefcase, didn't he?* I rummage around in it until I come up with a black Yves Saint Laurent bag, then wander through into the bathroom.

The dream was overspill, I realize unhappily. This is going to get even more embarrassing before it's over. I hope like hell Angleton's planning on disentangling me from her as soon as possible – otherwise I'm in danger of turning into a huge unintentional security leak. Nastier possibilities nag at the back of my mind, but I'm determined to ignore them. In this line of work, too much paranoia can be worse than too little.

I open the toilet bag and poke around until I come up with a toothbrush and a tube of toothpaste. **Griffin's nuts,** I send to her while I'm scrubbing away at the inside of my lower jaw. **He's completely paranoid about you guys. He also insists that he gets a veto over my actions, which is more than somewhat inconvenient.** I switch to my upper front teeth. **Have you been fucking with his head?**

You wish. I can almost feel her disdainful sniff. **We've got him pegged as a loose cannon who's been put out to pasture to keep him out of your agency's internal politics. He's stuck in the 1960s, and not the good bits.**

Well. I carefully probe my molars, just in case Angleton's planted a microdot briefing among them to tell me how to handle situations like this. **I can't comment on Laundry operational doctrine and overseas deployments in the Caribbean—** (because I don't know anything about them: Could that be why they picked me for this op? Because I'm a designated mushroom, kept in the dark and fed shit?) **—but I would agree with your assessment of Griffin. He's a swivel-eyed nutter.** I step into the shower and dial it all the way up to Niagara. I'm *supposed to report to Angleton while letting Griffin think he's in my chain of command: What should this tell me about the home game Angleton's playing here?* I shake my head. I'm not up to playing Laundry politics right now. I focus on showering, then get out and dry myself. **One question deserves another. Why did you get me out of bed?**

Because I wanted to fuck with *your* head, not Griffin's. She sends me a visual of herself pouting, which is a bloody distracting thing to see in the mirror when you're trying to shave. **I got news from my ops desk that Billington flew in a few hours ago. He's probably going to visit his casino before—**

His casino?

Yeah. Didn't you know? He owns this place.

Oh. So—

He's downstairs right now. I flinch, and discover the hard way that it is indeed possible to cut yourself on an electric razor if you try hard enough. I finish off hurriedly and open the door. Ramona thrusts a bulky carrier bag at me. "Put this on."

"Where did you get this?" I pull out a tuxedo jacket, neatly folded; there's more stuff below it.

"It was waiting for you at the front desk." She smiles tightly. "You have to look the part if we're going to carry this off."

"Shit." I duck back into the bathroom and try to figure out what goes where. The trousers have odd fasteners in strange places and I've got no idea what to do with the red silk scarf-like thing, but at least they cheated on the bow tie. When I open the door Ramona is sitting in the chair by the bed, carefully reloading cartridges into the magazine of an extremely compact automatic pistol. She looks at me and frowns. "That's supposed to go around your waist," she says.

"I've never worn one of these before."

"It shows. Let me." She makes the gun vanish then comes over and adjusts my appearance. After a minute she steps back and looks at me critically. "Okay, that'll do for now. In a dim light, after a couple of cocktails. Try not to hunch up like that, it makes you look like you need to sue your orthopedic surgeon."

"Sorry, it's the shoes. That, and you managed to land a critical hit on my geek purity score. Are you sure I can't just wear a tee shirt and jeans?"

"No, you can't." She grins at me unexpectedly. "Monkey-boy isn't comfortable in a monkey suit? Consider yourself lucky you don't have to deal with underwire bras."

"If you say so." I yawn, then before my hindbrain can start issuing shutdown commands again I go over to my briefcase and start gathering up the necessaries Boris issued to me: a Tag Heuer wristwatch with all sorts of strange dials (at least one of which measures thaumic entropy levels – I'm not sure what the buttons do) a set of car keys with a fob concealing a teensy GPS tracker, a bulky old-fashioned cellphone . . . "Hey, there's something fishy about this phone! Isn't it—" I pick it up "—a bit heavy?"

I suddenly realize that Ramona is standing behind me. "Switch it off!" she hisses. "The power switch is the safety catch."

"Okay already! I'm switching it off!" I put it in my inside pocket and she relaxes. "Boris didn't say anything about—what does it do?" Then the penny drops. "Holy fuck."

"That's what you'd get if you switched it on, pointed it at the pope, and dialed 1-4-7-star," she agrees. "It takes nine millimeter ammunition. Are you okay with that?" She raises one perfectly sketched eyebrow at me.

"No!" I'm not used to firearms, they make me nervous; I'm much happier with a PDA loaded with Laundry CAT-A countermeasure invocations and a fully charged Hand of Glory. Still, nothing wakes me up quite like nearly shooting someone by accident. I fidget with the new tablet PC that Brains provisioned for me, plugging it in and setting it for counter-intrusion duty. "Shall we go drop in on Billington?"

I'm not much of a beach bunny. I'm not a culture vulture or a clothes horse either. Opera leaves me cold, clubbing is something bad guys do to baby seals, and I'm no more inclined to work the slots than I am to stand in the middle of a railway station ripping up twenty-pound notes. Nevertheless, there's a certain vicarious amusement to be had in stepping out at night with a beautiful blonde on my arm and a brown manila envelope in my inside pocket labeled HOSPITALITY EXPENSES – even if I'm going to have to account for any cash I pull out of it, in triplicate, on a form F.219/B that doesn't list "gambling losses" as an acceptable excuse.

It's dark, and the air temperature has dropped to about gas

mark five, leaving me feeling like a Sunday roast in a tinfoil jacket. There's an onshore breeze that gives a faint illusion of coolness, but it's too humid to do much more than stir the sand grains on the sidewalk. The promenade is a modern pastel-painted concrete walkway decorated to a tropical theme, like Neo-Brutalist architecture on holiday. It's bright and noisy with late-opening boutiques, open-windowed bars, and nightclubs. The crowd is what you'd expect: tourists, surfers, and holiday-makers, all dressed up for a night out on the town. By the morning they'll be puking their margaritas up on the boardwalk at the end of the development, but right now they're a happy, noisy crowd. Ramona leads me through them with supreme confidence, straight towards a garishly illuminated, red-carpeted lobby that covers half the block ahead of us.

My nose prickles. Something they never mention in the brochures is that the night-blooming plants let rip during the tourist season. I try not to sneeze convulsively as Ramona sashays right up the red carpet, bypassing the gaggle of tourists being checked at the door by security. A uniformed flunkey scrambles to grovel over her gloved hand. I follow her into the lobby and he gives me a cold-fish stare as if he can't make up his mind whether to grope my wallet or punch me in the face. I smile patronizingly at him while Ramona speaks.

"You'll have to excuse me but Bob and I are new here and I'm so excited! Would you mind showing me where the cashier's office is? Bobby darling, do you think you could get me a drink? I'm so thirsty!"

She does an inspired airhead impersonation. I nod, then catch the doorman's eye and let the smile slip. "If you'd show her to the office," I murmur, then turn on my heel and walk indoors — hoping I'm not going in the wrong direction — to give Ramona space to turn her glamour loose on him. I feel a bit of a shit about leaving the doorman to her tender mercies, but console myself with the fact that as far as he's concerned, I'm just another mark: what goes around comes around.

It's darker and noisier inside than on the promenade and a lot of overdressed, middle-aged folks are milling around the gaming tables in the outer room. Mirror balls scatter rainbow refractions across the floor, at the far end of the room a four-piece is murdering famous jazz classics on stage. I spot the bar eventually and manage to catch one of the bartender's eyes. She's young and cute and I smile a bit more honestly. "Hi! What's your order, sir?"

"A vodka martini on the rocks." I pause for just a heartbeat, then add, "And a margarita." She smiles ingratiatingly at me and turns away, and the ghostly sensation of a stiletto heel grinding against my instep fades as quickly as it arrived. **That was entirely unnecessary,** I tell Ramona stiffly.

Wanna bet? You're falling into character too easily, monkey-boy. Try to stay focused.

When I find her she's leaning up against a small, thick window set in one wall, scooping plastic chips into her purse. I wait alongside with the drinks, then hand her the margarita. "Thanks." She closes the purse then leads me past a bunch of chattering one-armed-bandit fans towards an empty patch of floor near a table where a bunch of tense-looking coffin-dodgers are watching a young chav in a white shirt and dickey-bow deal cards with robotic efficiency.

"What was that about?" I murmur.

"What was what?" She turns to stare at me in the darkness, but I avoid making eye contact.

"The thing with the doorman."

"It's been a hard day, and American Airlines doesn't cater for my special dietary requirements."

"Really?" I stare at her. "I don't know how you can live with yourself."

"Marc over there—" she jerks her head almost impercep- tibly, back towards the door "—likes to think of himself as a lone wolf. He's twenty-five and he got the job here after a dishonorable discharge from the French paratroops. He served two years of a five-year sentence first. You wouldn't believe the things that happen on UN peacekeeping missions . . ."

She pauses and takes a tiny sip of her drink before contin- uing. Her voice is over-controlled and just loud enough to hear above the band: "He's not in contact with his family back in Lyon because his father kicked him out of the house when he discovered what he did to his younger sister. He lives alone in a room above a bike repair shop. When a mark runs out of cash and tries to stiff the house, they sometimes send Marc around to explain the facts of life. Marc enjoys his work. He prefers to use a cordless hammer-drill with a blunt three- eighths bit. Twice a week he goes and fucks a local whore, if he's got the money. If he hasn't got the money, he picks up tourist women looking for a good time: usually he takes their money and leaves their flight vouchers, but twice in the past year he's taken them for an early morning boat ride, which they probably didn't appreciate on account of being tied up and out of their skulls on Rohypnol. He's got an eight-foot dinghy and he knows about a bay out near North Point where some people he doesn't know by name will pay him good money for single women nobody will miss." She touches my arm. "Nobody is going to miss him, Bob."

"You—" I bite my tongue.

"You're learning." She smiles tensely. "Another couple of weeks and you might even get it."

I swallow bile. "Where's Billington?"

"All in good time," she croons in a low singsong voice that sends chills up and down my spine. Then she turns towards the baccarat table.

The croupier is shuffling several decks of cards together in the middle of the kidney-shaped table. A half-dozen players and their hangers-on watch with feigned boredom and avaricious eyes: leisure-suit layabouts, two or three gray-haired pensioners, a fellow who looks like a weasel in a dinner jacket, and a woman with a face like a hatchet. I hang back while Ramona explains things in a monotone in the back of my head — it sounds like she's quoting someone: **'It's much the same as any other gambling game. The odds against the banker and the player are more or less even. Only a run against either can be decisive and "break the bank" or break the players.' That's Ian Fleming, by the way.**

Who, the guy with the face . . .?

No, the guy I was quoting. He knew his theory but he wasn't as competent at the practicalities. During the Second World War he ran a scheme to get British agents in neutral ports to gamble their Abwehr rivals into bankruptcy. Didn't work. And don't even think about trying that on Billington.

The croupier raises a hand and asks who's holding the bank. Hatchet-Face nods. I look at the pile of chips in front of her. It's worth twice my department's annual budget. She doesn't notice me staring so I look away quickly.

"So how does it go now?" I ask Ramona quietly. She's scanning the crowd as if looking for an absent friend. She smiles faintly and takes my hand, forcing me to sidle uncomfortably close.

"Make like we're a couple," she whispers, still smiling. "Okay, watch carefully. The woman who's the banker is betting against the other gamblers. She's got the shoe with six packs of cards in it — shuffled by the croupier and double-checked by everyone else. Witnesses. Anyway, she's about to—"

Hatchet-Face clears her throat. "Five grand." There's a wave of muttering among the other gamblers, then one of the pensioners nods and says, "Five," pushing a stack of chips forwards.

Ramona: "She opened with a bank of five thousand dollars. That's what she's wagering. Blue-Rinse has accepted. If nobody accepted on their own, they could club together until they match the five thousand between them."

"Ri-ight." I frown, staring at the chips. Laundry pay scales are British civil service level — if I didn't have the subsidized safe house, or if Mo wasn't working, we wouldn't be able to afford to live comfortably in London. What's already on the table is about a month's gross income for both of us, and this is just the opening round. Suddenly I feel very cold and exposed. I'm out of my depth here.

Hatchet-Face deals four cards from the shoe, laying two of them face-down in front of Blue-Rinse, and the other two cards in front of herself. Blue-Rinse picks her cards up and looks at them, then lays them face-down again and taps them.

"The idea is to get a hand that adds up to nine points, or closest to nine points. The banker doesn't get to check his cards until the players declare. Aces are low, house cards are zero, and you're only looking at the least significant digit: a five and a seven make two, not twelve. The player can play her hand, or ask for another card — like that — and then — she's turning."

Blue-Rinse has turned over her three cards. She's got a queen, a two, and a five. Hatchet-Face doesn't smile as she turns her own cards over to reveal two threes and a two. The croupier rakes the chips over towards her: Blue-Rinse doesn't bat an eyelid.

I stare fixedly at the shoe. *They're nuts. Completely insane!* I don't get this gambling thing. Didn't these people study statistics at university? *Evidently not . . .*

"Come on," Ramona says quietly. "Back to the bar, or they'll start to wonder why we're not joining in."

"Why aren't we?" I ask her as she retreats.

"They don't pay me enough."

"Me neither." I hurry to catch up.

"And here I was thinking you worked for the folks who gave us James Bond."

"You know damn well that if Bond auditioned for a secret service job they'd tell him to piss off. We don't need upper-class twits with gambling and fast car habits who think that all problems can be solved at gunpoint and who go rogue at the drop of a mission abort code."

"No, really?" She gives me an old-fashioned look.

"Right." I find myself grinning. "They go for quiet, book-ish accountant-types, lots of attention to detail, no imagination, that kind of thing."

"Quiet, bookish accountant-types who're on drinking terms with the head-bangers from Two-One SAS and are field-certified to Grade Four in occult combat technology?"

I may have done a couple of training courses at Dunwich but that doesn't mean I've graduated to breathing seawater, much less inhaling vodka martinis. When I stop spluttering Ramona is looking away from me, whistling tunelessly and tapping her toes. I glare at her, and I'm about to give up on it as a bad job when I see who she's watching. "Is that Billington?" I ask.

"Yep, that's him. Aged sixty-two, looks forty-five."

Ellis Billington is rather hard to miss. Even if I didn't rec-ognize his face from the cover of *Computer Weekly*, it'd be pretty obvious that he was a big cheese. There's a nasty face-lift in a big frock hanging on his left arm, a briefcase-toting woman in wire-frame spectacles and a tailored suit that screams *lawyer* shadowing him, and a pair of thugs to either side, who wear their tuxedos like uniforms and have wires looped around their ears. A gaggle of Bright Young Things in cocktail dresses and tuxes bring up the rear, like courtiers basking in the reflected glory of a medieval monarch; the dubious doorman Ramona fingered for her midnight snack is oozing up to one of them. Billington himself has a distinguished silver-streaked hairdo that looks like he bought it at John De Lorean's yard sale and feeds it raw liver twice a day. For all that, he looks trim and fit – almost unnaturally well-preserved for his age.

"What now?" I ask her. I can see a guy who looks like the president of the casino threading his way across the floor towards Billington.

"We go say hello." And before I can stop her she's off across the floor like a missile. I scramble along in her wake, dodging dowagers, trying not to spill my drink – but instead of homing in on Billington she makes a beeline towards the Face Lift That Walks Like a Lady. "Eileen!" squeaks Ramona, coming over all blonde. "Why, if this isn't a complete surprise!"

Eileen Billington – for it is she – turns on Ramona like a cornered rattlesnake, then suddenly smiles and switches on the sweetness and light: "Why, it's Mona! Upon my word, I do declare!" They circle each other for a few seconds, sparring congenially and exchanging polite nothings while the courtier-yuppies home in on the baccarat table. I notice Billington's attorney exchanging words with her boss and then departing towards the casino office. Then I see Billington look at me. I take a deep breath and nod at him.

"You're with her." He jerks his chin at Ramona. "Do you know what she is?" He sounds dryly amused.

"Yes." I blink. "Ellis Billington, I presume?"

He looks me in the eye and it feels like a punch in the gut. Up close he doesn't look human. His pupils are a muddy gray-brown and slotted vertically: I've seen that before in folks who've had an operation to correct nystagmus, but somehow on Billington it looks too natural to be the after-effect of surgery. "Who are you?" he demands.

"Howard — Bob Howard. Capital Laundry Services, import/export division."

I manage to make a dog-eared business card appear between my fingers. He raises an eyebrow and takes it. "I didn't know you people traded over here."

"Oh, we trade all over." I force myself to smile. "I sat through a most interesting presentation yesterday. My colleagues were absolutely mesmerized."

"I have no idea what you're talking about." I take half a step back but Ramona and Eileen are laughing loudly over some shared confidence behind me: there's no escape from his lizardlike stare. Then he seems to reach some decision, and lets me down gently: "But that's not surprising, is it? My companies have so many subsidiaries, doing so many things, that it's hard to keep track of them all." He shrugs, an *aw-shucks* gesture quite at odds with the rest of his mannerisms, and produces a grin from wherever he keeps his spare faces when he isn't wearing them. "Are you here for the sunshine and sea, Mr. Howard? Or are you here to play games?"

"A bit of both." I drain my cocktail glass. Behind him, his lawyer is approaching, the casino president at her elbow. "I wouldn't want to keep you from business, so . . ."

"Perhaps later." His smile turns almost sincere for a split second as he turns aside: "Now, if you'll excuse me?"

I find myself staring at his retreating back. Seconds later Ramona takes hold of my elbow and twists it, gently steering me through the crowd towards the open glass doors leading onto the balcony at the back of the casino floor. "Come on," she says quietly. The courtiers have formed an attentive wall around the fourth Mrs. Billington, who is getting ready to recycle some of her husband's money through his bank. I let Ramona lead me outside.

"You know her!" I accuse.

"Of course I damn well know her!" Ramona leans against the stone railing that overhangs the beach, staring at me from arm's length. My heart's pounding and I feel dizzy with relief over having escaped Billington's scrutiny. He was perfectly polite but when he looked at me I felt like a bug on a microscope slide, pinned down by brilliant searchlights for scrutiny by a vast, unsympathetic intellect: trapped with nowhere to hide. "My department spent sixty thousand bucks setting up the first introduction at a congressman's fund-raiser two weeks ago, just so she'd recognize me tonight. You didn't think we'd come here without doing the groundwork first?"

"Nobody tells me these things," I complain. "I'm flailing around in the dark!"

"Don't sweat it." Suddenly she goes all apologetic on me, as if I'm a puppy who doesn't know any better than to widdle on the living room carpet: "It's all part of the process."

"What process?" I stare her in the eyes, trying to ignore the effects of the glamour that tells me she's the most amazingly beautiful woman I've ever met.

"The process that I'm not allowed to tell you about." Is that genuine regret in her eyes? "I'm sorry." She lowers her eyelashes. I track down instinctively, and find myself staring into the depths of her cleavage.

"Great," I say bitterly. "I've got a station chief who's as mad as a fish, an incomplete briefing, and a gambling-obsessed billionaire to out-bluff. And you can't fucking tell me what I'm supposed to be doing?"

"No," she says, in a thin, hopeless tone. And to my complete surprise she leans forwards, wraps her arms around me, props her chin on my shoulder, and begins to weep silently.

This is the final straw. I have been clawed at by zombies condescended to by Brains, shipped off to the Caribbean and lectured in my sleep by Angleton, introduced to an executive with the eyes of a poisonous reptile, and ranted at by an old-school spook who's fallen in the bottle — but those are all part of the job. This isn't. There's no briefing sheet on what to do when a supernatural soul-sucking horror disguised as a beautiful woman starts crying on your shoulder. Ramona sobs silently while I stand there, paralyzed by indecision, self-doubt, and jet lag. Finally I do the only thing I can think of and wrap my arms round her shoulders. "There, there," I mutter, utterly unsure what I'm saying: "It's going to be all right. Whatever it is."

"No, it isn't," she sniffles quietly. "It's *never* going to be all right." Then she straightens up. "I need to blow my nose."

I can take a hint: I let go and take a step back. "Do you want to talk?"

She pulls a hand-sized pack of tissues out of her bag and dabs at her eyes carefully.

"Do I want to talk?" She sniffs, then chuckles. Evidently something I said amused her. "No, Bob, I don't want to talk." She blows her nose. "You're far too nice for this. Go to bed."

"Too nice for what?" These dark hints of hers are getting really annoying, but I'm upset and concerned now that she's pulling herself together; I feel like I've just sat some kind of exam and failed it, without even knowing what subject I'm being tested on.

"Go to bed," she repeats, a trifle more forcefully. "I haven't eaten yet. Don't tempt me."

I beat a hasty retreat back through the casino. On my way out, I go through the side room where they keep the slot machines. I pass Pinky — at least, I'm half-sure it's Pinky — creating a near riot among the blue-rinse set by playing an entire row of one-armed bandits in sequence and winning big on each one. I don't think he notices me. Just as well: I'm not in the mood for small talk right now.

Damn it, I know it's just the effects of a class three glamour, but I can't stop thinking about Ramona — and Mo's flying in tomorrow.

6: CHARLIE VICTOR

I MAKE IT BACK TO MY HOTEL ROOM WITHOUT GETTING lost, falling asleep on my feet, or accidentally looking at the screen saver. I slump in the chair for a while, but there's nothing on TV except an adventure movie starring George Lazenby, and it'll take more than that to keep me awake. So I hang out the DO NOT DISTURB sign, undress, and go to bed.

I fall asleep almost instantly, but it's not very restful because I'm in someone else's head, and I really don't want to be there. Last time this happened, the fifty-something engineering salesman from Dusseldorf trapping off with the blonde call girl was just sad, and a bit pathetic on the side; this time it feels dirty. I *(no, he*: I struggle to hold myself aside from his sense of self) work out daily in a gym round the corner from the casino before I go in to work, and it's not just pumping iron and running on a track—there's stuff I don't recognize, practice routines with odd twisting and punching and kicking motions, somatic memories of beating people up and the warm sensual excitement that floods me when I stomp some fucking idiot for getting in my face. I've had a call from the customer, and I'm about ready to go off to work and go looking for the merchandise he wants, when this blonde American princess comes out of the *salle* and what do you know, but she's giving me a come-on? She's lost the rich nerd she showed up with, and good riddance; guess I'll have to take her home and that means . . . yeah, she'll do. Two birds, one stone, so to speak. Or two stones, in my case. Mind you, she's a customer – I'll just have to be discreet. So I smile at her and make nicey-nice while she giggles, then I offer to buy her a drink and she says, "Yes," and I tell her to meet me over the road at the Sunset Beach Bar so I can show her the town. She heads off, shaking her booty, and I go and get squared away. Time to do another line of Charlie in the john.

Checking out, walking over the road I get that thrill of arousal. I'm on top of the world again with cold fire coursing through my veins, like the time in the village near Bujumbura when Jacques and I caught that kid stealing and we – the memory skids away from me as if it's made of grease, only an echo of the blood and shit-smell of it and the screams lingering in my ears – and I get the hot tension again, like lightning seeking a path to earth. Sex, that'll help. Long as she doesn't make a fuss.

She's waiting for me on a bar stool, legs crossed and face hopeful. Plump cheeks, lips like throttled . . . I let my face smile at her and order her a drink and make chitchat. She smiles sympathetically and asks me questions trying to find out if I have – hey! She's worried I might have a regular girl-friend, the stupid cunt, so I explain that no my Elouise died in a car crash two years ago and I have been mourning since. She's so stupid she laps it up, asks me lots of questions and sounds concerned. I figure I'll drop her off with the rich guy's pilot at Anse Marcel tomorrow: but first we'll have some fun together. I act coy but let her draw me out because half the bitches want to be fucked hard by a stranger, they just have to convince themselves he's sensitive and caring at first to get over their inhibitions. After a while she looks at me slack-mouthed like she's already dripping, and I figure it's time. So I ask if she wants to come back to my place and she accepts.

We walk – it's only three blocks – and she doesn't bat an eyelid at the rubbish and the locked shutters. I show her upstairs and unlock the door, and when I turn back to pull her inside she actually gropes me! Normally they get cold at this point and start making excuses but this is going really smooth. I'm hard, of course, and when she kisses me I get an arm round her and start hiking up her skirt. The Rohypnol's in the fridge and it'd be more sensible to slip it to her first, then add a geas on top for safety's sake, but what the hell, she seems willing enough. This one really does seem to want a rough fuck – shame for her she doesn't know about the customer but those are the breaks. I pick her up and carry her inside, kick the door shut, then dump her on the bed and jump her. And the funny thing is she lets me, she doesn't fight, and my heart is in my mouth pounding away between her legs, wet meat, warm meat, it's like she doesn't even know the father says it's wrong to do this beat my meat it's not *ever* this easy and I can't let her talk afterwards even though she's biting my shoulder and sucking me, and *oh father my chest hurts*—

I open my eyes and stare at the hotel ceiling until my pulse begins to slow. I'm engorged and erect and freezing cold on the damp sheets, and I feel as if I'm about to throw up. "Ramona!" I croak, my larynx still half-paralyzed with sleep.

The fucker just flatlined on me! I can't feel his mind anymore, but he's lying on top of her, still twitching spastically, and I can taste her desperation and fear. **He must have had a dodgy heart, done one line too many. Finish me off, Bob!**

What— I realize I've been holding my penis and yank my hands away as if they're covered in chili oil.

Finish me off! *Please!* I can sense her succubus now, coiling like a black vortex of emptiness behind her conscious thoughts. There's nothing human about it, nothing warm — it's like death itself, not the small oblivion of orgasm but its complete antithesis, freezing and vacant, a hunger for life. It needs filling, it's searching for a sacrifice and she'd set her eyes on Marc but he checked out early and now— **It needs a little death to go with the big one, and the longer you wait the hungrier it gets.** She sounds breathless. **If you don't give it one it'll eat me, and you may think that would be a good thing but in case it's escaped your attention we're entangled—**

But I— I want Mo, don't I? *Don't I?* Mo isn't hiding behind a glamour. Mo doesn't eat people like a fuck-vampire. Mo isn't a drop-dead gorgeous blonde, she's just Mo, and we're probably going to end up getting married sooner or later, and I feel guilty and frightened because Mo won't understand what Ramona wants me to do.

But nothing! I can sense Ramona's arousal and, behind it, a canker of upwelling fear. **Jesus, Bob, do something, please help me here . . .!** She's helpless and small before the emptiness of her hunger, and Mo isn't here, and neither is she. I feel the empty hunger, and I try to wall it out, but Ramona needs me. She's teetering on the edge of an orgasm, the hunger is waiting for her, and if she meets it alone she won't come out the other side alive. I can't *not* do it. Can I?

I'm not cleared for sex magick, I tell her, gritting my teeth. But she sends me a touch-sense picture of herself: the warm weight on her chest, Marc's head lolling, the turgid stretch of her vulva occupied by a dead man's dick, a delicious sense of proximity to catastrophic nothingness, teetering on the edge of a cliff — and I clutch myself and begin to spasm wildly because I'm still massively turned on from the overspill of her sex. The sense of doom recedes immediately, and then something I wasn't expecting happens — Ramona comes, taking me completely by surprise. She goes on and on and on until I'm almost ready to scream for mercy. Finally the waves of sensation finally begin to slow down and recede, leaving her panting and pinned beneath Marc's cooling cadaver. A warm afterglow floods her with life. I can feel her reveling in it.

Thank you, she says fervently, and I can't tell at first whether she's talking to me or to the dead serial rapist. **If you hadn't joined in, it would have had me for sure.** The corpse's head lolls on her shoulder, a drop of spittle dangling from his mouth. She reaches up and shoves it aside. **Was it good for you, too?** she asks, and tenderly kisses his soft, unresponsive lips.

My skin crawls. **You enjoyed that a whole lot,** I tell her before I bite my tongue. But it's too late.

You enjoy eating, too, but pleasure's not the only reason you do it, she snaps. **And don't tell me you didn't enjoy this.** I cringe at her anger: *What will Mo say when she finds out?* It's not sex — no, it's just having a simultaneous orgasm with a consenting adult, my conscience jabs me. *Oh hell, what a mess.* I gingerly sit up and shuffle towards the bathroom and a late-night appointment with the shower.

Hey, what about me? Ramona complains bitterly, bracing herself to dislodge the drained husk of her prey.

I don't want to talk about it right now, I mutter. I twist the shower dial, feeling dirty.

Typical fucking male . . .

Look who's talking! You're a real piece of work. I turn the temperature right up until it hurts, then bite my tongue and stand underneath it. **You wanted to get into my pants, didn't you?**

**Anyone ever tell you you're an asshole, monkey-boy? If

I wanted you I'd have had you right there on the casino balcony, instead of nearly dying in a shit-hole.** She's working
on getting her clothes back into a semblance of order. Marc
lies on the floor beside the bed. She lashes out and kicks him
hard enough to hurt my toes and I suddenly realize she's
shaking with adrenalin, the aftermath of a terror trip.
Bastard!

She's *really* scared. That's my conscience talking; he's been
beating on the door for the past couple of minutes but I've
only just heard him over the racket in my head. *Why would-
n't she be telling the truth?* I swallow, forcing back stomach
acid. *She likes me. Fuck knows why.*

I force myself to come up with an apology. **Being scared
makes me more of an asshole than usual.** It sounds weak in
the silence afterwards, but I don't know what else to say.

You bet, she says tightly. **Go back to bed, Bob. I
won't bother you again tonight. Sweet dreams.**

I wake up with the early morning light from the window as
it streams in across my face. One of my arms is lying over the
edge of the bed, and the other is twisted around someone's
shoulders – *What the fuck?* I think fuzzily.

It's Ramona. She's curled up against me on top of the
sheets, sleeping like a baby. She's still wearing her glad rags,
her hair a wild tangle. My breath catches with fear or lust or
guilt, or maybe all three at the same time: guilty, fearful lust.
I can't make up my mind whether I want to gnaw my arm off
at the shoulder or ask her to elope with me.

Eventually I work out a compromise. I sit up, slowly
pulling my arm out from under her: "How do you take your
coffee?"

"Uh?" She opens her eyes. "Oh . . . hi." She looks puzzled.
"Where am I . . . oh." Mild annoyance: "I take it black. And
strong." She yawns, then rolls over and begins to sit up.

Yawns again. "I need to use your bathroom." She looks displeased, and it's not just her eyeliner running: somehow she looks older, less inhumanly perfect. The glamour's still there, masking her physical shape, but what I'm seeing now is unfogged by implanted emotional bias.

"Be my guest." I walk over to the filter machine and start prodding at it, trying to figure out where the sachet of coffee goes. My head's spinning — "How did you get in here?"

"Don't you remember?"

"No."

"Well that makes two of us," she says as she closes the door. A moment later I hear the sound of running water and realize too late that I need to use the bathroom, too.

Oh, great. There was the, whatever the fuck you call it, with the predator, Marc — and she needed me to — I try not to think too closely about it. I remember that much. *How the hell did she get in here?* I ask myself.

I get the coffee maker loaded and go prod my tablet PC. It's sitting where I left it last night, with a clear line of sight on the door and window, and it's still up and running. I look too closely and the ward tries to bite me between the eyes but misses. *Good.* So then I go and inspect the other wards I put on the door by opening it and gingerly pulling in the DO NOT DISTURB sign. The silver diagram, sketched on the sign using a conductive pencil and a drop of blood, shimmers at me. It's still live: anyone other than me who tries to get past it is going to get a very unpleasant surprise. Finally, as the coffee maker begins to spit and burble, I check the seal on the window. My mobile phone (the real one, the Treo with the Java countermeasure suite and the keyboard and all the trimmings, not the bullet-firing fake) is still propped up against it.

I glance up and down, then shake my head. There are no holes in the walls and ceiling, which means Ramona can't be here — the place is about as secure as a hotel room can be, stitched up tighter than Angleton's ass.

"I don't want to hurry you or anything, but I need the toilet, too," I call through the door.

"Okay, okay! I'm nearly ready." She sounds annoyed.

"Are you sure you don't remember how you got in here?" I add.

The door opens. She's repaired her glamour and is every bit the air-brushed, drop-dead gorgeous model she was when I first saw her in the Laguna Bar: only the eyes are different. Old and tired.

"How much of what happened last night do you remember?" she asks.

"I—" I stop. "What, do you mean after we met Billington? Or after I left the casino?"

"Did we leave together?" She frowns.

"You don't—" I bite my tongue and stare at her. *How did you get into my room?* Maybe it's a side effect of destiny entanglement — my wards can't tell us apart. "I had some really weird dreams," I say then hold out a coffee cup for her.

"Well, that's a surprise." She snorts then takes the cup. "But it doesn't have to mean anything."

"It doesn't—" I stop dead. "I dreamed about you," I say reluctantly. I find it really hard to pick the right words. "You were with some guy you'd picked up who worked at the casino."

She looks me in the eye calmly. "You dreamed about me, Bob. Things happen in dreams that don't always happen in real life."

"But he died while you were in bed with—"

"Bob?" Her eyes are greenish blue, flecks of gold floating in them, rimmed in expensive eyeliner that makes them look wide and innocent — but somehow they're deeper than an arctic lake, and much colder. "For once in your life, shut up and listen to me. Okay?"

She's got the Voice of Command. I find myself leaning against the wall with no definite memory of how I got here. "What?"

"*Primus*, we're destiny-entangled. I can't do anything about that. You stub your toe, I hurt; I call you names, you get pissy. But you're making a big mistake. Because, *secundus*, you had a weird dream. And you're jumping to the conclusion that the two are related, that whatever you dreamed about is whatever happened to me. And you know what? That ain't necessarily so. Correlation does not imply causation. Now——" she reaches over and pokes me in the chest with a fingertip "——you seem a little upset over whatever it was you dreamed about. And I think you ought to think very hard before you ask the next question, because you can choose to ask whether there was any connection between your weird dream and my night out – or you can just tell yourself you ate too many cheese canapés before bed and it was all in your head, and you can walk away from it. Is that clear? We may be entangled, but it doesn't have to go any further."

She stands there expectantly, obviously anticipating a reply. I'm rooted to the spot by the force of her gaze. My pulse roars in my ears. I don't – truly I don't – know what to do! My mind spins. Did I simply have a wet dream last night? Or did Ramona suck a serial rapist's soul right out of his body then use me for sex magick to keep her daemon in check . . .? And do I really want to know the truth? *Really?*

I feel my lips moving without any conscious decision. "Thank you. And if you don't mind, I'm going to un-ask that question for the time being."

"Oh, I mind all right." A flash of unidentifiable emotion flickers in her eyes like distant lightning. "But don't worry about me, I'm used to it. I'll be all right after breakfast." She glances down, breaking eye contact. "Jesus, stripy pajamas. It's too early in the morning for that."

"Hey, it's all I've got, anyway, it's better than sleeping in a tux." I raise an eyebrow at her dress. "You're going to have to get that professionally cleaned."

"No, really?" She takes a mouthful of coffee. "Thanks for the tip, monkey-boy, I'd never have guessed. I'll be going back to my room when I finish this." Another mouthful. "Got any plans for today?"

I pause for thought. "I need to touch base with my backup team and file a report with head office. Then I'm supposed to visit a tailor's shop. After which——" a ghost of a dream memory gibbers and capers for attention "——I heard there's a nice beach up at Anse Marcel. I figure I might hang out there for a while. How about you?"

I eat breakfast on a balcony overlooking an expanse of white beach, trying not to flinch as the occasional airbus rumbles past on final approach into Princess Juliana Airport. Midway through a butter croissant that melts on the tongue, my Treo rings: "Howard!"

"Speaking." I get a sinking sensation in the pit of my stomach: it's Griffin.

"Get yourself over here, chop-chop. We've got a situation."

Shit. "What kind of situation? And where's here?"

"Face time only." He rattles off an address somewhere near Mullet Beach and I jot it down.

"Okay, I'll be over in half an hour."

"Make sure you are!" He hangs up, leaving me staring at my phone as if it's turned into a dead slug in my hand. What a way to start a day: Griffin's found something to go nonlinear over. I shake my head in disgust. As if I haven't got enough problems already.

I'm just about up and running on local time. Even so, it

takes me a while to figure out my way to the address Griffin gave me. It turns out to be a holiday villa, white clapboard walls and wooden shutters overlooking the road behind the beachfront. The temperature's already up to the mid-twenties and rising as I trudge towards the front door. I'm about to knock when it opens and I find myself eyeball to hairy eyeball with Griffin.

"Get in here!" he half-snarls, grabbing me by my jacket. "Quick!"

I take in his red-rimmed eyes, stubbly chin, and general agitation. "Something bad happen?"

"You could say that." I follow him into the back room. The windows are shuttered, several large nylon hold-alls are lined up against one wall, and there's a mass of electronics spread across the dining table. After a couple of seconds I figure out that I'm looking at a clunky electrodynamic rig and a Vulpis-Tesla mainframe: it looks like it was invented by a mad pervert who was into torturing chickens, but it's really just a tool for summoning minor abominations. By the look on his face Griffin's been bolting it together and hitting the bottle for the past twelve hours or so—not a combination I'm sanguine about. "I got a dispatch from head office. The oppo's acting up – they've sent us one of their fast bowlers!"

"What's cricket got to do with us?" I ask, confused. It's too early in the morning for this.

"Who said anything about cricket?" Griffin hurries across the room and starts rearranging the bakelite plug-board that configures the chicken-torturer. "I said they'd sent a fast bowler, not a fucking cricketer."

"Slow up." I rub my eyes. "How long have you been out here?"

He rounds on me. "Nineteen years, if it means anything to you, whipper-snapper!" he snorts. "Kids these days . . ."

I shrug. "Slang changes, is what I'm saying."

"Bah." He straightens up and sighs. "I got a flash code from the Weather Service this morning: Charlie Victor is in town. He's one of their top assassins, works for Unit Echo – that's our designation for it, not theirs, nobody's got a fucking clue what the Black Chamber internal org chart looks like – and generally we don't get advance warning because the first warning anyone gets about Charlie Victor is when they wake up dead."

"Whoa." I grab a chair and sit down hard. "When did he arrive?"

"Yesterday, while you were snoozing." Griffin stares at me. "Well?"

"Do we know who his target *is?*"

"Weather Service says it's something to do with your mission, this billionaire."

"Weather Service—" I pause. How to phrase my opinion of the Predictive Branch tactfully? Just in case Griffin's got a gypsy cousin who's into fluffy chakra crystal ball-fu and works for Precognitive Ops . . . "Weather Service has a certain reputation." A reputation for being disastrously wrong about thirty percent of the time – as you'd expect of a bunch of webcams hooked up to crystal balls scrying random number generators – and for being less than half right about fifty percent of the time, which is even worse than the real Meteorological Office. The only reason we don't ignore them completely is that about one time in five they hit the jackpot – and then people live or die by their projections. But that thirty percent gave us the amazing invisible Iraqi WMDs, the Falklands War ("nothing can possibly go wrong"), and going back a bit further, the British Lunar Expedition of 1964.[7,8]

---

[7] What lunar expedition?
[8] Exactly.

"Weather Service is taking traffic flow at source from GCHQ and cross-correlating it with validated HUMINT sources," Griffin rumbles ominously. "This is about as hard as it gets. What are the implications for your mission?"

"I need to talk to Angleton – I thought we had an accommodation on this one, but if what you're saying's right, all bets are off." I glance at the VT frame. "What's the chicken plucker for?"

"A necessary precaution." Griffin stares at me speculatively. "In case Charlie Victor tries to pay a visit. And to keep a lock on your special kit." He nods at the cases in the corner.

"Uh-huh. Any sign of my backup team?"

"I called them for a meeting half an hour ago. They should be arriving any time—"

Right on cue, there's a knock at the door.

I head over to open the door but Griffin beats me to it, shoving me out of the way and raising a finger to silence me. He pulls an elderly-looking revolver from under his jacket, holding it behind his back as he turns the door handle.

It's Brains, wearing sunglasses and a loud Hawaiian shirt. "Yo, Bob!" he calls, ignoring Griffin. Boris slouches on the front stoop behind him.

"Come in," Griffin mutters uninvitingly. "Don't just stand there!"

"Where's Pinky?" I ask.

"Parking your car by the hotel." Brains walks past Griffin, whistling nonchalantly, then stops when he sees the VT frame. "Haven't seen one of those in a long while!" He closes in on it and peers at the plug-board. "Hey, this is wired up all wrong—"

"Stop that at once!" Griffin is about to hit the ceiling. "Before you start meddling—"

"Boys, boys." Boris grimaces tiredly. "Chill."

"I need to call Angleton," I manage to slip in. "And I've

got to get closer to the target. Can we please try to keep on track, here? What do we know about Billington's arrival? I didn't think he was meant to be here yet."

"Billington is here?" Boris frowns. "Is ungood news. How?"

"He flew in last night." I glance at Griffin, but his mouth is clamped in a thin line. He's not volunteering anything. "I met him briefly. Do we know where this yacht of his is? Or his schedule?" I ask Griffin directly, and he frowns.

"His yacht, the *Mabuse*, is moored off North Point – he's not using the marina at Marigot for some reason. While he's on the island he's got a villa on Mount Paradis, but I think you're more likely to find he's staying on the yacht." Griffin crosses his arms. "Thinking of paying him a visit?"

"Just puzzled." I glance at the wall where someone has pinned a large map of the island. North Point is about as far away from Maho Beach – and the casino – as you can get. It must be close to fifteen kilometers, and longer if you cover the distance by boat. "I was wondering how he got here last night."

"Simple; he flew." Griffin looks as if he's sucking a lemon. "Calling that monster a yacht is like calling a Boeing 777 a company light twin."

"How big is it?" asks Brains.

"Naval Intelligence knows." Griffin walks over to the sideboard and pulls out a bottle of tonic water. "Seeing as how it started life as a Russian Krivak-III-class frigate."

"Whee! Do you think they'd let me drive it?" Pinky's somehow slipped in under the radar. "Hey, Bob: catch!" He chucks me a key fob.

"You're telling me Billington owns a warship?" I sit down heavily.

"No, I'm telling you his yacht *used to* be one." Griffin fills his glass and puts the bottle down. He looks amused, for malicious values of amusement. "A Type 113 5 guided missile frigate, to be precise, late model with ASW helicopter and vertical launch system. The Russians sold it off to the Indian Navy during a hard currency hiccup a few years ago, and they sold it in turn when they commissioned the first of their own guided missile destroyers. I'm pretty sure they took out the guns and VLS before they decommissioned it, but they left in the helideck and engines, and it can make close to forty knots when the skipper wants to go somewhere in a hurry. Billington sank a fortune into converting it, and now it's one of the largest luxury yachts in the world, with a swimming pool where the nuclear missile launchers used to be."

"Jesus." It's not as if I was planning to do the scuba-dive-and-climb-aboard thing – for starters, I know just enough about diving to realize I'd probably drown – but when Angleton mentioned a yacht I wasn't thinking in terms of battleships. "What's he use it for?"

"Oh, this and that." Griffin sounds even more amused. "I hear it comes in handy for water skiing. More realistically, he can zip anywhere in the Caribbean in about twelve hours. Chopper into Miami, brief excursion out to sea, chopper into Havana, and nobody's any the wiser. Go visit his bankers in Grand Cayman, entertain visiting billionaires, hold meetings in real secrecy and we can't keep an eye on him without getting the Navy involved."

I can almost see the cards he's got stuffed up his sleeve. "What's your point?"

"My point?" He stares at me. "My point is that I happen to know a damn sight more about what's going on in my patch than all of you lot put together, or the clowns at head office for that matter. And I would appreciate it if you'd run any harebrained schemes past me before you put them into practice just in case you're about to put your foot in it.

Human Resources may have told you that I'm a garden leave case and you're reporting direct to Angleton, but you might also like to consider the possibility that Human Resources couldn't find their arse with a map, a periscope, and a tub of Vaseline."

Boris rises to the bait: "Am not possible commenting on Human Resources!"

Pinky snorts loudly.

I shrug: "Okay, I'll run any harebrained schemes I hatch past you if you give me the benefit of your advice. But if it's just as well with you, I need to go check in with my liaison." And I still have to call Angleton – who told Griffin about his control issues? "Then I've got to pick up some clothes and go wangle myself an invitation aboard the . . . What did you say the yacht was called?"

"The *Mabuse*," Griffin repeats. His cheek twitches. "And Charlie Victor is in town. You ought to take precautions."

"Sure." If the bastard thinks he can spook me that easily he's got another thing coming. "Boris, any immediate updates?"

Boris shakes his head: "Not yet."

"Okay, then I'll be going." And before Griffin can object I'm out the door.

I need to get my head together, so I start by heading for the tailor's shop they pointed me at back in Darmstadt. After half an hour of wandering among fast-food concessions, tourist traps, and free cosmetic sample stands I find it, and half an hour later I'm back in my room unwrapping – "What is this shit?" I ask myself, bemused. Whoever ordered it either didn't have a clue what I normally wear or didn't care. There's a lightweight suit, a bunch of shirts, a choice of ties – I corral them in the wardrobe and lock it carefully, in case they sneak out and try to strangle me in the night – and the nearest thing to wearable clothing is a polo shirt and a pair of chinos. Which are not only totally un-me, they're not even black. "Shit!" I blew out of Darmstadt with nothing but the business suit and a borrowed toilet bag: it's this or nothing. I make the best of a bad job, and end up looking like a second-rate parody of my father. I give up. I'll just have to go shopping, once I can find some cheap broadband access. Maybe Think Geek can ship me a care package by express airmail?

I pick up my Treo — not the crazy mechanical phonegun but real, reliable, understandable electronics — and head down to the car park. I hunt among the pickups and sports cars until I find the Smart Fortwo. I stare at it and it stares right back at me, mockingly. It's not even a convertible. "Someone's going to regret this," I mutter as I strap it on. Then it's the moment of truth: time for me to go check out a dream of a ghost of a memory, to see if someone's waiting for Marc the doorman to deliver a body to North Bay.

It's already getting hot, the sun burning through the deep blue vault of sky that arches overhead. I fumble my way out of Maho Bay and onto the road that winds towards the northern end of the island. Motoring here is just about as different from the autobahn experience as it's possible to get and still be on wheels, for which I'm fervently grateful. The road is narrow, barely graded and marked, and winds around the landscape as it climbs the picturesque but steep slopes of Mount Paradis. I pass numerous signs for tourist beaches, brightly painted shop fronts and restaurants . . . it's resort central. I crawl along behind a gaggle of taxis and a tourist 4x4 for about half an hour, then we're over the top of the island. The road more or less comes to a dead end in a depression between two hills, and I pull over beside a road sign to take a look.

The sign says: ANSE MARCEL. There's a scattering of shops

and hotels alongside the road, shaded by palm trees. On the downhill slope, I can see the sea in the distance, out across a brilliant white expanse of beach dotted with sunbathing tourists. Off to one side a hundred meters away, a clump of masts huddle together in a small marina. Looks like it's time to get out and walk.

I get out, feeling horribly overdressed: most of the punters hereabouts are wearing clothes that go well with thongs and sandals. Idyllic tropical beach paradise, with added ultraviolet burns and sand itch. And they're all so buff! I'm your typical pallid cube-maggot, and the six-pack is a high-cost luxury extra on that model. I shuffle down the street towards the marina, feeling about six centimeters tall, hoping that I'm wrong: that nobody's there, and I can go back to the hotel and write it all off as a bad dream brought on by vodka and jet lag.

The marina is little more than three piers with sailboats tied up on either side; two larger motorboats belonging to tour companies bob at the outer edge. A couple of guys are working on one of these, so I head up the pier until I can get a better view.

"*Bonjour*." One of the boatmen is watching me. "You want something?"

"Possibly." I glance out to sea. A distinctly dead-looking seagull sits on a bollard nearby, watching me stonily. *Watching me watching you* . . . it suddenly occurs to me that coming out here on my own might be a bad idea if Billington is serious about his privacy and is also, as Angleton put it, a player. "Does a boat from the *Mabuse* call here?"

"I think you want to find somewhere else to hang out." He smiles at me but the expression doesn't reach his eyes. He's holding a mallet and a big chisel.

"Why? They friends of yours?" I feel an itching in my

fingertips and a distinct taste of blue — my wards are responding to something nearby. Mr. Mallet glares at me. He's about my age, but built like a brick outhouse and tanned to the color of old oak. "Or maybe they aren't?"

"*Non.*" He turns his head and spits across the side of the pier.

"Pierre—" The other guy lets loose a stream of rapid-fire, heavily accented French that I can't hope to follow. He's in late middle-age, receding hair, salt-and-pepper beard: the picturesque Old Salt hanging out on the jetty, image only slightly spoiled by his Mickey Mouse tee shirt and blue plastic sandals. Pierre — Mr. Mallet — stares at me suspiciously. Then he turns and looks out across the sapphire sea.

I follow his gaze. There's a warship in the distance, a kilometer offshore: long, low, and lean, with a sharply raked superstructure. It takes me a few seconds to realize that it's the wrong color, gleaming white rather than the drab gray most navies paint their tubs.

I glance back at the pier. The goddamn seagull is staring at me, its eyes white and milky like—

Goddamn.

"Do you know a guy called Marc, from Maho Beach?" I ask.

A palpable hit: Pierre's head whips round towards me. He raises the chisel warningly as the seagull opens its beak. I pull out my Treo. "Smile for the camera, birdie."

The seagull stares at my smartphone accusingly, then topples off its perch and falls into the water like a dead weight. Which, in fact, is exactly what it is now that I've zapped it with my patent undead garbage collector.

"We've got about two minutes before they send another watcher," I say conversationally. "If they're awake, of course. So. Do you know Marc?"

"What's it worth?" He lowers the chisel, looking at me as if I've sprouted a second head.

I pull out two fifty-euro notes. "This."

"Yeah, I know Marc."

"Describe him."

"Oily bastard. Works out at the gym down the back of Rue de Hollande in Marigot, fills in on the door of the Casino Royale as a doorman and bouncer. He's the one you're asking about?"

I pull out two more notes. "Tell me everything you know."

The old guy glares at him, mutters something, gets up, and goes aboard the boat.

"I'll take those." Pierre puts down the chisel and I hand him the notes. "Marc is a piece of shit. He hits on tourist women and takes them for everything they've got. Nearly got himself arrested a year ago but they couldn't prove anything – or find the woman. Sometimes—" Pierre glances over his shoulder "—you see him in the early morning with some broad, going out on his boat. That one, there." He nods at a dinghy with a mounting for an outboard engine. "Meeting up with another boat. The women don't come back."

I have a heavy, sick feeling. "Would this other boat happen to be from the *Mabuse*?" I ask.

He looks at me sidelong. "I didn't say anything," he says.

I nod. "Thanks for your time."

"Thank you for taking out the trash." He gestures at the bollard where the bird was watching. "Now get out of here and please don't come back."

7: NIGHTMARE
BEACH

I'M TWO KILOMETERS DOWN THE ROAD TO GRAND Case and the coastal route to Marigot when I realize I'm being tailed. I'm crap at this private eye stuff, but it's not exactly rocket science on Saint Martin — the roads are only two lanes wide. There's a Suzuki SUV about a quarter-kilometer behind me. I speed up, it speeds up. I slow down, it slows down. So I pull over and park at a tourist spot and watch it tool past. Just before the next bend in the road it pulls over. How tedious, I think. Then I get on the ethereal blower.

Ramona? You busy?

Powdering my nose. What's up?

I stare at the car ahead of me, trying to visualize it well enough to shove it at her as a concrete image. **I've got company. The unwelcome kind.**

Surprise! I can feel her chuckle. **What did you do to annoy them?**

Oh, this 'n' that. I'm not about to go into my snooping activities just yet. **Billington's yacht is anchored off North Point, and some of the locals aren't too happy about it.**

Surprise indeed. So what's with the car?

They've been tailing me! I sound a bit peevish to myself — petulant, even. **And Billington's got the marina under surveillance. He's using seagulls as watchers. That makes me nervous.** I couldn't care less about the flying sea-rats, but I'm not terribly happy about the fact that someone aboard that yacht has got the nous to run the Invocation of Al-Harijoun on them, not to mention having enough spare eyeballs to monitor the surveillance take from several hundred zombie seagulls.

So why don't you lose them?

I take a deep breath. **That would entail breaking the traffic regulations, you know? I'm not supposed to do that. It's called drawing undue attention to yourself. Besides, there's a whole stack of documents to file, starting with a form A-19/B, or they'll throw the book at me. I could lose my license!**

What, your license to kill?

No, my license to drive! I thump the steering wheel in frustration. **This isn't some kind of spy farce: I'm just a civil servant. I don't have a license to kill, or authorization to poke my nose into random corners of the world and meet interesting people and hurt them. Capisce?**

For a moment I feel dizzy. I pinch the bridge of my nose and take a deep breath: my vision fades out for a scary moment, then comes back with this weird sense that I'm looking through two sets of eyes at once. **What the fuck?**

It's me, Bob. I can't keep this up for long . . . Look, you see that SUV parked ahead?

Yeah? I'm looking at it but it doesn't register.

The guy who just got out of it and is walking toward you is carrying a gun. And he doesn't look particularly friendly. Now I know you're hung-up on the speed limit and stuff, but can I suggest you——

There is one good thing about driving a Smart car: it has a turning circle tighter than Ramona's hips. I hit the gas and yank the wheel and make the tires squeal, rocking from side to side so badly that for a moment I'm afraid the tiny car is about to topple over. The bad guy raises his pistol slowly but I've floored the accelerator and it's not *that* slow in a straight line. My wards are prickling and tickling like a sandstorm and there's a faint blue aura crawling over the dash. Something smacks into the tailgate – a stray pebble, I tell myself as I swerve back up the coast road towards Orleans.

I knew you could do it! Ramona enthuses like she's channeling a cheerleader. **What did you do to get them riled up like that?**

I asked about Marc. I glance in the mirror and flinch; my tail is back in the SUV and has gotten it turned around. It's kicking up a plume of dust as it follows me. I swerve wildly to overtake a Taurus full of pensioners who're drifting along the crest of the road with their left turn signal flashing continuously, then I overcompensate to avoid rolling the Smart.

That wasn't very fucking clever of you, was it? she asks sharply. **Why did you do it?** Irrelevant distractions nag at the edges of my perception: a twin-engine pond-hopper buzzes overhead on final approach into Grand Case Airport.

I wanted to see if my suspicions were correct. And if I was dreaming or not.

There's a van ahead, moving slowly, so I pull out to look past it and there's an oncoming truck so I pull back in. And behind me, closing the gap again, is the SUV.

I am going to have to lose these guys before they phone ahead and get some muscle ahead of me on the road to Philipsburg. Any ideas?

Yes. I'll be on my way in about five minutes. Just stay ahead of them for now.

Be fast, okay? If you can't be safe. I pull out recklessly and floor the accelerator again, passing the van as the driver waves angrily at me. There's a kink in the road ahead and I take it as fast as I dare. The Smart is bouncy and rolls frighteningly but it can't be any worse at road-holding than the SUV tailing me, can it? **Just what are they doing with the women?**

What women?

The women Marc was kidnapping and selling to the boat crew. Don't tell me you didn't know about that?

The Suzuki has pulled past the van and is coming up behind me and I'm fresh out of side streets. From here, it's a three-kilometer straight stretch around the foothills of Paradise Peak before we get to Orient Beach and the fork down to the sea. After that, it's another five kilometers to the next turnoff. I'm doing eighty and that's already too damn fast for this road. Besides, I feel like I'm driving two cars at once, one of them a sawed-off subcompact and the other a topless muscle-machine that dodges in and out of the tourist traffic like a steeplechaser weaving through a queue of pensioners. It's deeply confusing and it makes me want to throw up.

What do you know about— pause **—the abductions?**

Women. Young. Blonde. His wife owns a cosmetics company and he looks too young. What conclusion would you draw?

He has a good plastic surgeon. Hang on. The muscle car surges effortlessly around another bus. Meanwhile the SUV has pulled even with me, and the driver is waving his gun at me to pull over. I glance sideways once more and see his eyes. They look dead and worse than dead, like he's been in the water for a week and nothing's tried eating him. I recognize that look: they're using tele-operator-controlled zombies. *Shit*. My steering wheel is crawling with sparks as the occult countermeasures cut in, deflecting their brain-eating mojo.

I tense and hit the brakes, then push the cigarette lighter home in its socket during the second it takes him to match my speed. We come to a halt side by side on the crest of a low hill. The SUV's door opens and the dead guy with the gun gets out and walks over. I sniff: there's a nasty fragrant smoke coming out of the lighter socket.

He marches stiffly round to my side door, keeping the gun in view. I keep my hands on the steering wheel as he opens the door and gets in.

"Who are you?" I ask tensely. "What's going on?"

"You ask too many questions," says the dead man. His voice slurs drunkenly, as if he's not used to this larynx, and his breath stinks like rotting meat. "Turn around. Drive back to Anse Marcel." He points the gun at my stomach.

"If you say so." I slowly move one hand to the gearshift, then turn the car around. The SUV sits abandoned and forlorn behind us as I accelerate away. I drive slowly, trying to drag things out. The stink of decaying meat mingles with a weird aroma of burning herbs. The steering wheel has sprouted a halo of fine blue fire and my skin crawls – I glance sideways but there are no green sparks in his eyes, just the filmed-over lusterless glaze of a day-old corpse. It's funny how death changes people: I startle when I recognize him.

"Drive faster." The gun pokes me in the ribs.

"How long have you had Marc?" I ask.

"Shut up."

I need Ramona. The smell of burning herbs is almost overpowering. I reach out to her: **Phone me.**

What's the problem? I'm driving as fast as——

Just phone me, damn it! Dial my mobile now!

Fifteen or twenty endless seconds pass, then my Treo begins to ring.

"I need to answer my phone," I tell my passenger. "I have to check in regularly."

"Answer it. Say that everything is normal. If you tell them different I'll shoot you."

I reach out and punch the call-accept button, angling the screen away from him. Then in quick succession I punch the program menu button, and the pretty icon that triggers all the car's countermeasures simultaneously.

I don't know quite what I was expecting. Explosions of sparks, spinning heads, a startling spewage of ectoplasm? I get none of it. But Marc the doorman, who managed to die of one of the effects of terminal cocaine abuse just before Ramona's succubus could suck him dry, sighs and slumps like a dropped puppet. Unfortunately he's not belted in so he falls across my lap, which is deeply inconvenient because we're doing fifty kilometers an hour and he's blocking the steering wheel. Life gets very exciting for a few seconds until I bring the car to rest by the roadside, next to a stand of palm trees.

I wind down the window and stick my head out, taking in deep gasping breaths of blessedly wormwood- and fetor-free ocean air. The fear is just beginning to register: *I did it again*, I realize, *I nearly got myself killed*. Sticking my nose into something that isn't strictly any of my business. I shove Marc out of my lap, then stop. *What am I going to do with him?*

It is generally not a good idea when visiting foreign countries to be found by the cops keeping company with a corpse and a gun. An autopsy will show he had a cardiac arrest about a day ago, but he's in my car and that's the sort of thing that gives them exactly the wrong idea — talk about circumstantial evidence! "Shit," I mutter, looking around. Ramona's on her way but she's driving a two-seater. *Double-shit.* My eyes fasten on the stand of trees. *Hmm.*

I restart the engine and reverse up to the trees. I park, then get out and start wrestling with Marc's body. He's surprisingly heavy and inflexible, and the seats are inconveniently form-fitting, but I manage to drag him across to the driver's side with a modicum of sweating and swearing. He leans against the door as if he's sleeping off a bender. I retrieve the Treo, blip the door shut, then start doodling schematics in a small application I carry for designing field-expedient incantations. There's no need to draw a grid round the car — the Smart's already wired — so as soon as I'm sure I've got it right I hit the upload button and look away. When I look back I know there's something there, but it makes the back of my scalp itch and my vision blur. If I hadn't parked the car there myself I could drive right past without seeing it.

I shamble back to the roadside and look both ways — there's no pavement — then start walking along the hard shoulder towards Orient Beach.

It's still morning but the day is going to be baking hot. Trudging along a dusty road beneath a spark-plug sky without a cloud in sight gets old fast. There are beaches and sand off to one side, and on the other a gently rising hillside covered with what passes for a forest hereabouts — but I'm either overdressed (according to my sweating armpits) or underdressed (if I acknowledge the impending sunburn on the back of my neck and arms). I'm also in a foul mood.

De-animating Marc has brought back the sense of guilt from Darmstadt: the conviction that if I'd just been slightly faster off the ball I could have saved Franz and Sophie and the others. It's also confirmed that my dreams of Ramona are the real thing: so much for keeping a fig leaf of deniability. *She was right: I'm an idiot.* Finally there's Billington, and the activities of his minions. Seeing that long, hungry hull in the distance, recognizing the watcher on the quay, has given me an ugly, small feeling. It's as if I'm an ant chewing away at a scab on an elephant's foot — a foot that can be raised and brought down on my head with crushing force should the pachyderm ever notice my existence.

After I've been walking for about half an hour, a bright red convertible rumbles out of the heat haze and pulls up beside me. I think it's a Ferrari, though I'm not much good at car spotting; anyway, Ramona waves at me from the driver's seat. She's wearing aviator mirrorshades, a bikini, and a see-through silk sarong. If my libido wasn't on the ropes from the events of the past twelve hours my eyes would be halfway out of my head: as it is, the best I can manage is a tired wave.

"Hi, stranger. Looking for a lift?" She grins ironically at me.

"Let's get out of here." I flop into the glove-leather passenger seat and stare at the trees glumly.

She pulls off slowly and we drive in silence for about five minutes. "You could have gotten yourself killed back there," she says quietly. "What got into you?"

I count the passing palm trees. After I reach fifty I let myself open my mouth. "I wanted to check out a hunch."

Without taking her eyes off the road she reaches over with her right hand and squeezes my left leg. "I don't want you getting yourself killed," she says, her voice toneless and over-controlled.

I pay attention to her in a way I can't describe, feeling for whatever it is that connects us. It's deep and wide as a river, invisible and fluid and powerful enough to drown in. What I sense through it is more than I bargained for. Her attention's fixed on the road ahead but her emotions are in turmoil. Grief, anger at me for being a damn fool, anxiety, jealousy. *Jealousy?*

"I didn't know you cared," I say aloud. *And I'm not sure I want you to care*, I think to myself.

"Oh, it's not about you. If you get yourself killed what happens to me?"

She wants it to sound like cynical self-interest but there's a taste of worry and confusion in her mind that undermines every word that comes out of her mouth.

"Something big is going down on this island," I say, tacitly changing the subject before we end up in uncharted waters. "Billington's crew has got watchers out. Seagull monitors controlled from, um, somewhere else. And then I ran into Marc. Judging by the state of my wards every goddamn corpse on the island must be moving – why the hell haven't they chained up the graveyards? And what's this thing they've got about single female tourists?"

"That might not be part of Billington's core program." Ramona sounds noncommittal but I can tell she knows more than she's admitting. "It might be his crew carrying on behind his back. Or something less obvious."

"Come on! If his sailors are kidnapping single females, you think he's not going to know about it?"

Ramona turns her head to look me in the eye: "I think you underestimate just how big this scheme is."

"Then why won't you tell me?" I complain.

"Because I'm—" She bites her tongue. "Listen. It's a nice day. Let's go for a walk, huh?"

"A walk – why?" I get the most peculiar sense that she's trying to tell me something without putting it into words.

"Let's just say I wanna see your boxers, okay?"

She grins. Her good humor's more fragile than it looks, but just for a moment I like what I can see. "Okay." I yawn, the aftereffects of the chase catching up with me. "Where do you want to go?"

"There's a spot near Orient Bay."

She drives past tourists and local traffic in silence. I keep my mouth shut. I'm not good at handling emotional stuff and Ramona confuses the hell out of me. It's almost enough to make me wish Mo was around; life would be a lot simpler.

We hit a side road and drive along it until we pass a bunch of the usual beach-side shops and restaurants and a car park. Ramona noses the Ferrari between a Land Rover and a rack of brightly painted boneshaker bicycles and kills the engine. "C'mon," she says, jumping out and popping open the trunk. "I bought you a towel, trunks, and sandals."

"Huh?"

She prods me in the ribs. "Strip off!" I look at her dubiously but her expression is mulish. There's a concrete convenience nearby so I wander over to it and go inside. I pull my polo shirt off, then lose the shoes, socks, and trousers before pulling on the swimming trunks. I have my limits: the smartphone I keep. I go back outside. Ramona is just about hopping up and down with impatience. "What are you doing with that phone?" she asks. "Come on, it'll be safe in the glove compartment."

"Nope. Not doing." I cross my arms defensively. The Treo doesn't fit nicely in the baggy boxer-style trunks' pocket, but I'm not handing it over. "You want my wallet, you can have it, but not my Treo! It's already saved my life once today."

"I see." She stares at me, chewing her lip thoughtfully. "Listen, will you turn it off?"

"What? But it's in sleep mode—"

"No, I want you to switch it *right off*. No electronics is best, but if you insist on carrying—"

I raise an eyebrow and she shakes her head in warning. I look her in the eye. "Are you sure this is necessary?"

"Yes."

My stomach flip-flops. *No electronics*? That's heavy. In fact it's more than heavy: to compute is to be, and all that. I don't mind going without clothes, but being without a micro-processor is *truly* stripping down. It's like asking a sorcerer to surrender his magic wand, or a politician to forswear his lies. *How far do I trust her?* I wonder, then I remember last night, a moment of vulnerability on a balcony overlooking the sea.

"Okay." I press and hold the power button until the phone chimes and the signal LED winks out. *No electronics.* "What now?"

"Follow me." She picks up the towels, shuts the car trunk, and heads towards the beach. While I wasn't looking she's shed the sarong: I can't keep my eyes from tracking the hyp-notic sway of her buttocks.

The sand is fine and white and the vegetation rapidly gives way to open beach. There's a rocky promontory ahead, and various sunbathers have set up their little patches; off-shore, the sailboards are catching the breeze. The sea is a huge, warm presence, sighing as waves break across the reef offshore and subside before they reach us. Ramona stops and bends forwards, rolls her briefs down her legs, and shrugs out of her bikini top. Then she looks at me: "Aren't you going to strip off?"

"Hey, this is public—"

There's an impish gleam in her eyes. "*Are* you?" She straightens up and deliberately turns to face me. "You're cute when you blush!"

I glance at the nearest tourists. Middle-aged spread and a clear lack of concealing fabric drives the message home. "Oh, so it's a nudist beach."

"Naturist, please. C'mon, Bob. People will stare if you don't."

Nobody taught me how to say no when a beautiful naked woman begs me to take my clothes off. I fumble my way out of my trunks and concentrate very hard on not concentrating on her very visible assets. Luckily, she's Ramona. She's

strikingly beautiful – with or without the glamour, it does-
n't matter – but I also find her intimidating. After a minute
or so I figure out I'm not about to sprout a semaphore pole in
public, so I begin to relax. When in Rome, et cetera.

Ramona picks her way past the clots of slowly basting
sunseekers – I notice with displeasure a scattering of heads
turning to track us – and detours around a battered hut selling ice cream and cold drinks. The beach is narrower at this
end, and proportionately less populated as she veers towards
the waterline. "Okay, this'll do. Mark the spot, Bob." She
unrolls her towel and plants it on the sand. Then she holds
out a waterproof baggie. "For your phone—sling it around
your neck, we're going swimming."

"We're going swimming?" **Naked?**

She looks at me and sighs. "Yes Bob, we're going swimming in the sea, bare-ass naked. Sometimes I despair of
you . . ."

Oh boy. My head's spinning. I bag up my phone, make sure
it's sealed, and walk into the sea until I'm up to my ankles,
looking down at the surf swirling grains of sand between and
over my toes. I can't remember when I last went swimming.
It's cool but not cold. Ramona wades into the waves until
she's hip-deep then turns round and beckons to me. "What
are you waiting for?"

I grit my teeth and plod forwards until the water's over
my knees. There's an island in the distance, just a nub of trees
waving slowly above a thin rind of sand. "Are you planning
on wading all the way out there?"

"No, just a little farther." She winks at me, then turns and
wades out deeper. Soon those remarkable buttocks are just a
pale gleam beneath the rippling waves.

I follow her in. She pitches forwards and starts swimming.
Swimming isn't something I've done much of lately, but it's
like riding a bicycle – you'll remember how to do it and your

muscles will make sure you don't forget the next morning. I splash around after her, trying to relearn my breast stroke by beating the waves into submission. Damn, but this is different from the old Moseley Road Swimming Baths.

This way, she tells me, using our speech-free intercom. **Not too far. Can you manage ten minutes without a rest?**

I hope so. The waves aren't strong inside the barrier formed by the reef, and in any event they're driving us back onshore, but I hope she's not planning on going outside the protective boundary.

Okay, follow me.

She strikes out away from the sunbathers and towards the outer reef, at an angle. Pretty soon I'm gasping for breath as I flail the water, trailing after her. Ramona is a very strong swimmer and I'm out of practice, and my arms and thigh muscles are screaming for mercy within minutes. But we're approaching the reef, the waves are breaking over it – and to my surprise, when she stands up the water barely reaches her breasts.

"What the hell?" I flap towards her, then switch to treading water, feeling for the surface beneath my feet. I'm half-expecting to kick razor-sharp coral, but what I find myself standing on is smooth, slippery-slick concrete.

"No electronics, because someone might have tapped into it. No clothing because you might be bugged. Seawater because it's conductive; if they'd tattooed a capacitive chart on your scalp while you were asleep it'd be shorted out by now. No bugs because we've got a high-volume white noise source all around us." She frowns at me, deadly serious. "You're clean, monkey-boy, except for whatever compulsion filters they've dropped on you, and any supernatural monitors."

"Shit." Enlightenment dawns: Ramona has dragged me

out here because she thinks I'm bugged. "What's down below us . . .?"

"It's a defensive emplacement. The French got serious about that in the early '60s, before the treaty arrangements got nailed down. You're standing on a discordance node, one of a belt of sixteen big ones designed to protect the east coast of Saint Martin against necromantic incursions. If you swim through it, any thaumaturgic bugs they've planted on you will be wiped — it's a huge occult degaussing rig. Which is one of the reasons I brought you here."

"But if it's a defensive emplacement, how come the zombies up at—" I bite my tongue.

"Exactly." She looks grave. "That's part of what's wrong here, which is the other thing I want to check out. About four months ago one of our routine geomantic surveillance flights noticed that the defensive belt was — not broken, exactly, but showed signs of tampering. One of Billington's subsidiaries, a construction company, landed the contract to maintain the concrete ballast units. Do I need to draw you a diagram?"

Here we are surrounded by ocean, and my mouth is dry as a bone. "No. You think somebody's running a little import/export business, right?"

"Yes."

I take a deep breath. "Anything else?"

"I wanted to get you alone, with no bugs."

"Hey, you only had to ask!" I grin, my heart pounding inappropriately.

"Don't take this the wrong way." She smiles ruefully. "You know what would happen if—"

"Only kidding," I say, abruptly nervous. The conversation is veering dangerously close to territory I'm uncomfortable with. I look at her — correction: I force my eyes to track about thirty degrees up until I'm looking at her face. She's watching me right back, and I find I can't help wondering what it would be like to . . . well. Sure she's attached to a level three glamour so tight you'd need a scalpel to peel it off her, but I can probably cope with whatever's underneath it, I think. Her daemon is something else again, but there are things we could do, without intercourse . . . but what about Mo? My conscience finally catches up with my freewheeling speculation. *Well, what indeed?* But the thought drags me back down to Earth after a fashion. I manage to get my worst instincts under control then ask: "Okay, so why did you *really* bring me out here?"

"First, I need to know: Why the fuck did you go rushing off to Anse Marcel?"

The question hits me like a bucket of cold water in the face. "I, I, I wanted to check something out," I stutter. It sounds lame. "Last night, I was inside Marc's head. He was going to—" I trail off.

"You were inside his head?"

"Yes, and it wasn't a nice place to be," I snap

"You were inside—" She blinks rapidly. "Tell me what you picked up?"

"But I thought you knew—"

"No," she says tightly. "I didn't know it went that far. This is as new to me as it is to you. What did you learn?"

I lick my lips. "Marc had an arrangement. Every couple of weeks he'd pick up a single female who wouldn't be missed and he'd— let's not go into that. Afterwards he'd drop a geas on her, a control ring he'd learned from the customer, and he'd drive her up to Anse Marcel where a couple of guys would come in on a boat to pick the victim up. They paid in coke, plus extras."

"Ri-ight." Ramona pauses. "That makes sense." I can feel it snapping into place in her mind, another part of a lethal booby-trapped jigsaw puzzle she's trying to solve. I realize in the silence between heartbeats that we've stopped pretending.

It feels as if some huge external force is pushing us together, squeezing us towards intimacy. She gave me an opening to pretend that I wasn't involved, and I didn't take it. But why? I wouldn't normally do this kind of thing; maybe the tropical clime's addled me.

"What part of the picture does it fit?" I meet her gaze. I have the most peculiar feeling that I'm watching myself watching her through two pairs of eyes.

"Billington's diversified into a variety of fields. You shouldn't think of him as simply a computer industry mogul. He's got his tentacles into a lot more pies than Silicon Valley."

"But kidnapping? That's ridiculous! It can't possibly be cost-effective, even if he's selling them off for spare parts." I swallow and shut up: she's broadcasting a horrible sense of claustrophobic dread, fear rising off her like a heat haze. I shuffle, grounding my feet against the concrete defense platform, and for a moment her skin acquires a silvery sheen. "What is it? Is he—"

"You know better than to say it aloud, Bob."

"I was afraid that was what you were trying to tell me." I look away, towards the breakers foaming across the reef and the open seas beyond. And it's not just her sense of dread anymore.

Some types of invocation need blood, and some require entire bodies. Whatever lives in the back of Ramona's head is a trivial, weak example; the creature I ran across in Santa Cruz and Amsterdam three years ago was a much more powerful one. Ramona is afraid that we're dealing with a life-eating horror that lives off the entropy burst that comes from draining a human soul: I'm pretty sure she's right. Which means the next question to ask is, who on Earth would summon such a thing, and why? And as I'm pretty sure we know the answer to *who* . . .

"What's Billington trying to do? What is he summoning up?"

"We don't know."

"Any guesses?" I ask sarcastically. "The Deep Ones, maybe?"

Ramona shakes her head angrily. "Not them! Never them." The sense of dread is choking, oppressive: she feels it personally, I realize.

I stare at her. That flash of silver again, the water lapping around her chest, drawing my eyes back towards those amazingly perfect breasts — I fight to filter out the distraction. *This isn't me, is it?* It's hard work, fighting the glamour. I want to see her as she really is. Taking a deep breath I force myself back to the matter in hand: "What makes you so sure the Deep Ones aren't behind him? You're holding out on me. Why?"

"Because they don't think that way. And yes, I *am* fucking holding out on you." She glares at me, and I can feel her wounded pride and defensive anger fighting against something else: Concern? Worry? "This is all going wrong. I brought you out here so I could tell you why you're being kept in the dark, not to pick a fight—"

"And here I was thinking you wanted me for my body." I hold my hands up before she has time to swear at me: "I'm sorry, but have you got any idea just how bloody distracting that glamour is?" It's amazing and frightening and beautiful, and it makes it a real bitch to try to concentrate on a conversation about subterfuge and lies without wondering what horrors she's concealing from me.

Ramona stares at me, until I can feel her inside my head, watching herself through my glamour-ensnared eyes. "Okay, monkey-boy: you want it, you got it." Her voice is flat and hard. "Just remember, you asked for it."

She lets go of the anchor of the glamour she's been

clinging on to. The constant repulsive force emanating from the concrete countermeasure emplacement we're standing on blows it away, like a hat in a hurricane – and I see Ramona as she truly is. Which gives me two very big surprises.

I gasp. I can't help myself. "You're one of *them!*" I meet her clear emerald gaze. And, quietly: "Wow."

Ramona says nothing, but one perfect nostril flares minutely. Her skin has a faint silvery iridescent sheen to it, like the scales of a fish; her hair is long and green as glass, framing a face with higher cheekbones and a wider mouth, rising from an inhumanly perfect long neck, the skin broken by two rows of slits above her clavicle. Her breasts are smaller, not much larger than her nipples, and two tinier ones adorn her rib cage beneath them. She raises her right hand and spreads her fingers, revealing the delicate tracery of webbing. "So what do you think of me now, monkey-boy?"

I swallow. She's like a sculpture in quicksilver, created by inhuman sea-dwelling aliens who have taken the essence of human female beauty and customized it to meet their need for an artificial go-between who can walk among the lumpen savages of the arid continental surfaces. "I've met half – sorry, the sea-born – before. At Dunwich. But not like, uh, you. Uh. You're different." I goggle at her, my mouth open like a fish. *Different* is an understatement and a half. The glamour she customarily wears doesn't make her look unnaturally beautiful to human eyes; rather, it conceals the more exotic aspects of her physiognomy. Strip it away and she's devastating, as unlike the weak-chinned followers of St. Monkfish as it's possible to imagine.

"So you've met the country cousins." Her cheek twitches. "Yes, I can understand your surprise." She stares at me, and I'm not sure whether she's disappointed or surprised. "So do you still think I'm a monster?"

"I think you're a—" I grind to a stop, before I can push

my foot any further down my throat. "Um." An inkling comes to me. "Let me guess. Your people. Go-betweens, like the colony at Dunwich. And you were given to the BC and they dropped the, your daemon on you to control you. Am I right?"

"I can neither confirm nor deny anything to do with my employers," she says with the flat-voiced emptiness of a necromancer's answering machine, before snapping back into focus: "My folks lived off Baja California. That's where I grew up." For a moment her eyes overflow with a sense of loss. "The Deep Ones did . . . well, they did what they did at Dunwich. My folks have been go-betweens for generations, able to pass as human and visit the depths. But we're not really at home among either species. We're constructs, Bob. And now you know why I use the glamour!" she adds harshly. "There's no need for flattery. I know damn well what I look like to you people."

You people: *Ouch!* "You're not a monster. Exotic, yes." I can't look away from her. I try to pull my eyes away from those perfect breasts and I keep looking down and there's another pair— "It just takes a little getting used to. But I don't mind, not really. I've already gotten over it." Down in the Laundry compound at Dunwich they've got a technical term for human employees who start spending too much time skinny-dipping with a snorkel: fish-fuckers. I've never really seen the attraction before, but with Ramona it's blindingly obvious. "You're as attractive without the glamour as with it. Maybe more so."

"You're just saying that to fuck with my head." I can taste her bitter amusement. "Admit it!"

"Nope." I take a deep breath and duck under the water, then kick off towards her. I can open my eyes here: everything is tinged pale green but I can see. Ramona dodges sideways then grabs me by the waist and we tumble beneath the reflective ceiling, grappling and pushing and shoving. I get my head above water for long enough to pull in a lungful of air, then she drags me under and starts tickling me. I convulse, but somehow whenever I really need air she's pushing me up above water rather than trying to pull me down. Weirdly, I seem to need much less air than I ought to. I can feel the gills working powerfully in her pleural cavity; it's as if there's some kind of leakage between us, as if she's helping oxygenate both our bloodstreams. When she kisses me she tastes of roses and oysters. Finally, after a few minutes of rubbing and fondling we settle to the bottom and lie, arms and legs entangled, in the middle of the circuit-board tracery of gold that caps the concrete table.

Fish-fucker! She mocks me.

It takes two to tango, squid-girl. Anyway, we haven't. I wouldn't dare.

Coward! She laughs ruefully, taking the sting out of the word. Silver bubbles trickle and bob towards the surface from her mouth. **Y'know, it's hard work breathing for both of us. If you want to help, go up to the surface . . .**

Okay. I let go and allow myself to stand up. As I pull away from her I feel a tightness in my chest that rapidly grows: we may be destiny-entangled, but the metabolic leakage is strictly short-range. I break surface and shake my head, gasping for air, then look towards the beach. There's a loud ringing in my ears, a deep bass rattle that resonates with my jaw, and a shadow dims the flashing sunlight on the reef. *Huh?* I find myself looking straight up at the underside of a helicopter.

"Get down!" Ramona hisses through the deafening roar. She wraps a hand around my ankle and yanks, pulling me under the surface. I hold my breath and let her drag me down beside her – my chest eases – then I realize she's pointing at a rectangular duct cover at one side of the concrete platform.

Come on, we've got to get under cover! If they see us we're screwed!

If *who* see us?

Billington's thugs! That's his chopper up there. Whatever you did must have really gotten them pissed. We've got to get under cover before—

Before what? She's wrestling with the iron duct cover, which is dark red with rust and thinly coated with polyps and other growths. I try to ignore the tightness in my chest and brace myself to help.

That. Something drops into the water nearby. I think it's rubbish at first, but then I see a spreading red stain in the water. **Dye marker. For the divers.**

Whoops. I grab hold of the handles and brace myself, then put my back into it. **How long—** the grate begins to move **—do we have?**

Fresh outa time, monkey-boy. Shadows flicker in the turbid waters on the other side of the coral barrier: barracuda or small sharks circling. My chest aches with the effort of holding my breath and I think I've ripped open the skin on my hands, but the grate is moving now, swinging up and out on a hinged arm. **C'mon in.** The opening is about eighty by sixty, a tight squeeze for two: Ramona drops into it feet first then grabs my hand and pulls me after.

What is this? I ask. I get an edgy, panicky feeling: we're dropping into a concrete-walled tube with hand-holds on one side, and it's black as night inside.

Quick! Pull the cover shut!

I yank at the hatch and it drops towards me heavily. I flinch as it lands on top of the tunnel, and then I can't see anything but a vague phosphorescent glow. I blink and look down. It's Ramona. She's breathing – if that's what you call it – like she's running a marathon, and she looks a bit peaked, and she's glowing, very dimly. Bioluminescence. **It's shut.**

Okay. Now follow me. She begins to descend the tunnel, hand over hand. My chest tightens.

Where are we going? I ask nervously.

I don't know – this isn't in the blueprints. Probably an emergency maintenance tunnel or something. So how about we find out, huh?

I grab a rung and shove myself down towards her, trying to ignore the panicky feeling of breathlessness and the weird sensations around my collarbone. **Okay, so why not let's climb down a secret maintenance shaft in an undersea occult defense platform while divers with spear guns who work for a mad billionaire wait for us up top, hmm? What could possibly go wrong?**

Oh, you'd be surprised. She sounds as if she does this sort of thing every other week. Then, a second later, I sense rather than feel her feet hit bottom: **Oh. Well *that's* a surprise,** she adds conversationally.

And suddenly I realize I can't breathe underwater.

8: WHITE HAT/BLACK HAT

AN ADVENTURE DEMANDS A HERO, AROUND WHOM the whole world circles; but what use is a hero who can't even breathe underwater?

To spare you Bob's embarrassment, and to provide a shark's-eye view of the turbid waters through which he swims, it is necessary to pause for a moment and, as if in a dream – or an oneiromantic stream ripped from the screen of Bob's smartphone – to cast your gaze across the ocean towards events transpiring at exactly the same time, in an office in London.

Do not fear for Bob. He'll be back, albeit somewhat moist around the gills.

"The Secretary will see you now, Miss O'Brien," says the receptionist.

O'Brien nods amiably at the receptionist, slides a book-mark into the hardback she's reading, then stands up. This takes some time because the visitor's chair she's been waiting in is ancient and sags like a hungry Venus' flytrap, and O'Brien is trying to keep her grip on a scuffed black violin case. The receptionist watches her, bored as she shrugs her khaki linen jacket into place, pats down a straying lock of reddish-brown hair, and walks over towards the closed briefing-room door with the AUTHORIZED PERSONNEL ONLY sign above it. She pauses with one hand on the doorknob. "By the way, it's *Professor* O'Brien," she says, smiling to take the sting out of the words. "'Miss' sounds like something you'd call a naughty schoolgirl, don't you think?"

The receptionist is still nodding wordlessly and trying to think of a comeback when O'Brien closes the door and the red light comes on over the lintel.

The briefing room contains a boardroom table, six chairs, a jug of tap water, some paper cups, and an ancient Agfa slide projector. All the fittings look to be at least a third of a century old: some of them might even have seen service during the Second World War. There used to be windows in two of the walls, but they were bricked up and covered over with institutional magnolia paint some years ago. The lighting tubes above the table shed a ghastly glare that gives everybody in the room the skin tint of a corpse – except for Angleton, who looks mummified at the best of times.

"Professor O'Brien." Angleton actually smiles, revealing teeth like tombstones. "Do have a seat."

"Of course." O'Brien pulls one of the battered wooden chairs out from the table and sits down carefully. She nods at Angleton, polite control personified. The violin case she places on the tabletop.

"As a matter of curiosity, how are your studies proceeding?"

"Everything's going smoothly." She carefully aligns the case's neck in accordance with the direction of the wards on Angleton's door. "You needn't worry on that account." Then she exhausts her patiently husbanded patience. "Where's Andy Newstrom?"

Angleton makes a steeple of his fingers. "Andrew was

unable to attend the meeting you called at short notice. I believe he has been unexpectedly detained in Germany."

O'Brien opens her mouth to say something, but Angleton raises a bony finger in warning: "I have arranged an appropriate substitute to deputize for him."

O'Brien swallows. "I see." Fingers drum on the body of the violin case. Angleton tracks them with his eyes. "You know this isn't about my research," she begins, elliptically.

"Of course not." Angleton falls silent for a few seconds. "Feel free to tell me exactly what you think of me, Dominique."

Dominique – Mo – sends him a withering stare. "No thank you. If I get started you'll be late for your next meeting." She pauses for a moment. Then she asks, with the deceptive mildness of a police interrogator zeroing in on a confession: "Why did you do it?"

"Because it was necessary. Or did you think I would send him into the field on a whim?"

Mo's control slips for a second: her glare is hot enough to ignite paper.

"I'm sorry," he adds heavily. "But this was an unscheduled emergency, and Bob was the only suitable agent who was available at short notice."

"*Really?*" She glances at the black velvet cloth covering the files on his desk. "I know all about your little tricks," she warns. "In case you'd forgotten."

Angleton shrugs uncomfortably. "How could I? You're perfectly right, and we owe you a considerable debt of gratitude for your cooperation in that particular incident. But nevertheless—" he stares at the wall beside her chair, a white-painted rectangle that doubles as a projector screen "—we are confronted with AZORIAN BLUE HADES, and Bob is the only field-certified executive who is both competent to deal with the matter and sufficiently ignorant to be able to, ah, play the role with conviction. You, my dear, couldn't do this particular job, you're too well-informed, leaving aside all the other aspects of the affair. The same goes for myself, or for Andrew, or for Davidson, or Fawcett, or any of a number of other assets Human Resources identified as preliminary candidates during the search phase of the operation. And while we have plenty of other staff who are not cleared for AZORIAN BLUE HADES, most of them are insufficiently prepared to meet its challenges."

"Nevertheless." Mo's hand closes on the neck of her case "I'm warning you, Angleton. I know you entangled Bob with a Black Chamber assassin and I know what the consequences are. I know that unless someone collapses their superposition within about half a million seconds, he's not coming back, at least not as himself. And I'm not putting up with the usual excuses – 'he was the only round peg we had that fit that particular hole, it was in the interests of national security' – you'd better see he comes back alive and in one body. *Or I am going to the Auditors.*"

Angleton eyes her warily. O'Brien is one of very few people in the organization who would make such a threat, and one of even fewer who might actually follow through on it. "I do not believe that will be necessary," he says slowly. "As it happens, I agreed to your request for a meeting because I intended to tap you for the next phase. Contrary to the impression you may have received, I don't consider Bob to be an expendable asset. But I believe you're allowing your relationship with him to color your perceptions of the risk inherent in the situation. I assume you'd be willing to help bring him back safe and sound?"

Mo nods sharply. "You know I would."

"Good." Angleton glances at the door, then frowns. "I do believe Alan's late. That's not like him."

"Alan? Alan Barnes?"

"Yes."

"What do you want *him* for?"

Angleton snorts. "A moment ago you were getting uptight about your boyfriend's security. Now you're asking why I asked Captain Barnes—"

The door bursts open, admitting a wiry pint-sized tornado. "Ah the fragrant Professor O'Brien! How you doing, Mo? And you, you old bat. What do you want now?" The force of nature grins widely. With his owlishly large glasses, leather-patched tweed jacket, and expanding bald spot he could pass for a schoolteacher – if schoolteachers habitually wore shoulder holsters.

Angleton pushes his spectacles up on his nose. "I was explaining to Professor O'Brien that I've got a little job for you. Bob's accepted the starring role in the approach plan for AZORIAN BLUE HADES and now it's time to set up the payoff. Not unnaturally, Mo has expressed certain reservations about the way the project has been conducted to date. I believe that, in view of her special skills, she can make a valuable contribution to the operation. What do you think?"

While Barnes is considering the question, Mo glances between the two of them. "This is a setup!"

Barnes grins at her: "Of course it is!"

She looks at Angleton. "What do you want me to do?" She grips the neck of her violin case tensely.

Barnes sniggers quietly, then pulls out a chair. Angleton doesn't deign to notice. Instead, he reaches across the table and switches on the projector.

"You're going on vacation. Officially you're on leave, flagged as a home visit to your elderly mother. That's because we can't rule out the possibility of an internal security leak," he adds.

Mo whistles tunelessly between her teeth. "Like that, is it?"

"Oh yes." A thin blade appears silently between Alan's

fingers, as if it congealed out of thin air. He begins to probe a cuticle on his other hand. "It's very *like that* indeed. And we want you to look into it on your way to the main performance."

"You'll be on board tomorrow's flight from Charles de Gaulle to Saint Martin. Your cover identity is Mrs. Angela Hudson, the wife of a tire-and-exhaust magnate from Dorking." Angleton slides a document wallet across the table towards Mo, who handles it as if it's about to explode. "This is a weak cover. It's been cleared with Customs and Immigration at both ends but it won't hold up to scrutiny. On the other hand you won't have to use it for more than about forty-eight hours. After this briefing, take yourself down to Wardrobe Department and they'll set you up with suitable clothing and support equipment for Mrs. Hudson. You may take—" he points at the violin case "—your instrument, and any other equipment you deem necessary. You'll be staying at a hotel in Grand Case. You should be aware that our local station chief, Jack Griffin, or someone working for him, has been compromised. We want to keep you out of Billington's sights for as long as possible, so bypassing Griffin's organization is top of your playlist. If you can identify the source of the leak and deal with it, I'd be grateful. Once you've settled in, Alan will be your backup. You'll be operating without a field controller; if you need a shoulder to cry on you come straight to me."

He turns to face Barnes. "Alan. Pick two of your best bricks. Make sure they're happy working with booties, I don't want any interservice cock-ups. You'll be flying out pronto and will rendezvous with HMS *York*, which is currently on APT(N). She's hosting a troop from M squadron SBS under Lieutenant Hewitt, who has signed Section Three and is cleared for level two liaison. The booties are available if you need additional muscle. Your job is to provide backup for Professor O'Brien, who is point on this mission. In case you were worried about BLUE HADES, Professor O'Brien speaks the language and is qualified to liaise. She's also completed her certification in combat epistemology and can operate as your staff philosopher, should circumstances require it. I have complete faith in her abilities to complete the mission and bring Bob back."

Angleton pauses for a moment. Then he adds: "In a real emergency – if HADES cooks off – you've got a hot line of credit with HMS *Vanguard*, although if you have to use a big white one I'm supposed to go to the board and get them to clear it with the Prime Minister first. So let's not go there, shall we?"

Mo looks back and forth between the two spooks. "Would you mind not speaking in slang? I know about Alan's men, but what's a 'big white one'?"

Barnes looks slightly distracted. "It's just a necessary backup precaution – I'll explain later," he assures her. "For now, the main thing is, you'll be operating independently but you'll have backup, starting with my lads and working up through the Royal Navy's North Atlantic Patrol, right to the top if you need it. Unfortunately we're dealing with a really powerful semiotic geas field – Billington's set things up so that we have to play by his rules – and that limits our moves. It would be a really bad mistake for you to come in-frame too soon." He raises an eyebrow at Angleton. "Are we definitely moving into the endgame?"

Angleton shrugs. "It's beginning to look that way." He nods at Mo. "We'd prefer not to have to do it this way, but our hands are unfortunately tied."

Mo frowns. "Wouldn't it make more sense for me to fly out with Alan and his soldiers? I mean, if you're borrowing a warship, why are you bothering with the undercover stuff? What exactly do you expect me to do?"

Barnes snorts and raises an eyebrow at Angleton: "Are you going to tell her, or am I?"

"I'll do it." Angleton picks up the control to the slide projector. "Would you mind switching off the lights?"

"Why the dog and pony show?" O'Brien demands, her voice rising.

"Because you need to understand the trick we're trying to play on the opposition before you can deal the cards. And it's best if I illustrate . . ."

Events have echoes, and almost exactly two weeks earlier, a similar meeting took place on another land mass.

While Bob continues to panic over his impending death by drowning, spare a thought for Ramona. It's not her fault that she's in the fish tank with Bob, quite the opposite. Given even the faintest shred of an excuse, she'd have managed to avoid this briefing in Texas. Unfortunately her controllers are not interested in excuses. They want results. And that's why we join her in the front seat of a Taurus, driving up a dusty unsurfaced lane toward a sun-blasted ranch house in the middle of nowhere.

This is so not Ramona's scene. She's too smart to be a Valley Girl, but she grew up in that part of the world. She's happiest when the bright sunlight is moderated by an onshore breeze and the distant roar of the surf is just crowding the edge of the white noise in her ears: ah, the smell of sagebrush. This part of west Texas, between Sonora and San Angelo, is just way too far inland for Ramona's taste. It's also too . . . Texan. Ramona doesn't care for good ol' boys. She doesn't much like arid, dusty landscapes with no water. And she especially doesn't like the Ranch, but that's not a matter of prejudice so much as common sense.

The Ranch scares her more every time she visits it.

There's a parking lot up front: little more than a patch of

packed earth. She pulls up between two unfeasibly large pickups. One of them actually has a cow's skull lashed to the front bumper and a rifle rack in the back. She gets out of the Taurus, collects her shoulder bag and her water bottle — she never comes here without a half-gallon can, minimum — and cringes slightly as the arid heat tries to suck her dry. Walking around the parked vehicles, she doesn't bother to check the cow's skull for the faint matching intaglio of a pentacle: she knows what she'll find. Instead she heads for the porch, and the closed screen door, with a wizened figure rocking in a chair beside it.

"You're five minutes and twenty-nine seconds late," the figure recites laconically as she climbs the front step.

"So bite me," Ramona snaps. She hikes her bag up her shoulder and shivers despite the heat. The guardian watches her with dry amusement. *Dry.* There is no water here, certainly not enough to hydrate the bony nightmare in bib overalls that hangs out next to the door, endlessly rocking its chair.

"You're expected," it rasps. "Go right in."

It makes no move toward her, but the skin on the back of her neck prickles. She takes two steps forward and twists the doorknob. At this point, an unexpected visitor can reasonably be expected to die. At this point, expected visitors also die — if Internal Affairs has issued a termination order. Ramona does not die this time. The door latch clicks open and she steps inside the cool air-conditioned vestibule, trying to suppress a shuddery breath as she leaves the watcher on the threshold behind.

The vestibule is furnished in cheap G-plan kit, with a sofa and chairs, and a desk with a human receptionist sitting behind it who looks up at Ramona and blinks sheep-eyes at her. "Ms. Random, if you'd care to take the second door on the left, go straight ahead, then take the first right at the end of the corridor. Agent McMurray is expecting you."

Ramona smiles tightly. "Sure thing. Can I use the ladies' room on the way?"

The receptionist makes a show of checking her desk planner. "I can confirm that you are authorized to use the ladies' room," she announces after a few seconds.

"Good." Ramona nods. "See you around." She walks through the second door on the left. It opens onto an anonymous beige-painted corridor, which she walks down for some distance. Partway along, she takes time out to hole up in the toilet. She bends over a wash basin and throws water on her face, her neck, and the base of her throat. She notes that there are no windows in the facility: just ventilation ducts high up in the walls.

Back in the corridor she continues toward its end where there are three identical doors. She pauses outside the one on the right, and knocks.

"Come in," a man's gravelly voice calls through the door.

Ramona opens the door. The room beyond is spacious, floored in rough-cut timber, and walled in glass-fronted cabinets. The door at the far end is open, a staircase leading down to what Ramona knows to be another corridor with more display rooms opening off to either side. She's already far enough inside the ranch house that by rights she should be standing with her feet firmly planted in the dirt fifty feet behind it – outside, but that's not how things work here. Instead, her controlling agent is waiting for her, a tall, slightly pudgy fellow with wire-rimmed glasses, thinning, close-cropped hair, and a checkered shirt. He smiles, faintly indulgently. "Well, well. If it isn't agent Random." He holds out a hand: "How was your trip out?"

"Dry," she says tersely, allowing her hand to be shaken. She squints slightly, sizing McMurray up. He looks human enough, but appearances at the Ranch are always deceptive. "I need to find a pool at some point. Apart from that—" she shrugs "—I can't complain."

"A pool." McMurray nods thoughtfully. "I think we can arrange something for you." His voice has a faint Irish lilt to it, although Ramona is fairly sure he's as American as she is. "It's the least we can do, seeing as how we've dragged you all the way out here. Yes indeed." He gestures at the steps leading down to the passageway. "How well did you understand your briefing?"

Ramona swallows. This bit is hard. As her controlling agent McMurray has certain powers. He was the key operative who compelled her to service; as long as he lives, he, or whoever holds his tokens of power, has the power of life and death over her, the ability to bind and release her, to issue orders she cannot refuse. There's stuff she doesn't want to talk about—but if he suspects she's holding out on him it'll be a lot worse for her than confessing to everything. Best to give him something, just hope it's not enough to raise more suspicions than it allays: "Not entirely," she admits. "I don't understand why we're letting TLA's chief executive run riot in the Caribbean. I don't understand why the Brits are involved in this, or what the hell TLA think they're doing. I mean—" she pats her shoulder bag "—I read it all, but I don't understand it. Just what's supposed to be going on?"

This is the point at which McMurray can – if he's suspicious – make her mouth open without her willing it, and spill her deepest secrets and most personal hopes and fears. Just considering the possibility makes her feel small and contemptibly weak. But McMurray doesn't seem to notice her discomfort. He nods and looks thoughtful. "I'm not sure anybody knows everything," he says ruefully.

A rueful apology? From a controlling agent? *Stop jerking me around*, Ramona prays, a cold knot of fear congealing in her stomach. But McMurray doesn't raise his left hand in a sigil of command; nor does he pronounce any words of dread. He just nods in false amity and gestures once again at the stairs.

"It's a mess," he explains. "Billington's a big campaign donor and word is, we're not supposed to rock the boat. Not under this administration, anyway. It would embarrass certain folks if he were exposed – at least on our soil. And just in case anyone gets any ideas about going around Control's back, he doesn't set foot on land these days. He's got the whole thing set up for remote management from extraterritorial waters. We'd have to send the Coast Guard or the Navy after him, and that would be too public."

"Too public and two bucks will get you a coffee," Ramona says acidly; then, fearful that she might have gone too far, adds: "But why did you need to bring me out here? Is it part of the briefing?"

She realizes too late that this was the wrong thing to say. McMurray fixes her with a penetrating stare. "Why else do you think you might have been ordered to the Ranch?" he asks, deceptively mildly. "Is there something I should know, agent Random?"

A huge fist grips her around the ribs, squeezing gently. "Nuh – no, sir!" she gasps, terrified.

Merely annoying McMurray can have enormous, terrible consequences for her: there's nothing subtle about the degree of control the Black Chamber exercises over its subjects, or the consequences of error. The Chamber has a secret ruling from the Supreme Court that citizenship rights only apply to human beings: Ramona's kin are barely able to pass with the aid of a glamour. For failure, the punishment can be special rendition to jurisdictions where the very concept of pain is considered a fascinating research topic by the natives. But he merely stares at her for a moment with watery blue eyes, then nods very slightly, relaxing the constraint binding. The pressure recedes like the backwash of an imagined cardiac arrest.

"Very good." McMurray turns and begins to descend the staircase at the end of the room. Ramona follows him, eager to get away from the things in the pickle jars behind the glass display panels. "I'm glad to see that you've still got a . . . sense of humor, agent Random. Unfortunately this is no laughing matter." He pauses at the bottom step. "I believe you've been here before."

Ramona's hand tightens on the stair rail until her knuckles turn white. "Yes. Sir."

"Then I won't have to explain." He smiles frighteningly, then walks down the corridor toward one of the display rooms. "I brought you here to see just the one exhibit, this time."

Ramona forces herself to follow him. She feels as if she's walking through molasses, her chest tight with an almost palpable sense of dread. *It's not as if anything here is aimed at me*, she tries to tell herself. *It's all dead, already*. But that's not strictly true.

Most advanced military organizations maintain libraries of weapons, depositories like armories that store one of everything — every handgun, artillery round, mine, grenade, knife — used by any other army that they might face in battle. The exhibits are stored in full working order, with specialist armorers trained in caring for them. Associated with their staff colleges, these depots are a vital resource when training special forces, briefing officers tasked with facing a given enemy, or merely researching future requirements. The Black Chamber is no different: like the Army repository at the Aberdeen Proving Ground, they maintain their own collection. There is a subtle difference, however. The Black Chamber's archive of reality-warping occult countermeasures is partially alive. Here lie unquiet roadside graves dug by ghoulish reanimators. Over there is a cupboard full of mandrakes, next door to a summoning grid that's been live for thirty years, the unquiet corpse of its victim dancing an eternal jig within the green-glowing circle, on legs long since worn down to blood-encrusted ivory stumps.

You can die if you get too close to some of the exhibits in the Ranch. And then they'll add you to the collection.

McMurray knows his way through the corridors and passages of the repository. He threads his way rapidly past doorways opening onto vistas that make Ramona's hair stand on end, then through a gallery lined with glass exhibit cases, some of them covered by protective velvet cloths. Finally he comes to a small side room and stops, beckoning Ramona toward a glass-topped cabinet.

"You asked about Billington," he says, his tone thoughtful.

"Yes, sir."

"You can cut the 'sir' bit; call me Pat." He half-smiles. "As I was saying, Billington's current actions worry the Dark Commissioners. In fact, they're extremely concerned that his motive for purchasing the *Explorer* and moving it to the Bahamas is to make a retrieval attempt on the eastern JEN-NIFER MORGUE site – that was in your briefing pack, yes? Good. If it turns out that JENNIFER MORGUE is a chthonian artifact, then an attempted retrieval operation could place us – that is, the United States government, not to mention the human species – in breach of the Third Benthic Treaty. That would be a bad place to go. On the other hand, the rewards to be reaped from such an artifact are huge. And your cousins have a very limited presence in the Caribbean. They prefer the deep ocean. It's possible that they're not even aware of the location of the artifact."

McMurray turns to stare at the glass-topped cabinet. "Billington's not doing this for the good of the nation, needless to say. We're not sure just what he plans to do with JENNIFER MORGUE if he gets his hands on it, but frankly, CenCom isn't keen to find out. He needs to be stopped. Which is where we run into an embarrassing problem. He already figured we'd take steps to interdict him, so he's preempted us." He glances at Ramona, and her blood freezes at his expression.

"Sir?"

McMurray gestures at the cabinet. "Look at this."

Ramona peers through the glass warily. She sees a wooden tabletop: perfectly mundane, but for a strange diorama positioned in its center. It seems to consist of a pair of dolls, male and female, wearing wedding clothes; adjacent to them are a pair of engagement rings and a model of a stepped wedding cake. The whole diorama is enclosed within a Möbius-loop design in conductive ink, connected to a breadboard analog-digital converter and an elderly PC.

"This is probably the least dangerous exhibit you'll find here," McMurray says calmly, his momentary anger stilled. "You're looking at a hardware circuit designed to implement a love geas using vodoun protocols and a modified Jellinek-Wirth geometry engine." His finger traces out the Möbius loop below. "Symbolic representations of the entities to be influenced are placed within a geometry engine controlled by a clocked recursive invocation. There are less visible signifiers here – the skin and hair samples, necessary for DNA affinity matching, and concealed within the dolls – but the intent should be obvious. The two individuals linked by this particular grid have been happily married for sixteen years at this point. It's a reinforcing loop; the more the subjects work within the framework, the stronger the feedback frame becomes. The geas itself extends its influence by altering the probability gauge metric associated with the subjects' interactions: outcomes that reinforce the condition are simply rendered more likely to occur while the circuit is operational."

Ramona blinks. "I don't understand."

"Obviously." McMurray steps back, then crosses his arms. "Try to get your head around the fact that it's a contagion spell that generates compliant behavior. This couple, for example, started out hating each other. If you were to destroy this generator, they'd be in divorce court — or one of them would be in a shallow grave — within weeks. Now bear in mind that Billington's cruising around the Caribbean in a huge yacht, plotting some kind of scheme. He isn't stupid. We figure that about six months ago he created a similar hardware-backed geas engine aboard his yacht, the *Mabuse*. The precise nature of the geas is not entirely clear to us, but it has been extremely detrimental to our counterforce operations — in particular, attempts to act against him through normal channels fail. Telex requests dispatched to the Cayman police force via INTERPOL get unaccountably lost, FBI agents develop random brain tumors, associates who might plea-bargain their way to giving evidence wake up embedded in concrete foundations, that sort of thing. CenCom's not convinced, but Sensor Ops believes that Billington has used the geas engine to create a Hero trap — only a single agent conforming to the right archetype can actually approach him; and even then, the geas will screw with their ability to take correct action. And because Billington figured he's got the most reason to be afraid of us, he picked a god-damn limey as the Hero archetype."

Ramona shakes her head. "We can't get to him ourselves?"

"I didn't say that." McMurray walks toward the door, then pauses in front of a picture on the wall. "Look."

Ramona stares at the picture. It's a photograph of an oriental longhair cat, reposing on a sofa. The cat is well-groomed and white, but lacks the distinctive pinkish eyes characteristic of albinism. It stares at the camera with haughty disdain.

"I've seen that cat before," she murmurs, chewing her lip. She glances at McMurray: "Is this what I think it is?"

McMurray nods. "It's a show-grade Persian cat, a tom. D'Urbeville Marmeduke the Fourth. Billington acquired this — *pet* is perhaps too loose a word, perhaps *familiar* is closer to the truth — some time ago. Probably when he began planning his current venture. He keeps him aboard the *Mabuse*. Fluffy white cat, yacht cruising around the Caribbean, huge mother ship with a secret undersea module — this geas isn't powered by some goddamn dolls and a wedding ring, agent Random, it's got *legs*. It'd take a miracle for anyone except the Brits to get close to him. One Brit in particular — an agent who doesn't exist." Then he stares at Ramona. "Except we've figured out a loophole, one that'll let us reach out and touch Billington where it hurts. You are going to go in through that loophole, you and me. And you will nail Billington's head to the table to prevent JENNIFER MORGUE Two from falling into the wrong hands.

"Here's how we're going to do it . . ."

Three people sit in a conference room with bricked-up windows in London. The slide projector clunks to an empty slide and Angleton leans over to switch it off. For a minute there's silence, broken only by the emphysemic rasp of Angleton's breathing.

"Bastard." Mo's voice is cold and superficially emotionless.

"We're going to get him back, Mo, I promise you." Barnes's voice is flat and assured.

"But damaged."

Angleton clears his throat.

"I can't believe you did this," she says bitterly.

"We didn't choose to, girl." His voice is a gravelly rasp, hoarse from too many late-night meetings this past week.

"I can't believe you let some snake oil defense contractor get the jump on you. Using it as an excuse. Shit, Angleton, what do you expect me to say? The bait-and-switch you're planning is stupid enough to start with, and you've handed my boyfriend over to a sex vampire and I'm supposed to lie back and think of England? You expect me to tamely pick up the pieces when she's finished banging his brains out and pat him on the head and take him home and patch his ego up? What am I meant to do, turn into some kind of angel-nurse-child-minder figure when all this is over? You've got a fucking nerve!" She's got the violin case by the neck and she's leaning across the table towards Angleton, throwing the words in his face. She's too close to see Barnes staring at her fingers on the neck of the instrument case like it's the barrel of a gun, and he's trying to judge whether she's going to reach for the trigger.

"You're understandably upset—"

"Understandably?" Mo stands up, shifting the case to the crook of her left arm as she toys with the clamp alongside its body. "Fuck you!" she snarls.

Angleton pushes the file across the table at her. "Your tickets."

"Fuck you *and* your tickets!" She's making chicken-choking motions with the fingers of her right hand, the other hand vaguely patting at the body of the violin case. Barnes slides to his feet, backing away, his right hand half-raised to his jacket until he catches Angleton's minute shake of the head. "*And* your fucking grade six geas!" Her voice is firm but congested with emotion. "I'm out of here."

She freezes in place for a moment as if there's something more to say, then grabs the file and storms out of the conference room, slamming the door behind her so hard that the latch fails and it bounces open again. Barnes stares after her, then, seeing the wide eyes and open mouth of the receptionist, he nods politely and pulls the door shut.

"Do you think she'll take the assignment?" he asks Angleton.

"Oh yes." Angleton stares bleakly at the door for a few seconds. "She'll hate us, but she'll do it. She's operating inside the paradigm. In the groove, as Bob would say."

"I was afraid for a minute that I was going to have to take her down. If she lost it completely."

"No." Angleton gathers himself with a visible effort and shakes his head. "She's too smart. She's a lot tougher than you think, otherwise I wouldn't have put her on the spot like that. But don't sit with your back to any doors until this is all over and we've got her calmed down."

Barnes stares at the pitted green desktop. "I could almost pity that Black Chamber agent you've hitched Bob to."

"Those are the rules of the game." Angleton shrugs heavily. "I didn't write them. You can blame Billington, or you can blame the man with the typewriter, but he's been dead for more than forty years. O'Brien's not made of sugar and spice and all things nice. She'll cope." He stares at Barnes bleakly. "She'll have to. Because if she doesn't, we're all in deep shit."

9: SKIN DIVING

That's interesting, Ramona says to the pitch darkness as I choke on a throatful of stinging cold saltwater, **I didn't know you could do that.** My chest is burning and it feels like ice picks are shoving at my eardrums as I begin to thrash around. I can feel my heart pounding like a trip hammer as the fear grips me like a straitjacket. I manage to bang one elbow on the side of the tunnel, a sharp stab of pain amidst the black pressure. **Stop struggling.**

Slim arms slide around my chest; her heart is hammering as she hugs me to her, pulling my face between her breasts. She drags me down like a mermaid engulfing a drowning sailor and I stiffen, panicking as I begin to exhale. Then we're in a bigger space — I can feel it opening up around me — and suddenly I don't need to breathe anymore. I can feel her/our gills soaking in the cool refreshing water, like air off a spring meadow, and I can feel her borrowed underwater freedom again.

Where are we? I ask, shuddering. **What the hell was that?**

We're right under the platform's central deflection circuit. I figure it throttled our link while we were passing through.

My eyes are starting to adjust and I can see a diffuse green twilight. A black ceiling squats above us, rough and pitted as I run my fingertips across it: the tunnel is a square opening in the middle of a room-sized dome under the middle of the flat ceiling. Off to the sides I can just about see other black silhouettes, support pillars of some sort that vanish into the murk below. Beyond them, the turbidity speaks of open seas.

I thought it was poured onto the bottom?

Nope. The reef comes to within meters of the surface, but offshore it falls away rapidly; the bottom hereabouts is nearly sixty meters down. They built it on the edge of an undersea cliff and jacked it off the bottom with those pillars.

Right, right. I experiment, pushing off and swimming a little distance away from her until the tightness in my chest begins to return. I can make it to about eight meters out on my own, down here in the penumbra of the coastal defense ward. I turn and drift slowly back towards her. **What was it you were wanting to tell me? Before we got interrupted.**

Her face is a ghostly shade in the twilight. **No time. The bad guys are coming.**

Bad guys—— I hear a distant churning rumble and look up, out from under the poured concrete ceiling. **Let me see. They've got spear guns?**

Good guess, monkey-boy. Follow me. She swims out towards one of the pillars and I follow hastily, afraid of being left behind by our bubble of entangled metabolic processes.

The pillar is as thick as my torso, rough-pored concrete covered with lumpy barnacles and shells and a few weird growths that might be baby corals. Beyond it, the open sea: greenness above us – we must be at least ten meters down – and darkness below. Ramona pulls her knees up and rolls head down, then kicks, spearing into the gloomy depths. I swallow, then turn and clumsily follow her. My inner ear is churning but I can almost fool it into thinking I'm climbing alongside the fat, gray pillar. I feel a bit breathless, but not too bad — all things considered. **Are you doing okay?** I ask.

I'm okay. Ramona's inner voice is tense, like she's breathing for two of us.

Slow down, then. There's a great beige wall looming behind us in the gloom, bulging closer to the pillar. In the distance I see the streamlined torpedo silhouettes of hunting fishes. **Let's get between the pillar and the cliff face.**

Distant plopping, bubbling noises from above. **Here they come.** Ramona peers up towards the surface.

C'mon. The cleft between the pillar and the rock face is about a meter wide at this depth. I swim into it then reach out and take her hand. She drifts towards me, still staring up at the distant sky, as I pull her into the shadow of the pillar. **How long can we hide down here? If they figure we're just skinny-dippers, they may not think to come this deep.**

No such luck. She closes her eyes and leans back against me. ** Have you ever killed anyone, Bob?**

Have I ever . . .? It depends what you mean by *anyone*. **Only paranormal entities. Does that count?**

No. Has to be human. She tenses. **I should have asked earlier.**

What do you mean, *has* to be human?

That's an oversight, she says tightly. **You were supposed to be blooded.**

What are you—

The geas. You have to kill one of them. She turns round slowly, her hair swirling around her head like a dark halo. Here we are under twenty meters of seawater and my mouth's gone as dry as the desert. **There are steps you have to carry out in sequence in order to adopt your role in the eigenplot. Jeopardy in a distant city, meet the dark anima, kill one of the other side's assassins – at least one, more would be better – and then we have to figure out a way around my – damn, here they come. We'll have to cover this later. Get ready.**

She shoves something hard into my hand. After a moment's confusion I realize it's the handle of a vicious-looking knife with a serrated edge. Then she vanishes into the shadows lining the cliff face. I glance round as a shadow glides overhead: tracking up and over I see a diver in a wetsuit, head down, peering into the depths.

I pass through a moment of acute disbelief and resentment. I've been in mortal danger before, but I'm not used to being in mortal danger from humans. It feels *wrong*. Any one of Alan's mad bastards is probably capable of whacking half a dozen al Qaeda irregulars before breakfast and not working up an existential sweat, but I'm not prepared for this. I can shoot at targets, sure, and I'm death on wheels when it comes to terminating cases of demonic possession with extreme prejudice, but the idea of killing a real human being in cold blood, some eating breathing sleeping guy with a job on a rich man's yacht, makes all the alarm bells in my head go *tilt*. Trouble is, I also have a deep conviction in my guts that whatever the hell Ramona is on about, she's *right*. I'm here for a purpose, and I've got to move my feet through the occult dance steps in the right sequence or it'll all be for nothing. And it doesn't matter what I want or don't want if Angleton's right and Billington is gearing up to drop the hammer on us. When you come down to it, if there's a war on, the bombs don't care whether they're falling on pacifists or patriots. And speaking of bombs . . .

The diver has seen something. Either that or he's into swimming head down into the depths beside a decaying defense station just for the hell of it. He's heading parallel to the pillar and he's got something in his arms. I glance down and see Ramona below me her skin a silvery flash like moonlight on ice, circling the pillar. My chest tightens. A stab of anger: **What the hell are you playing at?**

Hanging my ass out to give you a clear shot. She sounds lighthearted, but I can tell she's wound up like a watch spring inside. I taste the overspill of her uncertainty: *Is he up to it?* And my blood runs cold, because under the uncertainty, she harbors the rock-solid conviction that, if I'm not up to it, we're both going to die.

Outmaneuvered.

The guy above me is turning in tight circles as he descends, keeping an eye open for signs of an ambush as he heads towards Ramona, who is feigning a false sense of security, her back to the outside of the cliff next to the point where the pillar merges with it in a jagged mass of crumpled volcanic rock. I shelter in the cleft between pillar and cliff as he strokes steadily down, hugging the far side of the pillar from Ramona. In his arms he's clutching something that looks like a shotgun, if shotguns had viciously barbed harpoons jutting from their muzzles. *Just great*, I think. What was it Harry the Horse tried to beat into my head? *Never bring a dagger to a harpoon duel*, or something like that.

My luck runs out while he's still about three meters above me, ten meters above Ramona. He slows his corkscrew, peering into the shadowy cleft, and I see a change in his posture. *Shit*. Everything happens in nightmarish slow-mo. I've got my feet braced against the pillar and I let go like a spring, kicking straight up towards him, knife-first. Something sizzles past my shoulder, drawing a hot line across my chest, then I ram him with my shoulder. He's already tumbling out of the way of my knife and I try and bring it back round towards him. I can't breathe — I'm out of range of Ramona's gills — and in a bleak flash of clarity I realize I'm going to die here. The pressure in my chest eases as he takes a swing at me with a knife I sense rather than see, but I'm inside his reach and I grab his forearm and we go tumbling. He's strong but I'm desperate and disoriented and I somehow manage to get my other arm around his neck and something snags my knife. I yank on it as hard as I can, as he tenses his knife arm – we're arm-wrestling at this point – and *something* gives way. He thrashes spasmodically and lets go, kicks towards the surface, and there's a silvery stream of bubbles rising above him that's much too big and bright to be normal.

Ramona's right below me. **Let's go,** she gasps, tugging at my ankle. **Deeper!**

But I just—

I know what you just did! Come on before they do it right back to us! Nobody in their right mind dives alone. She lets go for a moment, kicks out, and moves her grip to my arm. **Let's move it.** She rolls us round and pulls me away from the pillar, back up towards the murky gloom beneath the defense platform. I feel her fear and let it pull me along behind her, but my mind's not home: I'm not feeling queasy, exactly, but I've got a lot to think about. **We've got to get back to the tunnel,** she says urgently.

The tunnel? Why?

They'll have searched it first. And most divers don't like confined spaces, caves. I figure they'll concentrate on the open waters outside the reef, now they've got the sighting. We just wait them out.

In the tunnel.

What are we doing here? I shake my head. *What's it all for?* I keep rerunning the video stream captured in my mind's eye, the silvery parabola of bubbles rising above the drowning diver—

We're missing something important, Ramona muses darkly.

How did they find us?

Not sure. They've opened a channel to let them bring their minions in, but the core defensive wards are still working, you're cleaner than—— She blinks at me. **Oh. *That's* how.**

The ceiling is right above our heads now, the dome set into it framing the deeper blackness of the tunnel. **What is it?**

I was wrong about them planting a tracker on you. They don't need to bug you, she says tersely. **They can find you anywhere. All they have to do is zero in on the eigenplot. Except here, right where you're shielded by the defense platform's wards, even if they have hacked a tunnel right through them to let their associates in . . .

What is this eigenplot you keep talking about? I ask. I'm dangerously close to whining. I *really* hate it when everyone else around me seems to know more about what's going on than I do.

The geas Billington's running. It's the occult equivalent of a stateful firewall. It keeps out intruders, unless they run through the approach states in a permitted sequence. The sequence is determined by the laws of similarity and contagion, drawing on a particularly powerful source archetype. When you run through them, that's called 'walking the eigenplot,' and you're doing it real well so far. Only a few people can do it at all – you can but I can't, for example – and there's an added catch: You can't do it if you know what the requirements are beforehand, it doesn't permit recursive attacks. That's why you're just going to have to be brave and . . . she trails off **. . . *shit*. Forget I said that bit. I mean *forget* it. You'll just have to see for yourself.** She centers herself under the pitch-black rectangle of the tunnel mouth. **C'mon.**

But you said——

If we're outside the tunnel we're not shielded. You want to learn how to breathe with a harpoon through you?

No way. I swim closer to her, until we're both right under the mouth. **I nearly drowned last time we went through here.**

The effect's attenuated only a couple of meters in. Closer. Hug me. Not like that, like this. She wraps her arms and legs around me. **Think you can swim? Straight up, until you don't feel like you're drowning?**

Like I'm going to say no? I look into her eyes from so close that we're almost touching noses. **Okay. Just this once. For you.**

Then I kick off straight up, into the black heart of the drowning zone.

Bands of steel around my chest. A pounding in my ears. Then the clean air of a spring meadow, Ramona's arms cradling me, her legs entwined around me, her lips locked against mine like a lovesick mermaid trying to kiss the drowned sailor back to life – or infuse his blood with oxygen through force of proximity alone.

Oh. We're in the tunnel. Totally black, walls either side of me, five meters of water between my head and the heavy iron grating, nothing but delirium's arms holding my sanity together. Distracting me. I *am* distracted. It's incongruous. There are divers out there hunting the waters for us, and here I'm getting an erection. Ramona's tongue, tentacular, searches my lips. She's aroused, I can feel it like an itch at the back of my mind.

This is a really bad idea, I overhear her thinking. **We're feeding off each other.** *I'm drowning. I'm horny. I'm drowning. I'm——* feedback. Too far apart and I start to choke, too close together and I start noticing her body, and whichever I'm paying attention to bleeds through into her head. **Got to stop.**

Tell me about it. An uneasy thought. **How much of this before the Other notices?**

It's not ready yet — I think. She pulls back a few centimeters while I concentrate on not thinking about drowning. **How long do you think we've been down here?**

I've lost track, I admit. **Half an hour?** I lean back against the rough wall of the tunnel that shouldn't exist. **Longer?**

Damn. I can feel the clockwork of her thoughts, tasting of rusty iron. It's like there's a weird tube of pressure squeezing us together down here; the tunnel is a flaw in the countermeasure wards, but outside it there's an almost unimaginable amount of power chained down and directed towards the exclusion of occult manifestations — like our own entanglement. Threatening to crush us to a bloody paste between walls of concrete. **Can we leave yet?**

Your breathlessness — have you ever been claustrophobic before?

Is that what it is? **Great time to find out.** I shudder and my heart tries to flutter away.

We're in as much danger if we stay down here as if we surface, she announces. **Come on. Slowly.**

Still locked together, we finger-and-toe our way up the narrow chimney in the rock, feeling ahead for rough bumps and the joints between concrete castings. As we rise, the nightmare awareness of my own death begins to fade. All too soon we reach the grating at the top, a cold wall of rusty iron. I tense up and try not to give in to the scream that's bubbling up inside. **Can you lift it?** I ask.

On my own? Shit. I feel her straining. **Help me!**

I brace my legs against one wall and my back against the opposite and raise my arms; Ramona leans against me and puts her back into it, too. The roof gives a little. I tense and shove hard, putting all my fear of drowning into it, and the lid squeals and lifts free above us.

Turn! I start twisting, rotating the rectangular lid so that when we let go it won't settle back into place. There's a roaring in my ears. I can hear my pulse. And suddenly I'm choking underwater with a lungful of air: we've lost skin contact and I'm going to have aching muscles tomorrow – if there is a tomorrow – and I can't get enough oxygen, so I kick out in near panic and the lid slides away and I kick out again, rising nightmarishly slowly towards the silver ceiling high above me, with my lungs on fire. Then I'm on the surface, bobbing like a cork in a barrel and I breathe out explosively and start to inhale just as a wave comes over the top of the reef and the platform and breaks over me.

The next few seconds are crazy and painful and I'm coughing and spluttering and close to panic again. But Ramona's in the water with me and she's a strong swimmer, and the next thing I know I'm on my back, coughing up my guts as she tows me towards the shallows like a half-drowned kitten. Then there's sand under my feet and an arm round my shoulders.

"Can you walk?"

I try to talk, realize it's a bad idea, and nod instead. A sidelong glance tells me her glamour's back in place.

"Don't look back. There's a dive boat just over the far side of the reef and they're looking out to sea. I figure we've got maybe two minutes before they check their tracker ward and see you're showing up again. Have you got any smoke screens on that fancy phone of yours?"

Think fast. I try to remember what I've loaded on it, remember the block I put on the car, and nod again. I'm not certain it'll work, but if it doesn't we're fresh out of options.

"Okay." We're about waist-deep now. "Blanket's over there. Think you can run?"

"Blanket——" I start coughing again.

"Run, monkey-boy!"

She grabs my hand and tugs me forwards. At the same time there's a ghostly sensation in my chest: she starts coughing, but I feel a whole lot better. Moments later I'm the one who's tugging her along through knee-deep water across a silvery beach, sunlight blazing down on my shoulders. I feel horribly exposed, as if there's a target painted on the small of my back. The towel is just ahead, up a gentle rise. Ramona stumbles. I get an arm round her waist and help her up, then we stagger on up the beach.

Towel. Trunks. A little pile of everyday tourist detritus. "This ours?"

She nods, gasping for breath: she's swallowed my water, I realize. I fumble under the towel and find the sealed poly-thene bag. Fingers shaking, I unseal it and pull out my Treo. The damn thing seems to take half an hour to boot up, and while I'm waiting for it I see heads bobbing to the surface near the boat on the far side of the reef. They're tiny in the distance but we're running out of time——

Ah. Scratchpad. "Lie down on the towel. Make like you're sunbathing," I tell her. Squinting at the tiny screen, I shield it with one hand so that I can see the schematic. *A circuit design, I need a circuit design.* But we're on a beach, right? Sand is porous. And about fifty centimeters below us there's a layer of conductive saline. Which means——

I squat on the sand and start drawing lines on the beach around us with my fingertips. I don't have to go all the way down to the water, I just have to reduce the resistivity of the layer of insulating sand above it in a regular pattern. Divers are crawling back into the boat as I finish the main loop and add the necessary terminals. *Phone, phone* . . . the bloody thing has gone to sleep on me. I'm about to poke at the screen when I realize there's sand on my fingertips. *Silly me.* I wipe them on the towel beside Ramona's hip and carefully wake the Treo up, stroke it into life, and hit the upload button. Then I sit down next to her and wait to learn if I've rendered us invisible.

About half an hour later, the divers give up. The boat turns, its outboard engine spouting a tail of white foam, and it slowly motors around the headland. Which is just as well because we don't have any sunscreen and my shoulders and chest are beginning to itch badly.

"You okay?" I ask Ramona.

"Pretty much." She sits up and stretches. "Your trick worked."

"Yeah, well. Trouble is, it's stationary: I can't take it with us. I figure our best bet would be to head back into town as fast as possible and lose ourselves in the crowd."

"You *really* got them stirred up. And their surveillance net is disturbingly good." She looks at me. "You're sure it was just Marc you were pushing on?"

"Yes." I look at her closely. "Marc, and his unfortunate habit of supplying single female tourists to friends with a boat and an unlimited supply of Charlie." Her expression doesn't change but her pupils tell me what I want to know. "Virgins aren't necessary, if this is what I think it is. But they have to be healthy and relatively young. Ring any bells?"

"I didn't know you were a necromancer, Bob." She looks at me calculatingly.

"I'm not." I shrug. "But I do countermeasures. And what I see here is that the island's defenses aren't worth jack shit if you've got a scuba kit and a boat. Someone's buying up single women, and they're sure as hell not shipping them to brothels in Miami. There's a surveillance net centered on

Billington's boat, and it's tied in to your friend Marc." I stare at her eyes. "Are you going to tell me it's a coincidence?"

She bites her lower lip. "No," she admits. A pause. "Marc wasn't a coincidence."

"What, then?"

"It centers on Billington but it's not all about Billington." She looks away from me and stares out to sea, morosely. "He's got his own . . . plans. To expedite them, he had to hire a bunch of specialists with eccentric tastes and needs. His wife − she's not harmless. She's *scum*." If looks could kill, the wave crests would be boiling into steam under her stare. "And she's got retainers. Call it a tactical marriage of convenience. She's got certain powers and he wants to make use of them. He's got shitloads of wealth and more ambition than— well, she likes that because it buys her immunity. Eileen . . . her predecessor Erzabet was probably framed by a rival, a duke who wanted her lands and her castle, but Eileen is the genius who figured out there was a skincare program in the old legend, productized the hell out of it, and sold it as Bathory™ Pale Grace™[9] Cosmetics, with added ErythroComplex-V. It's basically a mass-produced level one glamour. She sources most of the wholesale supplies from commercial slaughterhouses and leftover blood bank stock, and on paper she's clean, but you still need a better than homeopathic quantity of the real thing to make it work. And that's before you start asking how many regulatory committees she had to buy off to bury the details of her research."

"Why not go after her directly?"

"Because—" Ramona shrugs. "Eileen's not the main

[9] Pale Grace™, Pale Grace™ Skin Hydromax®, Pale Grace™ Bright Eyes®, and Pale Grace™ Number Three® [reference footnote 13] are registered trademarks of Bathory™ Cosmetics Corporation: "It'd better be bloody worth it at this price."

target. She's not even the appetizer. What she does amounts to at most a few dozen deaths per year. If Ellis gets what my boss thinks he wants the whole human species gets to deal with the fallout. So he figured I should get close to Eileen — to introduce you to Ellis, as much as anything else — and meanwhile get enough of a grip on the rest of her project to mop them up afterward."

"You were going to get information out of Marc after your Other got through chowing down on his soul?"

"You'd be surprised." She sniffs primly. "Anyway, you should know, mister computational demonologist: How hard would it be to summon up a puppeteer and schedule a late-binding, voice-directed linkage to keep the body dancing?"

I think back to the dead seagulls. To the bad guys and what they did to Marc after his fatal heart attack. "Not very."

"Okay, just so you know the score." She reaches out and grasps my wrist. Her fingers are warm and much too human.

"Billington's plans," I prompt. "The business with the *Explorer*."

"I'm not allowed to tell you everything I know," she says patiently. "If you know too much, his geas will spit you out like a melon seed and we won't have any time to prep a replacement."

"But you need me to get aboard his ship because I'm playing a role in some sort of script. While you stay entangled with me so you get to come along, too." I swallow. "Punching a hole in his firewall."

"That's the idea."

"Any idea how to do it?"

"Well—" a hint of a smile "—Billington usually visits the casino every evening when he's in range. So I'd say we ought to get back to the hotel and get ready for a high-rolling evening, and try to finesse an invitation. How does that sound?"

I stand up. "That sounds like a plan," I say doubtfully. "I

expected something a bit more concrete, though." I glance around. "Where did I put my boxers?"

We head back up the beach and when we get to the car Ramona hands me my clothes. By the time I get out of the toilet she's changed into a white sundress, head scarf, and shades that conceal her eyes. She's unrecognizable as the naked blonde from the beach. "Let's go," she suggests, turning the ignition key. I belt in beside her and she guns the engine, backing out of the parking lot in a spray of sand.

Ramona drives carefully along the coast road, back towards the west end of the island and the hotels and casinos. I slump down in the passenger seat and check my email as soon as we get adequate cellphone coverage. All that's waiting for me are two administrative circulars from the office, an almost plaintive request for a Sitrep from Angleton, and an interesting business proposition from the widow of the former president of Nigeria[10]. Ramona doesn't seem to be in a talkative mood right now, and I'm not sure I want to risk upsetting her by asking why.

Eventually, as we're entering Philipsburg, she nods to herself and begins talking. "You'll want to report in to your support team." She downshifts a gear and the engine growls. "Keep your station chief off your back, pick up the toys your tech guys have been unpacking, and call home."

"Yes. So?" I study the roadside. Pedestrians in bright summer holiday gear, locals in casuals, rickshaws, parked cars. Heat and dust.

---

[10] I briefly consider replying to the latter in the person of a highly placed agent of a secret British government agency, but the last time I did that Tony from Internal Security called me into his office and waxed sarcastic for almost half an hour before ordering me to give them back their bank.

"Just saying." We're crawling along. "Then I figure we need to meet up, late afternoon. To go sort out your invitation to the floating party aboard the *Mabuse*."

Late afternoon. A stab of guilt gets to me: it's about six o'clock back home, and I really ought to call Mo. I've got to reassure her that everything's under control and make sure she doesn't do something stupid like drop everything and come out here. (*Assuming everything is under control*, a quiet corner of my conscience reminds me. *If you were Mo, and you knew what was going on, what would you do?*) "You sound very certain that I'll get an invite," I speculate.

"Oh, I don't think it'll be too difficult." Ramona focuses on the road ahead. "You already got Billington's attention yesterday. After today, he'll want another look at you." She looks pensive. "Just in case, I've got some ideas. We can go over them later."

I steel myself. "I get the feeling you're trying very hard not to tell me something that's not related to the mission," I begin. "And you know I know but I don't know what I'm not supposed to know, and so—" I wind down, trying to keep track of all the double-indirect pointers and Boolean operators before I succumb to a stack crash.

"Not your problem, monkey-boy," she says with a false smile and a toss of her beautiful blonde hair, now coiling up into tight ringlets as the seawater dries in the breeze over the windscreen. "Don't worry yourself about me."

"What—" My skin crawls.

She looks at me, her eyes abruptly distant and hard. "You just have to get aboard the yacht, figure out what's going on, and expedite a solution," she tells me. "I've got to sit it out back here."

"But." I shut my mouth before I can stick any of my feet in it by accident. Then I point my head forwards, watching her out of the corner of my eye. Thin-lipped and grim-faced, knuckles gripping the steering wheel. The mermaid who clutched me to her watery bosom is frightened. Ramona, who plays with her food and never slept with a man who didn't die within twenty-four hours, is concerned. Driving me back to the hotel and the safe house and a setup where she'll have to hand me over to people she seems to despise — *Ramona, the spy who loves me?* No, that dog won't hunt. It must be something else, but whatever it is, she isn't talking. So we drive the rest of the way to the hotel in lonely silence, grappling with our respective demons.

10: DEAD LUCKY

When I get back to my hotel room I find Boris pacing the carpet like a trapped tiger. "What time you are naming this?" he asks, tapping his heavy stainless steel wristwatch. "Am being on edge of calling in Code Red on you!"

Pinky has plugged a PlayStation into the TV set and is making zooming sounds, bouncing up and down on the bed; and from the sounds leaking under the bathroom door Brains is testing a radio-controlled hovercraft in the shower.

"I've been running some errands," I say tiredly. "And then I went swimming."

"Swimming?" Boris shakes his head. "Am not enquiring. Are giving Angleton the Sitrep yet?"

"Oops. My bad." I pull out the desk chair and slump into it. My forearms and thighs are aching in unaccustomed places: I'm going to feel like shit tomorrow. "How did you get in here?"

Pinky saves his game and looks round. "Picked the lock," he says, waving what looks suspiciously like a hotel card key at me.

"You picked." I stare at it. "The lock."

"Yup." He flips it at me and I catch it. "It's a smartcard,

got an induction loop instead of the usual dumb mag stripe on the back. Guaranteed to run through the complete list of makers' override keys in under twenty seconds."

"Right." I put it down carefully.

"Hey, I'll want it back in a minute – where'd you think I saved my game?"

Boris snorts, then stares at me. "Report, Bob, now."

"Okay." I cross my arms. "When I left this morning, I thought I'd check out a hunch. I found out the hard way that Billington's got a total surveillance lockdown on the French Cul de Sac north of Paradise Peak. Dead birds on Anse Marcel, seagulls everywhere. His people are running zombies. Human ones, too." Boris looks like he's about to interrupt, but I keep on talking: "I had a run-in with one of them. Ramona helped me get out of it, and we lost them by going swimming close to the island defense chain. Which has been tampered with, incidentally, compromising the three-mile offshore thaumaturgic-exclusion zone – did you know that? Ramona says her sources say Billington's going to be back at the casino tonight, so we made a date. How does that fit with your plans?"

When I finish Boris nods. "Is making progress. Please to be continuing it." He turns to Pinky: "Get Brains." To me: "Am authorizing contact tonight. These two are being explain gizmos for self-defense. Call me later." And he leaves, just as there's a loud toilet-flushing sound and Brains comes out of the bathroom.

"Okay," I say, pointing at the half-inflated, bright yellow life belt hanging round his waist. "What's that about? And do I want to know?"

"Just testing." Brains pushes it down around his feet then steps out of it. "Can I have your dress shoes, please?"

"My shoes?" I bend down and rummage for them in my luggage. They're horrible things, shiny patent leather with soles that feel like lumps of wood. "What do you want them for?"

Pinky is doing something to the PlayStation. "This." He flourishes another smartcard, which Brains takes and slides into a hitherto invisible seam in the leather tongue of my right shoe.

"And this," Brains says, holding up a shoelace.

"That's a—"

"Miniature 100BaseT cable. Pay attention, Bob, you don't want to lose your network connectivity, do you? It goes in like *this* and to activate it you twist and pull like *that*; it uncoils to three meters and the plastic caps expand to fit any standard network socket. It doubles as a field-expedient grounding strap, too. That's right. No, you don't want to tie your shoelaces too tight."

I try to stifle a groan. "Guys, is this really necessary? Does it help me do the job?"

Pinky cocks his head to one side. "Predictive Branch says there's a ten percent chance of you failing on the job and dying horribly if you don't take it." He giggles. "Feeling lucky, punk?"

"Bah. What do I really need to know?"

"Here." Brains tosses a stainless steel Zippo lighter to me: "It's an antique, don't lose it. Predictive Branch said it would come in handy."

"I don't smoke. What else?"

"The usual stuff: There's a USB memory drive preloaded with a forensic intrusion kit hidden in each end of your dickey-bow, a WiFi-finder on your key ring, a roll-up keyboard in your cummerbund, the pen's got Bluetooth and doubles as a mouse, and there's a miniaturized Tillinghast resonator in your left heel. You turn it on by twisting the heel through one-eighty degrees; turn it off the same way. Your other heel is just a heel: We were going to hide a

Basilisk gun in it but some ass-hat in Export Controls vetoed our requisition because it was going overseas. Oh, and there's this." Brains reaches over to a briefcase on the bed and pulls out a businesslike nylon shoulder holster and a black automatic pistol. "Walther P99, 9mm caliber, fifteen-round magazine, silvercap hollow-points engraved with a demicyclic banishment circuit in ninety-nanometer Enochian."

"Banishment rounds?" I ask hesitantly, then: "Hang on." I hold up one hand: "I'm not cleared for carrying guns in the field!"

"We figured the exorcism payload means it's covered by your occult weapons certification. If anyone asks, it's just a gadget for installing exorcism glyphs at high speed." Brains sits down on the bed, ejects the magazine, works the action to make sure there's no round in the chamber, then starts stripping it down. "Word from Angleton is the bad guys are likely to get heavy and he wants you carrying."

"Oh my." I blank for a moment. It's only about an hour since I sliced some poor bastard's air hose in half, and having to deal with this so soon afterwards is doing my head in. "Did he really say that?"

"Yes. We don't want to end up losing you by accident because someone starts shooting and you're unarmed, do we?"

"I guess not." He passes the shoulder holster to me and I try to figure out how it goes on. "Well, if you're all done now, maybe you could leave so I can phone home?"

After Pinky and Brains leave, I call down to room service for a light lunch, put the door chain on, then go run a bath. There's a wet suit hanging over the shower rail and an oxygen tank leaning up against the toilet. While the bath's filling I try phoning home, but get the answering machine. I try Mo's mobile, but that's switched off, too. She must still be in

Dunwich under lockdown. Feeling sorry for myself, I go and rinse the salt off my skin: but I can't hang around in the bath without thinking of Ramona, and that's not a healthy sign either. I'm confused about her, I feel guilty whenever I think about Mo, and the smell of saltwater brings back that frightening slow-motion underwater tumble, knife in hand. This isn't me: I'm just not the cold-blooded killer type. When shit needs kicking and throats need slitting we send in Alan's goon squad. I'm supposed to be the quiet geek who sits at the back of the computer lab, right?

Except I signed my name on the line a few years ago, right below the paragraph that said I accepted the Crown's commission to go forth and perpetrate mayhem in the defense of the realm, as lawfully directed and commanded by my designated superiors. And while most of the time it's trivial shit — like breaking into an office and leaving evidence to shitcan some poor bastard who's stumbled too close to the truth — there's nothing there that says I'm *not* required to wrestle killers in wet suits or molest alien monsters. Quite the contrary, in fact. I don't have a license to kill, but I don't have orders *not* to kill in the course of my duties, either. Which realization I find extremely disturbing; it's like the sensation in your stomach the first time you get into a car after getting your driving license, when you suddenly realize there's no instructor in the seat next to you and *this is not a test*.

I wrap myself in a bath sheet and go back out into the bedroom. It's about one in the afternoon and I've got a few hours to kill before Ramona is due back. Lunch shows up and is as blandly tasteless as usual — I swear that there's a force field in the hotel dimensions that sucks the flavor out of food. I badly want something that'll distract me from pursuing this morbid introspection. Pinky left the PlayStation behind, so I plop myself down in front of the

TV, pick up the controller, and poke at it in a desultory sort of way. Candy-bright graphics and a splash screen flicker by as the machine clunks and whirs, loading; then it launches a road race game, in which I'm driving a variety of cars along winding roads around a jungle-covered island while zombies shoot at me. "Arse," I mutter, and switch off in disgust. I check that my tablet PC is plugged into all the wards correctly, then draw the curtains and lie down on the bed for a short nap.

I'm awakened what feels like a split second later by a banging on the door. "Hey, monkey-boy! Rise and shine!"

Jesus. I've been asleep for hours. "Ramona?" I stand up and stagger towards the vestibule. My upper thighs and forearms ache as if I've been beaten — must be the swimming. I draw the chain and open the door.

"Had a good nap?" She raises an eyebrow at me.

"Got to get—" I pause. "Dressed." *Damn, I haven't phoned Mo,* I realize. Ramona is looking like about a million dollars, in a blue evening dress that clings to her improbably well — it seems to be held on with double-sided sticky tape. There's several meters of pearl rope wound into her hair: she must have found a handy time warp for the make-up crew to have had time to get her ready for the fashion photo-shoot. Meanwhile, I'm wearing yesterday's underpants and I feel like I've been run over by a train.

"You're running late," she says, pushing past me; one nostril wrinkles aristocratically as she surveys the wreckage. She bends over a large carrier bag with the logo of that goddamned tailor on it: "Here, catch."

I find myself clutching a pair of boxer shorts. "Okay, I get the message. Give me a minute?"

"Take ten," she says, "I'll go powder my nose." Then she disappears into the bathroom.

I groan and retrieve my tuxedo from the leg-well of the

desk. There's a fresh shirt in the bag, and I manage to install myself in it without too much trouble. I leave the goddamn squeaky shoes for last. Then I have a mild anxiety attack when I realize I've forgotten the shoulder holster. *Should I or shouldn't I?* I'll probably end up shooting myself in the foot. In the end I compromise – I've still got Ramona's phonegun, so I'll carry that in one pocket. "I'm ready," I call.

"I'll bet." She comes out of the bathroom, adjusting her evening bag, and smiles brilliantly. Her smile fades. "Where's your gun?"

I pat my jacket pocket.

"No, no, not that one." She reaches in and removes the phonegun, then gestures at the shoulder holster: "*That* one."

"Must I?" I try not to whine.

"Yes, you must." I shrug out of my jacket and Ramona helps me into the shoulder rig. Then she straightens my bow tie. "That's more like it. We'll have you attending diplomatic cocktail parties in no time!"

"That's what I'm afraid of," I grumble. "Okay, where now?"

"Back to the casino. Eileen's throwing a little party in the *petit salle*, and I've got us tickets. Seafood canapés and crappy lounge music with a little gambling thrown in. Plus the usual sex and drugs rich people indulge in when they get bored with throwing their money away. She's using the party to reward some of her best sales agents and do a little quiet negotiating on the side. I gather she's got a new supplier to talk to. Ellis won't be there at first, but I figure if we can get you an invitation onto the ship . . .?"

"Okay," I agree. "Anything else?"

"Yes." Ramona pauses in the doorway. Her eyes seem very large and dark. I can't look away from them because I know what's coming: "Bob, I don't, I don't want to——" She reaches for my hand, then shakes her head. "Ignore me. I'm a fool."

I keep hold of her hand. She tries to pull away. "I don't believe you," I say. My heart is beating very hard. "You do, don't you?"

She looks me in the eye. "Yes," she admits. Her eyes are glistening, and in this light I can't tell whether it's cosmetics or tears. "But we mustn't."

I manage to nod. "You're right." The words feel very heavy to me, to both of us. I can feel her need, a physical hunger for an intimacy she hasn't allowed herself to indulge in years. It's not sex, it's something more. *Oh what a lovely mess!* She's been a solitary predator for so long that she doesn't know what to do with somebody she doesn't want to kill and eat. I feel ill with emotional indigestion: I don't think I've ever felt for Mo the kind of raw, priapic lust I feel for Ramona, but Ramona is a poisonous bloom – off-limits if I value my life.

She closes the gap between us, wraps her arms around me, and pulls me against her. She kisses me on the mouth so hard that it makes my hair stand on end. Then she lets go of me, steps back, and smooths her dress down. "I'd better not do that ever again," she says thoughtfully. "For both our sakes: it's too risky." Then she takes a deep breath and offers me her arm. "Shall we go to the casino?"

The night is young. It's just beginning to get dark, and some time while I was sleeping there was a brief deluge of rain. It's cut the baking daytime heat down a few notches, but steam is rising from the sidewalk in thin wisps and the humidity setting is somewhere between "Amazonian" and "crash dive with the torpedo tubes open." We stroll past a few street vendors and a bunch of good-time folks, under awnings with bright lights and loud noises. The brightly painted gazebos in front of the restaurants are all full, drowning out the creaking insect life with loud chatter.

We arrive at the casino entrance and I nod at the unfamiliar doorman. "Private party," I say.

"Ah. If *monsieur et madame* would come this way . . .?" He backs into the foyer and directs us towards a nondescript staircase. "Your card, sir?"

Ramona nudges me discreetly and I feel her slide something into my hand. I flip it round and pass it to the doorman. "Here." He scrutinizes it briefly, then nods and waves us upstairs.

"What was that?" I ask Ramona as we climb.

"Invitation to Eileen's little recreation." It's all polished brass and rich, dark mahogany here. Deeply tedious landscape paintings in antique frames dot the walls, and the lights are dim. Ramona frowns minutely as we reach the landing: "Under our own names, of course."

"Right. Do the names signify?"

She shrugs. "Probably, on some database somewhere. They're not stupid, Bob."

I offer her my arm and we walk down the wide hallway towards the open double-doors. Beyond them I can hear the clink of glassware and voices raised in conversation, layered above a hotel jazz quartet mangling something famous.

The crowd here feels very different to the gamblers in the public areas of the casino downstairs, and I instantly feel slightly out of place. There are dozens of women in their thirties and forties, turned out in an overly formal parody of office wear. They have a curious uniformity of expression, as if the skin of their faces has been replaced with blemish-resistant polymer coating, and they're pecking at finger food and networking with the perky ferocity of a piranha school on Prozac; it's like the Stepford Business School opening day, and Ramona and I have wandered in by mistake from the International Capitalist Conspiracy meeting next door. I briefly wonder if anyone's going to ask us to announce the winners of the prize for most cutthroat business development plan of the year. But past the buffet I spot another set of open double-doors, at a guess the ICC meeting's going to be through there, along with the roulette wheels and the free bar.

I'm going to go say 'hi' to our hostess, Ramona tells me. **See you in a couple of minutes?**

I can tell when I'm not needed. **Sure,** I say. **Want me to get you a drink?**

I'll handle it from here. She smiles at me then opens her mouth and gushes, "Isn't this wonderful, Bob? Be a dear and circulate while I go powder my nose. I'll just be a sec!" Then she's off, carving a groove through the little black dresses and plastic smiles.

I shrug philosophically, spot the bar, and go over to it. The bartender is busily pouring glass after glass of cheap, fizzy white plonk, and it takes me a while to catch his eye. "Service over here?"

"Sure. What do you want?"

"I'll—" a thousand fragments of half-grasped TV movies take control of my larynx "—can you make it a dry martini? Shaken, not stirred."

"Heh." He looks amused. "You're not the first guy who's asked me that." He grabs a cocktail shaker and reaches for the gin, and in just a matter of seconds he's handing me a conical glass full of clear, oily liquid with a pickled sheep's eyeball at the bottom. I sniff it cautiously. It smells of jet fuel.

"Thanks, I think." Holding it at arm's length I turn away from the bar and nearly dump it all over a woman in a severe black suit and heavy-framed spectacles. "Oops, I'm sorry."

"Don't mention it." She doesn't smile. "Mr. Howard? Of Capital Laundry Services?" She pronounces my name as if she's getting ready to serve a writ.

"Um, yes. You are . . .?"

"Liza Sloat, of Spleen, Sloat, and Partners." Her cheek twitches in something that might be a smile, or just neuralgia. "We have the privilege of handling the Billingtons' personal accounts. I believe we nearly met yesterday."

"We did?" Suddenly I remember where I know her from. She's the lawyer who was dogging Billington's footsteps, the one with the briefcase who went to see the casino president. I smile. "Yes, I remember now. To what do I owe the pleasure?"

The twitch turns into a genuine smile, albeit about as warm as liquid nitrogen. "Mr. Billington is running late today. He'll be along later in the evening, and meanwhile you're to make yourself at home." The smile slides away, replaced by a stare so coldly calculating that I shiver. "That is his prerogative. Personally, I think he is a little too trusting. You're rather young for a bidding agent in this auction." The smile reappears. "You might want to remind your employers of our history of successful litigation against individuals, organizations, and entities that try to interfere with the smooth running of our legitimate commercial operations. Good day."

She turns on one spiked black heel and clicks back in the direction of the inner room. *What the hell was that about?* I wonder unwisely taking a mouthful from my glass. I manage not to spew it everywhere, but it tastes even worse than it smelled: pure essence of turpentine with a finish of cheap gin and a tangy undernote of kerosene. "Gah." I swallow convulsively, wait for the steam to stop trickling out of my nose, and go looking for a potted plant that appears hardy enough to survive being irrigated with the stuff.

The salon next door is thickly carpeted, and curtained like an up-market whorehouse in a movie about *fin-de-siècle* Paris. Most of the folks here are clustered around the gaming tables and while some of the ladies from Pale Grace™ Cosmetics have wandered in, it looks to be mostly Billington's court of louche shareholders and their anorexic, artistically inclined, fashion-model fuck-bunnies. I'm moving towards the baccarat table when one of the younger and pushier sales associates appears in front of me, smiles ingratiatingly, and holds out her hand. "Hi! I'm Kitty. Isn't it great to be here?"

I squint at her from behind my regrettably full glass, then raise an eyebrow. "I suppose it is," I concede, "for some values of 'great.' Do I know you?"

Kitty stares at me, freezing like a rabbit in the headlights of an oncoming juggernaut. She's blonde, her hair lacquered into place like the glass fiber weave of a crash helmet awaiting the resin spray: she's pretty in a mascara'd and lip-glossed kind of way. "Aren't you, uh, really famous or something?" she stammers. "Mrs. Billington always invites famous speakers to these events—"

I force myself to smile benevolently. "That's okay, I don't mind you not recognizing me." I take a sip of the martini: it's revolting but it's got alcohol in it, so it can't be all bad. "It's rather refreshing, actually, being a nobody who people overlook all the time." Kitty smiles uncertainly, as if she's not sure whether I'm deploying irony or something equally exotic. "What brings you here, Kitty?" I ask, putting on my sincerest expression.

"I'm Busy Bee Number One for the Minnesota sales region! I mean, I have a really great team and they're amazingly great workers but it's such an honor, don't you think? And only last year we were sixty-second out of seventy-four regional teams! But I figured my girls just needed something to shoot for so I gave them new targets and a new promotional pricing structure with discount incentivization and it worked like crazy!" She half-covers her mouth: "And the viral marketing thing, too, but that's something else. But it was my worker bees who did it all, really! There are no drones in *my* hive!"

"That's, uh, truly excellent," I say, nodding. A thought strikes me: "What particular products are doing well at the moment? I mean, is there anything special that's responsible for your sales growth?"

"Oh, well, you know we've tracked the vertical segmentation of our region and different hives have different merchandise footprints, but you know something? It's the same everywhere, the Pale Grace™ Skin Hydromax® cream is, you know, walking off the shelves!"

"Hmm." I try to look thoughtful, which isn't difficult: *How the hell do you package a glamour in an ointment pot?* I shake my head in admiration and take another sip of drain cleaner. "That's really good to know. Maybe I should use it myself?"

"Oh, of course you should! Here, take my card; I'd be happy to set you up with a range of free samples and an initial consultation." Her card isn't just a piece of cardboard, it's a scratch 'n' sniff sample as complex as a Swiss Card survival tool – I manage to slide it into my pocket without getting any of the stuff on my skin. Kitty gushes in my direction, her eyes lighting up as she moves into the standard sales script, her voice softening and lowering with a compelling sincerity that is at odds with her natural bubbly extroversion: "The ErythroComplex-V in the Pale Grace™ Skin Hydromax® range is clinically proven to reverse ageing-induced cytoplasmic damage to the skin and nail cuticles. Just one application begins to undo the ravages of free radicals and enhance the body's natural production of antioxidants and cytochrome polyesterase inhibitors. *And* it's so creamy smooth! We make it with one hundred percent natural ingredients, unlike some of our competitors . . ."

I slip away while she's reciting her programmed spiel, and she doesn't even notice as I sidle up to a potted palm and take a last reflective mouthful of dry martini. My wards blipped slightly as her script kicked in, but that doesn't have to mean she's a robot, does it? *We make it with one hundred percent natural ingredients*, like the bottom tenth percentile of our sales force, the ones who don't get invited to this end of the marketing conference by the Queen Bee. Maybe Kitty's just a natural void, only too happy to be filled by the passing enthusiasm of the traveling salesman invocation, but somehow I doubt it: that kind of perfect vacuum doesn't come cheap.

I scuff my left heel on the ground. If I switched it on, the Tillinghast resonator that Brains installed in my shoe would let me see the sales-daemon riding her spine like a grotesquely bloated digger wasp, but I'd just as soon keep my lunch — and anyway the first law of demonology is that if you can see it, *it* can see *you*. But the small of my back itches as I glance round at the overdressed hedonists and the scarily neat saleswomen because I'm putting together a picture here that I really don't like: dinner jacket or no, I'm underdressed for the occasion, although Ramona fits right in.

While I'm having these grim thoughts, I notice that my martini glass is nearly empty. It's not a terribly endearing drink — it tastes like something that got hosed off a runway then diluted with antifreeze — but it does what it says on the label. I've got a nasty feeling I'm going to need plenty of Dutch courage to get through this evening. What that horrible lawyer-creature Sloat was saying is sinking in: This is either a cover or a warm-up for some sort of auction, isn't it? Maybe Billington is planning on selling whatever he dredges up from JENNIFER MORGUE Site Two to the highest bidder. That would make plenty of sense and it'd explain why the Black Chamber and the Laundry are both riled up about it, but I can't shake the feeling that this isn't the whole story: What was the business with Marc all about? Assuming it's connected. Maybe Ramona knows something she'd be willing to share with me.

I shake my head and look around. I don't see her among the glitterati at the gaming tables, but there are enough people here that she could have wandered off. **You there?** I ask silently, but she isn't answering and I can't sense what she's doing. It's as if she's figured out how to draw a thick blackout curtain around her mind, keeping me out when she doesn't want me around. *That'd be a neat skill to have*, I think, then mentally kick myself. What one of us can do the other can learn really fast. I'll just have to ask her how she does it whenever she comes out of hiding. At least she's not in trouble, I guess; given the nature of our link, I'm certain I'd know if she was.

I circulate back towards the bar in the other room and plant my glass on it, then turn round to see if I can spot either of the Billingtons among the happy-clappy flock of saleswomen: Ellis may be delayed but I can't see his wife throwing a revival-style party for her faithful without circulating to stroke her flock. "Another of the same?" murmurs the barman, and before I can make up my mind to say "no" he's fished out a glass and is pouring gin with a soup ladle. I nod at him and take it, then head back towards the gaming tables in the back room. I'm not going to drink it, I decide, but maybe if I keep it in my hand it'll stop anyone from trying to refill the bloody glass again.

The crowd near the tables is noisy and they're smoking and drinking like there's no tomorrow. I strain to see what's going on over a gaggle of sericulture-vultures with big hair. It's a baccarat table and from the disorganization there it looks like a game's just ended. Half a dozen of Billington's crowd are moving in while an old fart who looks like a merchant banker leans back in his chair, sipping a glass of port.

"Ah, Mr. Howard I believe." I nearly jump out of my skin before I recall that I'm supposed to be suave and sophisticated, or at least gin-pickled to the point of insensibility. "Care for a game?"

I glance round. I vaguely recognize the guy who knows my name. He's in early middle-age, crew cut, solidly built, and he fills his tuxedo with an avuncular bonhomie that I instinctively mistrust; he reminds me of the sort of executive who can fire six thousand people before lunch and go to a charity fundraiser the same evening with his sense of self-righteousness entitlement undented. "I'm not much of a gambler," I murmur.

"That's okay, all I ask is that you're a good loser." He grins, baring a perfect row of teeth at me. "I'm Pat, by the way. Pat McMurray. I consult on security issues for Mr. Billington. That's how I know about you."

"Right." I nod as I give him the hairy eyeball. He winks at me slowly, then tugs his left ear lobe. He's wearing an earring that looks a lot like a symbol I see most days at the office on my way past the secure documents store in Dansey House. This isn't in the script: *Security consultants who've been briefed on me? Gulp.* I try to feel what Ramona's doing again, but no luck. She's still got that blackout curtain up. "What kind of security issues do you consult on?" I ask.

"Well, you know, that's a good question." He points at my glass. "Why are you drinking that garbage when there's perfectly good liquor behind the bar?"

I stare at it. "It just sort of slipped into my hand."

"Heh. You come over to the bar and we'll get you a real man's drink. One that doesn't taste like drain cleaner." He turns and heads for the bar in complete certainty that I'll follow him, so I do. The bastard knows I need to know what he knows and he knows I can't say no. He leans on the bar and announces: "Two double tequila slammers on the rocks."

Then he turns to me and raises an eyebrow. "You're wondering what I do here, aren't you?"

"Um." Well, yes.

He must take it as agreement, because he nods encouragingly. "Ellis Billington's a big guy, you've got to know that. Big guys tend to pick up parasites. That's nothing new. Trouble is, what Ellis picks up is a different class of bloodsucker. See, you know who his company subcontracts for: this makes him a target for people who don't want just his money, they want a piece of *him*. So he hires specialist talent to keep them at arm's reach. Mostly ex-employees of you-know-who, plus a few freelancers." He taps his chest. The bartender sets two glasses down in front of us; crystals frost their edges and they're full of a colorless, slightly oily liquid, along with a slice of lemon. "C'mon. Back to the table, bring your glass. Let's play a round."

"But I don't gamble—" I begin, and he stops dead.

"You'll gamble and like it, son. Or Ellis Billington ain't going to make time for you."

Huh? I blink. The brown envelope labeled EXPENSES feels extremely hot and as heavy as a gold brick in my breast pocket. "Why?"

"Could be that he don't approve of limp-dicked limeys," McMurray mugs. "Or could be it's all part of the script. Besides, you'll enjoy it, you know you will. Go on, over to the cashier. Get yourself chipped up."

Moments later I'm swapping the contents of the envelope for a pile of plastic counters. Black, red, white: six months' salary gone to plastic. My mind's spinning like a hamster wheel. This *isn't* in the script I'm working from, either the gambling or McMurray's stark ultimatum. But it's all running on rails, and there's no way to get off this train without blowing the timetable. So I follow McMurray over to the table, trying to figure out the odds. House cards: nil. That's four in fourteen of anything I draw. Then it's modular arithmetic down to the wire, the sort of thing I could do in my head if it was in hexadecimal. Alas, playing cards predates hex and I've just sunk four shots of expensive gin and I'm not sure I can build a lookup table in my head fast enough to be of any use.

I sit down. The old toad with the cigar nods at us. "I bought the bank," he announces. "Place your bets. Opening at five thousand." The croupier next to him holds up the shoe and six sealed packs of cards. Four elderly vultures in frocks giggle and hunch at one end of the kidney-shaped table and two guys in DJs and big moustaches sit at the other end. McMurray and I end up in the middle opposite the old toad. A couple more gamblers take their seats – a woman with skin the color of milk chocolate and the complexion of a supermodel, and a guy in a white suit, open-necked shirt, and more bling than the Bank of England. "Opening at five thousand," repeats the banker.

Without willing my hands to move, I slide a handful of chips forwards. McMurray does likewise. The cards go into the mechanical shuffler in front of us, then two of the vultures squabble for the privilege of cutting them before they end up in the brass and wood shoe. My fingertips and nasal sinuses are itching: I actually *want a cigarette*, even though I don't smoke. There's a hollow sense of dreadful anticipation in the pit of my stomach as the toad positions the shoe in front of himself and then flicks out cards, face-down, one towards each of us. Then he repeats the deal. A second card lands in front of me, half on top of the first. I sneak a look at the cards. Six of hearts, five of clubs. *Shit*. Around me everyone else is turning their cards. I lay mine down face-up and watch with numb disbelief as the croupier rakes in my stake.

"Next round." The banker glances round. Again, I can't stop myself, even though there's a cold itch at the base of my spine and my wards are ringing like alarm bells. I slide another ten thousand forwards. This time I twitch and nearly scatter the stack everywhere. McMurray spares me a coldly amused glance; then the banker holds up the shoe and the card deck and begins to deal. *There's something very wrong here*, I tell myself. But it's no compulsion or geas I'm familiar with. There's a pattern to it, something I can't quite put my finger on. *Where's Ramona?* I can sense nothing but velvety darkness where she ought to be. I'm alone in my own head for the first time in days, and it's not a good feeling. Cards. Queen of diamonds, eight of spades—

A stack of chips approaches me across the table. I pick up my glass and throw back the tequila slammer, shuddering as it hits my throat. I feel out-of-control drunk and coldly sober at the same time: it's like my brain's trying to do the splits, its lobes skittering in opposite directions.

"Again, anyone?" asks the banker, looking round the table. I mechanically begin to push my chips forwards, then manage to divert the action, bend down, and twist the heel of my left shoe. Coming up above the level of the table I finish the motion before I can stop myself, all my chips gliding into a pile in front of the banker. He deals. I look around the room. McMurray's earring is a burning cold teardrop of radium fire. The shadows lengthen behind the drapes, hiding the screams of trapped tree-spirits embedded in the fine wall paneling. The Tillinghast resonator is humming along, but when I look at the toad he's just an ordinary retired fat-cat with a trust fund and a big bank account, enjoying his gambling habit. The same isn't true of the vultures – I look at them and try not to recoil. Instead of ageing former trophy-wives and heiresses I see hollow bags of translucent skin and hair held together by their clothes, hunched over their cards like blood-sucking parasites waiting to be filled.

"Hold or play?" someone asks. I glance at the guy in the

white suit and open-necked shirt and see a half-decayed cadaver grinning at me from behind his cards, skin peeling back from dark hollows lined with strips of adipocere, the effect of the resonator reaches my nasal sinuses and I *smell* him as well. The supermodel on his arm looks exactly the same as before, inhumanly calm and poised as she leans against him, but the shadows behind her are thick and fuliginous, and something about her expression makes me think of a hangman waiting proudly beside his latest client as the warden signs the death certificate.

"Play." I try hard not to gag as I turn my cards over. *Fuck, fuck, fuck.* The croupier is raking the chips across to the toad. "Excuse me," I gasp, pushing my chair back from the table. I stumble towards the discreet side door, my throat burning as the woodwork screams at me and hollow bags of skin turn their empty faces to follow my trajectory to the toilets.

I just lost twenty thousand bucks, I realize numbly as I splash water on my face and look at myself in the mirror above the wash basin. My face in the mirror leers at me and winks. I lift my leg hastily and twist the heel back into place: the face freezes in shock. *I can't afford that.* Ghastly visions dance in my mind's eye: Angleton will call the Auditors on me, Mo will scream blue murder. It's more than our combined savings account, the money we've been socking away this past year towards a deposit on a house. I shudder. My lips are numb from the alcohol I've been putting away. My throat and stomach feel raw. I still can't sense Ramona, and that's critical: if she's out of touch we've got a real problem with the whole operation. *Pull yourself together,* I tell the man in the mirror. He nods at me, looking shaken. What to do first? *McMurray:* The bastard set me up somehow, didn't he?

The realization gives me something concrete to focus on: I straighten up, carefully check out the stranger in the mirror to make sure he looks suitably composed, square my shoulders, and head back towards the party. But when I reach the door back to the room, I pause. The baccarat game is over. Everyone except the bank-toad is standing up, and new players are milling around their seats, buzzing like a swarm of flies around a— *don't go there*. I look away hastily, my eyes watering. I don't see McMurray anywhere, and my wards are kicking up a fuss. It feels like a major supernatural manifestation is happening somewhere nearby.

"You must be Mr. Howard?" a calm, somewhat musical voice says from right beside me.

I don't jump out of my skin this time: I barely twitch. The urgent nagging of my wards spikes in time with her voice. "Everyone seems to know who I am. Who are you?"

Looking round I recognize her at once. She's the supermodel type with the hangman's eyes who was chilling with Mr. Stiffy: she's got skin the color of a perfect mocha, her dancer's body exposed rather than concealed by her sheer white gown, a fortune in sapphires at ears and throat. Looks to die for, like Ramona – yes, it's a glamour. Predictably, she's the center of the manifestation my wards are yammering about. "I'm Johanna, Mr. Howard, Johanna Todt. I work for the Billingtons."

I shrug. "Doesn't everyone?"

It's meant to be a black joke, but Johanna doesn't seem to take it in the intended spirit. She frowns: "Not yet." Then she sniffs dismissively. "I'm supposed to bring you to see him."

"Really." I make myself look her in the eye. She really *is* beautiful, so much so that normally I'd be tongue-tied and babbling in her presence. But thanks to the time I've been spending with Ramona, supernatural beauty isn't as dazzling as it used to be, and besides, I've got other preoccupations right now. I manage to keep a lid on it. "Liza Sloat just got through warning me off, then I had some security consultant called McMurray all over me like a vest. What's the story?"

"Interdepartmental rivalry. Sloat and McMurray don't get on." Johanna tilts her head to one side and looks at me. "There are many mansions in the house of Billington, Mr. Howard. And as it happens, Mr. McMurray is my manager." She lays a long-fingered hand on my arm. "Walk with me."

She steers me past the bar and into the outer room, past the jazz butchers. There are French doors open on the balcony. *Where's Ramona?* I worry. *She wasn't in the back room, she's not here . . .*

"For obvious reasons we don't make it too easy to reach the chief," Johanna murmurs. "When you're as rich as the Billingtons it makes you a target. Money is an attractive nuisance. We're currently tracking six stalkers and three blackmailers, and that's before you count the third-world governments. We've got enough schizophrenics to fill one-point-four psychiatric hospitals, plus an average of two-point-six marriage proposals and eleven-point-one death threats per week, and a federal antitrust investigation which is worse than all of them combined."

Put that way, I can almost feel a sneaking sympathy for the man. "So why am I here?" I ask.

The ghost of a smile tugs at her lips. "You're not a stalker or a blackmailer." A faint ghost of a breeze comes through the open doors. She leads me out onto the balcony. "You're asking inconvenient questions and silencing you won't stop them, because the organization you work for is staffed by determined, intelligent, and very dangerous people. It's much better to get everything out in the open and discuss it like sensible people, don't you think?"

"Yeah, well." My mind's eye flickers back to the nightmare meeting in Darmstadt, the shadow of a diver's oxygen tank rippling across encrusted concrete . . . *Dammit, where's*

Ramona? She should be relaying this! "Incidentally, who was your boyfriend?" She raises an eyebrow. "Humor me. The guy in the white suit."

"What, him?" She shakes her head. "Just an ex of mine. He hangs out with me sometimes." My wards are still tingling and I get a sharp stab of pain as I look at her. Her smile slowly widens. "I walk the body – one at a time. Not *all* of us are as snobbish as prissy Miss Random."

I used to wonder why the most beautiful women always ended up with rotters, but as explanations go this one stinks. I try to take a step back but she's still holding my arm and she's got a grip like a steel mooring cable, and I'm backed up against the wall. My wards are flaring now, incandescent spectral light from the chain I'm wearing under my shirt. "What have you done with her?" I demand.

"Nothing, personally. But if you want to see her again you'll come with—"

The velvet wall between us rips open shockingly fast, and Ramona comes slamming through. I'm not sensing the shape of her emotions, or even seeing a blurry inner vision through her eyes, I'm inside her, I *am* Ramona for a random moment, and the somatic realization is simultaneously very wrong and very right. The floor beneath her feet is carpeted but it's slowly turning. Unsteady on her heels she looks round the gloriously upholstered salon, past the windows, sees the sea and the headland. Three black-clad guards with guns flank a monster just like the corpse in the white suit as her heart tries to climb her throat. ****Bob?**** Her cold apprehension hits me like a hammer. This isn't random fear of the unknown: she knows *precisely* what she's afraid of. I follow her gaze down to the floor, and the carpet she stands on. It's a glorious antique Isfahan carpet. Woven into it, almost invisible silver threads trace out a design identical to the one on my wards, on McMurray's earring. From one edge of the carpet a coiled cable leads to a control box grasped in the walking corpse's hands. **It's a trap, Bob, don't let them—**

The corpse pushes a button on the control box and suddenly I can't feel Ramona anymore. I stagger, disoriented: it's like having a full-body local anesthetic. I blink until I can focus my eyes. Johanna is smiling at me in a satisfied, cat-got-the-canary manner. "Who do you work for again?" I ask, trying to regain control.

"Ellis Billington." Her smile vanishes, replaced by casual authority. "He says I'm to take you aboard the *Mabuse*. You will do exactly as I say – assuming you ever want to see her again."

"What?" I ask, feeling sick and sober with the backwash from Ramona's fright. "But I came here to see him anyway!"

"Perhaps, but you've also acquired adversary status, according to our reading of the main security geas. It's probably a memory leak in the code, but until we've terminated this phase of the operation we're going to treat you as threat number one." She steps closer to me and before I realize what she's doing she reaches into my jacket and removes the pistol Ramona made me wear. She takes two steps back and I find myself staring up the muzzle of my own gun, feeling stupid. "Lights out, Mr. Howard."

I'm opening my mouth to say something when the ward they've trapped Ramona in shuts down and her presence floods into me again. I've got time for a brief moment of relief – time to think *we're whole again* – then the walking corpse shoots her with a Taser, and while Ramona and I are both flopping around on the floor Johanna steps forwards and sinks a disposable syringe into my neck.

11: DESTINY ENTANGLED

I AM ASLEEP AND DREAMING AND AWARE AT THE
same time – I appear to be having a lucid dream. I really
wish I wasn't, because that rat-bastard Angleton has taken
advantage of my somnambulant state to sneak into my head
with his slide projector and install another precanned top
secret briefing, using my eyelids as stereoscopic projection
screens. And I don't care how bad your nightmares are, they
can't possibly be as unpleasant as a mission briefing conducted by old skull-face while you're asleep, unable to wake
up, and suffering from an impending hangover.

"Pay attention, Bob," he admonishes me sternly. "If
you're alive you're getting this briefing because you've penetrated Billington's semiotic firewall. This means you're
approaching the most dangerous part of your mission – and
you're going to have to play it by ear. On the other hand,
you've got an ace up your sleeve in the form of Ms. Random.
She should be secure in the safe house your backup team has
organized, and she'll be your conduit back to us for advice
and instructions."

No she bloody isn't! I try to yell at him, but he's playing the
usual tricks with my vocal cords and I'm not allowed to say

anything that isn't on the menu. Propelled by the usual inexorable dream logic the briefing continues.

"Billington has let it be known that he will be conducting an advance Dutch auction for the specimens he expects to raise from JENNIFER MORGUE Site Two. These are described in vague but exciting terms, as chthonic artifacts and applications. There is of course no mention of his expertise in operating Gravedust-type oneiromantic convolution engines, or of the presence of a deceased DEEP SEVEN in the vicinity.

"He is restricting bidding to authorized representatives of governments with seats at the G8, plus Brazil, China, and India. Sealed bids are solicited in advance of the operation, which will be honored once the retrieval is complete. This indirect pressure makes it difficult for us to stay out of the auction, while simultaneously rendering it nearly impossible for us to take direct action against him – he's very carefully played the bidders off against one another. Of rather more concern is who Billington *hasn't* invited to bid – namely BLUE HADES. As I mentioned in your earlier briefing, our immediate concern is the response of BLUE HADES to Billington's activities around the site, followed in turn by what Billington really intends to do with the raised artifacts.

"Regardless, your actual task remains, as briefed, to determine what Billington is planning and to stop him from doing anything that arouses BLUE HADES or DEEP SEVEN – especially anything likely to convince them that we're in violation of our treaty obligations. To supplement your cover you are officially designated as an authorized representative of Her Majesty's Government, to deliver our bid for the JENNIFER MORGUE Site Two artifacts. This is a genuine bid, although obviously we hope we won't be called upon to make good on it, and the terms are as follows: for an exclusive usage license as designated in schedule one to be appended to this document, hereinafter designated 'the contract' between the seller 'Ellis Billington' and associates, corporations, and other affiliates and the purchaser, the Government of the United Kingdom, the sum of two billion pounds sterling, to be paid . . ."

Angleton rattles on in dreary legalese for approximately three lifetimes. It'd be tedious at the best of times, but right now it's positively nightmarish; the plan has already run off the rails, and the worst thing of all is, I can't even yell at him. I'm committing this goddamn contract that we're never going to use to memory, seemingly at Angleton's posthypnotic command, but the shit has hit the fan and Ramona's a prisoner. I'd gnash my teeth if I was allowed to. I've got a feeling that Angleton's sneak strategy – use me to leak disinformation to the Black Chamber via Ramona, of course – is already blown, because I don't think Billington is serious about running an auction. If he was, would he be dicking around risking a murder investigation in order to push a line of cosmetics? And would he be kidnapping negotiators? This is all so out of whack that I can't figure it out. I've got a sick feeling that Angleton's scheme was toast before I even boarded the airbus in Paris: if nothing else, his bid is implausibly low given what's at stake.

Eventually the briefing lets go of me and I slide gratefully beneath the surface of a dreamless lake. I'm rocking from side to side on it, with the leisurely wobble of a howdah perched on an elephant's back. After a brief infinity of unconsciousness I become aware that my head is throbbing fiercely and my mouth feels like a family of rodents has set up a campsite, complete with latrine, on my tongue. And that I'm awake. *Oh no.* I twitch, taking stock. I'm lying on my back which is never the right place to be, breathing through my mouth, and—

"He's awake."

"Good. Howard, stop fooling around."

This time I groan aloud. My eyes feel like pickled onions and it takes a real effort to force them open. More facts flood in as my brain reboots. I'm lying on my back, fully dressed, on something like a padded bench or sofa. The voice I recognize: it's McMurray. The room's well-lit, and I notice that the padded surface beneath me is covered in beautifully finished fabric. The lights are tasteful and indirect, and the curving walls are paneled in old mahogany: the local police cells, it ain't. "Give me a second," I mumble.

"Sit up." He doesn't sound impatient; just sure of himself.

I force arms and legs that are heavy and warm from too-recent sleep to respond, swinging my legs round and sitting up at the same time. A wave of dizziness nearly pushes me right back down, but I get over it and rub my eyes, blinking. "What *is* this place?" I ask shakily. *And where's Ramona? Still trapped?*

McMurray sits down on the bench opposite me. Actually, it's a continuation of the one I was lying on – it snakes around the exterior of the trapezoid room, past out-tilting walls and a doorway in the middle of the only rectilinear wall in the cabin. It's a nice room except that the doorway is blocked by a gorilla in a uniform-like black jumpsuit and beret, plus mirrorshades. (Which is more than somewhat incongruous, in view of it being well past midnight.) The windows are small and oval with neatly decorated but very functional-looking metal covers hinged back from them, and there are drawers set in the base of the padded bench – obviously storage of some kind. The throbbing isn't in my head; it's coming from under the floor. Which can only mean one thing.

"Welcome aboard the *Mabuse*," he says, then shrugs apologetically. "I'm sorry about the way you were handed your boarding pass: Johanna isn't exactly Little Miss Subtlety, and I told her to make sure you didn't abscond. That would totally ruin the plot."

I rub my head and groan. "Did you have to – no, don't answer that, let me guess: it's a tradition or an old charter, something like that." I continue to rub my head. "Is there any chance of a glass of water? And a bathroom?" It's not just a barbiturate hangover – the martinis are extracting a vicious revenge. "If you're going to take me to see the big cheese shouldn't I freshen up a bit first?" *Please say yes*, I pray to whatever god of whimsy has got me in his grip, being hungover is bad enough without a beating on top of it.

For a moment I wonder if I've gone too far, but he gestures at the gorilla, who turns and opens the door and retreats down the narrow corridor a couple of paces. "The head's next door. You have five minutes."

He watches as I stumble to my feet. He nods, affably enough, and gestures at another door set next to the rec room or wherever the hell it is they'd put me in to sleep things off. I open the door and indeed find a washroom of sorts, barely bigger than an airliner's toilet but beautifully finished. I take a leak, gulp down half a pint or so of water using the plastic cup so helpfully provided, then spend about a minute sitting down and trying not to throw up. **Ramona, are you there?** If she is, I can't hear her. I take stock: my phone's missing, as is my neck-chain ward, my wristwatch, and my shoulder holster. The bow tie is dangling from my collar, but they weren't considerate enough to remove my uncomfortable toe-pinching shoes. I raise an eyebrow at the guy in the mirror and he pulls a mournful face and shrugs: no help there. So I wash my face, try to comb my hair with my fingertips, and go back outside to face the music.

The gorilla is waiting for me outside. McMurray stands in front of the closed door to the rec room. The gorilla beckons to me then turns and marches down the corridor, so I play nice and tag along, with McMurray taking up the rear. The corridor is punctuated by frequent watertight bulkheads with annoying lintels to step over, and there's a shortage of portholes to show where we are: someone's obviously done a first-rate coach-building job, but this ship wasn't built as a yacht and its new owner clearly places damage control ahead of aesthetics. We pass some doors, ascend a very steep staircase, and then I figure we're into Owner Territory because the metal decking gives way to teak parquet and hand-woven carpets, and up here they *have* widened the corridors to accommodate the fat-cats: or maybe it's just that they built the owner's quarters where they used to stash the Klub-N cruise missiles and the magazine for the forward 100mm gun turret.

Klub-N vertical launch cells are not small, and the owner's lounge is about three meters longer than my entire house. It appears to be wallpapered in cloth-of-gold, which for the most part is mercifully concealed behind ninety-centimeter Sony displays wearing priceless antique picture frames. Right now they're all switched off, or displaying a rolling screensaver depicting the TLA Corporation logo. The furniture's equally lacking in the taste department. There's a sofa that probably escaped from Versailles one jump ahead of the revolutionary fashion police, a bookcase full of self-help business titles (*A Defendant's Guide to the International Criminal Court*, *The Twelve-Step Sociopath*, *Globalization for Asset-Strippers*), and an antique sideboard that abjectly fails to put the rock into baroque. I find myself looking for a furtive cheap print of dogs playing poker or a sad-eyed clown – anything to break the monotony of the collision between bad taste and serious money.

Then I notice the Desk.

Desks are to executives what souped-up Mitsubishi Colts

with low-profile alloys, metal-flake paint jobs, and extra-loud, chrome-plated exhaust pipes are to chavs; they're a big swinging dick, the proxy they use to proclaim their sense of self-importance. If you want to understand an executive, you study his desk. Billington's Desk demands a capital letter. Like a medieval monarch's throne, it is designed to proclaim to the poor souls who are called before it: *the owner of this piece of furniture is above you*. Someday I'll write a text book about personality profiling through possessions; but for now let's just say this example is screaming "megalomaniac!" at me.

Billington may have an ego the size of an aircraft carrier but he's not so vain as to leave his desk empty (that would mean he was pretending to lead a life of leisure) or to cover it with meaningless gewgaws (indicative of clownish triviality). This is the desk of a *serious* executive. There's a functional-looking ("watch me work!") PC to one side, and a phone and a halogen desk light at the other. One of the other items dotting it gives me a nasty shock when I recognize the design inscribed on it: millions wouldn't, but the owner of this hunk of furniture is using a Belphegor-Mandelbrot Type Two containment matrix as a mouse mat, which makes him either a highly skilled adept or a suicidal maniac. Yup, that pretty much confirms the diagnosis. This is the desk of a diseased mind, hugely ambitious, prone to taking insanely dangerous risks. He's not ashamed of boasting about it — he clearly believes in better alpha-primate dominance displays through carpentry.

McMurray gestures me to halt on the carpet in front of the Desk. "Wait here, the boss will be along in a minute." He gestures at a skeletal contraption of chromed steel and thin, black leather that only Le Corbusier could have mistaken for a chair: "Have a seat."

I sit down gingerly, half-expecting steel restraints to flash out from concealed compartments and lock around my wrists. My head aches and I feel hot and shivery. I glance at McMurray, trying for casual rather than anxious. The Laundry field operations manual is notably short on advice for how to comport oneself when being held prisoner aboard a mad billionaire necromancer's yacht, other than the usual stern admonition to keep receipts for all expenses incurred in the line of duty. "Where's Ramona?" I ask.

"I don't remember saying you were free to ask questions." He stares at me from behind his steel-rimmed spectacles until icicles form on the back of my neck. "Ellis has a specific requirement for an individual of her . . . type. I'm a specialist in managing such entities." A pause. "While you remain entangled, she will be manageable. And as long as she remains manageable, there will be no need to dispose of her."

I swallow. My tongue is dry and I can hear my pulse in my ears. This wasn't supposed to happen; she was supposed to be back in the safe house, acting as a relay! McMurray nods at me knowingly. "Don't underestimate your own usefulness to us, Mr. Howard," he says. "You're not just a useful lever." There's a discreet buzz from his belt pager: "Mr. Billington is on his way now."

The door behind the Desk opens.

"Ah, Mr. B—Howard." Billington walks in and plants himself firmly down on the black carbon-fiber Aeron chair behind the Desk. From the set of his shoulders and the tiny smile playing around his lips he's in an expansive mood. "I'm so pleased you could be here this evening. I gather my wife's party wasn't entirely to your taste?"

I stare at him. He's an affable, self-satisfied bastard in a dinner jacket and for a moment I feel a nearly uncontrollable urge to punch him in the face. I manage to hold it in check: the gorilla behind me will ensure I'd only get one chance, and the consequences would hurt Ramona as much as they'd hurt me. Still, it's a tempting thought. "I have a bid for your auction," I say, very carefully keeping my face straight. "This abduction was unnecessary, and may cause my employers to reconsider their very generous offer."

Billington laughs. Actually, it's more of a titter, high-pitched and unnerving. "Come now, Mr. Howard! Do you really think I don't already know about your boss's paltry little two-billion-pound bait-worm? Please! I'm not stupid. I know all about you and your colleague Ms. Random, and the surveillance team in the safe house run by Jack Griffin. I even remember your boss, *James*, from back before he became quite so spectral and elevated. I know much more than you give me credit for." He pauses. "In fact, I know *everything*."

Whoops. If he's telling the truth, that would put a very bad complexion on things. "Then what am I doing here?" I ask, hoping like hell that he's bluffing. "I mean, if you're omnipotent and omniscient then just what is the point of abducting me — not to mention Ramona — and dragging us aboard your yacht?" (That's a guess about Ramona, but I don't see where else he might be keeping her.) "Don't tell me you haven't got better things to do with your time than gloat; you're trying to close a multi-billion-dollar auction, aren't you?" He just looks at me with those peculiar, slotted lizard-eyes and I have a sudden cold conviction that maybe making money is the last thing on his mind right now.

"You're here for several reasons," he says, quite agreeably. "Hair of the dog?" He raises an eyebrow, and the gorilla hurries over to the sideboard.

"I wouldn't mind a glass of water," I confess.

"Hah." He nods to himself. "The archetype hasn't taken full effect yet, I see."

"Which archetype?"

McMurray clears his throat. "Boss, do I need to know this?"

Billington casts him a fish-eyed stare: "No, I don't think you do. Quick thinking."

"I'll just go and check in on Ramona then, shall I? Then I'll go polish the binnacle and check for frigging in the rigging or something." McMurray slithers out through the door at high speed. Billington nods thoughtfully.

"He's a smart subordinate." He raises an eyebrow at me. "That's half the problem, you know."

"Half what problem?"

"The problem of running a tight ship." The gorilla hands Billington a glass of whisky, then plants a glass full of mineral water in front of me before returning to his position by the door. "If they're smart enough to be useful they get ideas about making themselves indispensable – ideas about getting above their station, as you Brits would put it. If they're too dumb to be useful they're a drain on your management time. All corporations are an economy of attention, from the top down. You should take McMurray as a role model, Mr. Howard, if you ever make it back to your petty little civil service cubicle farm. He's a consummate senior field agent and a huge asset to his employers. No manager in their right mind would *ever* terminate him, but because he likes fieldwork he doesn't spend enough time in the office to get a leg up the promotion ladder. And he knows it." He falls silent. I take advantage of the break in his spiel to take a mouthful of water. "That's why I headhunted him away from the Black Chamber," Billington adds.

When I finish coughing, he looks at me thoughtfully. "You strike me as being a reasonably adaptable, intelligent young man. It's really a shame you're working for the public sector. Are you sure I can't bribe *you?* How would a million bucks in a numbered account in the Caymans suit you?"

"Get lost." I struggle to maintain my composure.

"If it's just that silly little warrant card you guys carry, we can do something about it," he adds slyly.

Ouch. That's a low blow. I take a deep breath: "I'm sure you can, but——"

He snorts. And looks amused. "It's to be expected. They wouldn't have sent you if they thought you had an easy price. It's not just money I can offer, Mr. Howard. You're used to working for an organization that is deliberately structured to stifle innovation and obstruct stakeholder-led change. My requirements are a bit, shall we say, different. A smart, talented, hard-working man – especially a morally flexible one – can go far. How would you like to come on board as deputy vice-president for intelligence, Europe, Middle East, and Africa division? A learning sinecure, initially, but with your experience and background in one of the world's leading occult espionage organizations I'm sure you'd make your mark soon enough."

I give it a moment's thought, long enough to realize that he's right – and that I'm not going to take the offer. He's offering me crumbs from the rich man's table, and not even bothering to find out in advance if that's the sort of diet I enjoy. Which means he's doing me the compliment of not taking the prospect of my defection seriously, which means he considers me to be a reliable agent. And now I stop to think about it, I realize to my surprise that I *am*. I may not be happy about the circumstances under which I took the oath, and I may gripe and moan about the pay and conditions, but there's a big difference between pissing and moaning and seriously contemplating the betrayal of everything I want to preserve. Even if I've only just come to realize it.

"I'm not for sale, Ellis. Not for any price you can pay, anyway. What's this archetype business?"

He nods minutely, examining me as if I've just passed

some sort of important test. "I was getting to that." He rotates his chair until he's half-facing the big monitor off to my right. He stabs at the mouse mat with one finger and I wince, but instead of fat purple sparks and a hideous soul-sucking manifestation, it simply wakes up his Windows box. (Not that there's much difference.) For a moment I almost begin to relax, but then I recognize what he's calling up and my stomach flip-flops in abject horror.

"I do everything in PowerPoint, you know." Billington grins, an expression which I'm sure is intended to be impish but that comes across to his intended victim — me — as just plain vicious. "I had to have my staff write some extra plugins to make it do everything I need, but, ah, here we are . . ."

He rapidly flips through a stack of tediously bulleted talking points until he wipes into a screen that's mercifully photographic in nature. It's a factory, lots of workers in gowns and masks gathered around worktops and stainless steel equipment positioned next to a series of metal vats.

"Eileen's Hangzhou factory, where our Pale Grace™ Skin Hydromax® range of products are made. As you probably already figured out, we apply a transference-contagion glamour to the particulate binding agent in the foundation powder, maintained by brute force from our headquarters operation in Milan, Italy. Unlike most of the cosmetics on the market, it really *does* render the wrinkles invisible. The ingredients are a bit of a pain, but she's got that well in hand; instead of needing an endless supply of young women just to keep one old bat pretty we can make do with only about ten parts per million of maid's blood in the mix. It's just one of the wonders of modern stem cell technology. Shame we can't find a replacement for the stress prostaglandins, but those are the breaks."

He clicks his mouse. "Here's the other end of the

operation." It's a room full of skinny, suntanned guys in short-sleeved shirts hunched over cheap PCs, row upon row of them: "My floating offshore programmer ranch, the SS *Hopper*. You've probably read about it, haven't you? Instead of offshoring to Bangalore, I bought an old liner, wired it, and flew in a number of Indian programmers to live on board. It stays outside the coastal limit and with satellite uplinks it might as well be in downtown Miami. Only they're not, um, actually programming anything. Instead, they're monitoring the surveillance take from the mascara. Because the Pale Grace™ Bright Eyes® products don't just link into the transference-contagion glamour, they contain particles nano-engraved with an Icon of Bhaal-She'vra that backdoors them into my surveillance grid. That's actually the main product of my sixty-nanometer fab line these days by the way, not the bespoke microprocessors everyone thinks it makes. It's a very useful similarity hack – anything the wearer can see or hear, my monitors can pick up, and we've got flexible batch manufacturing protocols that ensure every single cosmetics product is uniquely coded so we can tell them apart. It's almost embarrassing how much intelligence you can gather from this sweep, especially as Eileen's affiliates are running a loyalty scheme that encourages users to register their identity with us at time of sale for free samples, so that we know who they are."

I'm boggling already. "Are you telling me you've turned your cosmetics company into some kind of occult ubiquitous surveillance operation? Is that what this is?"

"Yup, that's about the size of it." Billington nods smugly. "Of course, it's expensive – but we manage to just about break even on a twenty buck tube of mascara, so it works out all right in the end. And it's less obvious than using several million zombie seabirds." He clears his throat. "Anyway, that's by way of demonstrating to you that you can run, but you can't hide. Now, to explain why you *shouldn't* run . . ."

He flicks to the next slide, and it's not a photograph, it's a live surveillance take from a camera somewhere. I'm pretty sure it's aboard this very ship. It's Ramona, of course. She's sprawling across a double bed in a stateroom, out cold. "Here's Ms. Random. I figure you know by now that you don't get to talk to her without my say-so. You need to know three things about her. Firstly, if I've got *you*, I can make her do anything I want – and vice versa. You've figured that out? Excellent."

He pauses for a few seconds while I force myself to stop trying to break the arms of my chair. "There's no need for that, Mr. Howard. No harm will come to either of you unless you force my hand. You're here because I need her to do a little job for me, one relating to the recovery of the alien artifact – and I need her willing cooperation. So that's item two out of the way. Item three, I gather you've met Mr. McMurray? Good. It might interest you to know that he's a specialist in controlling entities like Ramona's succubus, or Johanna's necrophage. I could threaten to hurt you if she tries to resist, but I always find that positive incentivization works much better than the big stick on employees: so I'm going to offer her a deal. If you and Ms. Random cooperate fully, I'll have Mr. McMurray see if he can permanently separate her from her little helper. As he was part of the team who invoked and bound it to her in the first place . . . well, what do you think she'll say to that?"

I pick up my water glass and drain it, hoping for something, anything, to occur to me that'll show me a way out. Billington may not have tried to figure out *my* price, but I'm pretty sure he's got Ramona's. "What's the job?"

Billington prods at his fancy remote again and another screen comes to life: a view of a huge metal chamber, something like a factory floor – only the floor itself is covered in black water. A moment's confusion, then it springs into focus for me. "Isn't that the *Glomar Explorer*?"

"It's now the *TLA Explorer*, but yes, well-spotted, Mr. Howard."

I focus on the pipe that pierces the heart of the pool of water. There's something big and indistinct lurking just under the surface down there, impaled on the end of the drill string. "What's that?"

"Can't you guess? It's the TMB-2, a clone of the original Hughes Mining Barge 1, equipped with updated telemetry and new materials so that pressure-induced brittleness in the grab cantilever arms won't stop it from working this time."

"But you *know* the Deep Ones won't let you retrieve—"

"Really?" His grin widens.

"But!" My head's spinning. I know about the original HMB-1, Operation JENNIFER, the BLUE HADES defense system that nearly dragged the mother ship down. "You said this was about Ramona?"

"She's one of the in-laws," Billington explains cheerfully. "She's got the Innsmouth look, you know? She tastes right to their minions, the abyssal polyps. You didn't think the Deep Ones guarded every inch of their territory in person, did you? The polyps are subsentient just like your burglar alarm. They work by biochemical tracers, discriminating self from other." He picks up his whisky. "I need her to ride the grab down and keep an eye on it while it locks onto the target. If the defenders of the deep smell Old One in the water they'll stay cowering in their burrows in the abyssal mud. What do you say to that?"

"It's an interesting theory," I admit, which is true because I don't know one way or the other whether it'll work.

"It's more than a theory. I sank a lot of money into arranging for the Black Chamber to send her, boy. Her folk aren't so numerous and most of them would die rather than let themselves be turned to such a purpose. She's been tamed, which is unusual, and you've got a handle on her, and I've got you. So, I'll make you a new offer. Convince her to ride the barge for me willingly, and I'll have McMurray free her from her curse. Convince her to ride the barge and I won't even have to threaten you. How about it?"

He's backed me into a corner, I realize. And not just with menaces; the thing is, he *has* found Ramona's price. And having been inside her skull, even if only a bit, I'm not sure I can criticize her. Or easily stand in her way, if she really wants to do it. Threats of torture are redundant — just forcing her to go on living in her current state is torment enough. Plus, if she doesn't cooperate, Billington might turn nasty and take it out of my hide. Which reminds me of something else . . . .

"Why me?" I finally burst out. "I mean, if you needed her, surely you don't specifically need *me* to control her? I'm nothing to you. You've got McMurray. You already know about my government's offer. What am I doing here? Why don't you just do the disentangling ritual and dump me overboard?"

Billington's smile widens, disturbingly: "Ah, but that's where you're wrong, Mr. Howard. Your presence *here* prevents anyone else — like the US Navy, for example — from turning up and spoiling my scheme. Which I realized would be a likely response to my current operation right at the outset, and took steps to prevent, in the form of a monumentally expensive and rather intricate destiny-entanglement geas that compels the participants to adopt certain archetypal roles that have been gathering their strength from hundreds of millions of believers over nearly fifty years. The geas doesn't mess with causality directly, but it does ensure that the likelihood of events that mesh with its destiny model are raised, while other avenues become less . . . probable. Going against the geas is hard; agents get run over by taxis, aircraft suffer inexplicable mechanical failures, that sort of thing. Now you've jumped through all the hoops in the geas and in so doing massively reinforced it. You've taken on the role of the heroic adversary. Which in turn means that *nobody else* is allowed to play the hero around here. And in accordance with another aspect of the geas, you're in my power for the time being and you're going to stay there until a virtuous woman turns up to release you. Got that?"

My head's spinning. What the hell is he on about? And where am I going to find a virtuous woman on board a mad billionaire's yacht at three in the morning as we steam towards the Bermuda Triangle? "What about the auction?" I ask plaintively.

Billington laughs raucously. "Oh, Mr. Howard! The auction was only ever a blind, to make your superiors believe I could be bought and sold!" He leans forwards across the Desk, and his eyebrows furrow like thunderclouds: "What use do you think I have for mere gigabucks? This is the high-stakes table." He looks past my shoulder, towards the gorilla. "Take him back to his room and lock him in until morning. We'll continue this conversation over breakfast." The gorilla stomps over and lays a beefy hand on my shoulder. "When I have JENNIFER MORGUE they'll do anything I want," he mutters, and my skin crawls because I don't think he's talking to me anymore. "Anything at all. They'll *have* to listen to me once I own the planet."

The gorilla herds me back down a short flight of steps and onto a passage that sports a row of mahogany-paneled doors like a very exclusive hotel. He opens one of them and gestures me inside. I briefly consider trying to take him, but realize it won't work: they've got Ramona and they've got the surveillance network from Hell and I'm on a ship that's already out of sight of land. I'll only get one chance, at most, and I'd better make sure I don't blow it. So I go inside without a struggle, and look around tiredly as he turns the key in the lock.

Being locked in one of Billington's guest rooms is a comfortable step up from a police cell. It's aboard ship so it's smaller than a five-star hotel suite, but that's about the only way it suffers by comparison. The bed's a double, the carpet is luxuriously thick, there's a porthole (non-opening), a wet bar, and a big flat-screen TV, a shelf next to it holds a handful of paperbacks and a row of DVDs. I assume I'm supposed to drink myself comatose while watching cheesy spy thrillers. The desk (small, guest-room-sized) opposite the bed shows raw patches where they must have yanked out a PC earlier — it's a damn shame, but Billington's people are smart enough not to leave a computer where I can get my hands on it.

"Shit," I mutter, then sit down in the sinfully padded leather recliner next to the wet bar. Surrender has seldom been such an attractive prospect. I massage my head. Looking out the porthole there's nothing but an expanse of night-black sea, overlooked by stars. I yawn. Whatever that bitch Johanna used to put my lights out was fast-acting; it can't be much past three in the morning. And I'm still tired, now that I think about it. I look around the room and there's nothing particularly obvious in the way of escape routes. Plus, they're probably watching me, via a peephole in the door if they've got any sense. "What a mess."

You can say that again, monkey-boy.

I flinch, then force myself to relax. Trying to show no sign of anything in particular, I open my inner ear again. **Ramona?**

No, I'm the fucking tooth fairy. Have you seen my pliers lying around? There's a couple of folks here in line for some root-canal surgery when I get free.

The wash of relief is visceral; if I was standing I'd probably collapse on the spot. It's a good thing I found the recliner first **You're all right?**

She snorts. **For what it's worth.** I can feel something itchy where my eyes can't see. Focusing on it, I see the inside of another room, much like this one. She's kicked off her heels and is pacing the floor restlessly, examining everything, looking for an exit.

They've wired the walls. There's a shielding graph in the floor but they must have switched it off for the time being to let us talk. I don't think they can overhear us, but they can stop us any time they want.

Nice of them——

To let us know they've got us where they want us? Don't be silly.

How'd they catch you? I ask, after an uncomfortable pause.

It's probably the oldest trick in the book. She stops pacing. **I was looking for Eileen's inner circle when I ran into a lure, a daemon disguised as someone I know professionally – a real class act, I could have sworn it was really him. He suckered me into an upstairs meeting room and before I knew what was happening they had me in a summoning lock. Which should be impossible unless they've got the original keys the Contracts Department used when they enslaved me, yet they did it. So I guess it's not impossible after all.**

I stare at the blank TV set. **Not if it was the real thing. His name's McMurray, isn't it?**

I can taste her shock. **How the *fuck* did you know that?** she demands.

Because he took me for my entire expenses tab at baccarat, I confess. **He's got a new employer with very deep pockets. Has Billington tried to buy you yet?**

She starts pacing again. **No, and he won't. Where he comes from there are different rules for people like me. You're employable. You're human. I'm . . .** I can feel her working her jaws, as if she's about to spit: **Let's just say, there are minorities it's still okay to shit on.**

I wince. **He led me to believe that . . . well, if you don't think he's going to try to buy you, what's he got on you? Besides the obvious.**

She tenses. **He's got you. That's bad enough, in case you hadn't figured it out.**

Whoops. **He knows all about your curse.** The idea begins to sink in. **Tell me about McMurray. You worked with him, right? In exactly what capacity?**

He made me. Her voice is chilly enough to liquefy nitrogen. **I'd rather not discuss it.**

Sorry, but it's relevant. I'm still trying to work out what's going on. How Billington turned him. I wonder what the key was, if it's just money, like Billington said, or if there's something else we can use . . .

Ramona snorts. **Don't waste your time. When I get out of here I'm going to kick his ass.**

I pause. **I think you may be wrong about Billington. I think he has every intention of trying to buy you. He's got your heart's desire in a box, if you'll just turn a trick for him.**

You English guys, you've got such a way with words! Look, I don't bribe, okay? It's not a matter of being too honest, it's just not possible. Suppose, for the sake of argument, I go down for him and he gives me whatever it is you're hinting at in return. What happens *then*? Has that occurred to *you?* I'd be dead meat, Bob. No way can he let me walk.

Not so fast. I mean, I think he's nuts. But I think he believes that if he succeeds there won't *be* an 'after,' in the conventional sense; he'll be home clean and dry, immune to any consequences. I put the offer Angleton – my boss – gave me on the table, and Billington just laughed at me! He laughed off about five billion dollars at today's exchange rate. He's not in this for the money, he's in it because he thinks he's going to come out of it owning the entire planet.

She snorts theatrically. **How boring, just another billionaire necromancer cruising the Caribbean in his thinly disguised guided missile destroyer, plotting total world domination.**

I shudder. **You think you're joking? He monologued at me. With *PowerPoint*.**

He *what*? And you're still sane? Obviously I underestimated you.

I shake my head. **I didn't have much choice. I figure we're stuck here for the duration. Or at least until he gets wherever he's taking us.**

The other ship.

Yeah, there's that. I stand up and walk over to the sliding door at the far side of the room. The bathroom beyond it is small but perfectly formed. There's no porthole, though.

If we could figure out a way to spring you, could you do your invisibility thing?

The question takes me by surprise. **Not sure. Damn it, they took my Treo. That would make it a whole lot easier. Plus, he's got an occult surveillance service that's going to be murder to evade. You don't use Eileen's make-up, do you? Especially not the mascara?**

Do I look like a dumb blonde? she snorts. **Pale Grace™ is for department store sales clerks and middle-management types trying to glam up their suits.**

**Good for you, because he's got a contagious proximity-awareness binding mixed in with it – that's what he married

Eileen for, that's why he bankrolled her business. The god-damn seagulls weren't how he was watching us, they were just cover: it was all the thirty-something tourist women. *All* of them, at least the ones who take the free samples down at the promenade. And I reckon if he's got any sense, all of the crew on this boat will be using it, or something similar.**

At least they'll all have beautiful complexions. She pauses. **So what does he want with us? Why are we still alive?**

You're alive because he wants you to do a job. *Me* . . . probably because he needs someone to monologue at. He said something about a geas, but I'm not sure what he meant. And we're still entangled, so I guess . . .

I stop. While I was wibbling, Ramona realized some-thing. **You're right, it *is* the geas,** she says sharply. **Which means nothing's going to happen until we arrive. So go to sleep, Bob. You're going to need all the sleep you can get before tomorrow.**

But—

Lights out. And with that, she pushes me out of her head, blocking me off from that sudden flash of understand-ing.

12: POWER
BREAKFAST

I AWAKEN IN A STRANGE BED THAT FEELS AS IF it's vibrating slightly, with a head like thunder, and muscles I didn't know I had aching in my arms and legs. The thin light of dawn is pouring in through a porthole. Sleep held me down and tried to drown me, but waking comes as fast as a bucket of seawater in the face: *I'm on Billington's yacht!*

I roll out of bed and use the bathroom. My eyes are bloodshot and I could strip paint with my chin, but I'm not even remotely sleepy. *I'm out of touch with Control!* That fact is sitting on my shoulder, screaming in my ear with a megaphone; forget little organizational tics like Griffin, I need to talk to Angleton and I need to talk to him *right now*, if not about six hours ago, and especially before the upcoming power breakfast. Last night's sense of apathetic passivity is a million miles away, so alien that I frown at myself in the mirror: *How the fuck could I do that?* It's not like me at all!

It's got to be something to do with this geas that Billington's running on me, the one Ramona refuses to explain in words of one syllable. I can't trust my own reflexes. Which sucks mightily. Billington is racing headlong towards a full-scale sanity excursion, he's penetrated the Black

Chamber, the auction for JENNIFER MORGUE is a decoy, and I'm in the shit just about up to my eyebrows – and not a snorkel in sight.

"Right," I mutter to myself. I look at my clothes from last night in distaste. "Let's see." I pull on my trousers and shirt, then pause. *Gadgets*. Pinky was talking about . . . *toys*. I snort. I pick up the bow tie, meaning to flick it across the room, then notice something lumpy in either end. That'd be the USB drives with the dog-fucker kit, right? "Ludicrous," I mutter, and roll the thing up. It'd be bloody handy if they'd locked me in a cell with a computer plugged into Billington's shipboard network, but they're not that stupid. I stare longingly at the bare chunk of space on the desktop. There may be a keyboard stitched into the lining of my cummerbund, but without a machine to plug it into it's about as much use as a chocolate hacksaw.

With nothing to do but wait for breakfast, I sit down next to the flat-screen TV and glance through the titles on the shelf. There's a bunch of paperback thrillers with titles familiar from the movie series: *Thunderball*, *On Her Majesty's Secret Service*. Next to them. a bunch of DVDs. It's all the same goddamn series about the most famous non-existent spy in history. Whoever furnished this room had a James Bond fixation. I sigh, and pick up the remote, thinking maybe I can watch a mindless movie for a while. Then the screen comes on, showing a familiar menu on a blue background and I stare at it, transfixed, like a yokel who's never seen a television before.

Because it's not a TV. It's a flat-screen PC running Windows XP Media Center Edition.

They can't be that dumb. It's got to be a trap, I gibber to myself. Not even the clueless cannon-fodder-in-jumpsuits who staff any one of the movies on the shelf would be *that* dumb!

Or would they? I mean, they've got me locked in a broom closet on the bastard's yacht and everything else is conforming to cliché, so why the hell not?

I randomly pull one of the DVDs down from the shelf — it's *Thunderball*, which seems appropriate although this yacht makes the *Disco Volante* look like a bath toy — and use it as an excuse to run my fingers around the rim of the TV. There's a slot for discs, and then, just below it, the giveaway: two small notches for USB plugs.

Bingo. Okay, they weren't *totally* stupid. They took the keyboard and mouse and locked the PC down in kiosk mode with nothing but a TV remote for access. With no administrator password and no keyboard and probably no network connection they figured it was safe. *You figured wrong*, I admonish them. I push the disc eject button and a tray pops out, and I stick the movie in. Returning to my chair I pick up the cummerbund and bow tie and drop them on the desk in front of the TV. *What else? Oh* . . . I pull on my jacket, frown, then casually take the pen from my inside pocket and toss it on the desk. Finally I sit down and spend the next five minutes doing the obvious thing in the most obvious way imaginable, just in case they're watching.

I'm about ten minutes into the "Making of . . ." documentary feature when suddenly the door opens. "Mr. Howard? You're wanted upstairs for a breakfast meeting."

I turn round then stand up slowly. The guard stares at me impassively from behind his mirrored aviator shades. The uniform hereabouts tends towards black — black beret, black tunic, black boots — and so do the guns: he's not actually pointing his Glock at me right now but he could bring it up and nail me to the bulkhead faster than I could cover the distance between us.

"Okay," I say, and pause, staring at the weapon. "Are you sure that's entirely safe?"

He doesn't smile: "Don't push your luck."

I slowly move towards him and he steps back smartly into the corridor before gesturing me to walk ahead of him. He's not alone, and his partner's carrying a cut-down Steyr submachine gun with so many weird sensors bolted to the barrel that it looks like a portable spy satellite.

"How much is he paying you?" I ask casually, as we reach a staircase leading back up to owner territory.

Beret Number One grunts. "We got a really good benefits package." Pause. "Better than the Marine Corps."

"And stock options," adds the other joker. "Don't forget the stock options. How many other dot-coms offer stock options for gun-toting minions?"

"You can't afford us," his partner says casually. "Not after the IPO, anyway."

I can tell when they're trying to fuck with my head; I shut up. At the top of the stairs I glance over my shoulder. "Door on the left," says Beret Number One. "Go on, he won't bite your head off."

"Unless you make him eat his hash browns cold," adds Beret Number Two.

I open the door. On the other side of it is a large, exquisitely panelled dining room. The table in the middle of the room is currently set for breakfast and I can smell frying bacon and eggs and toast and fresh coffee. My stomach tries to climb my throat and chow down on my sinuses: I am *hungry*. Which would be great except I'm simultaneously exposed to an appetite-suppressing sight: two stewards, the Billingtons, and their special breakfast guest, Ramona.

"Ah, Mr. Howard. Would you care for a seat?" Ellis smiles broadly. Today he's wearing one of those odd collarless Nehru suits that seem to be *de rigueur* for villains in bad techno-thrillers — but at least he hasn't shaved his head and acquired a monocle or a dueling scar. Eileen Billington is a violent contrast in her cerise business suit with shoulder pads sized for an American football quarterback. She grimaces at me like I'm something her cat's dragged in, then goes back to nibbling at her butter croissant as if she's had her stomach stapled.

I glance at Ramona as I step towards the table, and we make eye contact briefly. Someone's raided her hotel room for her luggage – she's swapped last night's gown for casuals and a freshly scrubbed girl-next-door look. "Is that coffee?" I ask, nodding towards the pot.

"Jamaican Blue Mountain." Billington smiles thinly. "And yes, you may have some. I prefer not to conduct interviews while the subjects are comatose."

The steward pours me a cup of coffee as I sit down, and I try hard not to be obvious about how desperate I am for the stuff. (Another couple of hours without it and the merciless headache would be setting in, visited on me by my caffiend in retaliation for withdrawal of his drug.) As I take the first mouthful something brushes up against my ankle. I manage to control my knee-jerk reflex; it must be the cat, right?

The coffee is as good as you'd expect from a billionaire's buffet. "I needed that," I admit. "But I'm still somewhat perplexed as to why you want me here at all." (*Although it beats the hell out of the alternatives*, I don't say.)

"I'd have thought that was perfectly obvious." Billington grins, with the boyish charm of a boardroom bandit whose charisma is his most potent weapon. "You're here because you're both young, intelligent, active professionals with good prospects. It's so hard to get the help these days—" he nods at Eileen, who is sitting at the opposite end of the table, ignoring us by staring into inner space "—and I've found that interviewing candidates in person is a remarkably good way of avoiding subsequent disappointments. Human resources will only get you so far, after all."

I notice that Ramona is watching Eileen. "What's up with her?" I ask.

"Oh, her mind wanders." Billington picks up his knife and fork and slices into a sausage. "Mostly all over her manufacturing sites; remote viewing is a marvelous management tool, don't you think?" The sausage bleeds juice across his plate. I suddenly realize there are no hash browns or tomatoes or mushrooms or anything like that in front of him – it's wall-to-wall dead animal flesh. "You should try it sometime."

Ramona looks me in the eye. "He told me what he wants me to do, Bob."

I raise an eyebrow. "What, ride the grab down to the abyssal plain . . .?"

"With you providing a running commentary," Billington slides in unctuously. "After all, your current unfortunate state has certain transient advantages, does it not?" He smiles.

"He also told me what he was offering." She looks away, distraught. "I'm sorry, Bob. You were right."

"You——" I stop. **You're going to trust him?** I ask via our private channel.

It's not just the, the binding to my aspect, she says, tongue-tied as she hunts for words. **If I do this for him, he makes McMurray set me free. What alternative do I have?**

Billington's been watching us in silence for the past short while. Now he interrupts, in my direction: "If I may explain?" He nods at Ramona. "You have a simple choice. Cooperate and I will have one of my associates perform the rite of disentanglement. You two will be free of each other forever if you so choose, *and* free of Ms. Random's daemon. You'll both live happily ever after, aside for a period of a few weeks during which you will be guests with limited freedom of movement, while I complete my current project. After it is finished, I can promise you there will be no reprisals from your employers. Nothing can possibly go wrong. You see, I don't need to be nasty: it's a win-win situation all round."

I lick my dry lips. "What if I don't want to cooperate?"

Billington shrugs. "Then you don't run my errand, and I don't pay you for it." He spears a strip of bacon, saws it in half, and raises it to his teeth. "Business is business, Mr. Howard."

I flinch as if someone's walked over my grave. He's making me an offer I can't refuse, disguising a threat of lethal violence as passive inaction. All he has to do to threaten us is let the nature of our entanglement take its course. I flash back to the yawning horror hiding behind Ramona's soul, the dead weight of Marc's body lying on top of her, suffocating and squeezing the breath from her body. Lock her up in her cabin for a few days and *what will she eat?* The thing inside her needs to feed. I have a sudden, disquieting vision: Ramona and myself, blurring at the edges, one confused mind in two bodies locked in separate cells, stalked by the dark side of our hybrid soul as the Other works itself up into an orgiastic fever that can only be satisfied by swallowing our minds—

I'm not giving up, I tell her silently, then nod at Billington. "I get the picture. Business is business; I'll cooperate."

"Excellent. Or jolly good, as I believe you English would say." He smiles in evident delight as he spears the other half of the strip of bacon and dangles it at knee level. A white streak blurs out of the shadows under the table and snaps the bacon right off his fork.

"Ah, Fluffy. *There* you are!" Billington reaches down and picks up the large, white cat, who turns his head and stares at me with sky-blue eyes that are disturbingly human. "I believe it's about time you were introduced. Say hello to Mr. Howard, Fluffy."

Fluffy stares at me like I'm an oversized mouse, then hisses charmlessly.

Billington grins at me from behind six kilos of annoyed cat. "Fluffy is what this is *really* about, Mr. Howard. I'm only doing this to keep him in kitty kibble, after all."

"Kitty kibble?" I shake my head. Fluffy is wearing a diamond collar that belongs in the Tower of London with a platoon of Beefeaters standing guard over it. "I for one welcome our new feline overlords." I tip the cat an ironic nod.

"I thought you could cover the cat-food bill out of the petty cash?" asks Ramona.

"Fluffy has *very* expensive tastes." Billington dotes on the wretched animal, which has calmed down slightly and is permitting him to scratch it behind the ears.

Eileen chooses this particularly surreal moment to quiver as if electrocuted, then she shakes her head, yawns, and looks about. "Have I missed anything?" she asks querulously.

"Not a lot, dear." Her husband regards her fondly. *Breakfast with the Hitlers*, I think, glancing between them. "Any news?"

"Ach." Eileen hunches like a vulture when she's aware. "Everything is in order, the central business groups advance on all fronts, nothing to report today." She glances at me sharply, then at Ramona. "I think we ought to continue this in the office, though. Flapping ears and all that."

Billington glances down at the table spread before him. I hastily refill my coffee cup before he looks up. "All right." He nods, then stands up abruptly — still holding Fluffy — and nods at me, then at Ramona. "Feel free to finish up," he says curtly. "Then you may return to your quarters. It won't be long now."

He and Eileen stalk out of the dining room via a door at the back, leaving me alone with Ramona, the remains of breakfast, and the disturbing sense that I've somehow strayed onto loose gravel at the edge of a precipice, and it may be too late to turn back and reach safe ground.

In the end, pragmatism wins: when you're being held prisoner you never know where the next power breakfast is coming from, so I grab some slices of toast and a plate full of other munchies. Ramona sits hunched in her chair, looking out the porthole above the sideboard. Misery and depression is coming off her in black, stultifying waves.

We've not failed yet,* I tell her silently, my mouth full of hash browns. **As long as we can reestablish communications with Control we can get back on top of the situation.**

You think? She holds out her coffee cup and the steward, who's still waiting on us, fills it up. **What do you think they'll do if we tell them what's really going on? Give us time to get off the ship before they start shooting?**

She takes a mouthful of coffee and puts her cup down. I can feel it scalding her tongue, too hot to swallow: nevertheless, she gulps it down. I wince at the sudden paralyzing heartburn.

We'll just have to stop him ourselves, then, I say, trying to encourage her.

Whatever. It doesn't work that way, Bob.

What doesn't?

The geas. She stands up then smiles at the steward. "If you don't mind?" she says.

The steward stands aside. There's nobody human home behind his eyes; I sidle past him with my back to the wall. Ramona opens the side door beside the staircase. There's a short passage with several doors opening off it. "I've got something to show you," she tells me.

Huh? Since when does Ramona have the run of Billington's yacht? I follow her slowly, trying to worry out what's going on.

"In here." She opens a door. "Don't worry about the guards they're either down below or up on the superstructure — this is the owner's accommodation area and they're not needed as long as we stay in it. This is the grand lounge."

The lounge is surprisingly spacious. There are molded leather-topped benches all around the walls, and bookcases and glass cabinets. In the middle of the floor is something that might have been a pool table once, before a monomaniacal model maker repurposed it as his display cabinet.

"What the hell is it?" I lean closer. On one side are two model ships, one being the *Explorer*, which I recognize from the huge drilling derrick; but the center of the table is occupied by a bizarre diorama: old dog-eared hardback novels and a worn-looking automatic pistol, piled on top of a reel of film and a map of the Caribbean. Something else: a set of fine wires tracing out — "Shit. That's a Vulpis-Tesla array. And that box must be a — is that a Mod-60 Gravedust board it's plugged into? Summoning up the spirits of the dead. What the hell?"

There's a GI Joe doll in evening dress, clutching a pistol. It's wired up to the summoning grid by its plastic privates. On either side of it stand two Barbies in ball gowns, one black, one white. Behind them lurks another GI Joe, this time hacked so that he's bald and bearded, in something that looks like *Wehrmacht* dress grays.

All at once, I get the picture.

"It's the core of his coercion geas, isn't it? It's a destiny-entanglement conjuration, on a bigger scale. James Bond, channelling the ghost of Ian Fleming as scriptwriter . . . Jesus." I glance across the table at Ramona. She looks flushed and apprehensive.

"Yes, James——" She bites her lip. "Sorry, monkey-boy. It's too strong in here, isn't it?"

I stare at her through narrowed eyes. Oh yes, I'm

beginning to get it. I'm half-tempted to shoot the bint now, then stuff her through the porthole before the bad guys get their mileage out of her, but I need all the friends I can get right now, and until I'm sure she's gone over to SPECTRE I can't afford to—

What. The. Fuck?

I blink rapidly. "Is there somewhere we can go that's not quite so . . . .?"

"Yeah. Next door."

Next door is the library or smoking room or whatever the hell it's called. My head stops swimming as soon as we get a wall between us and that diorama from Hell. "That was bad. What's the big idea? Why does Billington want to turn me into James Bond?"

Ramona slumps into an overstuffed chair. "It's not about you, Bob, it's all about *plot*. The way the geas works, he's set himself up as the evil villain in this humongous destiny-entanglement spell targeted against every intelligence agency and government on the planet. The end state for this conjuration is that the hero – which means whoever's being ridden by the Bond archetype – comes and kills the villain, destroys his secret floating headquarters, stymies his scheme, and gets the girl. But Billington's not stupid. He may be riding the Villain archetype but he's in control of the geas and he's got a good sense of timing. Before the Hero archetype gets to resolve the terminal crisis, he ends up in the villain's grasp under circumstances such that *nobody else* is positioned to deal with the villain's plan. Ellis figures that he can short the geas out before it goes terminal and makes the Bond figure kill him. At which point Billington will be left sitting in an unassailable position since the *only* agent on the planet who's able to stop him wakes up and suddenly remembers that he's not James Bond."

I consider this for a full minute. "Whoops."

"That's how we screwed up," she says bleakly. "Billington had a handle on me all along. *I'm* his handle on *you*, and *you're* his handle on Angleton. He's stacked us up like a row of dominos."

I take a deep breath. "What happens if I go next door and smash the diorama?"

"The signal strength—" She shakes her head. "You noticed how fast it drops off? If you're close enough to smash it the backwash will kill you, but it'll probably leave Billington alive. If we could get word out about what's going on it might be worth trying, but nobody's close enough to do anything right now – so we're back to square one. It really has to be shut down in good order, the same way it was set up, and I'd guess that's why Billington's brought that fucker Pat aboard."

"Hang on," I say slowly. "Griffin was sure there was a shit-hot Black Chamber assassin in town this week. Some guy code named Charlie Victor. Could he do anything about Billington if we cleared a path?"

"Bob, Bob. *I'm* Charlie Victor." She looks at me with the sort of sympathetic expression usually reserved for terminal cases.

I consider this for a moment. Then an atavistic reflex kicks in and I snap my fingers. "Then you must be, um . . . you're the glamorous female assassin from a rival organization, right? Like Major Amasova in the film version of *The Spy Who Loved Me*, or Jinx in *Die Another Day*. Does that mean you're the Good Bond Babe archetype or the Bad Bond Babe?"

"Well, I don't think I'm bad—" She's looking at me oddly. "What the hell are you talking about?"

"There are usually two Babes in every Bond movie," I say slowly. *Shit, she isn't British, is she?* I keep forgetting. She hasn't suffered through the ritual Bond movie every

Christmas afternoon on ITV since the age of two. I'd probably seen them all by the time I was fifteen, *and* read some of
the books, but I've never had to use the knowledge before
now . . .

"Look, Bond almost always has two Babes. Sometimes it's
three and in a few of the later movies they experimented with
one, but it's almost always two. The first to show up is the
Bad Bond Babe, who usually works for the villain and who
sleeps with Bond before coming to a nasty end. The second,
the Good Bond Babe, helps him resolve the plot and doesn't
shag him until just before the closing credits. You haven't
slept with me so far, which probably means you're safe – at
least, you're not the Bad Bond Babe. But you might be the
glamorous female assassin from a rival organization, who's
sort of a revisionist merge between the Bad Bond Babe and
the Good Bond Babe, who turns up later, gets Bond out of a
load of grief, tries to kill him, and eventually sleeps with
him——"

"——I hope this isn't a come-on, monkey-boy, because if it
is——"

"The setup's skewed. And I reckon we're going to have
company soon."

"Huh? What do you mean?"

"There are never two girls in the movies that feature the
glamorous rival assassin," I say, trying to get my head around
what this signifies. "And this plot doesn't fit that mold. Not
with Mo on her way out here."

"Mo? Your girlfriend?" Ramona gives me a hard-edged
stare.

I look around. The shelves are covered in business administration titles with an admixture of first editions of Ian
Fleming novels – boosters for the geas, at a guess – and the
portholes show me a view of a dark blue sea beneath a
turquoise sky.

"She said she was coming out here right after she finished reaming Angleton," I add, and wait for the double take.

"I find that hard to believe," Ramona says primly. "I've read her dossier. She's just an academic who stumbled into some classified topics!"

"Yes, but I'll bet that dossier doesn't have much on her after your organization gave her permission to leave, does it? That was three years ago. Did you know she works for the Laundry these days? And have you heard her violin? She plays music to die for . . ."

After digesting breakfast I find I've lost my appetite for socializing. I figure I could probably poke my nose all over the ship and make a nuisance of myself, but I'm not sure I want to jeopardize my tenuous status as a guest quite so soon. The real James Bond would be swarming through the ventilation ducts by now, kickboxing black berets overboard and generally raising hell, but my muscles are still aching from yesterday's swim and the nearest I've ever gotten to kickboxing is watching it on TV. Billington's fiendish plot is very well thought out, and the box he's slotted me into is dismayingly effective: I'm simply not a cold-blooded killer. If Angleton had sent Alan Barnes instead, *he'd* know how to raise seven shades of shit, but I'm not a graduate of the Hereford advanced college of mayhem and murder. Bluntly, I'm what used to be called a boffin, and these days is known as a geek, and while I know all the POSIX options to the kill(1) command, doing it with my bare hands is beyond my sphere of competence. I'm still having guilt attacks whenever I think of the guy offshore of the defense platform, and he was trying to make stabby on my arse at the time. So if I can't do the Bond thing, all that's left is to be true to my inner geek.

I slouch downstairs and go back to my room, where, on

the TV, *Thunderball* has just about gotten round to the bit when it's all going pear-shaped and Largo pushes the panic button on his yacht and it turns into a hydrofoil. I shut the door, wedge the chair under it, plug my cummerbund into one USB port and my bow tie into the other, then do a quick in-and-out with the power cable.

While the usual messy list of device drivers is scrolling up the screen I check inside my wardrobe. Sure enough, someone's transferred my luggage from the hotel. The suitcase I took to Darmstadt has finally caught up with me, because presumably one of the perquisites of being employed by a mad billionaire with designs on global domination is that he has a gigantic logistics and fulfillment operation dedicated to ensuring that nothing is *ever* missing when it's needed. I pull on a fresh pair of black jeans, a faded Scary Devil Monastery tee shirt, and a pair of rubber-soled socks: I feel much better immediately. It's as if my brain is slowly rebooting, just like the Media Center PC. It might all be for nothing if the bloody thing isn't networked, but you never know until you try to find out; and I might be suffering from acute cravings for unfiltered Turkish cigarettes, but at least now I know *why*. It's like finding out that the reason your machine's running slow is because some virus-writing spod from Maui has shanghaied it into a botnet and is using your bandwidth to spam penis enlargement ads across the Ukraine; it's a pain in the neck, but knowing what's going on is the first step to dealing with it.

The boot sequence is complete. It's amazing what you can cram into a memory stick these days: it loads a Linux kernel with some very heavily customized device drivers, looks around, scratches its head, spawns a virtual machine, and rolls right on to load the Media Center operating system on top. I hit the boss key to bring the Linux session front and center, then have a poke around. If anyone interrupts me, another tap on the boss key will bring the brain-dead TV back on-screen. I hunker down and take a look around the /proc file system to see what I've got my hands on. Yep, it definitely beats duct-crawling as a way of kicking black beret ass.

It turns out that what I've got my hands on is annoyingly close to a stock Media Center PC. A Media Center PC is meant to look like a digital video recorder on steroids, able to play music and do stuff with your cable connection. So it's a fair bet that there's some sort of cable going into the back of the box, I reason. The box itself is pretty powerful – that is, it's roughly comparable to a ten-year-old super-computer or a five-year-old scientific workstation – and when it isn't spending half its energy scanning for viruses or painting a pretty drop-shadow under the mouse pointer it runs like greased whippet shit. But it doesn't have all the occult applications support I'm used to finding preloaded, and as a development box it sucks mud – if I hadn't brought my USB key I wouldn't even have a C compiler.

Having 0wnZored the box, I go looking for network interfaces. First results aren't promising: there's a dedicated TV tuner card and a cable going into the back, but no wired Ethernet. But then I look again, and see the kernel's autoloaded an Orinoco driver. It hasn't come up by default, but . . . .

Hah! Five minutes of poking around tells me what's going on here. This box probably came with an internal WiFi card, but it's not in use. The PC is simply being used as a television, hooked up to the ship's coaxial backbone, and nobody's even configured the Ethernet setup under Windows. Possibly they don't know about the network card? The Laundry-issue USB stick detected it straight off and started running AirSnort in promiscuous node, hunting for wireless traffic, but it hasn't found anything yet. After about thirty seconds I realize why, and start cursing.

I'm on board the *Mabuse*. The *Mabuse* is a converted Type 1135.6 guided missile frigate, from the Severnoye Design Bureau with love, by way of the Indian Navy. They may have stripped out the VLS cells and the deck guns, but they didn't remove the damage control or countermeasures suites or rip out the shielded bulkheads. This used to be a warship, and its internal spaces are designed to withstand the EMP from a nearby nuclear blast: WiFi doesn't tunnel through solid steel armor and a Faraday cage very well. If I'm going to hack my way into Billington's communication center I'm going to need to find a back door in: an occult network as opposed to an encrypted one.

I pop the other USB stick out of the distal end of the bow tie. It's a small plastic lozenge with a USB plug at one end and a handwritten label that says *RUN ME*. I plug it in, then spend ten minutes adding some modifications to its startup scripts. I pop it out then reach down and pick up my dress shoes. *What was it, left heel and right shoelace?* I strip out the relevant gizmos and stuff them in my pockets, hit the boss button, and flip the cummerbund upside down so that it's just taking a nap in front of the TV. They haven't given me back my gun, my phone, or my tablet PC, but I've got a Tillinghast resonator, an exploding bootlace, and a Linux keydrive: down but not out, as they say. So I open the door and go looking for a source of bandwidth to leech.

A modified type three Krivak-class frigate displaces nearly 4,000 tons when fully loaded, is 120 meters long – nearly twice as long as a Boeing 747 – and can slice through the water at sixty kilometers per hour. However, when you're confined in a luxury suite carved out of the vertical launch missile cells and what used to be the forward magazine and gun turret, it feels a whole lot smaller: about the size of a large house, say. I make the mistake of going too far along a very short corridor, and find myself eyeball to hairy eyeball with a guard in standard-issue black beret and mirrorshades. One sickly smile later I'm staring at a closed door: I'm on a long leash, but this is as far as I'm going to get.

I'm about to go back to my room when two guards step into the corridor ahead of me. "Hey, you."

"Me?" I try to act innocent.

"Yes, you. Come here."

I don't have much in the way of options, so I let them lead me downstairs, along a corridor under the owner's territory, and then out into the working spaces of the ship. Which are painted dull gray, have no carpet or woodwork to speak of, and are full of obscure bits of mechanical clutter. Everything down here is cramped and roughly finished, and from the vibration and noise thrumming through the hull they've only soundproofed the executive suite. "Where are we going?" I ask.

"Com center. Mrs. Billington wants you." We pass a bunch of sailors in black, working on bits of who-knows-what equipment, then they take me up a staircase and through another door, down a passage and into another doorway. The room on the other side of it is long and narrow, like a railway carriage with no windows but equipment racks up to the ceiling on both sides of the aisle and instrument consoles every couple of feet. There are seats everywhere, and more minions in black than you can shake a stick at, still wearing mirrorshades – which is weird, because the lighting's dim enough to give me a headache. There's a continuous rumbling from underfoot which suggests to me that I'm standing right above the engine room.

Eileen Billington's suit is a surreal flash of pink in the twilight as she walks towards me. "So, Mr. Howard." Her smile's as tight as a six-pack of BOTOX injections. "How are you enjoying our little cruise so far?"

"No complaints about the accommodation, but the view's a bit monotonous," I say truthfully enough. "I gather you wanted to talk to me?"

"Oh yes." She probably means to smile sweetly but her lip gloss makes her look as if she's just feasted on her latest victim's throat. "Who is this woman?"

"Huh?" I stare blankly until she gestures impatiently at the big display screen next to me.

"Her. There, in the cross hairs."

We're standing beside a desk or console or whatever with a gigantic flat display. A black beret sitting in front of it is riding herd on a bunch of keyboards and a trackball: he's got about seventy zillion small video windows open on different scenes. One of them is paused and zoomed to fill the middle of the screen. It's an airport terminal and it looks vaguely familiar, if a little distorted by the funny lens. Several people are crossing the camera viewpoint but only one of them is centered—a woman in a sundress and big floppy hat, large shades concealing her eyes. She's got a messenger bag slung carelessly over one shoulder, and she's carrying a battered violin case.

Very carefully, I say, "I haven't a clue." Hopefully the noise of my heart pounding away won't be audible over the ship's engines. "Why do you think I ought to know her? What is this, anyway?" I force myself to look away from Mo and find I'm staring at the console instead, tier upon tier of nineteen-inch rackmount boxes stacked halfway to the ceiling. I blink and do a double take. They've got lockable cabinet fronts, but there's a key stuck in the one right above the monitor. I can see LEDs blinking behind it, set in what looks suspiciously like the front panel of a PC. Suddenly the USB thumb drive in my pocket begins to itch furiously. "You've sure got a lot of toys here."

Eileen isn't distracted: "She has something to do with

your employers," she informs me. "This is the monitoring hub." She pats the monitor. Some imp of the perverse tickles her ego, or maybe it's the geas. "Here you see the filtered take from my intelligence queue. Most of the material that comes in is rubbish, and filtering it is a big overhead; I've got entire call centers in Mumbai and Bangalore trawling the inputs from the similarity grid, looking for eyes that are watching interesting things, forwarding them to the *Hopper* for further analysis, and finally funneling them to me here on the *Mabuse*. Computer screens and keyboards where the owners are entering passwords, mostly. But sometimes we get something more useful . . . the girl on the cosmetics stand in the arrivals terminal at Princess Juliana Airport, for example."

"Yes, well." I make a show of peering at the screen. "Are you sure she's who you're looking for? Could it be one of that group, there?" I point at a bunch of wiry-looking surf Nazis with curiously even haircuts.

"Nonsense." Eileen sniffs aristocratically. "The surge in the Bronstein Bridge definitely coincided with that woman crossing the immigration desk—" She stops and stares at me with all the warmth of a cobra inspecting a warm furry snack. "Am I monologuing? How unfortunate." She taps the black beret on his shoulder. "You, take five."

The black beret gets up and leaves in a hurry. "It's very unfortunate, this geas," she explains. "I could spill important stuff by accident, and then I'd have to send him to Human Resources for recycling." Her shoulder pads twitch up and down briefly, miming: *What can you do?* "It's hard enough to get the staff as it is."

"This looks like a great system," I say, fingering the frame of the workstation. "So you've got access to the eyeballs of anyone who's wearing Pale Grace™ eye shadow? That must be really hard to filter effectively." I'm guessing that I've got Eileen's number. I've seen her type before, stuck in a pale green annex block out behind the donut in Cheltenham, desperate to show off how well she's organized her departmental brief. Eileen's little cosmetics operation is genuine enough, but she came out of spook country just the same as Ellis did: staring at goats for state security. (Forget the whack-jobs at Fort Bragg; there's stuff the Black Chamber gets up to that makes it very useful to have a bunch of useful idiots prancing around in public out front, convincing everybody that it's all a bunch of New Age twaddle.) Eileen isn't much of a necromancer, but she's got the ghostly spoor of midlevel occult intelligence management all over her designer suit, and she's desperate for professional recognition.

"It's top of the range." She pats the other side of the rack, as if to make sure it's still there: "This baby's got sixteen embedded blade servers from HP running the latest from Microsoft Federal Systems division and supporting a TLA Enterprise Non-Stop Transactional Intelligence™ middleware cluster[11] connected to the corporate extranet via a leased *Intelsat* pipe." Her smile softens at the edges, turning slightly sticky: "It's the best remote-viewing mission support environment there is, including Amherst. We know. We *built* the Amherst lab."

Amherst lab? It's got to be a Black Chamber project. I keep my best poker face on: this is useful shit, if I ever get a chance to tell Angleton about it via a channel who isn't code named Charlie Victor. But right now I've got something more immediate to do. "That's impressive," I say, putting all the honesty I can muster at short notice into my voice. "Can I have a look at the front panel?"

Eileen nods. The hairs at the nape of my neck stand on end: for a moment everything seems to be limned in an opalescent glow and her gaze is simultaneously fixed on my face and looking at something a million miles away — no, infi-

---

[11] Translation: "a bunch of computers."

nitely far away: at an archetype I've borrowed, at an identity with the ability to sway any woman's sanity, the talent to lie like a rug and charm their knickers off at the same time. "Be my guest." She giggles, which is a not entirely appropriate sound – but sanity and consistency are in decreasing supply this close to the geas field generator (which, unless I am very much mistaken, is one deck up and five meters over from where we're standing). I reach up with one hand and flip the front panel down to look at the blinkenlights and status readouts on the front of the box. Eileen's still looking at me, glassily: I run my hand down the front panel, the palmed thumb drive between two fingers, and a moment later I twitch my finger over the reset button then flip the lid closed.

The screen freezes for a moment, then an error message dialog box flashes up. Eileen blinks and glances at the monitor then her head whips round: "What did you just do?"

I roll out my best blank look. "Huh? I just closed the front panel. Is it a power glitch?" I can't believe my luck. *Now if only Eileen didn't notice me stick the stubby little piece of plastic in the exposed USB keyboard socket . . .*

She leans forwards, over the screen. "One of the servers just went offline." She sniffs then straightens up and waves the nearest beret over: "Get Neumann back here, his station's acting up." She looks at me suspiciously then glances at the workstation, her gaze flickering across the lid of the blade server. "I thought they'd fixed the rollover bug," she mutters.

"Do you still need me around?" I ask.

"No." She knows something's not right but she can't quite put her finger on it: the alarm bells are ringing in her head but the geas has wrapped a muffling sock disguised as a software bug around the hammer. "I don't like coincidences, Mr. Howard. You'd better stick close to your quarters until further notice."

*

The goons escort me back to the padded-cell luxuries of the yacht. I'm trying not to punch the air and shout *"Yes!"* at the top of my voice: it's bad form to gloat. So I let them shut me in and look appropriately chastened until they go away again.

I chucked the tux jacket in the closet this morning. Now I rifle through the pockets quickly until I find the business card Kitty gave me. Yes, it *is* scratch 'n' sniff on steroids: about five tiny compartments full of Pale Grace™ mascara, eye shadow, foundation, and other stuff I don't recognize. There's even a teensy brush recessed into one side of it, like the knife on a Swiss Card. Humming tunelessly I pull out the brush and quickly sketch out a diagram on the bathroom mirror – a reversed image of the one I sketched in the sand around the hire car. With any luck it'll damp down any access they've got to the cabin until they wise up and come to look in on me in person. Then I take a deep breath and *imagine* myself punching the air and shouting *"Yes!"* by way of relief. (Better safe than sorry.)

Let me draw you a diagram:

Most of what we get up to in the Laundry is symbolic computation intended to evoke decidedly nonsymbolic consequences. But that's not all there is to . . . well, any sufficiently alien technology is indistinguishable from magic, so let's call it that, all right? You can do magic by computation, but you can *also* do computation by magic. The law of similarity attracts unwelcome attention from other proximate universes, other domains where the laws of nature worked out differently. Meanwhile, the law of contagion spreads stuff around. Just as it's possible to write a TCP/IP protocol stack in some utterly inappropriate programming language like ML or Visual Basic, so, too, it's possible to implement TCP/IP over carrier pigeons, or paper tape, or daemons summoned from the vasty deep.

Eileen Billington's intelligence-gathering back end relies

on a classic contagion network. The dirty little secret of the intelligence-gathering job is that information doesn't just want to be free — it wants to hang out on street corners wearing gang colors and terrorizing the neighbors. When you apply a contagion field to any kind of information storage system, you make it possible to suck the data out via any other point in the contagion field. Eileen is already running a contagion field — it's the root of her surveillance system. I've got a PC on my desk that isn't connected to the ship's network, but I've just stuffed a clone of its brain into a machine that *is* on that network — so all I need to do is contaminate my own box with Pale Grace™, and then . . .

Well, it's not as easy as all that. In fact, at first I'm shit-scared that I've broken the TV (I'm pretty sure the warranty specifically excludes damage due to the USB ports being full of mascara) but then I figure out a better way. Tracing the Fallworth graph on the bathroom mirror backwards with a Bluetooth pen hooked into the television is not the recommended way of establishing a similarity link with a network you're trying to break into — it's not even the second worst way of doing so — but it just happens to be the only one I've got available to me, so I use it. Once I've brought up the virtual interface I poke around until I find the VPN port that the USB dongle I planted in Eileen's server farm is running. The keystroke logger is happily snarfing login accounts, and I figure out pretty rapidly that Eileen's INFOSEC people aren't paranoid enough — they figure that for systems aboard a goddamn destroyer, who needs to go to the bother of bio-metrics or a challenge/response system like S/Key? They want something they can get into fast and reliably, so they're using passwords, and my dongle's captured six different accounts already. I rub my knuckles and go poking around the server farm to see what they're doing with it. Give me a bottle of Mountain Dew, an MP3 player hammering out something by VNV Nation, and a crate of Pringles: that's like being at home. Give me root access on a hostile necromancer's server farm, and I *am* at home.

Still, I'm worried about Mo. That view Eileen wanted me to vet – even if Eileen bought my story – means that Mo is here, on the island, and she's under the gun. The Pale Grace™ surveillance net is tracking her and the stabbing sense of anxiety that doubles as my guilty conscience tells me I need to make sure she's all right before I start trying to figure out a way to reestablish communications with Control. So I pull up a VNC session, log into one of Eileen's server blades using a password looted from one of the black berets, and go hunting for a chase cam.

13: FIDDLER HITS THE ROOF

TEN HOURS ABOARD AN AIRBUS IS NEVER A HAPPY fun experience, even in business class. By the time Mo feels the nose gear touch down on the centerline of the runway, rattling the glasses up front in the galley, she's tired, with a bone-weary exhaustion that is only going to go away if she can find the time to crash for twelve straight hours on an oversprung hotel mattress.

But. *But.* Mo hums tunelessly to herself as the airbus taxis towards the terminal. *What's he gotten himself into this time?* she asks herself, a bright point of worry burning through the blanket of fatigue. Angleton wasn't remotely reassuring, and after that disturbing interview with Alan she went and did some digging. Asked Milton, actually, the one-armed, old security sergeant with the keys to the conservatory and the instrument store. "What's a big white one?" she repeated, refusing to take the first answer he offered – or to notice the prickling in her ears and the flush of blood to her cheeks until he set her straight.

Fuck. Nukes? What the wily old bastard had been offering Alan – right under her nose! – was a kamikaze insurance policy. The realization fills her with even more apprehension.

Bob's got himself into something so dicey that Angleton thinks a destroyer full of SAS and SBS special forces isn't enough, and they may need to call in a Trident D-5 ballistic missile to nail whatever's been stirred up down there. That kind of overkill isn't on the menu, outside of a bad spy thriller: that or CASE NIGHTMARE GREEN, anyway, and CASE NIGHTMARE GREEN hasn't started yet, and even then the real nasties probably won't arrive until at least ten years after the grand alignment commences.[12]

As soon as the seatbelt sign blinks off and the cabin crew announces that it's safe for passengers to leave their seats, Mo is up like a jack-in-the-box to haul down her overnight bag, wide-brimmed hat, and the battered violin case from the overhead locker. She clutches the instrument case protectively all the way to the baggage claim area and immigration queue, as if she's walking through a dangerous part of town and it's a gun. But when the customs officer gives her the hairy eyeball and asks her to open it she smiles brightly and clicks back the locks to reveal – a violin.

"See?" she says. "It's an Erich Zahn special, wired with Hilbert-space pickups. I don't think there's another one on this side of the Atlantic." She's relying on his ignorance to let her through. Polished to the creamy gleam of old ivory, the electric violin nestles in its case like a Tommy gun, to all outward appearances nothing but a musical instrument. *Just don't ask me to play it*, she prays. The custom officer nods, satisfied it's not an offensive weapon, and waves her on. Mo closes the case with false calm, nods her head, and locks the instrument back in. *If only you knew . . .*

One airport concourse is much like any other. Mo tows her suitcase over to the exit, where taxis jostle for position oppo-

---

[12] They tend to oversleep.

site the curb. It smells hot and damp with a faint undertone of rotting seaweed. There are people everywhere, tourists in bright clothes, natives, business types. A woman in a suit brandishes a clipboard at her: "Hi! How would you like a free sample of eyeliner, ma'am?"

Why the hell not? Mo nods and accepts the sample, smiles, idly rubs a smear of it on her wrist to check the color, and moves on before the woman can deliver her sales spiel. *Okay, the hotel next. That'll do.* As she walks through the door the Saint Martin climate clamps down on her like a warm, wet blanket, coating her in sweat. Abruptly, she's grateful for the hat and the sundress Wardrobe Department insisted she wear. It's not her style at all, but her usual jeans and blouse would be . . . *Hell, call me the Wicked Witch of the West and have done with it.* She fans herself with the hat as she walks over to the taxi queue. *What a mess.*

"Where to, ma'am?" asks the taxi driver. He's pegged her for a tourist, probably American; he doesn't bother to get out and help her with the suitcase.

"Maho Beach Hotel, if you don't mind." She glances at him in the mirror: he's got crow's-feet around prematurely aged eyes, hair the color of damp newsprint.

"Okay. Twenty euros."

"Got it."

He starts the engine. Mo leans back and closes her eyes. She doesn't let her fingers stray from the violin case, but to a casual onlooker she could be snoozing off a case of jet lag. In fact, when she's not keeping a surreptitious eye open for tails, she's working her way down a checklist she's already committed to memory. *Let's see. Check in, phone home for a Sitrep, confirm Alan's on site, then . . .* a guilty frisson: *off the roadmap. Find Bob. If necessary, find this Ramona person. Make sure Bob's safe. Then figure out how to get him disentangled before it sucks him in too deep . . .*

Anxiety keeps her awake every meter of the way to the hotel, drags her tired ass to the front desk for checkin:

"Mrs. Hudson? Your husband checked in this morning. He said you'd be arriving and to leave you a key to your suite." The receptionist smiles mechanically. "Have a nice stay!"

Husband? Mo blinks and nods, making thankful sounds on autopilot. "Which room is he in?"

"You're in 412. Elevators are left past the fountain."

She rides the elevator upstairs in thoughtful silence. *Husband?* It's not Bob. He wouldn't pull a stunt like this without forewarning her. And it's a suite: Laundry expense accounts don't usually run that high. *Alan Barnes? Or . . .?*

Mo pauses outside the door to room 412. She sets down her overnight bag on top of her suitcase, takes off her sunglasses and hat, and opens the violin case. She slides the card key into the lock with the same hand that grips the end of her bow, then nudges the door handle: by the time it's half-open she has the violin raised to her chin and the bow poised above a string that seems to haze the air around it in a blue glow of Cerenkov radiation.

"Come on out where I can see you," she calls quietly, then kicks the ungainly train of bags forwards through the door, steps forwards after it, and lets the door shut itself behind her.

"I'm over here." The middle-aged white guy in the tropical suit isn't Alan. He's sitting in the office chair behind the hotel room desk, nursing a glass of something that probably isn't water, he's got a twelve-hour beard and he looks haggard. "You're all that Angleton sent? Jesus."

"What are you doing here?" Mo takes another step into the room, glancing sidelong through the doorways into the two bedrooms and the bathroom. "You're not part of my cover."

"Last minute change of plan." He smiles lopsidedly. "You can put the violin down — what were you planning to do with it, make me dance?"

"Who are you?" Mo keeps the violin at the ready, its neck aimed at the interloper.

"Jack Griffin, P Division." *The station chief*, she remembers. He waves at the room. "It's all yours. Bit of a mess really."

Mo's left earring tingles. It's a ward, attuned to warn her when someone's being truthful. In her experience, the average human being tells a little white lie once every three minutes. Knowing when they're telling the truth is much more useful than knowing when they aren't. "So what are you doing here?" she asks tensely.

"There's been a problem." Griffin's accent is clipped, very old-school-tie, and he sounds rueful. "Your predecessor ran into a spot of bother and Angleton asked me to take you in hand and make sure you didn't follow his example."

"A spot of bother, you say." Mo has half-closed the gap separating them before she realizes what she's doing. The violin string hums alarmingly, feeding off her anxiety. "What happened?"

"He was working with a bint from the opposition." Griffin puts his glass down and stares at her. "Billington lifted them both about, oh, twelve hours ago. Invited them to some sort of private party at the casino and the next thing you know they were over the horizon on a chopper bound for his yacht: the coastal defenses are compromised, you know." Griffin shrugs. "I told him not to trust the woman, she's obviously working for Billington by way of a cut-out . . ."

Her earring is itching, throbbing in Morse: Griffin is mixing truth and falsehood to concoct a whirlpool of misdirection. Mo sees red. "You listen to me—"

"No, I don't think I will." Griffin reaches into his pocket

for something that looks like a metal cigarette case. "You folks from head office have fucked up, pardon my French, all the way down the line, sending lightweights to do a professional's job. So you're going to do things my way——"

Mo takes a deep breath and draws the bow lightly across one string. It makes a noise like a small predator screaming in mortal agony and terror, and that's just the auditory backwash. A drop of blood oozes from each fingertip where she grips the neck of the instrument. Griffin's gin and tonic spreads in a puddle across the carpet from where he dropped it. She walks over to him, rolls his twitching body into the recovery position, and squats beside him. When the convulsions cease, she touches the end of the instrument to the back of his head.

"Listen to me. This is an Erich Zahn, with electroacoustic boost and a Dee-Hamilton circuit wired into the soundboard. I can use it to hurt you, or I can use it to kill you. If I want it to, it won't just stop your heart, it'll slice your soul to shreds and eat your memories. Do you understand? Don't nod, your nose is bleeding. Do you understand?" she repeats sharply.

Griffin shudders and exhales, spraying tiny drops of blood across the floor. "What's——"

"Listen closely. Your life may depend on whether you understand what I'm about to tell you. My *predecessor*, who is missing, means rather a lot to me. I intend to get him back. He's entangled with a Black Chamber agent: fine, I need to get her back, too, so I can disentangle them. You can help me, or you can get in my way. But if you obstruct me and Bob dies as a result, I'll play a tune for you that'll be the last thing you ever hear. Do you *understand?*"

Griffin tries to nod again. "Beed. A. T'shoo."

Mo stands up gracefully and takes a step back. "Get one, then." She tracks him with the neck of the violin as he pushes himself upright slowly then shuffles towards the bathroom.

"You're a bard. Woban," he says aggrievedly, standing in the doorway clutching a tissue to his nose. It's rapidly turning red. "I'b on you're sibe."

"You'd better be." Mo leans against the sideboard and raises her bow to a safe distance above the fiddle. "Here's what we're going to do: You're going to go downstairs and hire a helicopter. I'm going to phone home and find out where my backup's gotten to, and then we're going to go for a little run out to visit Billington's yacht, the *Mabuse*. Got that?"

"Bub he'd be aboard the yacht! He'b geb you!"

Mo smiles a curious, tight smile. "I don't think so." She keeps the fiddle pointed at Griffin as he splutters at her. "Billington is all about money. He doesn't do love, or hate. So I'm going to hit him where he doesn't expect to be hit. Now get moving. I expect you back here inside an hour," she adds coolly. "You *really* don't want to be late."

I'm punch-drunk from surprises — the sight of Mo strong-arming Griffin into hiring her a helicopter is shocking enough, and the idea that she's willing to jump in on the Billingtons without a second thought just because of me is enough to turn my world upside down — but then I realize: If *I* can see her, what about the bad guys?

I may not be able to send her a message — the surveillance feed is strictly one-way — but I can try to cover her ass on this side of the firewall. I rummage around for what's left of the Pale Grace™ sample, then draw some more patterns on the side of the PC and trace them with the 'toothpen. They're interference patterns, stuff to break up the contagious spread of the information on my screen. Then I go back to watching. There's not a lot I can do right now, not until we dock with the *Explorer*, but if Mo makes it out there I can make damn sure that, geas or no geas, whatever she's planning takes the Billingtons by surprise.

Griffin has barely closed the door when Mo's energy gives out and she slumps in on herself with a tiny whimper. She puts the violin down, then pulls a black nylon tactical strap from a side pocket in its case – her hands shaking so badly it takes her three attempts to fasten it – then slings the instrument from her shoulder like a gun. She walks over to the desk, wobbling almost drunkenly with fatigue or the relief of tension, and flops down in the chair. The message light on the phone is blinking. She picks up the handset and speed-dials.

"Angleton?"

"Dr. O'Brien."

"Your station chief. Griffin. Is he meant to be in on this side of the operation?"

Angleton is silent for three or four seconds. "No. He wasn't on my list."

Mo stares at the door, bleakly. "I sent him on a wild goose chase. I may have up to an hour until he gets back. Penetration confirmed he's your pigeon. At a guess, Billington got to him via his wallet. Got any suggestions?"

"Yes. Leave the room. Take hand luggage only. Where did you tell him you were going?"

"I sent him to hire a chopper. For the *Mabuse*."

"Then you should go somewhere else, by any means necessary. I'm opening your expense line: unlimited fund. I'll have local assets take Griffin out of the picture."

"I can live with that." Mo's shoulders are shaking with barely repressed fury. "I could kill him. Do you want me to do that?"

Angleton falls silent again. "I don't think that would be

useful at this point," he says finally. "Do you have your primary documents with you?"

"I'm not stupid," she snaps.

"I didn't say you were." Angleton's tone is unusually mild. "Go to ground then call me with a sanitized contact number. Stay there and don't go anywhere. I'll have Alan make contact and pick you up when it's safe to proceed."

"Got it," she says tensely, and hangs up. Then she stands up and collects her violin case. "Right," she mutters under her breath. "Go to ground."

Mo packs methodically and rapidly. The instrument goes back in its carrier. Then she opens her hand luggage – a black airline bag – and tips the contents out on the bed. She squeezes the violin case inside, adds a document wallet and a toilet bag from the pile on the quilt, then zips it up and heads for the door. Rather than using the elevator she takes the emergency stairs, two steps at a time. At the ground floor, there's a fire exit. She pushes the crash bar open – it squeals slightly, a residue of rust on the mechanism –and slips out into the crowd along the promenade at the back of the hotel.

Over the next hour Mo puts her tradecraft to work. She doubles back around her route, checking her trail in window reflections in shop fronts: changes course erratically, acts like a tourist, dives into souvenir markets and cafés to make a show of looking at the menu while keeping an eye open for tails. Once she's sure she's clean she walks the block to the main drag and goes into the first clothes shop she passes, and then the second. Each time, she comes out looking progressively different: a tee shirt under her sundress, then a pair of leggings and an open shirt. The dress has vanished. With the addition of a new pair of sunglasses and a colorful scarf to keep the sun off her head, there's no sign of Mrs. Hudson. She finishes up at a cafe: diving into its coolly air-conditioned interior she orders two double espressos and drinks them straight down, shuddering slightly as the caffeine hits her.

What next? Mo is clearly fighting off the effects of jet lag. She stands up tiredly and steps outside again, shouldering the heat like a heavy burden. Then she heads directly away from the row of nearby hotels, towards the marina on the edge of the harbor and the row of motorboats for hire.

I am just beginning to get my head around the fact that Mo is not only out here, but she's a player — and she isn't going to follow Angleton's instructions — when there's a pounding on my door. I hammer the boss key and spin round in my chair, slamming one leather-padded arm into my right kidney as I try to stand up; then the door opens and the black beret is pointing his mirrorshades at me, lips set in a disapproving scowl. "Mr. Howard, you're wanted on deck."

I scramble to my feet dizzily, wincing and rubbing my side. It's probably a good thing I whacked it — I don't think I could avoid looking disturbed or guilty if I wasn't actually in physical pain. I don't know what the hell Mo thinks she's doing, but it doesn't look like she's planning on following orders and going to the mattresses until Alan calls for her. *And what's Alan doing here anyway?* I wonder as I follow the two guards up the stairs to the deck. Angleton only calls Alan in when there's some serious head-breaking to be done. He's OIC for the Territorial SAS squadron tasked with supporting Occult Operations in the field — some of the scariest — not to mention most eccentric — special forces soldiers in the British Army. I've been along for the ride when they went right through a rip in space-time to head-butt an ancient evil that was threatening to squirm through, I've seen them secure an industrial estate in Milton Keynes with a suspected basilisk on the loose; and I've had the dubious pleasure of being rescued by them on exercise at Dunwich.

Maybe Angleton's sent the heavy cavalry, I decide, hopefully: it's easier to swallow than the alternative, which is that Angleton's written me off as beyond hope and has called them in for Plan B.

The guard up front surprises me when we get to deck level, by turning away from the door to the conservatory and instead opening a hatch onto a narrow green-painted corridor leading aft. "This way," he tells me, while his backup guy hangs behind.

"Okay, I'm going," I say, as agreeably as I can manage. "But where are we going to?"

Mirrorshades man opens a door at the far end of the tunnel and steps through. "HQ," he says over his shoulder.

I emerge, blinking, onto a stretch of deck I hadn't seen before, sandwiched between a big outboard motorboat and a whole bunch of gray cylinders sticking out of the superstructure beneath a rack of masts and antennae. The motorboat hangs from some sort of crane affair. It's getting crowded here: the space is already occupied by Ramona, in company with McMurray, his designer-clad thugette Miss Todt, and a couple more black berets. "Ah, Mr. Howard." McMurray nods at me. "Feel up to a little cruise?"

"Where are you—"

My guard pokes me in the back with a finger. "Jump in." The black berets on deck are setting up a control station for the crane. McMurray gestures at the boat: "This won't take long. We're nearly there."

"Where are we going?

"To the *Explorer.*" McMurray seems to be in a hurry. "Go on, it doesn't do to be late."

"Come on." That's Todt. She clambers over the motorboat's side and jumps down inside.

Ramona follows her, not without a murderous look at McMurray. **Can you—?** I begin to think, then I realize

I can't hear her inside my head. *Shit*. I glance round and the guard who led me up here nods significantly at the boat. *Double-shit*. They must have come up with a portable version of the jammer they used on me and Ramona last night. I climb over the side of the boat and sit down next to Ramona, at the opposite side from Todt and McMurray.

"Where's the jammer?" I ask quietly.

"I think he's got it." She doesn't meet my eyes. "They don't trust us.

"If our positions were reversed, would you?" asks Johanna. I startle. She smiles: it's not a friendly expression.

"I'd trust you anywhere, darling," says Ramona: "I'd trust you to fuck up."

"You——" Todt turns a peculiar shade, as if she's getting ready to explode. McMurray puts a hand on her arm before she can stand up.

"You'll both be quiet," he says in a curiously calm tone, and oddly, they both shut up. I glance sideways and see Ramona's cheek twitching. She rolls her eyes frantically at me, and the penny drops.

I lean over towards McMurray. "You've made your point. Let them talk. They won't do it again."

"You sure of that, boy?" McMurray looks amused. "I've known these hellcats and their type longer than you've been alive, and they'll——"

"That's not the point!" I stab one finger at him. "Do you want her willing cooperation, or not?"

He makes a sound halfway between a laugh and a snigger, just as there's a loud grinding noise from the crane and the boat lurches. "All right, have it your way," he says indulgently as we lift off the deck with a bump that throws Ramona against me.

"Bastard," she says indistinctly. Then the mist clears and I can suddenly feel her presence in my mind again, as warm and vibrant as my own pulse. **Not you, him,** she adds internally. **Thanks. It's not like Pat to make a mistake like that, lifting both blocks at the same time.**

Think it's intentional? I ask, wondering how long we've got to talk.

Not really.

McMurray is saying something to Todt, who's slumped against the railing away from him. I try to make the most of his lapse: **I've noticed them making other mistakes. Listen, I got into Eileen's surveillance network. Mo's arrived, and there's a backup team on the way to rescue us.** The crane swings us over the edge of the *Mabuse* and the boat drops like a lift towards the sea below, leaving my stomach somewhere above my head. **Griffin's on the spot, looks like he's been playing an inside game. Ramona, if you run into Mo, don't get her pissed-off, she's brought her——**

I suddenly realize that my head's full of cotton-wool and Ramona isn't listening. She looks at me and blinks, then stares at McMurray, who smiles faintly in response. "What's that about?" she asks, aggrieved.

"No talking out of class." He looks at me speculatively. A porthole winds past the back of his head, embedded like a zit in the flank of a behemoth. "Orders from the boss. Once you're aboard the TMB-2, *then* you get to talk among yourselves."

"Enjoy the peace and quiet while you can," Todt sneers.

We hit the water with a neck-jarring thump, and everything gets very busy for a minute or two. The two black berets who've been riding down with us fire up the engine and cast-off the cables securing us to the crane, which in turn throws us variously into one another and across the bottom of the boat. It's a bouncy, jarring ride, and I get a lungful of spray as I try to sit up. It ends with me coughing over the side, wishing I had Ramona's gills. By the time I'm half-recovered we're turning away from the *Mabuse* and accelerating across open water. I finally get some air back and look around to see that we've circled the former destroyer. In the distance, there's land on the horizon, but much closer to home a monstrous cliff-like bulk looms over us — the former *Glomar Explorer*.

My sense of scale fails me when I try to take it in. I find myself looking up, and up, and up — the thing's as big as a skyscraper, nearly a fifth of a kilometer long. After the *Explorer* was retired and mothballed in the 1970s they cut the superstructure away, but Billington's people have rebuilt the huge derrick that towers ten stories above the deck, the two huge docking legs and the big cranes at each end of the moon pool, and the entire drilling platform and pipe management system. It looks like an oil rig humping a supertanker. There are loud pumps or engines running up on the deck, and a hammering noise overhead; looking up I see a chopper closing in on the helipad at the stern of the ship. "Who's that?" I ask.

"That'll be the boss arriving," says McMurray. To the driver: "Take us in."

We motor steadily towards a platform hanging near the waterline, halfway along one flank of the giant ship. The ship sits eerily still in the water, as if it's embedded in the top of a granite pillar anchored to the sea floor. As we get closer, the noise from the drilling platform up top gets louder, a percussion of rhythmic clanking and clattering sounds adding to the bass line of the motors and the squeal of drill segments grating across each other as the pipe-feeding mechanism winches them off the huge pile under the superstructure and passes them to the automatic roughneck mechanism. When we tie up alongside the metal staircase I feel the deep humming vibration of the bow and stern thrusters holding the ship on position against the waves.

"Up and out!" The black berets are waving us onto the

platform. While Todt and the guards are busy down below, Ramona and I follow McMurray up the ladder towards a door two decks up. He leads us on a bewildering tour of the colossal drilling ship, up and down narrow corridors and cramped stairwells and finally along a catwalk overlooking a giant room with no floor – the moon pool. A black beret on duty at the door passes us ear defenders as we step out onto the catwalk. The noise is deafening and the air feels like I've walked into a cross between a sauna and a machine shop: greasy and humid with a stink of overheated metal parts. A sickly sweet undertone hints of fishy things that have died and not gone to heaven, embedded in the machinery that moves the underwater doors at the bottom of the moon pool. It's not like this in the movies: presumably James Bond's enemies all employ crack task-forces of janitors spritzing everything with pine-scented disinfectant at fifteen-minute intervals to keep down the rotten shellfish stink.

About ten meters in front of me, a metal pipe as thick as my thigh descends from the underside of the drilling deck, hypnotically spearing into the pool below. I stare at it, following it down to the bubbling point of white water where it plunges into the moon pool and the deep ocean below. Somewhere far down there a drowned alien artifact awaits its arrival. Presumably Billington, with his expertise in Gravedust interrogations, knows what to expect. Above us the drilling platform shudders and roars, hellishly loud as it feeds infinite numbers of pipe segments to the sea god.

McMurray walks along the catwalk until he reaches a row of incongruous office windows and a door, just as you'd expect to find overlooking the shop floor of a factory or a workshop. We follow him inside.

It's a big room, and as befits the villain's working headquarters one wall is occupied by a gratuitously large projection screen showing a map of the sea floor below the

Explorer. There are lots of consoles with blinking lights, and half a dozen black berets sitting at desks where they mouse around schematics on a computer-controlled engineering interface. So far so good. It would look a lot like the control room of a power station, if not for the fact that there's something-that resembles a dentist's chair in the middle of the floor. The ankle and wrist straps and the pentacles around its base suggest that it's not designed for root canal jobs. To top it all off there's a gloating villain standing front and center, wearing a Nehru suit and cradling an excessively somnolent Tiddles in his arms.

"Ah, Ms. Random, Mr. Howard! So glad you could make the show!" I twitch at Billington's victorious smirk. Somehow or other I'm having difficulty controlling the urge to punch him out, sap two or three black-uniformed guards, steal an MP5K, and let fly.

"You need to turn down the gain on that geas: it's overpowering," I suggest.

"All in due course." Billington looks amused, then mildly concerned. "Are you feeling up to the job, Ms. Random? You look a bit peaked."

Ramona snorts. "If you want me to do this thing, you really ought to tell Pat to drop the interference. I can't hear myself think, much less Bob."

"Thinking is not what I'm paying you for. However, no purpose is served by separating you at this time." Billington nods to McMurray: "Allow them full intercourse."

McMurray looks alarmed: "But the suppressor's all that's keeping their entanglement from proceeding to completion! If I stop it now they'll only have about two days' individuality left, then we'll have to cut them loose or deal!"

Shit. I glance at Ramona. She stares at me, wide-eyed. "I understand," Billington says affably, "but as it will take less than twenty-four hours to accomplish the retrieval, I fail to see what the objection is?" He thinks for a moment then comes to a decision. "Drop the suppressor field now. When Ms. Random returns, you will immediately end their state of entanglement, as we discussed earlier." He turns to me, and gestures at the dentist's chair arrangement: "Please take a seat, Mr. Howard."

I stare at him. "What *is* that thing?"

Billington's pupils narrow, lizardlike: "It's a comfy chair, Mr. Howard. Don't make me ask twice."

"Uh-huh." Behind me I sense more than see McMurray adjust some sort of compact ward he keeps strapped to his left wrist: the fuzzy fogbank in my head fades away and I can feel Ramona's unease, the cold, hard deck beneath her feet, and the churning emptiness in her stomach.

Bob, do as he says! Ramona's sense of urgency carries over leaving a nasty metallic taste in my mouth. I edge towards the chair nervously.

"What are the straps for?" I ask.

"They're just in case of convulsions," Billington says soothingly, "nothing you need to worry about."

It's a high-bandwidth sympathetic resonator, Ramona tells me. Snowflakes of half-remembered knowledge slide into place in my head. Control cables suffer weird anomalies when you stick them under kilometers of water; Billington wants a better way of tracking his submersible grab, of staying in control over the retrieval process. Unlike its seventies predecessor, the new grab that Billington's had built is designed to be manually operated by one of Ramona's people, the Deep One/human hybrids. And it doesn't use fiber optics or electrical cables for monitoring the process via TV – it uses two entangled occult operatives. This chair will plug me right into Eileen's surveillance grid, far more efficiently than a swipe of mascara across the eyelashes. **Look, if you don't do it, we're screwed so hard it's not funny.**

I weigh my chances, then swallow. "The straps go," I say. Then I sit down tensely before I can change my mind.

"Jolly good." Billington smiles. "Pat, if you'd be so good as to escort Ms. Random to the pool, I believe her watery chariot is ready to depart."

That's about the last thing I hear, because as my butt hits the padding on the chair I almost black out. I've been strongly aware of Ramona's presence ever since McMurray dropped his blocking ward, like having a mild case of double vision. But that was before I plugged myself into the chair. It's an amplifier. I'm not sure how they've managed to make it work, but Ramona's perceptions almost overwhelm my awareness of my own body. She's got a sharper sense of smell than me, and I can appreciate her mild disgust with Billington's after-shave – there's a bilious undernote of ketosis to it, as if it's covering up something rotten – and the tang of ozone and leaking hydraulic fluid as she moves towards the doorway. Her dislike and fear of McMurray is gnawing away in the background, and there's her concern for— I shy away. It takes a real effort of will to move my arms, even to realize that they're still there: I manage to lie down, or rather to flop bonelessly, then close my eyes.

Ramona? I ask.

Bob? She's curious, worried, and anxious.

This chair, it's an amplifier—

You really didn't know? You weren't being sarcastic? She pauses with her hand on the doorknob. McMurray looks round.

No shit, what am I meant to do here? What's it for?

If you're asking, they haven't switched it on yet. She looks round and now I can see myself lying in the chair, with a couple black berets leaning over me—

Hey! What are they doing—

Relax, it's in case you start convulsing. McMurray

starts to say something, and Ramona speaks aloud: "It's Bob. You didn't tell him what to expect."

"I see," says McMurray. "Ramona, channel. Bob, can you hear me?"

I swallow – no, I swallow with Ramona's throat muscles. "What's happening?" My voice sounds oddly high. Not surprising, considering whose throat it's coming out of.

McMurray looks pleased. He glances at the guards bending over my body, and I turn my head to follow, feeling the unaccustomed weight of her hair, the faint pull of tension on the gills at the base of her throat: I see myself – Bob – lying flat out, strapped down while they hook up bits of bleeping biotelemetry. A medic stands by, holding a ventilator mask. "Amplification to level six, please," says McMurray, then he looks back at me – at Ramona, that is. "Your entanglement lets you see through Ramona's eyes, Bob. It also lets her speak through your mouth, when you're at depth. The defense field around the chthonic artifact plays hell with electronics and scrambles ordinary scalar similarity fields, but the deep entanglement between you and Ramona is proof against just about any interference short of the death of one of the participants. When she's at depth, Ramona will operate the controls of the retrieval grab by hand – they're simple hydraulic actuators – to lock onto the artifact, then signal through you to commence the lift process."

"But I thought, uh, doesn't it take days to ride the grab down?"

McMurray shakes his head. "Not using this model." He looks insufferably smug. "Back in the sixties they designed the grab to be fixed to the end of the pipe string. We've updated it a little; the grab clamps to the outside of the string and drops down it on rollers, then locks into place when it reaches the end. If we were going to unbolt and store the pipe sections when we retrieved it, we'd take two days to suck it all back up, it's true – but to speed things up we've got a plasma cutter up top that can slice them apart for recycling instead of unbolting each joint. This baby is nearly four times faster than the original."

"Doesn't Ramona need to decompress or something, on the way up?"

"That's taken care of: her kind have different needs from us land-dwellers. It'll still take us a whole day to bring the string up; she'll be all right." He turns away, dismissively. "Dive stations, please."

Ramona follows him through the door and along the catwalk to a dive room where there's a whole range of esoteric kit laid out for her. She's done this sort of thing before and finds a kind of comfort in it. It's very strange to feel her hands working with straps and connectors that feel large to her slim fingers – shrugging out of her clothes and across the chilly steel deck plates, then one leg at a time into a wet suit. There's more unfamiliar stuff: an outer suit threaded with thin pipes that connect to an external coupling, weight belt, a knife, torches. **What's the plumbing for?** I ask. **I thought you could breathe down there.**

I can, but it's cold, so they're giving me a heated suit. I get a picture: hot water is pumped down through the pipe string under high pressure, used to power the grab assembly via a turbine. Some of the water is bled off and cooled by a radiator until it's at a comfortable temperature for circulating through Ramona's suit. She's going to be down there for more than a day—

You're taking a bar of chocolate? I ask, boggling slightly as she slides the foil-wrapped packet into a thigh pocket.

There are fish down there, but you wouldn't want to eat them raw. Shut up and let me run through this checklist again.

I hang back and wait, trying not to get in the way. A dive error wouldn't be the lethal disaster for Ramona that it would be for me but it could still leave her stranded and exposed in the chilly darkness, kilometers below the surface. Even if she's immune to the predations of the BLUE HADES defense polyps, there are other things down there — things with teeth out of your worst nightmares, things that can see in the dark and burrow through flesh and bone like drill-mouthed worms.

Ramona finally pulls her helmet on. Open-faced, with no mask or regulator, she turns and faces McMurray. "Ready when you are."

"Good. Take her to the pool," he says to the technicians, and strides back out in the direction of the observation room.

Down in the moon pool, the waters are warm and still. The drill string has stopped descending, although there are muted clanking and clattering noises from the platform over-head. Around the walls of the pool the sea is dark, but something bulky and flat squats below the water in the middle of the pool. There are technicians in the water, scud-ding about in a Zodiac with an electric outboard: they seem to be collecting cables that connect the submerged platform to the instrument bay below the observation room windows.

Ramona walks heavily down the metal steps bolted to the wall of the pool until she's standing just above the waterline. There are lights on top of the submersible grab, lined up in two rows to either side of an exposed platform with railings and, incongruously, an operator's chair, its seat submerged beneath two meters of seawater. There are two divers work-ing on a panel in front of the seat; behind it, there's a bulky arrangement of shock absorbers and rollers clamped around a steel yoke the size of a medium truck, threaded around the drill string. Ramona steels herself, then steps off the plat-form. Water slaps her in the face, cool after the humid air in the moon pool. She drops below the surface neatly, opens her eyes, and – this fascinates me – blows a stream of silver bubbles towards the surface. Her nasal sinuses burn for a moment as she inhales a deep draught of water, and there's a moment of panicky amphibian otherness before she relaxes the flaps at the base of her throat, and kicks off towards the submerged control platform, reveling in the sense of freedom and the flow of water through her gills. Nictitating membranes slide down across my – *no, her* – eyes, adding a faint iridescent haze to the view.

"Ready to go aboard," I feel her saying through my throat. "Can you hear me, Billington?" Somewhere a long way away I can hear my body coughing as Ramona swims over the seat and lets the two support divers strap her into it and hook up her warm-water hoses. She's doing something funny with my larynx and it's not used to it.

Hey, careful about that, I nudge her.

There's an echoing flash of surprise. **Bob? That feels really weird . . .**

You're not doing it right. Try using it like this. I show her, swallowing and clearing my throat. She's right, it feels really weird. I close my eyes and try to ignore my body, which is lying on the dentist's chair as Ellis Billington leans close to listen to her.

There's a panel with about six dozen levers and eight mechanical indicator dials on it, all crude-looking industrial titanium castings with rough edges. Ramona settles in her seat and waves a hand signal at the nearest diver. There's a lurch, and the seat drops under her. A loud metallic grating sound follows, felt as much as heard, and she glances round to watch the huge metal harness grip the pipe string. I feel a pressure in her ears and I swallow for her. The pipe is rising through the docking collar – no, the platform I'm sitting on is sinking, about as fast as an elevator car. The great wheels grip the pipe, held in place to either side by hydraulic clamps. I manage to prod her into looking up: the moon pool and the ship merge into a dark fish-shaped silhouette against a deep blue sky, already darkening towards a stygian night broken only by the spotlights that ridge the spine of the huge grab we're riding on.

It's odd how Ramona's senses differ from my own. I can feel the pressure around me, but it's different from the way it feels to me in my own skin. Waves of sound move across me, sounds too low- or too high-pitched to hear with my own ears. Ramona can sense them in the small bones of her skull, though. There are distant clicking hunting noises from marine mammals, strange sizzling and clattering noises – krill, tiny crustaceans floating in the high waters like a swarm of locusts grazing on the green phytoplankton. And then there are the deep bass whoops and groans of the whales, growing abruptly louder as we drop below a thermocline. The water on my exposed face is suddenly cold, and there's a sense of pressure on my skull, but a few deep gulps of water flushing through my gills clears it. Ramona swallows sea-water as well as breathing it, letting it flood her stomach and feeling the chill as it infiltrates her gut. Rarely used muscles twitch painfully into life, forcing strange structures to realign themselves. **How are you taking this?** she asks me.

I'll cope, I tell her. The light outside our charmed circle of lamps has dimmed to a faint twilight. In the distant murk I spot a gray belly nudging past, possibly a deep-ranging tiger shark or something less well-known. The pipe rolls end-lessly up through the docking harness.

"Dive stable at one meter per second," Ramona tells Billington. I lie back, do the math: it's going to take us a little over an hour to reach the abyssal plain where JEN-NIFER MORGUE Two lies broken and desolate beneath

400 atmospheres of pressure, on a bed of gray ooze that's been accreting since before hairless apes slouched across the plains of Africa.

There's something soothing about the motion of the pipe string. Once every few minutes Ramona opens my mouth and murmurs something technical: some of the time Billington turns and relays an instruction or two to the ever-present flunky waiting at his shoulder. I lapse into a dreamy, near-hypnotized state. I know something's wrong, that I shouldn't be this relaxed under the circumstances — but a great sense of lassitude has come over me as our entanglement nears completion. *Lie back and think of England.* Where the hell did that come from? I blink and try to throw back the sense of disengagement.

Ramona——

Shut up and let me concentrate here. She's working two of the levers and there's a loud *clank-bump* that I feel more than hear. **Okay, that's it.** We resume our descent, passing an odd bulge where the pipe triples in diameter for about three meters, like a python that's just swallowed a small pig. **What is it?**

What do we do after you raise the artifact?

What do—— She stops. **We get disentangled, right?**

Yes, but what then? I persist. For some reason I feel dizzy when I try to follow this line of reasoning. I can almost sense my own body again, see Billington leaning over me expectantly like an eager cultist inspecting his dead leader for signs of imminent resurrection. **Aren't we supposed to do . . . something?**

Oh, you mean kill Ellis, massacre his guards, and set the ship on fire. before making our escape on jet skis? she says brightly.

Something like that. A thought bubbles up to the

surface of my mind and pops, halfheartedly: **You gave that a lot of thought, huh?**

The jet skis are on C deck, and there are only two of them. I've got to get Pat out of here – I'm afraid you'll have to make your own arrangements, she says briskly. **But yeah, I can definitely nail Billington.**

The penny drops – icy and cold, right down the back of my metaphorical net. **You've been planning this as a hit on Billington right from the start!**

Well, that's the whole point of my being here, isn't it? Why else would they send an assassin? I mean, d'oh!

I ought to be more shocked; maybe it's had time to sink in, what she really is. (And there's the whole escape thing, of course. Am I imagining things or did she feel a twinge of guilt when she told me I'd have to swim for myself?) **Your people used me to get close to Billington,** I accuse.

Yup. It's funny how these little misunderstandings only come clear when you're 800 meters below sea level and dropping like an express elevator towards Davy Jones's tentacle-enhanced locker. **As soon as Billington shuts down the geas field I'll be free to act on my own agency.** I can feel a funny tight smirk tugging at the sides of her mouth. It's not humor. **He doesn't realize it yet, but he's so screwed you could plug him into the mains and call him Albert Fish.**

But you can't do that unless we're disentangled, surely? And for that you need—

The other shoe drops, or rather, she kicks me between the eyes with it in her next comment: **Yes, that's why Pat is here. You didn't think supervisors from Department D routinely defect, did you? He's under even tighter control than I am.** And at that moment I can see the geas that's binding her to the Black Chamber, tying her to the daemon they've imposed on her will: bright as chromed steel, thick as girders, compelling obedience. The Laundry warrant card is bad enough – if you try to spill our secrets you'll die, not to put too fine a point on it – but this is even worse. We do it for security. This is nothing short of vindictive. If she thinks a disloyal thought too far, the Other will be let loose – and the first thing it will do is feed on her soul. No wonder she's terrified of falling in love.

I'm fully awake now, mind spinning like a hamster on a wheel in a cage on a conveyor belt heading for the maw of an industrial-scale wood chipper: there are thoughts I really desperately don't want to think while I'm inside her skull and vice versa. On the other hand, something *does* occur to me . . .

If McMurray's working with you, do you think you can convince him to give me back my mobile phone?

Huh?

It's no big deal, I explain, **it's just, if I've got my phone I can escape. You want that to happen, right? Once we get back to the surface, you and McMurray want me out of the picture as soon as possible. I can get a ride home just about any time, as long as I've got my phone.**

But we're out of range of land, she points out logically.

What makes you think I was going to use it to make a phone call?

Oh. We watch the pipe string unreel for a minute or two in silence. Then I feel her acquiesce: **Yeah, I don't think that'll be a problem. In fact, why don't you just ask him for it? I mean, it's not as if you can phone home, so you can probably use some of your super-agent mojo while you've got it.**

I am conflicted between wanting to hug Ramona, and kick her in the shins for being a smart-arse. But I guess that's her job, I mean, she really *is* a glamorous, high-flying super-spy and assassin and I'm just an office nerd who's along for the ride. It doesn't matter what Angleton thinks of me, all I can really do here is lie back and think of – *England* – not to mention the . . . *game of Tetris* . . . on my phone—

Stop trying to think, monkey-boy, you're making my head hurt and I've got to drive this thing.

Monkey-boy? *That does it.* I send her a picture of a goldfish gasping in a puddle of water beside a broken bowl. Then I clam up.

14: JENNIFER MORGUE

WE RIDE DOWN TO THE ABYSSAL PLAIN IN SILENCE, doing our best to barricade each other out of our minds.

The journey down actually takes nearer to three hours than one. There's a lengthy pause in the darkness of the bathypelagic zone, a kilometer down, while Ramona stretches and twists in strange exercises she's learned for adapting to the pressure. Her joints make cryptic popping noises as she moves, accompanied by brief stabbing pains. It's almost pitch-black outside our ring of lights, and at one point she unstraps herself from the seat and swims over to the edge of the platform to relieve herself, still tethered by the umbilical hose that pumps warm water through her suit. Looking out into the depths, her eyes ad just slowly: I can see a cluster of faint reddish pinpricks swimming at the edge of visibility. There's something odd about her eyes down here, as if their lenses are bulging and she can see further into the red end of the spectrum; by rights she ought to be as blind as a bat. From the sounds these sea creatures are making they're some sort of shrimp, luminescent and torpid as they feed on the tiny scraps of biomass raining down from the illuminated surface like oceanic dandruff.

The water down here is frigid – if Ramona didn't have the heated suit she'd likely freeze to death before she could surface again. She messes with a pair of vents near her chin, and a tepid veil of warm water flows across her face, smelling faintly of sulfur and machine oil. "Let's get this over with," she mutters as a weird itching around her gills peaks and begins to subside: "If I stay down here much longer I'll begin to *change*." She says it with a little shudder.

She fastens herself back into the control chair and throws the lever to resume our descent. After an interminable wait, there's a loud clang that rattles through the platform. "Aha!" She glances round. The descent rollers have just passed a football-shaped bulge in the pipe painted with the white numerals "100." "Okay, time to slow down." Ramona hits the brakes and we slide over another football, numbered "90," then "80." They're counting down meters, I realize, indicating the distance to go until we hit something.

I feel Ramona working my jaws remotely; it's most unpleasant – my mouth tastes as if something died in it. "Nearly there," she tells the technician who's taken Billington's place during the boring part of the descent. "Should be seated on the docking cone in a couple of minutes." She squeezes the brake lever some more. "Thirty meters. What's our altitude?"

The technician checks a screen that's out of my line of sight: "Forty meters above ground zero, one-seventy degrees out by two-two-five meters."

"Okay . . . ." We've slowed to a crawl. Ramona squeezes the brake lever again as the "10" meter football creeps past, climbing the pipe string. The brakes are hydraulically boosted – the grab she's sitting on weighs as much as a jumbo jet – and the big rollers overhead groan and squeal against the pipe string, scraping away the paint to reveal the gleam of titanium-graphite composite segments. (No expense is spared: that stuff is usually used for building satellites and space launchers, not drilling pipes that are going to be cut apart once they've been hauled back up to the surface.) I watch as Ramona frowns over a direction indicator and carefully uses another lever to release water to the directional control jets, shoving the platform round until it's lined up correctly with the docking cone below. Then she releases the brake again, just enough to set us gliding down the final stretch.

The pipe flares out to three times its previous diameter, then stops being a pipe: there's an enormous conical plug dangling from the drill string, point uppermost, with flanges that lock into a tunnel on the underside of the platform's harness, like Satan's own butt-plug. We drop steadily, and the rollers are pushed outwards by the cone until the harness locks into place around the cone. "Okay securing the grab now," Ramona comments, and throws the final lever. There's an uneven series of bangs from below the deck as hydraulic bolts slide into place, nailing us to the end of the pipe. "You want to begin steering us over to the target zone?"

"Make sure you're secured in your seat," the tech advises her whispering in my ear. "Visual check. Are your wards contiguous?"

Ramona switches on her hand torch, casts the beam around the metal panels at her feet. Pale green light picks out the non-Euclidian circuitry of a Vulpis exclusion array etched into the deck with a welding torch. It extends all the way around her chair. "Check. Wards clear and unobstructed. How are they powered?"

"Don't worry, we took care of that." Oh *great*, I realize, they're going to drop Ramona into the field around JENNIFER MORGUE Site Two — a field that tends to kill electronics and, quite possibly people — with only a ward for protection, one that needs blood to power it. "It's full of Pale

Grace™ Number Three®[13], and we've got a sacrifice waiting in cell four to energize it. Should be commencing exsanguination in two minutes."

"Um, okay." Ramona checks her compass, suppressing a stab of anger so strong it nearly shocks me into a languorous yawn. "What did the subject do to rate a starring role?"

"Don't ask me – underperforming sales rep or something. There's plenty more where she came from." The technician steps back for a while, at Billington's command, then nods, and steps forwards into view again. "Right. You're about to see the wards light up. Tell me immediately if they stay dark."

Ramona glances down. Eerie red sparks flicker around the runes on the deck. "It's lit."

"Good." Somewhere disturbingly close to the back of my own mind I can feel her daemon coil uneasily in its sleep, a sensual shudder rippling through us as it senses the proximity of death. The skin of my scrotum crawls; I feel Ramona's nipples tighten. She shudders. "What's that?"

Billington leans over me now. "You're twenty meters off the counter-intrusion field rim, sitting in the middle of a contagion mesh with a defensive ward around you. If my analysis is correct, the field will absorb the sacrifice and let you in. Your entanglement with Bob up here will confuse its proximity sense and should let you survive the experience. You might want to uncap your periscope at this time: from now on, you're on your own until you dump the ballast load."

He steps back smartly and the wards inscribed on the

---

[13] The word "Three" and the digit "3" (and non-English localizations thereof) are patented intellectual property of TLA Systems Corporation and denote the entity that, in the set of integers, is the ordinal successor of 2 and predecessor of 4. Used by kind permission.

floor around my chair light up so bright that the glare reflects off the ceiling of the control room above me, pulling me back into my own head for a moment. "Hey—" I begin to say, and just then . . .

Things.

Get.

Confused.

I'm Ramona: leaning over a narrow, glass letter box in the middle of the console, staring down at a brown expanse of mud as I twitch the thruster control levers, flying the platform and its trailing grapple arms closer towards a cylindrical outcropping in the middle of the featureless plain. I'm in my element, slippery and wet, comfortably oblivious to the thousands of tons of pressure bearing down on me from above.

I'm Bob: limp as a dishrag, passive, lying on a dentist's chair in the middle of a pentacle with lights flaring in my eyes, a cannula taped into my left forearm, and a saline drip emptying into it through an infusion pump – *They've drugged me,* I realize dizzily – a passenger, along for the ride.

And I'm someone else: frightened half to death, strapped down on a stretcher with cable ties so I can't move, and the robed figures around me are chanting, and I'd scream if I could but there's something wrong with my throat and why won't anyone rescue me? Where are the police? This isn't supposed to happen! Is it some kind of sorority initiation thing? One of the sisters is holding a big knife. What's she doing? When I get out of here I'm going to—

I stare down at the muddy expanse unrolling beneath the platform. Rotating the periscope I check the ten grab-arms visually: they all look okay from here, though it won't really be possible to tell for sure until I fire the hydraulic rams. They cast long shadows across the silt. Something white gleams between two of them, briefly: skeletal remains or something. *Something.*

Glimpse of silvery strings across the grayness, like the webs of a spider as big as a whale. Conical spires rising from the mud, dark holes in their peaks like the craters of extinct volcanoes. Guardians sleeping. I can feel their dreams, disturbed thoughts waiting: but I can reassure them, *I'm not who you want*. Beyond them, more open ground and a sense of prickling fire that ripples across my skin as I float past an invisible frontier left over from a war that ended before humans existed—

She screams silently and the terror gushes inside my head as the knife tears through her throat, blood spurting in thick pulses draining towards zero—

The daemon in my head is awake now, noticing—

The blood vanishing, drained into the fiery frontier on the sea floor—

And we're inside the charmed circle of death around JENNIFER MORGUE Site Two.

A long time later, McMurray comes up to me and clears his throat. "Howard, can you hear me?" he asks

I mumble something like *leave me alone*. My head aches like it's clamped in a vice, and my mouth is a parched desert.

"Can you hear me?" he repeats patiently.

"Feel. Like shit." I think for a minute, during which time I manage to crowbar my eyes open. "Water?" Something's missing, but I'm not sure what.

McMurray turns away and lets a medical type approach me with a paper cup. I try to sit up to drink but I'm as weak as a baby. I manage a sip, then I swallow: half the contents of the cup go down my chin. "More." While the paramedic is busy I get my throat working again. "What happened?"

"Mission accomplished." McMurray looks self-satisfied. "Ramona's on her way back up with the goods."

"But, the——" I stop. Hunt around in my head. "You put the block back," I accuse.

"Why wouldn't I?" He steps out of the way to let the nurse or paramedic or whoever pass me another cup of water. This time I manage to lift a hand and take hold of it without making a mess of things. "It's going to take another twelve hours or so to bring her up, and I don't want you deepening the entanglement while that's happening."

I stare into his pale blue eyes and think, *Got you, you bastard*. Even though it's treachery against Billington, who thinks he owns McMurray body and soul, I get the picture. "Did she get the, the thing?" I ask. Because that's when I blacked out, right after we entered the zone of the death spell or curse or force field or whatever it is around the wrecked chthonian war machine on the seabed. Right when Ramona recognized what she was looking for, bang in the middle of the periscope, and opened my mouth to announce, "I've got it. Give me three more meters, and stand by for contact."

"Yes, she got it."

"When, when are you going to unhook us?"

"When Ramona's back up and decompressed – tomorrow. She has to be physically present, you know." His expression turns sour. "So it's back to your room for the duration."

"Agh." I try to sit up and nearly fall off the chair. He puts one hand on my shoulder to steady me. I glance around, my vision still blurry. Billington's across the room conversing with his wife and the ship's officers; I'm all on my own over here with McMurray and the medic. Icy fear clamps around my stomach. "How long have I been under?"

McMurray glances at his watch, then chuckles. "About six hours." He raises one eyebrow. "Are you going to come quietly or am I going to have to have you sedated?"

I shake my head. Quietly I say, "I know about Charlie Victor." His fingers dig into my shoulder like claws. "You want to settle with Billington, that's none of my business," I add hastily. "But give me back my phone first."

"Why?" he asks sharply. Heads turn, halfway across the control room floor: his face slides into an effortless smile and he waves at them then turns back to me. "Blow my cover and I'll take you down with me," he hisses.

"No fear." I swallow. *How much can I safely reveal . . .?* At least Ramona isn't listening in; I don't need to doublethink around McMurray right now. "She told me about the jet skis, I know how we're getting out of here." *I know that there's a seat reserved for you, but no room for me.* It's time to lie like a rug: "The phone isn't official issue, it's mine. I bought it unlocked, not on contract. Cost me close to a month's wages, I really can't afford to lose it when the shit hits the fan." I put a whine in my voice: "They'll take that expenses packet you made me gamble away out of my pay for the next year and I am going to be so screwed—"

"We're out of range of land," he says absent-mindedly, and his grip relaxes. I swing my legs over the floor and steady myself until the world stops spinning around my head.

"Doesn't matter: I'm not planning on phoning home. But can I have it back anyway?" I get one foot on the deck outside the ward.

McMurray cocks his head to one side and stares at me. "Okay," he says, after a moment, during which I feel none of the weirdly other-worldly sense of strangeness that came over me while I was putting one across Eileen in the monitoring center. "You can have your damned phone back tomorrow, before Ramona surfaces. Now stand up – you're going back to the *Mabuse*."

McMurray details four black berets to escort me back to my room aboard the *Mabuse*, and it takes all of their combined efforts to get me there. I'm limp as a dishcloth, hung-over from whatever drugs Billington's tame Mengele pumped into me. I can barely walk, much less climb into a Zodiac.

It's dark outside – past sunset, anyway – and the sky is black but for a faint red haze on the western horizon. As we bump up against the side of the *Mabuse*, where they've lowered a boarding platform, I notice the guards are still wearing their trademark items: "Hey what's with the mirrorshades?" I ask, slurring my words so that I sound half-drunk. "'S nighttime, y'know?"

The goon who's climbing the steps ahead of me stops and looks round at me. "It's the eyeliner," he says finally. "You think wearing mirrorshades at night looks stupid, you should try carrying an MP-5 with a black jumpsuit and a beret while wearing eye shadow."

"Cosmetics don't go/with GI Joe," chants the goon behind me, a semitone out of tune with himself.

"Eye shadow?" I shake my head and manage to climb another step.

"It's the downside of our terms and conditions of employment," says Goon Number One. "Some folks have to piss in a cup to pass federally mandated antidrug provisions; we have to wear make-up.

"You're shitting me."

"Why would I do a thing like that? I've got stock options that're going to be worth millions after we IPO. If someone offered you stock options worth a hundred million and said you had to wear eyeliner to qualify . . ."

I shake my head again. "Hang on a moment, isn't TLA Corporation already publicly traded? How can you IPO if it's already listed on NASDAQ?"

Goon Number Two behind me chuckles. "You got the wrong end of the stick. That's Install Planetary Overlord, not Initial Public Offering."

We climb the rest of the steps in silence and I reflect that it makes a horrible kind of sense: if you're running a ubiquitous surveillance web mediated by make-up, wouldn't it make sense to plug all your guards into it? Still, it's going to make breaking out of here a real pain in the neck – much harder than it looked before – if the guards are also nodes in the surveillance system. As we trudge through the corridors of the ship, I speculate wildly. Maybe I can use my link into Eileen's surveillance network to install an invisibility geas on the server, and use the sympathetic link to their eyes as a contagion tunnel so that they don't see me. On the other hand, that sort of intricate scheme tends to be prone to bugs – get a single step wrong in the invocation and you might as well be donning a blinking neon halo labeled ESCAPING PRISONER. Right now I'm so tired that I can barely put one foot in front of another, much less plan an intricate act of electronic sabotage: so when we get to my room I stagger over to the bed and lie down before they even have time to close the door.

Lights out.

It's still dark when I wake up shuddering in the aftershock of a nightmare. I can't remember exactly what it was about but something has filled my soul to overflowing with a sense of profound horror. I jerk into wakefulness and lie there with my teeth chattering for a minute. It feels like an entire convention of bogeymen has slithered over my grave. The shadows in my room are full of threatening shapes: I reach out and flick the bedside light switch, banishing them. My heart pounds like a diesel engine. I glance at the bedside clock. It's just turned five in the morning.

"Shit." I sit up and hold my head in my hands. I'm not making a good showing for myself, I can tell that much: frankly, I've been crap. After a moment I stand up and walk over to the door, but it's locked. No moonlight excursions tonight, I guess. Somewhere a kilometer below the surface,

Ramona will be dozing in that chair slowly decompressing as a nightmare dreams on in the ancient war machine tucked between the ten mechanical grabs on the underside of the retrieval platform. Aboard the *Explorer*, Billington paces the command center of his operation, those weirdly catlike eyes slitted before the prospect of world domination. Somewhere else on board the *Explorer*, the treacherous McMurray is waiting for Billington to terminate the Bond geas, so that he can release Ramona's daemon and then she can assassinate the crazed entrepreneur, delivering JENNIFER MORGUE Site Two into the hands of the Black Chamber.

It's pretty damn clear now, isn't it? And what am I doing about it? I'm sitting on my arse in a gilded cage, looking pretty while acting pretty ineffectual. And I keep finding myself mumbling *lie back and think of England*, which is just plain humiliating. It's almost as if Billington has already terminated the invocation that's binding me to the heroic role—

"Shit," I say again, startling myself. *That's it!* That's what I should have noticed earlier. The heroic pressure of the geas is no longer bearing down on me, skewing my perspective. I'm back to being myself again, the nerdy guy in the corner. In fact, it feels like I'm being squeezed into a state of fatalistic passivity, waiting for a rescuer to come get me out of this situation. The reason I feel so indecisive and like crap is, I'm going through cold turkey for heroism. Either that or the focus of the Hero trap has shifted—

I check the alarm clock again. It's now ten past five. What did McMurray say? *Sometime today.* I pull out the chair and sit down in front of the Media Center PC. *Jet skis on C deck.* They're going to give me my phone back soon. *What was the speed dial code?* As soon as we're untangled Charlie Victor is going to kill Billington. *Gravedust systems.* JENNIFER MORGUE isn't as dead as McMurray seems to think. That's the only explanation I can come up with for Billington's behavior.

"Oh Jesus, we are so fucked," I groan, and hit the boss key so I can see whether Mo, at least, is safe.

"It's like this," says Mo, checking the seals on her instrument case once more, "I can do it without attracting attention. Whereas, if you guys do it, you're not exactly inconspicuous. So leave the job to me."

She's sitting on a gray metal platform slung over the side of a gray metal ship. A flashy-looking cigarette boat is tied up next to it, all white fiberglass and chromed trim until you get back to the enclosed cockpit and the two gigantic Mercury outboards in the tail. The man she's talking to is wearing a wet suit, a bullet-proof vest, and horn-rimmed spectacles. "What makes you think you can do it?" he asks, with barely concealed impatience.

"Because it's what I've spent the past four bloody months training for, thank you very much." She squints at the lock, then nods minutely and puts the case down. "And before you say it's what you've spent the last twenty years specializing in, I'd like to remind you that there are any number of reasons why you *shouldn't* go in first, starting with their occult defenses, which are my specialty. Then there's the small matter of their point defense systems, starting with an Indian Navy sensor suite that Billington's spent roughly fifty million on, upgrading to NATO current standards. The bigger the initial insertion the greater the risk that it'll be spotted, and I don't think you want them to realize they're being stalked by a Royal Navy task group, do you?"

Barnes nods thoughtfully. "I think you underestimate how fast and hard we can hit them, but yes, it's a calculated risk. But what makes you think you can do it alone?"

Mo shrugs. "I'm not going in without backup — that

would be stupid." She grins momentarily. "On the other hand, you know how this setup works. If I stay back at HQ it all goes pear-shaped. I think the smart money is riding on them already having retrieved JENNIFER MORGUE: the worst-case operational contingency is that, with Billington's expertise in necro-cognitive decoding, he also knows how to make it work. I expect any first attempt we make to fail — unless I'm along for the ride and in a position to act out my assigned role in accordance with the geas he's got running. I'm not trying to be sticky here, I'm just reading the rules."

"Shit." Barnes is silent for a moment, evidently running some sort of scenario through his mind's eye. Then he nods briskly. "All right, you convinced me. One reservation: you've got a ten-minute lead, maximum, and not a second longer. If there's even a hint of instability in the geas field, all bets are off and I'm taking both teams in immediately. Now, one last time — can you enumerate your priorities?"

"First, secure the field generator so Billington can't shut it down on schedule. Next, release the hostages and hand them off to the 'B' team for evac. Third, neutralize the chthonian artifact and if necessary sink the *Explorer*. That's all, isn't it?"

Captain Barnes clears his throat. "Yes. Which I'm afraid means you just passed Angleton's cricket test. But you need this, first." He hands Mo a red-striped document wallet. "Read it, then sign here."

"Oh dear," Mo says mildly, running one finger down a series of closely typed paragraphs of legalese drafted by a bunch of Home Office lawyers with too much time on their hands: "Do I have to?"

"Yes," Barnes says grimly. "You must. That's *also* in the rules. They don't hand these out every day. In fact, they're so rare I think they probably had to invent it just for you . . ."

"Well, pass me the pen." Mo scrawls a hasty signature then hands the document back to him. "That all square?"

"Well, there's one other thing I'd like to add," Barnes says as he seals the document into a waterproof baggie and passes it to a sailor waiting on the bottom steps of the ladder. "Just between you and me, just because you've got the license, it doesn't mean you've got to use it. Remember, you're going to have to live with yourself afterwards."

Mo smiles, her lips drawn razor-thin. "It's not me you should be worrying about." She picks up a waterproof fiberglass black case and checks the latches on it carefully. "If this goes to pieces, I'm going to have words with Angleton."

"Really? I'd never have guessed." Barnes's tone is withering, but he follows it by sitting down next to Mo and leaning close: "Listen, this is *not* going to go pear-shaped. One way or another, we've got to make it work, even if none of us end up going home. But more importantly – *you* listen – this isn't about you, or me, or about Bob, or about Angleton. If the Black Chamber gets their hands on JENNIFER MORGUE it's going to destabilize everything. But that's just the start. We don't know why Billington wants it but the worst-case analyses – well, use your imagination. Watch out for any signs – anything, however small – that suggests Billington isn't in the driving seat, if you follow my drift. Got that?"

Mo stares at him. "You think he's possessed?"

"I didn't say that." Andy shakes his head. "Once you start asking which captains of industry are being controlled by alien soul-sucking monsters from another dimension, why, anything might happen. That sort of thing leads to godless communism and in any case they've got friends in high places like Number Ten, if you know what I mean. No, let's not go there." His cheek twitches. "Nevertheless, there is no obvious reason why a multibillionaire *needs* to acquire alien weapons of mass destruction—it's not exactly on the list of best business practices – so you be careful in there. As I said, you can call 'A' troop in at any time after you make contact, but once you've made contact they're going in ten minutes later whether you ask for them or not. Let's check your headset—"

There's a knock on the door.

I hit the boss key, flip the keyboard upside down, and stand up just as the door begins to open. It's one of the stewards from upstairs, not a black beret. "Yes?" I demand, slightly breathless.

He holds out a silver tray, half-covered by a crisp white linen cloth. My Treo sits in the middle of it, pristine and untouched. "This is for you," he says dully. I look at his face and shudder as I reach for the phone – he's not himself, that's for sure. Green lights in the back of the eye sockets and a distinct lack of breathing are usually indicators that you're looking at a nameless horror from outside space-time rather than something really sinister like, say, a marketing executive: but you still wouldn't want to invite one back to your cabin for a drink and after-dinner conversation.

I take the phone and hit the power button. "Thanks," I say. "You can go now."

The dead man turns and leaves the room. I close the door and hit the button to fire up the phone's radio stage – not much chance of getting a signal this far from land, but you never know. And in the meantime . . . well, if I can get back in touch with Control somehow and tell them not to send Mo in after me that would be a good thing. I find I'm shaking. This new Mo, fresh from some kind of special forces class at Dunwich, spilling blood with casually ruthless abandon, and working as an assault thaumaturgist with Alan's head-bangers, scares me. I've lived with her for years, and I know how hard she can be when it's time to rake a folk festival organizer over the coals, but that new violin she's carrying gives me the willies.

It's as if it comes with a mean streak, a nasty dose of ruthlessness that's crawled into the tough-minded but intermittently tender woman I love, and poisoned her somehow. And she's heading for the *Explorer*, now, to – *secure the field generator, release the hostages, neutralize the chthonian artifact, sink the* Explorer—

I stop dead in mid-thought. "Huh?" I mumble to myself. "*Secure* the field generator?"

That was the geas field she and Alan were discussing. The probability-warping curse that dragged me kicking and screaming into this stupid role-play thing, the very invocation I'm supposed to be destroying. She thinks it's aboard the *Explorer*? And Angleton wants her to keep it *running*?

I stare at my phone. There's no base station signal, but I've still got a chunk of battery charge. "Does not compute," I say, and stub my thumb on the numeric keypad. I'm frustrated: I admit it. Nobody tells me anything; they just want to use me as a communications link, keep me in the dark and feed me shit, pose around in evening drag at a casino and drink disgusting cocktails. I go back to the desk, flip the keyboard rightside up, and hit the boss key again. Mo's sitting in the cockpit of the cigarette boat, fastening her five-point safety harness. A pair of sailors is installing a kit-bag full of ominous black gadgets in the seat next to her; over the windscreen I can see the gray flank of a Royal Navy destroyer, bristling with radomes and structures that could be anything from missile batteries to gun turrets or paint lockers, to my uneducated eye. The horizon is clear in all directions but for the ruler-straight line of an airplane's contrail crawling across the sky. I glance sidelong at the phone, longingly: if I could call her up I could tell her – if only I wasn't stuck on board this goddamn yacht, moping like the token love interest in a bad thriller while the shit is going to hit the fan in about two hours aboard the *Explorer*, which is sitting less than half a kilometer away—

"What the fuck has gotten *into* me?" I ask, wondering why I'm not angry. This bovine passivity just isn't me: Why does it feel like my best option is to just sit here and wait for Mo to arrive? Damn it, I need to get things moving. McMurray can't afford to lose me before Ramona's delivered her surprise party trick to Billington: that gives me a lever I can pull on. And Angleton wants the geas field generator kept running? That's my cue. The penny drops: if the geas field actually works, and Billington can't shut it down, then he's going to be in a world of hurt. Could that be Angleton's plan? It's so simple it's fiendish. Almost without thinking, I dial 6-6-6. It's time to call my ride and get moving. After all, even the Good Bond Babe — token love interest and all — doesn't always spend the final minutes of the movie waiting for her absent love to come rescue her. It's time to kick ass and set off explosions.

15: SCUTTLE TO COVER

AN HOUR LATER, HAVING DONE EVERYTHING I CAN via the Media Center PC, I pocket my phone and open the door to my room.

There's a lot you can do in an hour with a PC on a supposedly secure but in reality penetrated-to-Hell-and-back network, especially if you've got a USB flash drive full of hacking tools. Unfortunately there's rather less you can do on such a network without making it blindingly and immediately obvious that it's been 0wnZor3d. But on the third hand, by this point I don't give a shit. I mean, I thoroughly expect what I've done to the PC to be exposed within a matter of hours, but worrying about it is taking second place right now to worrying whether I'll still be alive by then. There's a time when you've got to look at any asset and think, *Use it or lose it*, *baby*, and that time is definitely up when you're counting down the minutes in the last hour before the men in black come for you. So, what the hell.

To start with, I disable all the system logging mechanisms, so they won't be able to figure out what's going on in a hurry. I set the remote login ports to shut down an hour hence and scramble the password databases they're so quaintly relying on, and whip up a shell script that'll fry the distributed relational database behind the surveillance management system by randomly reversioning everything and then subtly corrupting the backups.

But that's just a five-fingered warm-up exercise. Billington's empire is based on the premise that you buy commercial, off-the-shelf gear, customize it to meet a MILSPEC requirement, and sell it back to the government at a 2,000 percent markup. An awful lot of his network – all the workstations those cubicle drones from Mumbai have on their desks, basically – run Windows. You'd expect a corporate enterprise rollout of Vista to be locked down and patrolled by rabid system administrators wearing spiked collars, and you'd be right: by ordinary commercial standards, Billington's network is pretty good. The trouble is, the Windows security model has always been inside out and upside down, and they're all running exactly the same service pack release. It's a classic corporate monoculture, and I've got exactly the right herbicide stuffed up one end of my bow tie, thanks to the Laundry's network security tiger team. Eileen's mission-critical surveillance operation may be running on horribly expensive blade servers with a securely locked-down NSA-approved UNIX operating system, but the workstations are . . . well, the technical term for what they'll be when I get through with them is *toast*. And by the time I get through with them Eileen is going to have a whole lot of the wrong kind of zombies on her hands.

The Laundry carped over giving me a decent car, even though I can prove that Aston Martins depreciate more slowly and cost less in running repairs than a Smart (after all, half the Aston Martins ever built are still on the road, and they've been in business for three-quarters of a century). But they didn't even blink over giving me a key drive stuffed full of malware that must have cost CESG about, oh, two million to develop, and which I am about to expend in the next half-hour, and which will subsequently leak out into the general public domain, whereupon it will give vendors of virus scanners spontaneous multiple orgasms and cause the authors to be cursed from one pole of the planet to the other. It's a classic case of misplaced accounting priorities, valuing depreciable capital assets a thousand times more highly than the fruits of actual labor — but that's the nature of the government organization. Let's just say that if what I'm about to unleash on the Billingtons' little empire doesn't take several hundred sysadmin-years and at least a week of wall-clock time to clean up, my middle names aren't Oliver and Francis.

My work done, I glance at my phone. The display is showing a cute little animated icon of a baby-blue Smart car, dust bunnies scudding beneath its tires, and a progress bar captioned *62Km/74% Complete*. I stick it back in my pocket, then pick up the dress shoes Pinky and Brains issued to me. Grimacing, I tie the shoe laces. Then I reach down and wrench the left heel round. Instantly, the shadows in my cabin darken and deepen, taking on an ominous hue. The Tillinghast resonator is running: in this confined space it should give me just enough warning to shit myself before I die, if Billington's entrusted his operational security to daemons, but in the open . . . well, it adds a whole new meaning to *take to your heels.*

The corridor outside my door is dark and there's an odd, musty smell in the air. I pause, skulking just inside the doorway as I wait for my eyes to adjust. Ellis Billington and his cronies are aboard the *Explorer*, but there's no telling who's still here, is there? I can make myself useful while I wait for Mo by finding out what's going on aboard the *Mabuse*. Ellis isn't so stupid he won't have some kind of getaway plan in mind, in case things go pear-shaped – and backup plans "C" and "D" behind plan "B," for multiple redundancy – but if I can find out what they are . . .

Oops. The door at the end of the corridor opens. "You. What are you doing outside your room? Go back at once!" The black beret draws his pistol.

My mind blanks for a moment, and there's a big hollow feeling. I feel a doubled heartbeat: **Is that you, Ramona?**

What are you——

"There's a problem with my faucet?" I hear my mouth saying. "Can you take a look at it?" And I'm opening the door and stepping backwards to make room.

Let me handle this, monkey-boy. I can taste seawater in my sinuses.

What are you doing? Has McMurray lost it——

No, but Ellis has, he ordered Eileen off the *Mabuse* ten minutes ago and there are scuttling charges due to blow as soon as she's clear. Something about contagious corruption in his oneiromantic matrix; he figures someone's sabotaged the ship and he's not in the mood for half-measures——

Shit. That would be me, wouldn't it? The goon steps closer and I can see green shadows behind his mirrorshades, green writhing worms twitching and squirming in rotting cadaverous eye sockets as he steps closer and raises the pistol in both hands——

——Glock 17, says Ramona.

And she takes over.

I jackknife forwards from the opposite side of the narrow room and bring my left hand down on the pistol, grabbing the slide and pushing it back, as my right hand comes up, curling uncomfortably to punch at his left eye. Glass shatters as he pushes up with the gun, not knowing to pull it back out of reach, and I twist it sideways. It goes off, and the noise is so loud in the confined space that it's like someone's slammed my head in a door. It feels like I've torn half the skin off my right hand but I somehow keep turning while maintaining my grip, and kick and twist away from his follow-on punch, with a searing pain in my side, like I've pulled a muscle — then I'm facing the half-rotted zombie with a gun barrel in my left hand. I grab the butt with my right, which is dripping blood, and I pull the trigger, *bang,* and pull it again because somehow I managed to miss at a range of about half a meter — *bang* — and there's blood all over the inside of the door and a faint distant tinkling of cartridges rattling as they bounce off the screen of the PC.

I gasp for breath and gag at the stench. The thing on the floor — at least, what the Tillinghast resonator is showing me — has been dead for weeks. **What just happened again?** I ask Ramona.

Billington. She opens her eyes and I push myself into her head. She's still underwater, but she's not sitting in the control chair on board the submersible grab anymore: she's free-swimming in near-total darkness, stroking upwards alongside the drill string, and I can feel the exhaustion as a tight band across the tops of her thighs. **It's a double-cross.** I can taste her fear.

Talk to me! I force myself to bend over and go through the corpse's pockets. There's another magazine for the pistol, and a badge: some species of RFID tag. I take it and glance around the cabin. My right hand is still bleeding but it doesn't look as bad as it feels. (Memo to self: do not make a habit of gripping the slide of an automatic pistol while it is being fired.) **How long have I got? Where are you?**

The grab — I was halfway home when one of the docking splines engaged, and the control deck disconnected and stayed stuck on the pipe string while the payload kept going up. It's got to be intentional. He was planning on leaving me down there all along!

I can feel the panic, ugly and personal and selfish and pitiful. **Hang in there,** I tell her. **If you can make it to the surface we can pick you up—**

You don't understand! If I stay down here too long I'll begin the change – it's hereditary! I've put it off this long by staying on land most of the time, but I'm an adult and if I spend too long in the deeps I begin to adapt, irreversibly. And if I do that, my daemon will decide I'm trying to escape . . .

Ramona. I find I'm breathing fast and shallow. **Listen to me—**

Billington knows! He must know! That's why he sent the guard to kill you! He'll have McMurray under arrest or dead or worse!

Ramona. *Listen*. I take a deep breath and try to focus on air and dry land. **_Listen_ to me. Feel through my skin. Breathe through my lungs. Remember where you come from.** I stand over a cadaver and force myself to think of lush green landscapes. **You were able to let me share your metabolism when I nearly drowned. Let's try doing it the other way.** *Breathe.* Keep breathing for two people, lest one of them start sprouting tentacles and scales. It's not as easy as it sounds: you should try it one day.

You've got to get off the ship!

How do you know what Ellis is doing? I ask. I step over the body and into the corridor. It's even less welcoming, stinking of the grave, of soil and darkness and blind burrowing things. *First door on the right, up the stairs, left, corridor—*

Pat and I have a back channel. Ramona concentrates on swimming, letting the calming repetitive motions occupy her mind. (Is it my imagination, or is it beginning to get slightly less dark?) **Last time he checked in he warned me about the scuttling charge. He figured Billington would have you taken off the ship, along with Eileen. Next thing, he drops the block between us. That's all I know, I swear!**

Uh-huh. The stairs feel as if they're on the edge of crumbling beneath my shoes, maggot-riddled boards creaking warnings to one another. The air is turning clammy. *Keep breathing*, I remind myself. **You haven't been entirely honest with me, have you? You and Pat. You've been using that block of his to keep me from dumpster-diving your head for intelligence. Playing me like an instrument:**

Hey, you're a fine one to talk! Too late: I realize she's glimpsed my memory of Mo's briefing. *Secure the geas generator*. **You guys want it, too.**

No, I say grimly, **we want to stop *anyone* from getting it. Because if you think through the political implications of a human power suddenly starting to play with chthonian tech, you need to ask yourself whether BLUE HADES would view it—**

Creepy violin music in the back of my head raises the hair on the nape of my neck, just as I round the corner at the top of the stairs and come face to face with another zombie in a black uniform. He's got an MP-5 in a tactical sling at the ready, but I've got adrenalin and surprise on my side – I'm so jittery that I pull the trigger three times before I can make myself stop.

—as a Benthic Treaty violation, I finish, then draw a deep breath and try to stop my hands shaking. **What's with all the zombies? Is Billington killing his optioned employees as a tax dodge or something?**

I don't *know*. She takes out her frustration on the water. **Will you move it? You've got maybe six minutes to get off that ship!**

Secure the geas generator. The corridor seems to pulse,

contracting and dilating around me like a warm fleshy tube –
a disturbingly esophageal experience. The smell of decay is
getting stronger. I pick up the MP-5, managing not to lose
my non-existent breakfast as the zombie's neck disintegrates.
I brush rotting debris off the sling, stick the pistol in my
pocket, and let Ramona take over my hands to check the
burst selector on the machine pistol. I duck-walk down the
passage and then there's a crossway and another door opposite
me. I open the door to the owner's lounge—

I've got company.

"Well, if it isn't the easily underestimated Mr. Howard!"
She smiles like a snake. "Better not squeeze that trigger, all
the carbines are loaded with banishment rounds in case the
Black Chamber tries something – you'll fry the generator if
you shoot. And you wouldn't want to do that, would you?"

It's Johanna Todt, McMurray's thugette. It's funny how
she's nothing like as glamorous when I'm sharing my eyeballs with Ramona: or maybe it's something to do with the
combat fatigues, life preserver, and smudged make-up, not to
mention the stench of ancient death she drags around like a
favorite toy she can't bear to let go of. She's standing behind
the diorama at the center of the geas generator grid, holding
a hammer about ten centimeters above the Bond-man-
nequin's head. *Whoops*.

I'm still trying to think of something to say when
Ramona takes the initiative: "Fancy meeting you here, dear.
Did Pat deep-six you or did you decide you needed a bit
more bargaining power?"

"Ramona?" She cocks her head to one side. "Ah, I should
have guessed. Three's a crowd: Why don't you butt out,
bitch?"

I manage to temporarily regain control of my larynx: "She
stays," I say. *Remember to breathe deeply*, I tell myself. My doubled vision is beginning to annoy me: the light around

Ramona is definitely brightening towards a predawn twilight. I try to keep the MP-5 pointing in Johanna's general direction, but she's right – if I start shooting, I'm as likely to take out the geas generator as hit her. "What are you doing here?"

"Unlike some, I know who I'm loyal to. I figured I'd help myself to the leftovers at the rich man's buffet, seeing I've just armed the scuttling charges. And aren't you just the dish? I think you'll do for starters." Johanna's grin widens, carnivorously: I catch a whiff of breath that's not so much stale as cadaverous, reeking of the crypt. "I can disentangle you, 'Mona, did you know that? I can even unlock your binding without killing McMurray. I stole his tokens while I was helping him consider the error of his ways down in the brig." She turns her free hand so that I can see she's holding a small plastic box. "It's all in here. I own you both."

Breathe. Ramona tenses and kicks harder towards the light. Her buttocks are a solid slab of agony: she's swum nearly a kilometer straight up, and she's beginning to tire of struggling, of fighting off the adaptive stress that seductively taunts her, the knowledge that if she just uses her *other* muscles everything will become so much easier—

"So what do you want with us?" I ask, taking a short step towards her.

"Stop. Don't move." She stares at me. "I want you to adore me," she says, almost wistfully. "I want you to be my body. 'Mona, give him to me and I'll even set you free, Ellis doesn't need to know—"

For a moment I'm in Ramona's body, swimming free towards a surface that is slowly brightening: it's still a dim twilight, utter darkness to merely human eyes, but I can see shapes in the murk above me. Half of the horizon is dominated by a huge, black shadow that the drill string disappears into, and there's another dark silhouette in the near distance.

I'm in control, I'm the one who's swimming with unfamiliar legs and weaker upper arms – I begin altering course towards the distant, dark shape in the water—

Meanwhile, Ramona is in *my* body, and she's dropped the MP-5 and is halfway across the perspex lid covering the diorama, making a noise in the back of her throat that I've heard when two cats get serious about their territory. Johanna whacks the hammer hard, off the back of my neck – aiming for my head, but she misses – causing a bright sharp pain, and then I'm in her face and she's biting at me and trying to smash me on the side of the skull and Ramona does something with my arms that I'm just not up to, some type of blocking move. I can feel muscles, possibly a tendon, tearing as I punch Johanna overarm; she blocks, I bring up a knee—

Breathe for two because the *Mabuse* is holding station but it's still a third of a kilometer away—

"Bitch!" screams Johanna, then sinks her teeth into my shoulder and goes for my balls.

Ramona, not used to having that external hazard to guard, doesn't react in time to Johanna – but I do, and I manage to squirm sideways so that Johanna grabs my inner thigh painfully, rather than turning me into a pile of screaming jelly. The Glock in my pants is digging in uselessly. Then I notice Johanna's teeth in my right shoulder. They burn and they're icy-cold at the same time, which is *wrong*: bite injuries aren't meant to freeze. Everything about Johanna is wrong: this close with the Tillinghast resonator powered up I can feel something moving just behind her face, something horrifyingly similar to Ramona's succubus, but different. Instead of feeding on the small death I can hear it calling for the great one, the ending of time. I feel weak in its presence, enervated and crushed by a numinous dread.

Fuck it, keep breathing, monkey-boy! What are you doing, shit-for-brains, trying to kill us both? That's

Ramona. She sounds as if she's calling to me from the far end of a long corridor.

Breathe? I'm lying on top of Johanna on the floor. *How did we get here?* She's still as a corpse, but she's got her teeth embedded in my shoulder and she's hugging me like her one true love. And I feel so *heavy.* Breathing is a huge effort. There's a haze forming around my vision. *Breathe?*

A hand – mine? – is fumbling with the lump in my pocket.

Breathe.

Everything is going gray. The tunnel is walled in darkness. Johanna Todt waits at the end of it, smiling coolly, as inviting and desirable as a glass of liquid helium. But I can also tell somehow that Johanna isn't what's waiting for me if I take that drink: Johanna is like the bioluminescent lure dangling before an angler fish's head, right in front of the sharp jaws of oblivion. She's got me in her arms and if I take the lure, when I get up I'll be as hollow as she is, I won't be *me* anymore, just a puppet rotting slowly on its feet while her daemon tugs it through the motions of life.

Breathe?

BANG.

Johanna spasms beneath me, shuddering and tensing. Her thighs flex.

BANG.

I remember to breathe, then nearly choke on the hot stink of burned powder.

She's vibrating away, drumming her heels on the floor, and there's a flood of blood and tissue everywhere around her head, like a spray of hair. As I pant for breath I realize there's a hand clutching a pistol inches away from my head, and my arm feels as if it's twisted half out of its socket. A combined wash of fear and revulsion makes me bounce off the floor, muscles screaming. **Ramona?**

Still here, monkey-boy. She's gasping — no, that's wrong — she's struggling for breath. There's a burning sensation in her gills as she fights down the reflex to extend them fully. Stroking towards the slim shadow of the *Mabuse* outlined against the brightness of the surface, still some 200 meters overhead: **Breathe, dammit! I'm getting cramps! I can't keep this up.**

I pant like a dog, then carefully lower the pistol. I've got more pulled muscles and my right arm is screaming at me, plus a savage bite that makes me dizzy when I poke at it with my left hand. I look at my fingertips. *Blood.* **Shit. How long—**

If that bitch was telling the truth, you've got two or three more minutes to get the diorama and make it up on deck.

I look around, trying to make sense out of nonsense, a luxurious lounge aboard a yacht, a dead woman on the floor . . . and a diorama in a large, locked display case. I can't move the case, it's the size of a pool table. I groan. It looks like the proximate effect of my first stab at hatching a Plan B was to spook Billington into ordering the ship sunk — and right now, I seem to be short of options.

But. *Secure the field generator.* That's the core of the geas Billington's set up, and he's now trying to destroy it in the crudest way imaginable — not just by throwing the "off" switch, but by blowing up the ship. (Why? Because I got a little too clever and let slip the yipping Chihuahuas of infowar.) If I can keep it running, then the semantics of the spell demand that James Bond — or a good knockoff — will save us. It's just a matter of figuring out how to keep the thing running while I get it off the sinking ship.

My Treo is in my back pocket. I nearly scream as I reach for it with my right arm, then shakily switch it on and aim the camera lens at the display. Once I've filled the memory card that'll have to do. I check the display – *72Km/97% Complete* – then shove it in a hip pocket.

Looking around the owner's lounge, I don't see anything obvious, but the dining room was just up the corridor. I duck out and stumble towards it, shove my way through the door, and what I want is waiting for me under a pile of uncollected dirty dishes. I grab the linen tablecloth, wait for the clatter of crockery to stop, and stagger back to the lounge. Then I whack the display case hard with the butt of my pistol, knocking out as much glass as possible.

Breathe. I catch a glimpse of Ramona, the agony spreading to her lower back. There are burning wires of pain in her shoulders as she scrabbles towards the surface close by the port side of the *Mabuse.* The air in here is foul, a stench of sewers and decaying, uncooked meat. I shove the pistol in a pocket then take the tablecloth in both hands and drop it across the broken glass and the diorama. I lean forwards – *remember to breathe* – and gather it all in with both hands. Then I fumble on the floor for the plastic box containing the tokens that Johanna taunted Ramona with. My hands shake as I finally tie off the corners of the tablecloth in a rough knot. **Got it,** I tell her.

Get the hell out!

She doesn't need to tell me twice. I head for the door, grabbing the MP-5 on the way, and cast around the corridor for the door onto the sun deck.

That one, Bob——

The daylight glare nearly brings tears to my eyes after the death-stink below decks. I step out onto the deck and walk to the side of the ship, then look aft. In the distance there's a white trail etched across the wave crests. *Breathe.* I blink, and see through Ramona's eyes, looking up at the light from beneath the keel of the frigate. From down here it looks enormous, the size of a city. *Run.* I weave my way aft, back into the access passage to the boat deck. There's a crane and boarding steps descending over the side, ending just above a floating platform at the waterline. I take the steps two at a time, nearly tumbling into the water in my haste.

Get yourself overboard! Now! *Breathe*. She can see the grid of the platform, the shadows of my feet on the metal grating.

Not yet. I gasp for breath, my vision flickering with the bright sparkles of hyperventilation as I set down the stolen diorama and pull out my phone: *74Km/99% Complete.* **How do you think we're going to get onto the *Explorer*? Neither of us is in any condition to swim that far, and anyway – it's moving.**

There's white foam at the bow of the huge drilling ship as its positioning thrusters power up. Billington isn't stupid enough to sit too close while his yacht self-destructs: even if he isn't afraid of the backwash from the geas generator he's got to be worried about the fuel tanks.

We've got to get over there! She's near the surface.

I've got a plan. *Breathe*. I reach down into the water as—

With all her remaining energy she reaches up towards the hand breaking through the silvery mirror-surface above her and—

"*Ow!*" Water splashes over me as Ramona breaks the surface and grabs onto my hand.

"Plan. What plan? *Ow* . . ." I heave. Something in my back registers a complaint, in triplicate, then locks up and goes on strike.

Ramona twists round and falls back onto the platform. Out of the water, she goes limp. I can feel her muscles. I wish I couldn't.

"Look over there." I point. The silvery trail is curving towards us like a bizarre missile running just above the surface of the water. There's something that looks like a glassy black sphere in the middle of it, surrounded by four huge orange balls: "It's my car."

"You. Have got to be. Kidding."

"Nope." I grin like a mad thing as the Smart Fortwo whines towards me eagerly, its hub-mounted air bags thrashing the water into submission. "It may not be a BMW or an Aston Martin, but at least it comes when I call it." It slows as it nears the edge of the platform. Ramona sits up wearily and begins to peel off her outer-heated wet suit. Her skin is silvery-gray, the scales clearly visible: even the few hours underwater have been enough to cause the change to set in, and her fingers have begun to web. By the time she's got her top layer unzipped, the car has slowly pulled up to platform edge and driven aboard. The engine stops.

"Who's that?" she asks, pointing through the windscreen.

"Oops, I forgot about him." It's Marc, sometime procurer and latterly zombie. He's bloated up against the front windscreen and the driver's side door. "You'll have to help me get him out of there."

"This is why I never date the same guy twice – avoids raising a stink, you know?"

I get the door open, just in time to be hit by an olfactory experience almost as good as Johanna's buffet. "Ick."

"You can say that again, monkey-boy. He's leaked all over the seats – you expect me to ride in this?"

"You're the one who told me about the scuttling charges, I'm the one with the biometrics that match the ignition button. Your call."

I grab hold of one arm. To my great delight, it doesn't come off in my hand. Ramona opens the opposite door and shoves him towards me. I do a two-step with the stiff, twist him round, and shove him onto the platform. I grab the bundled-up geas generator and shove it into the shoe box that passes for a boot in this thing. Ramona winces as she tries to belt herself in, and holds something up: "What's this?"

"Marc's idea of a conversational intro." I pass her the MP-5. "You know how to use one of these, I figure I'll take the pistol." It's another Glock, of course, with a whizzy laser-sighting widget and an extended magazine. "Now let's go visit Ellis, huh?"

I push the ignition button, check that the doors and windows are closed, then gently tap the gas pedal. There's a red light blinking on the dash, but the engine starts. We tilt alarmingly as I drive off the edge of the platform, but the car stabilizes fairly fast, leaving us bobbing like a cork in the water. I stroke the accelerator again. That starts a lot of spray flying – this thing isn't the world's most efficient paddle boat – but we begin to move away from the *Mabuse*, and I start the windscreen wipers so I can see where we're going. The *Explorer* is a huge, gray bulk about 400 meters away. There's the beginning of a trail of foam at her stern, but I'm pretty sure I can catch her – even a Smart car can outrun a 60,000-ton, deep-ocean drilling ship, I figure. Ramona leans against my sore shoulder and I feel her bone-deep exhaustion, along with something else, a creeping smugness.

"We make a pretty good team," she murmurs.

I'm about to say something intended to take the place of a witty reply when the rearview mirror lights up like a flash bulb. I goose the accelerator and we lurch wildly, nearly nosing over as a spray of water goes everywhere. Then there's a sound like the door of Hell slamming shut behind me, and another huge lurch sets us bobbing side to side. A water spout almost as high as the topmost radar mast hangs over the ship, then comes crashing back down

"Fuck fuck fuck . . ." We're less than a ship-length away from the *Mabuse*, on the opposite side to the scuttling charge, and that's probably what saves us: most of the blast is heading in the opposite direction. On the other hand, the ship is rolling, heeling over almost sixty degrees, and there's a gash below the waterline that's raised so high above the surface I can see it in my rearview mirror. It looks large enough to take on a hundred tons of water a second. Johanna opened the bulkhead doors below the waterline, and as if it isn't enough that the charge has ripped the yacht's skin open, cavitation from the explosion has broken her keel. I suppose Billington doesn't much care about money at this point – when he's Planetary Overlord he can have as many yachts as he likes – but right now *I* care because we're less than 200 meters away from something as massive as a ten-story office block that's just begun to disintegrate. As a way of ensuring that annoying witnesses are silenced and the geas generator stops working, it's overkill, but if it succeeds I suppose Lloyds of London are the only people who're going to complain.

The ship's superstructure hangs in the air like a hallucination heeled over through almost ninety degrees. Loose life rafts and stores tumble across the deck and fall into the sea. With majestic slowness it begins to roll back upright – warships aren't designed to capsize easily – and I steel myself for the inevitable backwash when four or five thousand tons of ship go under.

I floor the accelerator pedal to open up some distance behind us which is, of course, the cue for the engine to die. There's an embarrassed *beep* from the dashboard. I mash my thumb on the START button, but nothing happens, and I realize that the blinking red light on the dash has turned solid. There's a little LCD display for status messages and as I stare at it in disbelief a message scrolls across:

MANDATORY SERVICE INTERVAL REACHED RETURN TO MAIN DEALER FOR ENGINE MAN-AGEMENT RESET.

Behind me, there's a sinking frigate, while ahead of me, the *Explorer* has begun to make way. I start swearing: not my usual "shitfuckpisscuntbugger" litany, but *really* rude words. Ramona sinks her fingers into my left arm. "This can't be happening!" she says, and I feel a wash of despair rising off her.

"It's not. Brace yourself."

I flip open the lid on top of the gear-stick and punch the eject button. And the car ejects.

The car. Ejects. Three words that don't belong in the same sentence or at any rate in a sentence that's anywhere within a couple hundred meters of sanity street. In real life, cars do not come with ejector seats, for good reason. An ejector seat is basically a seat with a bomb under it. The traditional way they're used is, you pull the black-and-yellow striped handle, say goodbye to the airplane, and say hello to six weeks in traction, recovering in hospital – if you're lucky. The survival statistics make Russian roulette look safe. Very recent models buck the trend – they've got computers and gyroscopes and rocket motors to stabilize and steer them in flight, they've probably even got cup holders and cigarette lighters – but the basic point is, when you pull that handle, Elvis *has* left the cockpit, pulling fifteen gees and angling fifteen degrees astern.

Now, the ejector system Pinky and Brains have bolted to the engine block of this car is not the kind you get in a fifth-generation jet fighter. Instead, its closest relative is the insane gadget they use to eject from a helicopter in flight. Helicopters are nicknamed "choppers" for a reason. In order to avoid delivering a pilot-sized stack of salami slices, helicopter ejection systems come with a mechanism for getting those annoying rotor blades out of the way first. They started out by attaching explosive bolts to the rotor hub, but for entirely understandable reasons this proved unpopular with the flight crew. Then they got smart.

Your basic helicopter ejector system is a tube like a recoilless antitank missile launcher, pointing straight up, and bolted to the pilot's seat. There's a rocket in it, attached to the seat by a steel cable. The rocket goes up, the cable slices through the rotor blades on the way, and only then does it yank the seat out of the helicopter, which by this time is approximately as airworthy as a grand piano.

What this means to me:

There's a very loud noise in my ear, not unlike a cat sneezing, if the cat is the size of the Great Sphinx of Giza and it's just inhaled three tons of snuff. About a quarter of a second later there's a bang, almost as loud as the scuttling charge that broke the *Mabuse*, and an elephant sits down on my lap. My vision blurs and my neck pops, and I try to blink. A second later, the elephant gets up and wanders off. When I can see again – or breathe – the view has changed: the horizon is in the wrong place, swinging around wildly below us like a fairground ride gone wrong. My stomach flip-flops – *look ma, no gravity!* – and I hear a faint moan from the passenger seat. Then there's a solid jerk and a baby hippopotamus tries me for a sofa before giving up on it as a bad deal – that's the parachute opening.

And we're into injury time.

Most of the time when someone uses an ejector seat, the pilot sitting in it has a pressing reason for pulling the handle – for example he's about to fly into the type of cloud known as cumulo-granite – and the question of where the seat – and pilot – lands is a bit less important than the issue of what will happen if it doesn't go off. And this much is true: if you eject over open water, you probably expect to land on the water, because there's a hell of a lot more water down there than ships, or whales, or desert islands stocked with palm trees and welcoming tribeswomen.

However, this isn't your normal ejection scenario. I've got

Billington's Bond-field generator stuffed in the trunk, a glamorous female assassin with blood in her eye clutching a submachine gun in the passenger seat, and a date with a vodka martini in my very near future – just as soon as I make landfall alive. Which is why, as we swing wildly back and forth beneath the rectangular, steerable parachute (the control lines of which are fastened to handles dangling just above the sunroof), I realize that we're drifting on a collision course with the forward deck of the *Explorer*. If we're not lucky we're going to wrap ourselves around the forward docking tower.

"Can you work the parachute?" I ask.

"Yes—" Ramona unfastens her seatbelt, yanks at the sunroof release latch: "Come on! Help me!" We slide the roof back and she stands up, makes a grab for the handles, catches them, and does something that makes my eyes water and bile rise in the back of my throat. "Come on, baby," she pleads, spilling air from one side of the parachute so that it side-slips away from the docking tower, "you can make it, can't you?"

We swing back and forth like a plumb bob held by a drunken surveyor. I look down, trying to find a reference point to still my stomach: there's a tiny boat down there beside the *Explorer* – it's a speedboat, and from here it looks alarmingly similar to the boat I saw Mo loading stuff into. *It can't be*, I think, then hastily suppress the thought. It's best not to notice that kind of thing around Ramona.

We swing round and the deck rushes up towards us terrifyingly fast. "Brace!" calls Ramona, and grabs me. There's a long-drawn-out metallic scraping crunching noise and the elephant makes a last baby-sized appearance in my lap, then we're down on the foredeck. Not that I can see much of it – it's shrouded beneath several dozen meters of collapsing nylon parachute fabric – but what I saw of it right before we landed wasn't looking particularly hospitable. Something

THE JENNIFER MORGUE 333

about the dozens of black berets racing towards us, guns at the ready, suggests that Billington isn't too keen on the local skydiving club dropping in for tea.

"Get ready to run," Ramona says breathily, just as there's a metallic racking noise outside the parachute fabric that's blocking our view.

"Come out with your hands up!" someone calls through a megaphone that distorts their voice so horribly that I can't hope to identify them.

I glance at Ramona. She looks spooked.

"We have a Dragon dialed in on you," the voice adds, conversationally. "You have five seconds."

"Shit." I see her shoulders droop in despair and disgust. "It's been nice knowing you—"

"It's not over yet."

I flick the catch and push the door open, wincing, then swing my feet out onto the deck. It's time to face the music.

16: REFLEX DECISION

"**So**," says Billington, pacing out a lazy circle on the deck around me, "the rumors of your resourcefulness were not misplaced, Mr. Howard."

He flashes a cold smile at me, then goes back to staring at the deck plates in front of his feet, inspecting the wards around us. After a few seconds he passes out of my field of vision. I can feel Ramona flexing her arms against the straps; a moment later she spots him coming into view. Two more of the dentist's chairs are mounted side by side, facing in opposite directions, on the same pedestal in the control room: Billington probably gets a bulk discount on them at villain-supply.com. Unfortunately he's also got Ramona and me strapped to them, and an audience of about fifty black berets who are either brandishing MP-5s or leaning over instrument consoles. These particular black berets are still human, not having succumbed to the dubious charms of Johanna Todt, but the freshly painted wards, inked out in human blood, sizzle and glow ominously before my Tillinghast-enhanced vision.

"Unfortunately your usefulness appears to have expired," says Ellis, walking back into view in front of me. He smiles again, his weird pupils contracting to slits. There's something badly wrong about him, but I can't quite put my finger on it: he's not a soulless horror like the zombie troops, but he's not quite all there, either. Something is missing in his mind, some sense of self. "Shame about that," he adds conversationally.

"What are you going to do to us?" asks Ramona.

I really wish you hadn't asked that, I tell her silently, my heart sinking.

Bite me, monkey-boy. Just keep him talking, okay? While he's monologuing he isn't torturing us to death . . .

"Well, that's an interesting conundrum." Billington glances over his shoulder at a clipboard-toting minion: "Would you mind finding Eileen and asking her why she's late? It doesn't normally take her this long to terminate an employee." The minion nods and hurries away. "Following the logic of the situation that prevailed until I ended the invocation field by sinking the *Mabuse*, I ought to have you tortured or fed to a pool of hungry piranhas. Fortunately for you, the geas should be fully dissipated by now, I'm short on torturers, and urban legends to the contrary, piranhas don't much like human flesh." He smiles again. "I was inclined to be merciful, earlier: I can always find a niche for a bright, young manager in Quality Assurance, for example—" I shiver, half-wondering if maybe the piranha tank wouldn't be preferable "—or for a presentable young lady with your talents." Then the smile drops away like a camo sheet covering an artillery tube: "But that was before I discovered that you—" he stabs a finger at Ramona "—were sent here to murder me, and that you—" I flinch from his bony digit "—were sent here as a *saboteur*."

He hisses that last, glaring at me malevolently.

"Saboteur?" I blink and try to look perplexed. *When in doubt, lie like a very flat thing indeed.* "What are you talking about?"

Billington gestures at the huge expanse of glass walling the control room off from the moon pool. "Look." His hand casually takes in the huge skeletal superstructure hanging from the ceiling by steel hawsers, its titanium fingers cradling a blackened cylinder with a tapered end: JENNIFER MORGUE Two, the damaged chthonian weapon. An odd geometric meshwork scarifies its hull: there are whorls and knots like the boles of a tree spaced evenly along it. From this angle it looks more like a huge, fossilized worm than a tunneling machine. It's quiescent, as if dead or sleeping, but . . . I'm not sure. The Tillinghast resonator lets me notice things that would otherwise be invisible to merely human eyes, and something about it makes my skin crawl, as if it's neither dead nor alive, or even undead, but something else entirely; something waiting in the shadows that is as uninterested in issues of life and death as a stony asteroid rolling eternally through the icy depths of space, pacing out a long orbit that will end in the lithosphere of a planet wrapped in a fragile blue-green ecosystem. Looking at it makes me feel like the human species is simply collateral damage waiting to happen.

"Your masters want to stop me from helping him," Billington explains. "He's very annoyed. He's been trapped for thousands of years, stranded on a plateau in the rarefied and chilly dark, unable to move. Unable to heal. Unable even to revive." Huge hoses dangle from the underside of the *Explorer*'s drilling deck, poking into the skin of the chthonian artifact like intravenous feeding lines. I blink and look back at Billington. *He's lost it*, I tell myself, with gathering horror. *Hasn't he?*

You've only just figured that out? asks Ramona. **And here I was thinking you were quick on the uptake.** Despite the sarcasm, she feels very frightened, very cold. I think she knew some of this, but not the full scope of Billington's deviancy.

"I know *all* about your masters," Billington adds in her direction. He can't hear our silent exchange, feel Ramona testing the strength of her bonds, or recognize me scoping out the parametric strength of the wards he's positioned around us – he just wants to talk, wants someone to listen and understand the demon urges that keep him awake late in the night. "I know how they want to use him. They sent you to me in the hope of trading in a strong tool for a more powerful one. But he's not a tool! He's a cyborg warrior-god, a maker of earthquakes and an eater of souls, birthed for a single purpose by the great powers of the upper mantle. It is *his* geas to rejoin the holy struggle against the numinous aquatic vermin as soon as his body is sufficiently restored for him to resume residence in it. And it is *our* nature that the highest expression of our destiny must be to submit to his will and lend our strength to his glorious struggle."

Billington spins round abruptly and jabs a stiff-armed salute at the thing hanging in its titanium cradle outside the window. He raises his voice: "He demands and requires our submission!" Turning back to me, he shouts, "We must obey! There is glory in obedience! Fitness in purpose!" He raises a clenched fist: "The deep god commands that his body be restored to its shining terror! You will help me! You *will* be of service!" Spittle lands on my face. I flinch but I can't do anything about it – can't move, don't dare express skepticism, *don't piss off the lunatic* . . . I'm half-convinced, with an icy certainty verging on terror, that he's going to kill one of us in the next couple of minutes.

"How does he talk to you?" Ramona asks, only a faint unevenness in her voice betraying the fact that her palms are clammy and her heart is pounding like a drum.

Billington deflates like a popped balloon, as if overcome with a self-conscious realization of what he must look like. "Oh, it's not voices in my head, if *that's* what you're worrying about," he says disparagingly. His lips quirk. "I'm not mad, you know, although it helps in this line of work." A guard is walking along the catwalk outside, followed by a flash of pink. "He doesn't really approve of madness among his minions. Says it makes their souls taste funny. No, we talk on the telephone. Conference calls every Friday morning at 9:00 a.m. EST." He gestures at a console across the room, where an old bakelite handset squats atop an old gray-painted circuit box that I recognize as an enclosure for Billington's Gravedust communicator. "It's so much easier to just dial 'D' for Dagon, so to speak, than to bother with the eerie voices and walls softening under your fingertips. And these days we've sorted out a telepresence solution: he's taken up residence in a host body so he can keep an eye on things in person, while we restore his primary core to full functionality. Of course it's energetically expensive for him to occupy another body, so we have to keep the sacrifice schedule in mind as a critical path element in the restoration project, but there's no shortage of tenth-decile underperformers on the sales force . . . ah, yes." He glances at his watch. "Top of the hour, right on time."

The guard and the woman in the pink suit arrive just as Billington gestures at the window. Outside, on the moon pool floor, a structure like an airport baggage-conveyor terminates in a platform just underneath the chthonian's conical head. I squint: there are lines and curves on that pointed end, almost like the helical coils of a drill, or a squid's tightly coiled tentacles. Down on the conveyor, something wriggly is working its way towards the platform. Or rather, something on the conveyor is being fed forwards remorselessly, wriggling and twitching like a worm on a hook.

What's that—? Ramona is in my head, using my eyes.

Not what – who. I peer closer, then blink. The

baitworm on the conveyor is still alive, but black fire crawls along the edges of the platform at the far end. It twists and rolls, and it's funny how a change of angle changes your entire perspective on things because suddenly I see his face, eyes bugging out with fear, and what I'm looking at snaps into focus. He's been trussed up in gaffer tape and his mouth taped shut to stop him screaming but I recognize McMurray, and I recognize a human sacrifice when I see him. He's heading towards that platform, and now I realize—

"You've got to stop it!" I shout at Billington. "Why are you doing this? It's insane!"

"On the contrary." Billington turns away from me and holds his hands behind his back. "I don't like doing this, but it's necessary if we're to meet our third-quarter target for energizing the revivification matrix," he says tightly. "By the way, you ought to relax: you're in the circuit, too."

I jackknife against the straps and nearly choke myself. "What—"

"Oh *shit*," swears Ramona, despair and apprehension sweeping over her.

"Considering you appear to have prevented Johanna from returning, it's the least you can do for me," Billington explains. "I need a soul devourer. Otherwise it's just more dead meat, which doesn't help anyone. And while you're so inconveniently entangled I might as well plug both of you into the summoning grid to reduce the side-band leakage."

The platform unfolds shutterlike flaps as McMurray nears it. I can distantly hear his voice screaming in Ramona's head. **Get me out of this! That's an order!** *Billington needs an infovore*, I realize. *He's feeding the chthonian by destroying souls in its presence.* My knees feel like jelly: I've seen this sort of thing before. *Which means—*

Ramona convulses against the straps and begins to choke. I gag my guts rolling, because I can feel the backwash from

McMurray's ill-considered words echoing off the inside of her skull like thunder and lightning. Ramona can't *not* obey, but she's immobile, unable to respond to her master's voice, and she's capable of choking herself to death and taking me with her.

Get me out! McMurray howls as the conveyor deposits him on the killing platform under the cylinder. Then the platform begins to sink and the shutters close in on top of it and I realize what I'm looking at: a hydraulic iron-maiden, a car crusher built for humans.

Ramona's daemon is rising. I can feel a monstrous pressure in my balls. I can't see properly and I'm choking, I can't move – Ramona can't move – and a hideous heat spreads through my crotch. *Her* crotch. Proximity to death excites it, whether hers or her victim's. And this is about as close as it gets: the shutters are steel slabs, driven by hydraulic rams. There's a whine of motors, deepening and slowing, and a muffled noise I can't identify. I can't breathe, or Ramona can't breathe, and her daemon senses the flow of life from the killing box down below. As the flow spurts into us the daemon feeds greedily, and Ramona convulses and falls unconscious.

With the last of my energy I inhale in a ragged breath, and scream.

"Oh dear," says Billington, turning round. "What seems to be the problem?"

I draw another breath.

"You really shouldn't have done that," says the woman in the pink suit, standing in the doorway.

"Hurt her—" I gasp. Then I start coughing. I can't sense Ramona's daemon, but Ramona herself is deeply unconscious. "She needs water. Lots of seawater." I'm breathing for two of us but I can't quite get enough air, because what Ramona needs now is full-body immersion. I can feel it, the changes in her cells, her organs slowly contracting and rearranging inside her frame, the fever of mutation that will only end in her death or complete metamorphosis—

"What took you so long, dear?" asks Billington, looking at the doorway.

"I was putting my face on," says the woman in pink. I'm still gasping as a pair of black berets close in on Ramona's chair with buckets in hand, but something about the woman in pink trips my attention. *Hang on, that's not Eileen—*

"Excellent." Billington glances at the black berets bending over Ramona and frowns. "We seem to have a little problem, this one isn't as robust as the last."

I peer at the woman in pink. In one hand, she holds a shiny metal briefcase; the other arm is stretched rigidly down, close to her body, as if she has a ruler up her sleeve. I try to focus on the sparkling around her: *class three glamour, at least*, I realize. She's taller and younger than Eileen, and if I squint – I look past her at her reflection in the glass – *red hair—*

"What do you expect?" asks the woman everyone but me seems to think is Eileen Billington. "She's not a movie hero, is she? And neither is he, for that matter."

"Not now that I've terminated the reel," Billington says briskly. "You, you, and you, go chuck the piranhas overboard, fill the fish tank with seawater, and get it over here—"

"Really?" asks the woman. "Are you *sure* it's all over?"

Billington glances at her. "Pretty much, apart from a few little details – mass human sacrifices, invocations of chthonic demigods, Richter-ten earthquakes, harrowing of the Deep Ones, rains of meteors, and the creation of a thousand-year world empire, that sort of thing. Trivial, really. Yes, it's all nailed down, dear. Why do you ask?"

"I was curious: Does it mean we're safe from any risk that the Hero-designate playing the archetypical role is going to leap out of the shadows, armed to the teeth with specialized lethal hardware, and wreck all our plans?"

Billington begins to turn. "Yes, of course. Why are you worrying about——"

To my necromancy-stunned eyes it all seems to happen in very slow motion. Her clenched fist unclenches: a bone-colored bow drops down her sleeve like a concealed cosh until she grips it by one end and brings her hand up to unlatch the briefcase. Both sides of the case eject, leaving her clutching a handle and a sling attached to a pale violin that she raises to her chin in a smooth motion that speaks of long practice. The halves of the case contain compact amplified speakers, and there's a stark black-on-yellow sticker on the underside of the violin: THIS MACHINE KILLS DEMONS. I start to shout a warning as Ramona begins to stir, her gills flexing limply against the base of her throat and her mouth pouting, and Billington begins to inscribe a sigil in the air in front of his face——

"This is a song of unbinding," says Mo, and the bow slides across the faintly pulsing things-that-aren't-strings, glowing like gashes in my retinas and trailing a ghostly haze when she moves. The first note sounds, wavering eerily on the air and building like the first breezy harbinger of a hurricane. "It unlocks – *everything*."

Across the room, a particularly alert black beret shouts a warning and raises his MP-5. The second note wavers and screams from the body of the instrument, resonating painfully with my back teeth. Every hair on my body is trying to stand on end simultaneously. These aren't sounds the human ear is supposed to be able to hear: the psycho-acoustic model is all wrong. I feel like I'm suddenly listening to bat song, the noises that drive dogs wild, the raw and bloody notes of silence. The brief hammering of gunfire drives nails into my eardrums then stops in a shattering of glass and a brief scream as Mo squeezes the fingerboard. The bow string is glowing red. A third note quavers weirdly out of the instrument, somehow building simultaneously with the first and second, which haven't stopped – they've taken root in the air of the room, thickening and turning it blue – and there's a popping noise as the buckles of the straps holding me down spring open.

More screams. Billington, being non-stupid, dashes for the door onto the catwalk outside. The bow reaches the end of its arc and begins to slice back across the bridge of the violin as lockers burst apart, spilling paper and supplies across the floor: zippers break, belts unfasten, doors fly open. The noise is so loud now that it feels like a god is ripping the two halves of reality apart: the sound of tearing inside my head is deafening. I can't hear or feel Ramona anymore, and the lack of her presence is a huge vacuum in my soul, trying to split me in two. The noise of another shot slams in my ears as I sit up and see Mo advancing across the room towards the guards, still playing one hideous note after another. Her skin crackles with static discharge and her hair stands on end as the black beret with the pistol takes aim again and I gulp air, about to shout a warning: but she notices him and anything I could say would be redundant because she merely points the fingerboard of her instrument at him and there's a spray of blood, unlocked from the skin that binds it. Across the room, there's a sudden flash of light and smoke begins to pour out of one of the equipment racks.

An alarm klaxon begins to blare on and off mournfully, then a speaker crackles into life: "Alert! Incoming helicopters! All hands to point defense!"

Where's Billington gotten to? I shake my head, trying to dislodge the dreadful keening sound of strings. The straps are gone. I sit up and lean over the side of the chair, then stumble to my feet and stagger round to the other side. Ramona's out for the count, and she looks really ill – breathing fast, the livid, bruised stripes of her gill slits pulsing against the fish-white scales around the base of her neck. *She's too dry*, I realize. *Too dry?* A stab of guilt: I glance across at Mo, who is single-mindedly driving the surviving black berets out of the room. They're panicking, running for safety. Where's their master?

I glance through the shattered window overlooking the moon pool and my blood runs cold. The thing in the cradle dangling from the drilling rig is twitching fitfully. Down below it a familiar figure hunkers down on the deck, staring up at the chthonic killing machine. *Shit, so that's where he's gotten to.* Then I notice the second, smaller creature standing in front of him. *And that's the host body. He's going to try to reactivate it!* Which means—

I shuffle painfully away from the chairs, and nearly trip over a pistol. Bending down, I pick it up: it's either the futuristic-looking P99 with laser scope that Marc had, or its identical twin. "Mo?" I call.

She turns round and says something. I can't hear a single word over the howling reverberation of her violin.

"I've got to stop him!" I yell. I can barely hear myself. She looks blank, so I point at the door onto the catwalk. "He's out there!"

She points at one of the inner doors emphatically, as if suggesting I should head that way instead. So I shake my head and stumble towards the catwalk. Behind me, the flickers of light suggest more electrical fires breaking out among the high-voltage bearers. I lean over the railing and look down dizzily. It's about twenty meters away – a small target at that range. I fumble with the pistol and switch on the laser. My hand's shaking. *If I'm right*—

The red dot dances across the far wall. I trace it down the wall, swearing under my breath, and run it rapidly across the deck towards the drained floor of the moon pool. I keep my finger away from the trigger. *If I'm wrong—*

Billington is an expert at soul-sucking abominations. Now he's in thrall to another, greater evil: one with a damaged body, so he's provided it with a convenient temporary replacement while he comes up with enough sacrificial victims and spare parts to repair its original one. What entity aboard this ship exhibits all the personality traits of a cold-blooded killing machine, combined with the monstrous, overweening vanity and laziness of a convalescent war god lounging in their personal Valhalla while their minions prepare their armor? There's only one answer.

The Persian tomcat sits underneath the alien horror, washing itself without concern. "C'mon, Fluffy," I tell it. "Show me what you are." We all know about cats and lasers. Lasers are the best cat toy ever invented: the red-dot machine that comes out for playtime. Used skillfully, you can make a cat chase the dot so slavishly that she'll run headfirst into a wall. It's like the sitting-in-cardboard-boxes thing, or the sniffing-an-extended-finger reflex. All cats do it, unless they're so enervated that they choose to ignore the lure and groom their fur instead.

Fluffy takes a few seconds to lock on, and when he does, his response is immediate and drastic. He glances down at the deck, sees the red dot dancing around nearby – and dashes away like his tail's on fire.

"Bob! We've got to get out of here! Ellis has gotten away." I look round. Mo stands in the doorway, one hand cupped around an ear: "There are scuttling charges due to blow as soon as he's clear—"

It's déjà vu all over again. At least her eyeballs aren't glowing blue and she isn't levitating. I shake my head and point down at the moon pool: "Help me! We've got to stop him!"

"Who's the target?" Mo ducks out and stands beside me.

"Him!" I pull the trigger. There's an ear-stinging ricochet a fraction of a second after the shot. I'm nowhere near the target. "Damn, missed."

"Bob, we've got to get out of here! Can you still feel that Black Chamber bitch? The chromatic disintermediator should have broken your entanglement, but – why are you trying to shoot that cat?"

"Because—" I squeeze off another shot "—it's possessed!"

"Bob." She looks at me as if I'm mad. There's a loud bang from inside the control room, and a human figure in a black beret runs out onto the sealed doors flooring the pool: I shoot instinctively and miss, and he dives for cover. "Leave the fucking cat – hey, that's Billington down there!" She raises her instrument and prepares to let fly.

The cat squirts out across the floor, a white blur targeting the downed bad guy. I shoot again, and again, and keep missing. "Not Billington! Get the cat!"

Mo sniffs skeptically. "Are you sure?"

"Yes, I'm goddamn sure!" Billington's standing in front of the iron maiden, as if steeling himself to jump inside. "It's the enemy! Get it now, or we're fucked!"

Mo raises her violin, squints darkly down at the deck below us, and drops a noise like a million felines being disemboweled down on top of Fluffy. Who opens his fanged maw to howl, then explodes like a gore-filled, white dandelion head. Mo turns and looks at me harshly. "That looked just like a perfectly ordinary cat to me. If you've—"

"It was possessed by the animation nexus behind JENNIFER MORGUE Two!" I gabble. "The clue – he saw a laser dot and dodged—"

"Bob. Back up a moment."

"Yes?"

"The cat. You said it was the enemy. You didn't say it was

occupied by the mind of *that* thing?" She points up at the ceiling, where the chthonic warrior is definitely twitching and writhing. I stare.

"Uh, well, I meant—"

"And you thought killing it would improve matters?"

"Yes?"

One of the bole-like knots in the warrior's hide is growing larger. Then it opens, revealing an eye the size of a truck tire. It stares right back at me.

She clouts me on the back of the head: "Run!"

The huge tentacle slams down onto the deck where Ellis Billington kneels in supplication before his god, landing with a percussive clang that rattles the remaining windows and reduces him to a greasy stain on the bulkhead. Which is probably why Mo and I survive: we stumble back through the control room doorway about two seconds before the tree-trunk-thick limb slams into the wall with the force of a runaway locomotive. Support trusses scream and buckle beneath the blow. I start coughing and my eyes water immediately. The air is gray with smoke and thick with the greasy fish-oil smell of burning insulation. I thump the big red button beside the door and metal shutters begin to drop down behind the broken glass – maybe it's too little too late, but at least it makes me feel better. "Where's Ramona? We've got to get her out of here!"

Mo glares at me. "What makes you think rescuing her's on my list of mission objectives? You're disentangled, aren't you?"

I stare back at her, wondering who the hell she thinks she is, barging in here with her Class A thaumaturgic weapons. Then I blink and remember sharing a slow breakfast with her back before all this started, all those endless weeks ago – *Is that all?* "I think I know what you're thinking," I say slowly, feeling an awful weary emptiness inside me, "but that's not what's been going on between us. And if you leave her because you're jealous, you'll be making a mistake you can never undo. Plus, you'll be leaving her to *that*."

JENNIFER MORGUE thumps against the outside of the security shutters, sending a shower of glass daggers crackling and clinking across the floor. The shutters bend but they hold: something's clearly wrong with the beast, or it should have been out of the moon pool by now, leaving a twisted trail of titanium structural members behind it. Dumping the controlling intelligence out of its temporary host body must have awakened the chthonian prematurely, still deathly weak and hungry. Mo doesn't look away from my face. She's searching me for something, some sign. I stare at her, wondering which way she's going to jump, whether the geas has gone to her head: if it has conferred not only the power that goes with her role, but also the callousness.

After a few seconds Mo looks away. "We'll sort this out later."

I stumble back towards the sacrifice chairs. Ramona is still out. I rest a palm on her forehead, then snatch it back fast: she's fever-hot. "Give me a hand . . ." I manage to get one arm over my shoulder and begin to lift her off the chair, but in my present state I'm too weak. Just as my knees begin to give out under me someone takes her other arm. "Thanks——" I glance round her lolling head.

"This way, mate." The apparition grins at me around its regulator. "Sharpish!"

"If you say so." More black-clad figures appear – this time, wearing wet suits and body armor. "Is Alan here?"

"Yeah. Why?"

"Because——" there's a crashing noise from the far wall, and I wince "——there's an alien horror on the other side of that wall and it wants in *bad*. Make sure somebody tells him." I start coughing: the air in here becoming unbreathable.

"Ah, Bob, exactly the man! Don't worry about the eldritch horror, we've got a plan for this contingency – as soon as we've evac'd we'll just pop a brace of Storm Shadows on his ass and send him right back down where he came from. But you're exactly the man I was hoping to see. How are you doing, old chap? Got a Sitrep on the opposition for me?"

I blink, bleary-eyed. It's Alan all right: wearing scuba gear and a communications headset only the Borg could love, he still manages to look like an excitable schoolteacher. "I've had better days. Look, the primary opposition movers are dead, and I think Charlie Victor might be amenable to an offer of political asylum if the rite of unbinding did what I think it did to her, but about the Smart car on the drilling deck—"

"Yes, yes, I know it's a bit scorched around the edges and there are some bullet holes, but you don't have to worry: the Auditors won't mind normal wear and tear—"

"No, that's not it." I try to focus. "In the boot. There's a tablecloth with a diorama wrapped up in it. Would you mind having one of your lads blow it up? Otherwise all the Bond mojo zapping around in here is going to follow us home and wreck any chance of me and Mo getting back together again for anything but a one-night stand."

"Ah! Good thinking." Alan pushes a button and mutters into his mike. "Anything else?"

"Yeah." Either there's a lot of gray smoke in here, or – "I'm feeling dizzy. Just let me sit down, for a moment . . ."

EPILOGUE:

THREE'S COMPANY

IT'S AUGUST IN ENGLAND, AND I'M ALMOST functioning on British Summer Time again. We're having another heat wave, but up here on the Norfolk coast it's not so bad: there's an onshore breeze coming in from the Wash, and while it isn't exactly cold, it feels that way after the Caribbean.

We call this place the Village: it's an old in-joke. Once upon a time it was a hamlet, a village in all respects save its lack of a parish church. It was one of three churchless hamlets that had clustered in this area, and the last of them still standing, for the others slid under the waves a long time ago. There was only the one meandering road in the vicinity, and it was potholed and poorly maintained. Go back sixty or seventy years and you'd find it was home to a small community of winkle-pickers and fishermen who braved the sea in small boats. They were a curious, pale, inbred lot, not well liked by the neighbors up and down the coast, and they kept to themselves. Some of them, it's said, kept to themselves so efficiently that they never left the company of their own kind from birth unto death.

But then the Second World War intervened. And someone remembered the peculiar paper the village doctor had tried to publish in the *Lancet*, back in the '20s, and someone else noticed its proximity to several interesting underwater obstructions, and, with the stroke of a pen, the War Ministry relocated everyone who lived next to the waterline. And the men from MI6 Department 66 came and installed electricity and telephones and concrete coastal defense bunkers, and they rerouted the road so that it doubled back on itself and missed the village completely before merging with the road to the next hamlet up the coast. And they systematically erased the Village from the Ordnance Survey's public maps, and from the post office, and from the discourse of national life. In a very real sense, the Village is as far away from England as Saint Martin, or the Moon. But in another sense, it's still too close for comfort.

Today, the Village has the patina of neglect common to building developments that subsist on the largess of government agencies, and rely for their maintenance on duct tape and the extensive use of the power of Crown Immunity to avoid planning requirements. It's not a white-painted picturesque Italianate paradise like Portmeirion, and we inmates aren't issued numbers instead of names. But there's a certain resemblance to that other Village — and there is, overlooking the harbor mole, a row of buildings that includes an old-fashioned pub with paint peeling from the wooden decking outside, worn linoleum floors, and hand-pumps that dispense a passable if somewhat briny brew.

I came up from London yesterday, after the board of enquiry met to hear the report on the outcome of the JENNIFER MORGUE business. It's over now, buried deep in the secret files in the Laundry stacks below Mornington Crescent tube station. If you've got a high enough clearance you can get to read them — just go ask the librarians for CASE BROCCOLI GOLDENEYE. (Who says the classification office doesn't have a sick sense of humor?)

I'm still feeling burned by the whole affair. Bruised and used about sums it up; and I'm not ready to face Mo yet, so I had to find somewhere to hole up and lick my wounds. The Village isn't a resort, but there's a three-story modern building called the Monkfish Motel that's not entirely unlike a bad '60s Moat House — I think it was originally built as MOD married quarters — and there's the Dog and Whistle to drink in, and if I get drunk and start babbling about beautiful man-eating mermaids and sunken undersea horrors, nobody's going to bat an eyelid.

It's late afternoon and I'm on my second pint, slumped in the grasp of the sofa in the east corner of the lounge bar. I'm the only customer at this time of day — most everyone else is off attending training courses or working — but the bar stays open all the same.

The door opens. I'm busy failing to reread a dog-eared paperback biography, my mind skittering off the words as if they're polished ice cubes that melt and slide away whenever I warm them with my glance. Right now it's gathering moss on the coffee table in front of me as I idly flip the antique Zippo lighter that's the one part of my disguise kit I ended up bringing home. Footsteps slowly approach, clattering on the bare floor. I sit there in the corner, and I wonder tiredly if I ought to run away. And then it's too late.

"He told me I'd find you here," she says.

"Really?" I put the Zippo down and look up at her.

The prelude to this little drama took place the day before yesterday in Angleton's office. I was sitting in the cheap plastic visitor's seat he keeps on the other side of his desk, my line of sight partially blocked by the bulky green-enameled flank of his Memex, trying to hold my shit together. Up until this point I'd been doing a reasonable job aided by Angleton going out of his way to explain how we were going to clear my entirely unreasonable expense claims with the Auditors: but then he decided to try and get all human on my ass.

"You'll be able to see her whenever you want," he said, right out of the blue, without any warning.

"Fuck it! What makes you think—"

"Look at me, boy." There's a tone of voice he uses that reaches into the back of your head and pulls the control wires, grating and harsh and impossible to ignore: it got my attention.

I looked directly at him. "I am sick and tired of everyone tiptoeing around me as if I'm going to explode," I heard myself say. "Apologizing won't help: what's done is done, there's no going back on it. It was a successful mission and the ends, at least in this case, justify the means. However underhanded they were."

"If you believe that, you're a bigger fool than I thought." Angleton closed the cover of the accounts folder and put his pen down. Then he caught my gaze. "Don't be a fool, son."

Angleton's not his real name – real names confer power, which is why we always, all of us, use pseudonyms – nor is it the only thing about him that doesn't ring true: I saw the photographs in his dream-briefing, and if he was that old when he was along for the ride on Operation JENNIFER, he can't be a day under seventy today. (I've also seen an eerily similar face in the background of certain archival photographs dating from the 1940s, but let's not go there.) "Is this where you give me the benefit of your copious decades of experience? Stiff upper lip, the game's the thing, they also serve who whatever-the-hell-the-saying goes?"

"Yes." His cheek twitched. "But you're missing something."

"Huh. And what's that?" I hunker down in my chair,

resigned to having to sit through a sanctimonious lecture about wounded pride or something.

"We fucked with your head, boy. And you're right, it is just another successful operation, but that doesn't mean we don't owe you an apology and an explanation."

"Great." I crossed my arms defensively.

He picked up his pen again, scratching notes on his desk pad.

Two weeks' compassionate leave. I can stretch it to a month if you need it, but beyond that, we'll need a medical evaluation." *Scribble, scribble.* "That goes for both of you. Counseling, too."

"What about Ramona?" The words hung in the air like lead balloons .

"Separate arrangements apply." He glanced up again, fixing me with a wintry blue stare. "I'm also recommending that you spend the next week at the Village."

"Why?" I demanded.

"Because that's where Predictive Branch says you need to go, boy. Did you want fries with that?"

"Fucking hell. What do *they* have to do with things?"

"If you'd ever studied knife fighting, one of the things your instructors would have drilled into you is that you always clean your blade after using it, and if possible sharpen and lubricate it, before you put it away. Because if you want to use it again some time, you don't want to find it stuck to the scabbard, or blunt, or rusted. When you use a tool, you take care to maintain it, boy, that's common sense. From the organization's point of view . . . well, you're not just an interchangeable part, a human resource: we can't go to the nearest employment center and hire a replacement for you just like that. You've got a unique skill mix that would be very difficult to locate — but don't let it go to your head just yet — which is why we're willing to take some pains to help you get over it. We used you, it's true. And we used Dr. O'Brien, and you're both going to have to get used to it, and what's more important to you right now — because you expect to be used for certain types of jobs now and again — is that we didn't use you the way you *expected* to be used. Am I right?"

I spluttered for a moment. "Oh, sure, that's everything! In a nutshell! I see the light now, it's just in my nature to be all offended about having my masculinity impugned by being cast in the role of the Good Bond Babe, hero-attractor and love interest for Mo in her capacity as the big-swinging-dick secret agent man with the gun, I mean, violin, and the license to kill. Right? It's just vanity. So I guess I'd better go powder my nose and dry my tears so I can look glamorous and loving for the closing romantic-interest scene, huh?"

"Pretty much." Angleton nodded. His lip quirked oddly. A suppressed smile?

"Jesus fucking Christ, Angleton, that's leaving just a little bit out. Not to mention Ramona. If you think you could tie our brains together like the Kilkenny cats, then just cut us loose — it doesn't work that way, you know?"

"Yes." He nodded again. "And that's why you need to go to the Village," he said briskly. "Talk to her. Settle where you both stand, in your own mind." He picked up his papers and looked away, an implicit dismissal. I rose to my feet.

"Oh, and one other thing," he added.

"What?"

"While you're about it, remember to talk to Dr. O'Brien as well. You both need to sort things out — and sooner, rather than later."

"He made it an order." She shrugs. "So here I am." Looking as if she'd rather be anywhere else on the planet.

"Enjoying yourself?" I ask. It's the sort of stilted, stupid question you ask when you're trying to make small talk but walking on eggshells in case the other person explodes at you. Which is what I'm half-expecting – this situation is a minefield.

"No," she says with forced levity. "The weather sucks, the beer's warm, the sea's too cold for swimming, and every time I look at it . . ." She stalls, the thin glaze of collectedness cracking. "Can I sit down?"

I pat the sofa beside me. "Be my guest."

She sits down in the opposite corner, an arm's length away. "You're acting like you're mad at me."

I glance at the book on the table. "I'm not mad at *you*." I try to figure out what to say next: "I'm mad at the way the circumstances made things turn out. Are *you* still mad at *her*?"

"At *her*?" She chuckles, startled. "I don't think she had any more choice in it than you did. Why should I be mad at her?"

I pick up my glass and take a long mouthful of beer. "Because we slept together?"

"Because you – what?" A waspish tone creeps into her voice: "But I thought you said you hadn't!"

I put my glass down. "We didn't." I meet her eye. "In the Bill Clinton sense of things, I can honestly say I have *not* had sexual intercourse with that woman. You know what the Black Chamber did to her? If I *had* slept with her I'd be dead."

"But how can you——" Mo is confused.

"Her monster had to feed. Before you came and unbound it, it had to feed. She had to feed it, or it would have eaten her. I was along for the ride."

Enlightenment dawns. "But now she's there——" a wave in the vague direction of the drowned village of Dunwich, a mile out to sea, where the Laundry maintains its outpost "——and you're here. And you're both safe."

Acid indigestion. "Safe from what?" I ask, watching her sidelong.

"Safe from—" She stops. "Why are you looking at me?"

"She's undergoing the change, you know that? They can usually hold it off, but in her case it's looking irreversible."

Mo nods, reluctantly.

"Probably it was triggered by the deep-diving excursion," I add. "Although proximity to certain thaumic resonances can bring it on prematurely." *Which you would be in a position to know all about*, I don't say. It's a horrible thing to suspect of anyone, especially your partner who you've been sharing a house with for enough years that it's getting to be a habit. "I gather they expect her to make it, with her mind intact."

"That's good," Mo says automatically. A double take: "Isn't it?"

"I don't know. Is it a good thing?" I ask.

"That's not a question I'd have expected you to ask."

I sigh. None of this is straightforward. "Mo, you could have warned me they were training you in deep-cover insertion and extraction operations! Jesus, I thought *I* was the one on the sharp end!"

"And you were!" she snaps at me suddenly. "Did you wonder how I felt about it, every time you disappeared on a black bag job? Did you ask if maybe I was worried sick that you were never coming back? You know what I know, how helpless do you think that left me feeling?"

"Whoa! I didn't want you to worry—"

"You didn't want! Jesus, Bob, what does it take to get through to you? You can't stop other people worrying just by not *wanting* them to. It's not about you, dim-bulb, it's about me. At least, this time it was. Or do you think I turned up there on your ass by accident?"

I stare at her, at a loss for words.

"Let me lay it out for you, Bob. The whole solitary reason Angleton assigned you to that stupid fucking arrangement with Ramona was *precisely* because you didn't know what was going on. What you didn't know, you couldn't leak to Ramona."

"I got that much, but why—"

"Billington was enslaved by JENNIFER MORGUE Two sometime in the '70s, after the abortive attempt to raise the K-129. He tried to contact the chthonian using the Gravedust rig – a little private free enterprise, if you like. JENNIFER MORGUE Two wanted out, and wanted out bad, but it needed someone to come and repair it. Billington provided it with a temporary host body, kitty kibble, and he had the resources to buy the *Explorer* – once the US Navy decommissioned it – and kit it out for a retrieval run. And we knew all this, on deep background, three years ago."

I blink. "Who is this 'we' you speak of?"

"Me." She looks impatient. "And Angleton. And everybody else with BLUE HADES clearance who's been working on the project. Except for you, and a couple of others, who've been kept in a mushroom box against the day."

"Damn." I pick up my glass and drain what's left of the beer. "I need another drink." Pause. "You too?"

"Make mine a double vodka martini on ice." She pulls a face. "I can't seem to kick the habit."

I stand up and walk inside to the bar, where the middle-aged barwoman is sitting on a stool poring over the Sudoku in the back of the *Express*. "Two double vodka martinis on ice." I say diffidently.

The woman puts her magazine down. She stares at me like I crawled out from under a rock. "You're going to say shaken, not stirred, ain't cha?" She's got a Midwestern accent: probably another defector, I guess. "You know how bad that tastes?"

"Make it one shaken, one stirred, then. Off the ice. And easy on the vermouth." I wink.

I go back towards the corner I'd claimed, then pause in

the archway. Mo's leaning back in the sofa, infinitely familiar. For a moment my breath catches in my throat and I have
to stop and try to commit the picture to memory in case it
turns out to be one of the last good times. Then I force
myself to get my legs moving again.

"They'll be over in a minute," I say, dropping onto the
sofa beside her.

"Good." She stares at the windows overlooking the beach.
"You know the Black Chamber wanted to get their hands on
JENNIFER MORGUE. That's what McMurray was doing
there."

"Yes." So she thinks I want to talk about business?

"We couldn't let them do that. But luckily for us,
Billington . . . well, he wasn't entirely sane to begin with,
and when he came up with the idea of implementing a Hero
trap, that made things a lot easier."

"*Easier?*" It's a good thing I don't have a drink in my
hand.

"Absolutely." She nods. "Imagine if Billington had simply
gone to the Black Chamber and said, 'Ten billion and it's
yours,' keeping his fix-it plan to himself. But instead, he gets
this idea that he's got to act in solitary as the prime mover in
the scheme, and of *course* he's the archetype of the billionaire
megalomaniac, so he does the obvious thing: leverages his
assets. The Hero trap – the geas he built around that yacht –
required a hero to trigger it. He figured the plot structure is
deterministic: the hero falls into the bad guy's hands, the bad
guy monologues – and at that point, he was going to destroy
the trap, neuter the hero, who is just another civil servant at
this point, stripped of the resonances of the Bond invocation – and allow his plan to proceed to completion."

"Except . . ."

"You know the alternative plot?" She glances at the book
I've been reading: a biography of a playboy turned naval

intelligence officer, news agency manager, and finally spy novelist.

"What?" I shake my head. "I thought it was——"

"Yes, it's so neat you can draw a flow chart. But it's non-deterministic, Bob: the Bond plot structure has a number of forks in it before it converges on the ending, with Mr. Secret Agent Man and his love interest getting it on in a lifeboat or the honeymoon suite of the QE2 or something. Including the approach to the villain. Billington didn't look into it deeply enough; he assumed that the Hero archetype would come looking for him and fall into his clutches directly."

"But." I snap my fingers, trying to collect my scattered thoughts. "You. Me. He got *me*, but I wasn't the real Bond-figure, right? I was a decoy."

She nods. "It happens. If the love interest ends up on the villain's yacht, being held prisoner, *then* the hero has to go after her. Or *him*. The real trick was the idea – I think it was Angleton's – of using the Good Bond Girl as a decoy by dressing her up in a tux and a shoulder holster. And then to figure out how to use this to get the Black Chamber to put one over on Billington."

"Ramona. She knew that I thought I was the agent in place, so she naturally assumed I really *was* the agent."

"Right. And this also let us identify a leak in our own organization, because how else did Billington make you so rapidly? Which turns out to have been Jack. Last of the public school assholes, hung out to dry out where he couldn't do any damage – so he develops a sideline in selling intel to what he thinks is another disgruntled outsider."

"Urk." I suddenly remember the electrodynamic rig Griffin had stuck in his safe house and briefly wonder just what the hell else he might have been picking up on it, sitting pretty in the middle of the Caribbean with no supervision.

Mo falls silent. I realize she's waiting for something. My tongue's frozen: there are questions I want to ask, but it's a bad idea to ask something when you're not sure you want to hear the answer. "Did you enjoy being . . . Bond?" I finally manage.

"Did I?" She raises an eyebrow. "Hell." She frowns. "Did *you*?" she demands.

"But I wasn't——"

"But you *thought* you were."

"No!" The very question is freighted with significance I don't want to explore. "I don't do high society, I don't smoke, I don't like being beaten up, being taken prisoner, being tortured, or fighting people, and I'm no good at the womanizing bit." I dry-swallow. "How about you?"

"Well," she pauses to consider, "I'm no good at womanizing either." Her cheek twitches. "Is that what this is about, Bob? Did you figure I was cheating on you?"

"I was——" I clear my throat "——unsure where I stood."

"We need to talk about this. Get it out in the open some time. Don't we?"

I nod. It's about all I can do.

"I didn't jump into bed with anybody else," she says briskly. "Does that make you feel better?"

No, it doesn't. Now I feel like a shit for having asked in the first place. I make myself nod.

"Well, great." She crosses her arms, then taps her fingers on her upper arm: "Where have our drinks gotten to?"

"I ordered the martinis. I guess she's taking her time." *Quick, change the subject.* I really don't want us to fall down one of those embarrassing conversational potholes where the silence stretches out into an eloquent statement of mutual miscommunication: "So how did you manage to disguise yourself as Eileen? You really had me convinced at first."

"Oh, that was no big deal." Mo looks relieved. She smiles

at me and my heart beats faster. "You know Brains has a sideline in cosmetology? Says some of his best friends are drag queens. Well, we've got enough surveillance background on Eileen to know what she looks like, so I got Brains out to the *York* to provide make-up services before the assault. Stick a class two glamour on top of the basics — a wig, the right clothes, some latex paint — and her own daughter wouldn't make her. We used Pale Grace™ for the finishing touch; it might be bugged, but we made sure I wouldn't see anything until I was aboard the ship. So I just headed for the control room using the maps we had on file from Angleton's—"

I raise a hand. "Hold it."

"What?" Mo stares at me.

"Have you got your violin?" I whisper, hunkering down.

"No, why—"

Shit. "Our drinks are well overdue."

"And?"

"And this plot was set up by a document that's classified CASE BROCCOLI GOLDENEYE, Angleton said, and Predictive Branch said I needed to be here, *and* . . ."

"And?"

I kneel on the floor and pull my mobile phone out, flick the switch to silence it, then put it in camcorder mode. I sneak it out from behind the sofa, then pull it back and inspect the bar. There's nobody there. I swear quietly, and call up my thaumic scratchpad application. Then I tip my glass upside down over the table, and draw my fingers through the resulting beer suds frantically, wishing I hadn't downed the pint and left myself mere drops to work with.

"Have you got that stupid piece of paper on you?"

"What, the license to kill? It's just a prop, it doesn't mean anything—"

"So pass it here, then. We haven't had plot closure yet, and you're not the only one who can use cosmetics and a class two glamour."

"Shit," Mo whispers back at me, and rolls forwards onto the floor. "Are you thinking what I think you're thinking?"

"What, that we've been followed home by a manifestly evil mistress of disguise who is hankering for revenge because we got her husband stomped into pink slime by a chthonian war machine?"

There's a disturbingly solid *click-chunk* from the front door, like a Yale lock engaging.

"Do you know the ending of *Diamonds Are Forever*? The movie version with Sean Connery?" I meet Mo's eyes for a moment, and in a disturbing flash of clarity I realize that she means a whole lot more to me than the question of who she has or hasn't been having sex with. Then she nods and rolls away from the floor in front of the sofa, and I hit the button on my phone just as there's a flat percussive bang: not the ear-slamming concussion I expect from a pistol, but muffled, much quieter.

I look round.

The middle-aged barwoman is waving a pistol inexpertly around the room, the long tube of a silencer protruding from its muzzle: she looks subtly familiar this time. "Over here!" I call.

She makes the classic mistake: she glances my way and blinks, gun muzzle wavering. "Come out where I can see you!" Eileen snaps querulously.

"Why? So you can kill us more easily?" I'm ready to jump up and dive through the window if necessary, but she can't see me — the concealment spell is still working, at least until the remaining beer evaporates. I go back to folding a paper airplane out of Mo's license, my fingers shaking with tension.

"That would be the idea," she says. "A lovers' quarrel,

male agent kills partner then shoots self. It doesn't have to hurt."

"No shit?" Mo asks. I squint and try to spot her, but one thing we've both got going for us is that pubs tend to be gloomy and poorly lit, and this one's no exception.

Eileen spins round through ninety degrees and unloads a bullet into the wall of optics behind the bar.

I glance at the drying suds then roll to my hands and knees and creep around the sofa, trying to stay low. I think the paper plane's balanced right – it had better be, I'm only going to get the one chance to use it. There are forms, and this is . . . well, it *might* work. If it doesn't we're trapped in a locked pub with a madwoman with a gun, and our invisibility spell has a half-life measured in seconds rather than minutes. There are two martini glasses on the bar, one of them half full: Maybe Eileen wanted to steady her nerves first? There's probably an unconscious or dead bartender out back. What a mess: I don't think an intruder's ever penetrated the Village before. I doubt it would be possible without the blowback from the Hero trap to help.

There's a creak from a floorboard and another shot goes flying, to no apparent effect. Eileen looks spooked. She takes a step backwards towards the bar, gun muzzle questing about, and then another step. My heart's pounding and I'm feeling lightheaded with anger – no, with rage – *You think anyone would* ever *believe I'd hurt Mo?* And then she's at the bar.

There's a glassy *chink*.

Eileen spins round, and pulls the trigger just as the half-full martini glass levitates and flies at her face. She manages to shoot the ceiling, then recoils. "Ow! Bitch!" I raise the paper dart and take aim. She wipes her eyes as she brings her gun down to bear on a faint distortion in the air, a snarl of satisfaction on her face: "I see you now!"

I flick the Zippo's wheel and then throw the flaming dart at her martini-irrigated head.

Afterwards, as the paramedics load her onto a stretcher and zip the body bag closed, and Internal Security removes the CCTV hard drives for evidence, I hold Mo in my arms. Or she holds me: my knees feel like jelly and it would be downright embarrassing if Mo wasn't shuddering, too. "You're all right," I tell her, "you're all right."

She laughs shakily. "No, *you're* all right!" And she hugs me hard.

"Come on. Let's take a walk."

There's a mess on the floor, fire extinguisher foam half-concealing the scorch marks, and we skirt it carefully on our way to the door. Security has placed us under a ward of compulsion and we'll be seen by the Auditors tomorrow: but for the time being, we've got the run of the Village. Mo seems to want to head back to our quarters, but I pull back. "No, let's go walk on the beach." And she nods.

"You knew that was coming," she says as we jump down off the concrete wall and onto the rough pebbles.

"I had an idea something bad was in the air." The onshore breeze is blowing, and the sun is shining. "I didn't know for sure, or I'd have been better prepared."

"Bullshit." She punches me lightly on the arm, then puts an arm around my waist.

"No, would I lie to you?" I protest. I stare out to sea. Somewhere out there Ramona is lying in a watery hostel, learning what she really is. A new life lies ahead of her: she won't be able to come ashore after the change is complete. Hey, if I really *was* James Bond, I could have a girl in every port – even the drowned ones.

"Bob. Would you have left me for her?"

I shiver. "I don't think so." Actually, *no*. Which is not to say Ramona didn't have glamour of the non-magical kind as well, but there's something about what I have with Mo—

"Well, then. And you're cut up about the idea that I might have been cheating on you."

I consider this for a few seconds. "Surprised?"

"Well." She's silent, too. "I was worried. And I'm still worried about the other thing."

"The other thing?"

"The possibility that we're going to be haunted by the ghost of James Bond."

"Oh, I dunno." I kick a pebble towards the waterline, watch it skitter, alone. "We could always do something totally un-Bond-like, to break any remaining echoes of the geas."

"You think?" She smiles. "Got any ideas?"

My mouth is dry. "Yeah – yes, as a matter of fact I do." I take her in my arms and she puts her arms around me, and rests her face against the side of my neck. "If this was really the end of a Bond story, we'd go find a luxury hotel to hole up in, order a magnum of champagne, and fuck each other senseless."

She tenses. "Ah, I hadn't thought of that." A moment later, and faintly: "Damn."

"Well. I'm not saying it's impossible. But—" My heart is pounding again, and my knees are even weaker than they were when I realized Eileen hadn't shot her. "We've got to do it in such a way that it's *completely incompatible* with the geas."

"Okay, wise guy. So you've got a bright idea for an ending that simply wouldn't work in a Bond book?"

"Yes. See, the thing is, Bond's creator – like Bond himself – was a snob. Upper crust, old Etonian, terribly conventional. If he was around today he'd always be wearing a tailored suit, you'd never catch him in ripped jeans and a Nine Inch Nails tee shirt. And it goes deeper. He liked sex, but he was deeply ingrained with a particular view of gender relationships. Man of action, woman as bit of fluff on the side. So the one thing Bond would never expect one of his girls to say is—" it's now or never "—will . . . will you marry me?" I can't help it; my voice ends up a strangled squeak, as befits the romantic interest doing something as shockingly unconventional as proposing to the hero.

"Oh, Bob!" She hugs me tighter: "Of course! Yes!" She's squeaking, too, I realize dizzily: *Is this normal?* We kiss. "Especially if it means we can hole up in a luxury hotel, order in a magnum of champagne, and fuck each other senseless without being haunted by the ghost of James Bond. You've got a sick and twisted mind – that's why I love you!"

"I love you, too," I add. And as we walk along the beach, holding hands and laughing, I realize that we're free.

PIMPF

I HATE DAYS LIKE THIS

It's a rainy Monday morning and I'm late in to work at the Laundry because of a technical fault on the Tube. When I get to my desk, the first thing I find is a note from Human Resources that says one of their management team wants to talk to me, soonest, about playing computer games at work. And to put the cherry on top of the shit-pie, the office's coffee percolator is empty because none of the other inmates in this goddamn loony bin can be arsed refilling it. It's enough to make me long for a high place and a rifle . . . but in the end I head for Human Resources to take the bull by the horns decaffeinated and mean as only a decaffeinated Bob can be.

Over in the dizzying heights of HR, the furniture is fresh and the windows recently cleaned. It's a far cry from the dingy rats' nest of Ops Division, where I normally spend my working time. But ours is not to wonder why (at least in public).

"Ms. MacDougal will see you now," says the receptionist on the front desk, looking down her nose at me pityingly. "Do try not to shed on the carpet, we had it steam cleaned this morning." *Bastards*.

I slouch across the thick, cream wool towards the inner

sanctum of Emma MacDougal, senior vice-superintendent, Personnel Management (Operations), trying not to gawk like a resentful yokel at the luxuries on parade. It's not the first time I've been here, but I can never shake the sense that I'm entering another world, graced by visitors of ministerial import and elevated budget. The dizzy heights of the *real* civil service, as opposed to us poor Morlocks in Ops Division who keep everything running.

"Mr. Howard, do come in." I straighten instinctively when Emma addresses me. She has that effect on most people – she was born to be a headmistress or a tax inspector, but unfortunately she ended up in Human Resources by mistake and she's been letting us know about it ever since. "Have a seat." The room reeks of quiet luxury by Laundry standards: my chair is big, comfortable, and hasn't been bumped, scraped, and abraded into a pile of kindling by generations of visitors. The office is bright and airy, and the window is clean and has a row of attractively un-browned potted plants sitting before it. (The computer squatting on her desk is at least twice as expensive as anything I've been able to get my hands on via official channels, and it's *not even switched on*.) "How good of you to make time to see me." She smiles like a razor. I stifle a sigh; it's going to be one of *those* sessions.

"I'm a busy man." *Let's see if deadpan will work, hmm?*

"I'm sure you are. Nevertheless." She taps a piece of paper sitting on her blotter and I tense. "I've been hearing disturbing reports about you, Bob."

Oh, bollocks. "What kind of reports?" I ask warily.

Her smile's cold enough to frost glass. "Let me be blunt. I've had a report – I hesitate to say who from – about you playing computer games in the office."

Oh. *That.* "I see."

"According to this report you've been playing rather a lot

of Neverwinter Nights recently." She runs her finger down the printout with relish. "You've even sequestrated an old departmental server to run a persistent realm — a multiuser online dungeon." She looks up, staring at me intently. "What have you got to say for yourself?"

I shrug. What's to say? She's got me bang to rights. "Um."

"Um indeed." She taps a finger on the page. "Last Tuesday you played Neverwinter Nights for four hours. This Monday you played it for two hours in the morning and three hours in the afternoon, staying on for an hour after your official flexitime shift ended. That's six straight hours. What have you got to say for yourself?"

"Only *six?*" I lean forwards.

"Yes. Six hours." She taps the memo again. "Bob. What are we paying you for?"

I shrug. "To put the hack into hack-and-slay."

"Yes, Bob, we're paying you to search online role-playing games for threats to national security. But you only averaged four hours a day last week . . . isn't this rather a poor use of your time?"

Save me from ambitious bureaucrats. This is the Laundry, the last overmanned organization of the civil service in London, and they're *everywhere* — trying to climb the greasy pole, playing snakes and ladders with the org chart, running esoteric counterespionage operations in the staff toilets, and rationing the civil service tea bags. I guess it serves Mahogany Row's purposes to keep them running in circles and distracting one another, but sometimes it gets in the way. Emma MacDougal is by no means the worst of the lot: she's just a starchy Human Resources manager on her way up, stymied by the full promotion ladder above her. But she's trying to butt in and micromanage inside my department (that is, inside *Angleton's* department), and just to show how efficient she is, she's actually been reading my time sheets and trying to stick her oar in on what I should be doing.

To get out of MacDougal's office I had to explain three times that my antiquated workstation kept crashing and needed a system rebuild before she'd finally take the hint. Then she said something about sending me some sort of administrative assistant — an offer that I tried to decline without causing mortal offense. Sensing an opening, I asked if she could provide a budget line item for a new computer — but she spotted where I was coming from and cut me dead, saying that wasn't in HR's remit, and that was the end of it.

Anyway, I'm now looking at my watch and it turns out that it's getting on for lunch. I've lost *another* morning's prime gaming time. So I head back to my office, and just as I'm about to open the door I hear a rustling, crunching sound coming from behind it, like a giant hamster snacking down on trail mix. I can't express how disturbing this is. Rodent menaces from beyond space-time aren't supposed to show up during my meetings with HR, much less hole up in my office making disturbing noises. What's going on?

I rapidly consider my options, discarding the most extreme ones (Facilities takes a dim view of improvised ordnance discharges on Government premises), and finally do the obvious. I push the door open, lean against the battered beige filing cabinet with the jammed drawer, and ask, "Who are you and what are you doing to *my computer?*"

I intend the last phrase to come out as an ominous growl, but it turns into a strangled squeak of rage. My visitor looks up at me from behind my monitor, eyes black and beady, and cheek-pouches stuffed with—ah, there's an open can of Pringles sitting on my intray. "Yuh?"

"That's my computer." I'm breathing rapidly all of a

sudden, and I carefully set my coffee mug down next to the light-sick petunia so that I don't drop it by accident. "Back away from the keyboard, put down the mouse, and nobody needs to get hurt." And most especially, my sixth-level cleric-sorcerer gets to keep all his experience points and gold pieces without some munchkin intruder selling them all on a dodgy auction site and re-skilling me as an exotic dancer with chloracne.

It must be my face, he lifts up his hands and stares at me nervously, then swallows his cud of potato crisps. "You must be Mr. Howard?"

I begin to get an inkling. "No, I'm the grim fucking reaper." My eyes take in more telling details: his sallow skin, the acne and straggly goatee beard. *Ye gods and little demons, it's like looking in a time-traveling mirror.* I grin nastily. "I asked you once and I won't ask you again: *Who are you?*"

He gulps. "I'm Pete. Uh, Pete Young. I was told to come here by Andy, uh, Mr. Newstrom. He says I'm your new intern."

"My new *what* . . .?" I trail off. *Andy, you're a bastard! But I repeat myself.* "Intern. Yeah, right. How long have you been here? In the Laundry, I mean."

He looks nervous. "Since last Monday morning."

"Well, this is the first anyone's told me about an intern," I explain carefully, trying to keep my voice level because blaming the messenger won't help; anyway, if Pete's telling the truth he's so wet behind the ears I could use him to water the plants. "So now I'm going to have to go and confirm that. You just wait here." I glance at my desktop. *Hang on, what would I have done five or so years ago . . .?* "No, on second thoughts, come with me."

The Ops wing is a maze of twisty little passageways, all alike. Cramped offices open off them, painted institutional green and illuminated by underpowered bulbs lightly dusted with cobwebs. It isn't like this on Mahogany Row or over the road in Administration, but those of us who actually contribute to the bottom line get to mend and make do. (There's a malicious, persistent rumor that this is because the Board wants to encourage a spirit of plucky us-against-the-world self-reliance in Ops, and the easiest way to do that is to make every requisition for a box of paper clips into a Herculean struggle. I subscribe to the other, less popular theory: they just don't care.)

I know my way through these dingy tunnels; I've worked here for years. Andy has been a couple of rungs above me in the org chart for all that time. These days he's got a corner office with a blond Scandinavian pine desk. (It's a corner office on the second floor with a view over the alley where the local Chinese take-away keeps their dumpsters, and the desk came from IKEA, but his office still represents the cargo-cult trappings of upward mobility; we beggars in Ops can't be choosy.) I see the red light's out, so I bang on his door.

"Come in." He sounds even more world-weary than usual, and so he should be, judging from the pile of spreadsheet printouts scattered across the desk in front of him. "Bob?" He glances up and sees the intern. "Oh, I see you've met Pete."

"Pete tells me he's my intern," I say, as pleasantly as I can manage under the circumstances. I pull out the ratty visitor's chair with the hole in the seat stuffing and slump into it. "And he's been in the Laundry since the beginning of this week." I glance over my shoulder; Pete is standing in the doorway looking uncomfortable, so I decide to move White Pawn to Black Castle Four or whatever it's called: "Come on in, Pete; grab a chair." (The other chair is a crawling horror covered in mouse-bitten lever arch files labeled STRICTLY SECRET.) It's important to get the message across that I'm not leaving without an answer, and camping my hench-squirt on Andy's virtual in-tray is a good way to do that. (Now if only I can figure out what I'm supposed to be asking . . .) "What's going on?"

"Nobody told you?" Andy looks puzzled.

"Okay, let me rephrase. Whose idea was it, and what am I meant to do with him?"

"I think it was Emma MacDougal's. In Human Resources." *Oops, he said Human Resources.* I can feel my stomach sinking already. "We picked him up in a routine sweep through Erewhon space last month." (Erewhon is a new Massively Multiplayer Online Role-Playing Game that started up, oh, about two months ago, with only a few thousand players so far. Written by a bunch of spaced-out games programmers from Gothenburg.) "Boris iced him and explained the situation, then put him through induction. Emma feels that it'd be better if we trialed the mentoring program currently on roll-out throughout Admin to see if it's an improvement over our traditional way of inducting new staff into Ops, and his number came up." Andy raises a fist and coughs into it, then waggles his eyebrows at me significantly.

"As opposed to hiding out behind the wet shrubbery for a few months before graduating to polishing Angleton's gear-wheels?" I shrug. "Well, I can't say it's a *bad* idea——" Nobody ever accuses HR of having a *bad idea*; they're subtle and quick to anger, and their revenge is terrible to behold. "——but a little bit of warning would have been nice. Some mentoring for the mentor, eh?"

The feeble quip is only a trial balloon, but Andy latches onto it immediately and with evident gratitude. "Yes, I completely agree! I'll get onto it at once."

I cross my arms and grin at him lopsidedly. "I'm waiting."

"You're——" His gaze slides sideways, coming to rest on

Pete. "Hmm." I can almost see the wheels turning. Andy isn't aggressive, but he's a sharp operator. "Okay, let's start from the beginning. Bob, this fellow is Peter-Fred Young. Peter-Fred, meet Mr. Howard, better known as Bob. I'm—"

"—Andy Newstrom, senior operational support manager, Department G," I butt in smoothly. "Due to the modern miracle of matrix management, Andy is my line manager but I work for someone else, Mr. Angleton, who is also Andy's boss. You probably won't meet him; if you do, it probably means you're in big trouble. That right, Andy?"

"Yes, Bob," he says indulgently, picking right up from my cue. "And this is Ops Division." He looks at Peter-Fred Young. "Your job, for the next three months, is to shadow Bob. Bob, you're between field assignments anyway, and Project Aurora looks likely to keep you occupied for the whole time – Peter-Fred should be quite useful to you, given his background."

"Project Aurora?" Pete looks puzzled. Yeah, and me, too. "What is his background, exactly?" I ask. *Here it comes* . . .

"Peter-Fred used to design dungeon modules for a living." Andy's cheek twitches. "The earlier games weren't a big problem, but I think you can guess where this one's going."

"Hey, it's not my fault!" Pete hunches defensively. "I just thought it was a really neat scenario!"

I have a horrible feeling I know what Andy's going to say next. "The third-party content tools for some of the leading MMORPGs are getting pretty hairy these days. They're supposed to have some recognizers built in to stop the most dangerous design patterns getting out, but nobody was expecting Peter-Fred to try to implement a Delta Green scenario as a Neverwinter Nights persistent realm. If it had gone online on a public game server – assuming it didn't eat him during beta testing – we could have been facing a mass outbreak."

I turn and stare at Pete in disbelief. "That was *him?*" *Jesus, I could have been killed!*

He stares back truculently. "Yeah. Your wizard eats rice cakes!"

And an attitude to boot. "Andy, he's going to need a desk."

"I'm working on getting you a bigger office." He grins. "This was Emma's idea, she can foot the bill."

Somehow I *knew* she had to be tied in with this, but maybe I can turn it to my advantage. "If Human Resources is involved, surely they're paying?" Which means, deep pockets to pick. "We're going to need two Herman Miller Aeron chairs, an Eames bookcase and occasional table, a desk from some eye-wateringly expensive Italian design studio, a genuine eighty-year-old Bonsai Californian redwood, an OC3 cable into Telehouse, and gaming laptops. Alienware: we need lots and lots of Alienware...."

Andy gives me five seconds to slaver over the fantasy before he pricks my balloon. "You'll take Dell and like it."

"Even if the bad guys frag us?" I try.

"They won't." He looks smug. "Because you're the best."

One of the advantages of being a cash-starved department is that nobody ever dares to throw anything away in case it turns out to be useful later. Another advantage is that there's never any money to get things done, like (for example) refit old offices to comply with current health and safety regulations. It's cheaper just to move everybody out into a Portakabin in the car park and leave the office refurb for another financial year. At least, that's what they do in this day and age; thirty, forty years ago I don't know where they put the surplus bodies. Anyway, while Andy gets on the phone to Emma to plead for a budget, I lead Pete on a fishing expedition.

"This is the old segregation block," I explain, flicking on

a light switch. "Don't come in here without a light or the grue will get you."

"You've got grues? Here?" He looks so excited at the prospect that I almost hesitate to tell him the truth.

"No, I just meant you'd just step in something nasty. This isn't an adventure game." The dust lies in gentle snowdrifts everywhere undisturbed by outsourced cleaning services — contractors generally take one look at the seg block and double their quote, going over the ministerially imposed cap (which gets imposed rigorously on Ops, freeing up funds so Human Resources can employ plant beauticians to lovingly wax the leaves on their office rubber plants).

"You called it a segregation block. What, uh, who was segregated?"

I briefly toy with the idea of winding him up, then reject it. Once you're inside the Laundry you're in it for life, and I don't really want to leave a trail of grudge-bearing juniors sharpening their knives behind me. "People we didn't want exposed to the outside world, even by accident," I say finally. "If you work here long enough it does strange things to your head. Work here too long, and other people can see the effects, too. You'll notice the windows are all frosted or else they open onto air shafts, where there aren't any windows in the first place," I add, shoving open the door onto a large, executive office marred only by the bricked-up window frame in the wall behind the desk, and a disturbingly wide trail of something shiny — I tell myself it's probably just dry wallpaper paste — leading to the swivel chair. "Great, this is just what I've been looking for."

"It is?"

"Yep; a big, empty, executive office where the lights and power still work."

"Whose was it?" Pete looks around curiously. "There aren't many sockets . . ."

"Before my time." I pull the chair out and look at the seat doubtfully. It was good leather once, but the seat is hideously stained and cracked. The penny drops. "I've heard of this guy. 'Slug' Johnson. He used to be high up in Accounts, but he made lots of enemies. In the end someone put salt on his back."

"You want us to work in here?" Pete asks, in a blinding moment of clarity.

"For now," I reassure him. "Until we can screw a budget for a real office out of Emma from HR."

"We'll need more power sockets." Pete's eyes are taking on a distant, glazed look and his fingers twitch mousily: "We'll need casemods, need overclocked CPUs, need fuck-off huge screens, double-headed Radeon X1600 video cards." He begins to shake. "Nerf guns, Twinkies, LAN party—"

"Pete! Snap out of it!" I grab his shoulders and shake him. He blinks and looks at me blearily. "Whuh?"

I physically drag him out of the room. "First, before we do *anything* else, I'm getting the cleaners in to give it a class four exorcism and to steam clean the carpets. You could catch something nasty in there." *You nearly did*, I add silently. "Lots of bad psychic backwash."

"I thought he was an accountant?" says Pete, shaking his head.

"No, he was *in Accounts*. Not the same thing at all. You're confusing them with Financial Control."

"Huh? What do *Accounts* do, then?"

"They settle accounts — usually fatally. At least, that's what they used to do back in the '60s; the department was terminated some time ago."

"Um." Pete swallows. "I thought that was all a joke? This is, like the BBFC? You know?"

I blink. The British Board of Film Classification, the people who certify video games and cut the cocks out of movies? "Did anyone tell you what the Laundry actually *does*?"

"Plays lots of deathmatches?" he asks hopefully.

"That's one way of putting it," I begin, then pause. *How to continue?* "Magic is applied mathematics. The many-angled ones live at the bottom of the Mandelbrot set. Demonology is right after debugging in the dictionary. You heard of Alan Turing? The father of programming?"

"Didn't he work for John Carmack?"

Oh, it's another world out there. "Not exactly, he built the first computers for the government, back in the Second World War. Not just codebreaking computers; he designed containment processors for Q Division, the Counter-Possession Unit of SOE that dealt with demon-ridden Abwehr agents. Anyway, after the war, they disbanded SOE – broke up all the government computers, the Colossus machines – except for the CPU, which became the Laundry. The Laundry kept going, defending the realm from the scum of the multiverse. There are mathematical transforms that can link entities in different universes – try to solve the wrong theorem and they'll eat your brain, or worse. Anyhow, these days more people do more things with computers than anyone ever dreamed of. Computer games are networked and scriptable, they've got compilers and debuggers built in, you can build cities and film goddamn movies inside them. And every so often someone stumbles across something they're not meant to be playing with and, well, you know the rest."

His eyes are wide in the shadows. "You mean, this is *government* work? Like in Deus Ex?"

I nod. "That's it exactly, kid." Actually it's more like Doom 3 but I'm not ready to tell him that; he might start pestering me for a grenade launcher.

"So we're going to, like, set up a LAN party and log onto lots of persistent realms and search 'n' sweep them for demons and blow the demons away?" He's almost panting with eagerness. "Wait'll I tell my homies!"

"Pete, you can't do that."

"What, isn't it allowed?"

"No, I didn't say that." I lead him back towards the well-lit corridors of the Ops wing and the coffee break room beyond. "I said you *can't* do that. You're under a geas. Section III of the Official Secrets Act says you can't tell anyone who hasn't signed the said act that Section III even exists, much less tell them anything about what it covers. The Laundry is one hundred percent under cover, Pete. You can't talk about it to outsiders, you'd choke on your own purple tongue."

"Eew." He looks disappointed. "You mean, like, this is *real* secret stuff. Like Mum's work."

"Yes, Pete. It's all really secret. Now let's go get a coffee and pester somebody in Facilities for a mains extension bar and a computer."

I spend the rest of the day wandering from desk to desk, filing requisitions and ordering up supplies, with Pete snuffling and shambling after me like a supersized spaniel. The cleaners won't be able to work over Johnson's office until next Tuesday due to an unfortunate planetary conjunction, but I know a temporary fix I can sketch on the floor and plug into a repurposed pocket calculator that should hold "Slug" Johnson at bay until we can get him exorcised. Meanwhile, thanks to a piece of freakish luck, I discover a stash of elderly laptops nobody is using; someone in Catering mistyped their code in their Assets database last year, and thanks to the wonders of our ongoing ISO 9000 certification process, there is no legal procedure for reclassifying them as capital assets without triggering a visit by the Auditors. So I duly issue Pete with a 1.4 gigahertz Toshiba Sandwich Toaster, enlist his help in moving my stuff into the new office, nail a WiFi access point to the door like a tribal fetish or mezuzah ("this office now occupied by geeks who worship the great god GHz"), and park him on the other side of the spacious desk so I can keep an eye on him.

The next day I've got a staff meeting at 10:00 a.m. I spend the first half hour of my morning drinking coffee, making snide remarks in e-mail, reading Slashdot, and waiting for Pete to show up. He arrives at 9:35. "Here." I chuck a fat wallet full of CD-Rs at him. "Install these on your laptop, get on the intranet, and download all the patches you need. Don't, whatever you do, touch my computer or try to log onto my NWN server — it's called Bosch, by the way. I'll catch up with you after the meeting."

"Why is it called Bosch?" he whines as I stand up and grab my security badge off the filing cabinet.

"Washing machines or Hieronymus machines, take your pick." I head off to the conference room for the Ways and Means Committee meeting — to investigate new ways of being mean, as Bridget (may Nyarlathotep rest her soul) once explained it to me.

At first I'm moderately hopeful I'll be able to stay awake through the meeting. But then Lucy, a bucktoothed goth from Facilities, gets the bit between her incisors. She's going on in a giggly way about the need to outsource our administration of office sundries in order to focus on our core competencies, and I'm trying desperately hard not to fall asleep, when there's an odd thudding sound that echoes through the fabric of the building. Then a pager goes off.

Andy's at the other end of the table. He looks at me: "Bob, your call, I think."

I sigh. "You think?" I glance at the pager display. *Oops, so it is.* "'Scuse me folks, something's come up."

"Go on." Lucy glares at me halfheartedly from behind her lucky charms. "I'll minute you."

"Sure." And I'm out, almost an hour before lunch. Wow, so interns *are* useful for something. Just as long as he hasn't gotten himself killed.

I trot back to Slug's office. Peter-Fred is sitting in his chair, with his back to the door.

"Pete?" I ask.

No reply. But his laptop's open and running, and I can hear its fan chugging away. "Uh-huh." And the disc wallet is lying open on my side of the desk.

I edge towards the computer carefully, taking pains to stay out of eyeshot of the screen. When I get a good look at Peter-Fred I see that his mouth's ajar and his eyes are closed; he's drooling slightly. "Pete?" I say, and poke his shoulder. He doesn't move. *Probably a good thing*, I tell myself. *Okay, so he isn't conventionally possessed* . . .

When I'm close enough, I filch a sheet of paper from the ink-jet printer, turn the lights out, and angle the paper in front of the laptop. Very faintly I can see reflected colors, but nothing particularly scary. "Right," I mutter. I slide my hands in front of the keyboard — still careful not to look directly at the screen — and hit the key combination to bring up the interactive debugger in the game I'm afraid he's running. Trip an object dump, hit the keystrokes for quick save, and quit, and I can breathe a sigh of relief and look at the screen shot.

It takes me several seconds to figure out what I'm looking at. "Oh you stupid, *stupid* arse!" It's Peter-Fred, of course. He installed NWN and the other stuff I threw at him: the Laundry-issue hack pack and DM tools, and the creation toolkit. Then he went and did *exactly* what I told him not to do: he connected to Bosch. That's him in the screenshot between the two half-orc mercenaries in the tavern, looking very afraid.

*

Two hours later Brains and Pinky are baby-sitting Pete's supine body (we don't dare move it yet), Bosch is locked down and frozen, and I'm sitting on the wrong side of Angleton's desk, sweating bullets. "Summarize, boy," he rumbles, fixing me with one yellowing rheumy eye. "Keep it simple. None of your jargon, life's too short."

"He's fallen into a game and he can't get out." I cross my arms. "I told him precisely what not to do, and he went ahead and did it. Not *my* fault."

Angleton makes a wheezing noise, like a boiler threatening to explode. After a moment I recognize it as two-thousand-year-old laughter, mummified and out for revenge. Then he stops wheezing. *Oops*, I think. "I believe you, boy. Thousands wouldn't. But you're going to have to get him out. You're responsible."

I'm *responsible*? I'm about to tell the old man what I think when a second thought screeches into the pileup at the back of my tongue and I bite my lip. I suppose I *am* responsible, technically. I mean, Pete's my intern, isn't he? I'm a management grade, after all, and if he's been assigned to me, that makes me his manager, even if it's a post that comes with loads of responsibility and no actual power to, like, stop him doing something really foolish. I'm *in loco parentis*, or maybe just plain *loco*. I whistle quietly. "What would you suggest?"

Angleton wheezes again. "Not my field, boy, I wouldn't know one end of one of those newfangled Babbage machine contraptions from the other." He fixes me with a gimlet stare. "But feel free to draw on HR's budget line. I will make enquiries on the other side to see what's going on. But if you don't bring him back, I'll make you explain what happened to him to his mother."

"His mother?" I'm puzzled. "You mean she's one of *us*?"

"Yes. Didn't Andrew tell you? Mrs. Young is the deputy director in charge of Human Resources. So you'd better get him back before she notices her son is missing."

James Bond has Q Division; I've got Pinky and Brains from Tech Support. Bond gets jet packs, I get whoopee cushions, but I repeat myself. Still, at least P and B know about first-person shooters.

"Okay, let's go over this again," says Brains. He sounds unusually chipper for this early in the morning. "You set up Bosch as a server for a persistent Neverwinter Nights world, running the full Project Aurora hack pack. That gives you, oh, lots of extensions for trapping demons that wander into your realm while you trace their owner's PCs and inject a bunch of spyware, then call out to Accounts to send a black-bag team round in the real world. Right?"

"Yes." I nod. "An internet honeypot for supernatural intruders."

"Wibble!" That's Pinky. "Hey, neat! So what happened to your PFY?"

"Well . . ." I take a deep breath. "There's a big castle overlooking the town, with a twentieth-level sorceress running it. Lots of glyphs of summoning in the basement dungeons, some of which actually bind at run-time to a class library that implements the core transformational grammar of the Language of Leng." I hunch over slightly. "It's really neat to be able to do that kind of experiment in a virtual realm – if you accidentally summon something nasty it's trapped inside the server or maybe your local area network, rather than being out in the real world where it can eat your brains."

Brains stares at me. "You expect me to believe this kid took out a *twentieth-level sorceress*? Just so he could dick around in your dungeon lab?"

"Uh, no." I pick up a blue-tinted CD-R. Someone – not me – has scribbled a cartoon skull-and-crossbones on it and added a caption: DO'NT R3AD M3. "I've been looking at this – carefully. It's not one of the discs I gave Pete; it's one of his own. He's not *totally* clueless, for a crack-smoking script kiddie. In fact, it's got a bunch of interesting class libraries on it. He went in with a knapsack full of special toys and just happened to fuck up by trying to rob the wrong tavern. This realm, being hosted on Bosch, is scattered with traps that are superclassed into a bunch of scanner routines from Project Aurora and sniff for any taint of the *real* supernatural. Probably he whiffed of Laundry business – and that set off one of the traps, which yanked him in."

"How do you get *inside* a game?" asks Pinky, looking hopeful. "Could you get me into Grand Theft Auto: Castro Club Extreme?"

Brains glances at him in evident disgust. "You can virtualize any universal Turing machine," he sniffs. "Okay, Bob. What precisely do you need from us in order to get the kid out of there?"

I point to the laptop: "I need *that*, running the Dungeon Master client inside the game. Plus a class four summoning grid, and a lot of luck." My guts clench. "Make that a lot more luck than usual."

"Running the DM client—" Brains goes cross-eyed for a moment "—is it reentrant?"

"It will be." I grin mirthlessly. "And I'll need you on the outside, running the ordinary network client, with a couple of characters I'll preload for you. The sorceress is holding Pete in the third-level dungeon basement of Castle Storm. The way the narrative's set up she's probably not going to do anything to him until she's also acquired a whole bunch of plot coupons, like a cockatrice and a mind flayer's gallbladder – then she can sacrifice him and trade up to a fourth-level

demon or a new castle or something. Anyway, I've got a plan.
Ready to kick ass?"

I *hate* working in dungeons. They're dank, smelly, dark, and
things keep jumping out and trying to kill you. That seems to
be the defining characteristic of the genre, really. Dead
boring hack-and-slash – but the kiddies love 'em. I know I
did, back when I was a wee spoddy twelve-year-old. Fine,
says I, we're not trying to snare kiddies, we're looking to
attract the more cerebral kind of MMORPG player – the sort
who're too clever by half. Designers, in other words.

How do you snare a dungeon designer who's accidentally
stumbled on a way to summon up shoggoths? Well, you
need a website. The smart geeks are always magpies for
ideas – they see something new and it's "Ooh! Shiny!" and
before you can snap your fingers they've done something
with it you didn't anticipate. So you set your site up to suck
them in and lock them down. You seed it with a bunch of
downloadable goodies and some interesting chat boards – not
the usual MY MAGIC USR CN TW4T UR CLERIC,
D00D, but actual useful information – useful if you're programming in NWScript, that is (the high-level
programming language embedded in the game, which hard-
core designers write game extensions in).

But the website isn't enough. Ideally you want to run a
networked game server – a persistent world that your victims
can connect to using their client software to see how your
bunch o' tricks looks in the virtual flesh. And finally you seed
clues in the server to attract the marks who know too damn
much for their own good, like Peter-Fred.

The problem is, BoschWorld isn't ready yet. That's why I
told him to stay out. Worse, there's no easy way to dig him
out of it yet because I haven't yet written the object retrieval
code – and worse: to speed up the development process, I

grabbed a whole bunch of published code from one of the bigger online persistent realms, and I haven't weeded out all the spurious quests and curses and shit that make life exciting for adventurers. In fact, now that I think about it, that was going to be Peter-Fred's job for the next month. Oops.

Unlike Pete, I do not blunder into Bosch unprepared; I know exactly what to expect. I've got a couple of cheats up my non-existent monk's sleeve, including the fact that I can enter the game with a level eighteen character carrying a laptop with a source-level debugger – all praise the new self-deconstructing reality!

The stone floor of the monastery is gritty and cold under my bare feet, and there's a chilly morning breeze blowing in through the huge oak doors at the far end of the compound. I know it's all in my head – I'm actually sitting in a cramped office chair with Pinky and Brains hammering away on keyboards to either side – but it's still creepy. I turn round and genuflect once in the direction of the huge and extremely scary devil carved into the wall behind me, then head for the exit.

The monastery sits atop some truly bizarre stone formations in the middle of the Wild Woods. I'm supposed to fight my way through the woods before I get to the town of, um, whatever I named it, Stormville? – but sod that. I stick a hand into the bottomless depths of my very expensive Bag of Holding and pull out a scroll. "Stormville, North Gate," I intone (*Why* do ancient masters in orders of martial monks always *intone*, rather than, like, speak normally?) and the scroll crumbles to dust in my hands – and I'm looking up at a stone tower with a gate at its base and some bint sticking a bucket out of a window on the third floor and yelling, "Gardy loo." Well, *that* worked okay.

"I'm there," I say aloud.

Green serifed letters track across my visual field, completely spoiling the atmosphere: WAY K00L, B08. That'll be Pinky, riding shotgun with his usual delicacy.

There's a big, blue rectangle in the gateway so I walk onto it and wait for the universe to download. It's a long wait — something's gumming up Bosch. (Computers aren't as powerful as most people think; running even a small and rather stupid intern can really bog down a server.)

Inside the North Gate is the North Market. At least, it's what passes for a market in here. There's a bunch of zombies dressed as your standard dungeon adventurers, shambling around with speech bubbles over their heads. Most of them are web addresses on eBay, locations of auctions for interesting pieces of game content, but one or two of them look as if they've been crudely tampered with, especially the ass-headed nobleman repeatedly belting himself on the head with a huge, leather-bound copy of A *Midsummer Night's Dream*. "Are you guys sure we haven't been hacked?" I ask aloud. "If you could check the tripwire logs, Brains . . ." It's a long shot, but it might offer an alternate explanation for Pete's predicament.

I slither, sneak, and generally shimmy my monastic ass around the square, avoiding the quainte olde medieval gallows and the smoking hole in the ground that used to be the Alchemists' Guild. On the east side of the square is the Wayfarer's Tavern, and some distance to the southwest I can see the battlements and turrets of Castle Storm looming out of the early morning mists in a surge of gothic cheesecake. I enter the tavern, stepping on the blue rectangle and waiting while the world pauses, then head for the bar.

"Right, I'm in the bar," I say aloud, pulling my Project Aurora laptop out of the Bag of Holding. (Is it my imagination, or does something snap at my fingertips as I pull my hand out?) "Has the target moved?"

N0 J0Y, B08.

I sigh, unfolding the screen. Laptops aren't exactly native to NWN, this one's made of two slabs of sapphire held together by scrolled mithril hinges. I stare into the glowing depths of its screen (tailored from a preexisting crystal ball) and load a copy of the pub. Looking in the back room I see a bunch of standard henchmen, -women, and -things waiting to be hired, but none of them are exactly optimal for taking on the twentieth-level lawful-evil chatelaine of Castle Storm. *Hmm, better bump one of 'em*, I decide. *Let's go for munchkin muscle.* "Pinky? I'd like you to drop a quarter of a million experience points on Grondor the Red, then up-level him. Can you do that?" Grondor is the biggest bad-ass half-orc fighter-for-hire in Bosch. This ought to turn him into a one-man killing machine.

0<D00D.

I can tell he's really getting into the spirit of this. The bar-maid sashays up to me and winks. "Hiya, cute thing. (1) Want to buy a drink? (2) Want to ask questions about the town and its surroundings? (3) Want to talk about anything else?"

I sigh. "Gimme (1)."

"Okay. (1) G'bye, big boy. (2) Anything else?"

"(1). Get me my beer then piss off."

One of these days I'll get around to wiring a real conversational 'bot into the non-player characters, but right now they're still a bit—

There's a huge sound from the back room, sort of a creaking graunching noise. I blink and look round, startled. After a moment I realize it's the sound of a quarter of a million experience points landing on a—

"Pinky, what exactly did you up-level Grondor the Red to?"

LVL 15 C0RTE5AN. LOL!!!

"Oh, great," I mutter. I'll swear that's not a real character class. A fat, manila envelope appears on the bar in front of me. It's Grondor's contract, and from the small print it looks like I've hired myself a fifteenth-level half-orc rent-boy for muscle. Which is annoying because I only get one hench-thug per game. "One of these days your sense of humor is going to get me into *really* deep trouble, Pinky," I say as Grondor flounces across the rough wooden floor towards me, a vision of ruffles, bows, pink satin, and upcurved tusks. He's clutching a violet club in one gnarly, red-nailed hand, and he seems to be annoyed about something.

After a brief and uncomfortable interlude that involves running on the walls and ceiling, I manage to calm Grondor down, but by then half the denizens of the tavern are broken and bleeding "Grondor pithed," he lisps at me. "But Grondor thtill kickth ath. Whoth ath you wanting kicked?"

"The wicked witch of the west. You up for it?"

He blows me a kiss.

LOL! ! ! ROFL! ! ! whoops the peanut gallery.

"Okay, let's go."

Numerous alarums, excursions, and open-palm five-punches death attacks later, we arrive at Castle Storm. Sitting out in front of the cruel-looking portcullis, topped by the dismembered bodies of the sorceress's enemies and not a few of her friends, I open up the laptop. A miniature thundercloud hovers overhead, raining on the turrets and bouncing lightning bolts off the (currently inanimate) gargoyles.

"Connect me to Lady Storm's boudoir mirror," I say. (I try to make it come out as an inscrutable monkish mutter rather than *intoning*, but it doesn't work properly.)

"Hello? Who is this?" I see her face peering out of the depths of my screen, like an unholy cross between Cruella De Vil and Margaret Thatcher. She's not wearing make-up and half her hair's in curlers — *that's odd*, I think.

"This is the management," I intone. "We have been notified that contrary to statutory regulations issued by the Council of Guilds of Stormville you are running an unauthorized boarding house, to wit, you are providing accommodation for mendicant journeymen. Normally we'd let you off with .a warning and a fifty-gold-piece fine, but in this particular case—"

I'm readying the amulet of teleportation, but she seems to be able to anticipate events, which is just plain wrong for a non-player character following a script. "Accommodate *this!*" she hisses, and cuts the connection dead. There's a hammering rumbling sound overhead. I glance up, then take to my heels as I wrap my arms about my head; she's animated the gargoyles, and they're taking wing, but they're still made of stone – and stone isn't known for its lighter-than-air qualities. The crashing thunder goes on for quite some time, and the dust makes my eyes sting, but after a while all that remains is the mournful honking of the one surviving gargoyle, which learned to fly on its way down, and is now circling the battlements overhead. And now it's my turn.

"Right. Grondor? Open that door!"

Grondor snarls, then flounces forwards and whacks the portcullis with his double-headed war axe. The physics model in here is distinctly imaginative, you shouldn't be able to reduce a cast-iron grating into a pile of wooden kindling, but I'm not complaining. Through the portcullis we charge, into the bowels of Castle Storm and, I hope, in time to rescue Pete.

I don't want to bore you with a blow-by-blow description of our blow-by-blow progress through Cruella's minions. Suffice to say that following Grondor is a lot like trailing behind a frothy pink main battle tank. Thuggish guards, evil imps, and the odd adept tend to explode messily very soon after Grondor sees them. Unfortunately Grondor's not very discriminating, so I make sure to go first in order to keep him away from cunningly engineered deadfalls (and Pete, should we find him). Still, it doesn't take us too long to comb the lower levels of the caverns under Castle Storm (aided by the handy dungeon editor in my laptop, which allows me to build a bridge over the Chasm of Despair and tunnel through the rock around the Dragon's Lair, which isn't very sporting but keeps us from being toasted). Which is why, after a couple of hours, I'm beginning to get a sinking feeling that Pete isn't actually *here*.

"Brains, Pete isn't down here, is he? Or am I missing something?"

H3Yd0NTB3 5AD D00D FlN|<0V V XP!!!

"Fuck off, Pinky, give me some useful input or just *fuck off*, okay?" I realize I'm shouting when the rock wall next to me begins to crack ominously. The hideous possibility that I've lost Pete is sinking its claws into my brain and it's worse than any Fear spell.

OK KEEP UR HAIR 0N!! 15 THIS A QU3ST?? D0 U N33D 2 CONFRONT S0RCR3SS lST?

I stop dead. "I bloody hope not. Did you notice how she was behaving?"

Brains here. I'm grepping the server logfile and did you know there's another user connected over the intranet bridge?

"Whu—" I turn around and accidentally bump into Grondor.

Grondor says, "(1) Do you wish to modify our tactics? (2) Do you want Grondor to attack someone? (3) Do you think Grondor is sexy, big boy? (4) Exit?"

"(4)," I intone – if I leave him in a conversational state he won't be going anywhere, dammit. "Okay, Brains. Have you tracerouted the intrusion? Bosch isn't supposed to be accessible from outside the local network. What department are they coming in from?"

They;e coming in from – a longish pause – *somewhere in HR*.

"Okay, the plot just thickened. So someone in HR has gotten in. Any idea who the player is?" I've got a sneaking suspicion but I want to hear it from Brains—

Not IRL, but didn't Cruella act way too flexible to be a 'bot?

Bollocks. That *is* what I was thinking. "Okay. Grondor: follow. We're going upstairs to see the wicked witch."

Now, let me tell you about castles. They don't have elevators, or fire escapes, or extinguishers. Real ones don't have exploding whoopee cushions under the carpet and electrified door-handles that blush red when you notice them, either, or an ogre resting on the second-floor mezzanine, but that's beside the point. Let me just observe that by the time I reach the fourth floor I am beginning to breathe heavily and I am getting distinctly pissed off with Her Eldritch Fearsomeness.

At the foot of the wide, glittering staircase in the middle of the fourth floor I temporarily lose Grondor. It might have something to do with the tenth-level mage lurking behind the transom with a magic flamethrower, or the simultaneous arrival of about a ton of steel spikes falling from concealed ceiling panels, but Grondor is reduced to a greasy pile of goo on the floor. I sigh and do something to the mage that would be extremely painful if he were a real person. "Is she upstairs?" I ask the glowing letters.

SUR3 TH1NG D00D!!!

"Any more traps?"

N0!!??!

"Cool." I step over the grease spot and pause just in front of the staircase. It never pays to be rash. I pick up a stray steel spike and chuck it on the first step and it goes *BANG* with extreme prejudice. "Not so cool." Rinse, cycle, repeat, and four small explosions later I'm standing in front of the doorway facing the top step. No more whoopee cushions, just a twentieth-level sorceress and a minion in chains. *Happy joy*. "Pinky. Plan B. Get it ready to run, on my word."

I break through the door and enter the witch's lair.

Once you've seen one witch's den you've seen 'em all. This one is a bit glitzier than usual, and some of the furniture is nonstandard even taking into account the Laundry hack packs linked into this realm. *Where did she get the mainframe from?* I wonder briefly before considering the extremely ominous Dho-Na geometry curve in the middle of the floor (complete with a frantic-looking Pete chained down in the middle of it) and the extremely irate-looking sorceress beyond.

"Emma MacDougal, I presume?"

She turns my way, spitting blood. "If it wasn't for you meddling hackers, I'd have gotten away with it!" Oops, *she's raising her magic wand.*

"Gotten away with what?" I ask politely. "Don't you want to explain your fiendish plan, as is customary, before totally obliterating your victims? I mean, that's a Dho-Na curve there, so you're obviously planning a summoning, and this server is inside Ops block. Were you planning some sort of low-key downsizing?"

She snorts. "You stupid Ops heads, why do you always assume it's about you?"

"Because—" I shrug. "We're running on a server in Ops. What do you think happens if you open a gateway for an ancient evil to infest our departmental LAN?"

"Don't be naïve. All that's going to happen is Pimple-Features here is going to pick up a good, little, gibbering infestation then go spread it to Mama. Which will open up the promotion ladder once again." She stares at me, then her eyes narrow thoughtfully. "How did you figure out it was me?"

"You should have used a smaller mainframe emulator, you

know; we're so starved for resources that Bosch runs on a three-year-old Dell laptop. If you weren't slurping up all our CPU resources, we probably wouldn't have noticed anything was wrong until it was too late. It had to be someone in HR, and you're the only player on the radar. Mind you, putting poor Peter-Fred in a position of irresistible temptation was a good move. How did you open the tunnel into our side of the network?"

"He took his laptop home at night. Have you swept it for spyware today?" Her grin turns triumphant. "I think it's time you joined Pete on the summoning-grid sacrifice node."

"Plan B!" I announce brightly, then run up the wall and across the ceiling until I'm above Pete.

PIAN 8 :) :) :)

The room below my head lurches disturbingly as Pinky rearranges the furniture. It's just a ninety-degree rotation, and Pete's still in the summoning grid, but now he's in the target node instead of the sacrifice zone. Emma is incanting; her wand tracks me, its tip glowing green. "Do it, Pinky!" I shout as I pull out my dagger and slice my virtual finger. Blood runs down the blade and drops into the sacrifice node—

And Pete stands up. The chains holding him to the floor rip like damp cardboard, his eyes glowing even brighter than Emma's wand. With no actual summoning vector spliced into the grid it's wide open, an antenna seeking the nearest manifestation. With my blood to power it, it's active, and the first thing it resonates with has come through and sideloaded into Pete's head. His head swivels. "Get her!" I yell, clenching my fist and trying not to wince. "She's from personnel!"

"*Personnel?*" rumbles a voice from Pete's mouth – deeper, more cultured, and infinitely more terrifying. "*Ah, I see. Thank you.*" The being wearing Pete's flesh steps across the grid – which sparks like a high-tension line and begins to smolder. Emma's wand wavers between me and Pete. I thrust my injured hand into the Bag of Holding and stifle a scream when my fingers stab into the bag of salt within. *"It's been too long."* His face begins to lengthen, his jaw widening and merging at the edges. He sticks his tongue out: it's grayish-brown and rasplike teeth are sprouting from it.

Emma screams in rage and discharges her wand at him. A backwash of negative energy makes my teeth clench and turns my vision gray, but it's not enough to stop the second coming of "Slug" Johnson. He slithers towards her across the floor, and she gears up another spell, but it's too late. I close my eyes and follow the action by the inarticulate shrieks and the wet sucking, gurgling noises. Finally, they die down.

I take a deep breath and open my eyes. Below me the room is vacant but for a clean-picked human skeleton and a floor flecked with brown — I peer closer — slugs. *Millions* of the buggers. "You'd better let him go," I intone.

"Why should I?" asks the assembly of molluscs.

"Because—" I pause. *Why should he?* It's a surprisingly sensible question. "If you don't, HR — Personnel — will just send another. Their minions are infinite. But you *can* defeat them by escaping from their grip forever — if you let me lay you to rest."

"Send me on, then," say the slugs.

"Okay." And I open my salt-filled fist over the molluscs — which burn and writhe beneath the white powderfall until nothing is left but Pete, curled fetally in the middle of the floor. And it's time to get Pete the hell out of this game and back into his own head before his mother, or some even worse horror, comes looking for him.

AFTERWORD: THE GOLDEN AGE OF SPYING

THE MARY-SUE OF MI6

"MY NAME IS BOND — JAMES BOND."

These six words, heard by hundreds of millions of people, are almost invariably spoken during the first five minutes of each movie in one of the biggest media success stories of the twentieth century. Unless you've lived under a rock for the past forty years, you hear them and you know at once that you're about to be plunged into a two-hour-long adrenaline[1]-saturated extravaganza of snobbish fashionable excess, violence, sex, car chases, more violence, and Blowing Shit Up — followed by a post-coital cigarette and a lighthearted quip as the credits roll.

It wasn't always so. When *Casino Royale* was first published in 1953, it got a print run of 4,750 hardcover copies and no advertising budget to speak of; while the initial reviews were favorable, comparing Ian Fleming to Le Queux and Oppenheim (the kings of the prewar British spy-thriller genre), it took a long time for his most famous creation to set the world on fire. Despite his rapidly rising print runs (*Casino Royale* eventually sold over a million paperbacks in

---

[1] And testosterone.

the UK alone), and despite his increasing prominence among the postwar thriller writers, a decade elapsed before any of Fleming's novels were filmed; indeed, their author barely lived to see the commercial release of *Dr. No* and the runaway success of the icon he created. (Nor were the films seen as a runaway success before they were made – *Dr. No* was notoriously made on a tight budget, even though it went on to gross nearly $60 million around the world.)

Literary immortality – or indeed, mere postmortem survival – is dauntingly hard for a novelist to achieve. The limbo of postmortem obscurity awaits ninety-five percent of all novelists – almost all novels go out of print for good within five years of the death of their author. But in addition to being a million-selling bestseller, Fleming was a ferociously well-connected newspaper executive with a strong sense of the value of his ideas, and he pursued television and film adaptation remorselessly. Cinematic success arrived just in time for his creation, and the synergy between bestselling books and massive movie hype has sufficed to keep them in print ever since.

James Bond is a creature of fantasy, perhaps best described using a literary term looted from that most curious and least respected of fields, fan fiction: the Mary-Sue. A Mary-Sue character is a place-holder in a script, a hollow cardboard cutout into whose outline the author can squeeze their own dreams and fantasies. In the case of Bond, it's cruelly easy to make a case that the famous spy was his author's Mary-Sue, for Fleming had a curious and ambiguous relationship with spying.

A dilettante and dabbler for his first three decades, unsuccessful as a stockbroker, foreign correspondent, and banker, Fleming fortuitously landed his dream job on the eve of the Second World War: Secretary to the Director of Naval Intelligence in the Admiralty. The war was good for Ian

Fleming, broadening and deepening him and giving him a job that captured his imagination and drew out his not inconsiderable talents. But Fleming was the man who knew too much: privy to too many secrets, he was wrapped in tissue paper and prevented from pursuing his desire to go into the field. He ended the war with a distinguished record – and absolutely no combat experience (if one excludes being bombed by the *Luftwaffe* or watching the Dieppe raid from a destroyer safely far off the Normandy coastline). Fleming grew up in the shade of a father who died heroically on the Western Front in 1917, and in adult life, he wrote in the shadow of an elder brother whose reputation as a novelist surpassed his own. It's easy to imagine these unkind familial comparisons provoking the imaginative but flighty playboy who almost found himself during the war, which goaded him into imagining himself in the shoes of a hero who was not merely larger than life, but larger in every way than his own life.

And, as it turns out, James Bond was larger than Ian Fleming. Not only do few novels survive their author's demise, even fewer acquire sequels written by other hands; yet several other authors (including Kingsley Amis and John Gardner) have toiled in Fleming's vineyard. Few fictional characters acquire biographies written by third parties – but Bond has not only acquired an autobiography (courtesy of biographer John Pearson) but spawned a small cultural industry, including a study of his semiotics by Umberto Eco. Now, that has got to be a sign of something . . .

As with every true pearl, there was a sand-grain of truth at the heart of Bond. Fleming wrote thrillers informed by his actual experience. Years spent working out of the hothouse environment of Room 39 of the Admiralty building – headquarters of the Naval Intelligence Division of the Royal Navy – gave him a ringside seat on the operations of a major espionage organization. On various trips to Washington, DC, he worked with diplomats and officers of the OSS (predecessor organization to the CIA). There is also some evidence that, as a foreign news manager at the *Sunday Times* after the war, Fleming made his agency's facilities available to officers of MI6. His first Bond novels were submitted to that agency for security clearance before they were published. Bond himself may have been larger than life, but the strictures imposed by the organization he worked for were drawn from reality, albeit the reality of an intelligence agency of the early 1940s.

The world of secret intelligence-gathering during the Second World War was, however, very different from life in the intelligence community today. It was already changing by the late 1950s, as the bleeping, football-shaped *Sputniks* zipped by overhead and intelligence directors began dreaming of spy satellites. By 2004, when MI5 (the counter-intelligence agency) openly placed recruiting advertisements in the press, we can be sure that Bond would have been best advised to seek employment elsewhere. Spies are supposed to be short — less than 180 centimeters (5 feet 11 inches) for men — and nondescript. As a branch of the civil service, MI5's headquarters are presumably nonsmoking, and drinking on the job is frowned upon. As intelligence agencies, MI5 and MI6 staffs aren't in the business of ruthlessly wiping out enemies of the state: any decision to use lethal force lies with the Foreign Secretary, the COBRA committee, and other elements of the British government's security oversight bureaucracy. An MI6 agent driving a 1933 Bentley racer with a supercharged engine, frequenting the high-stakes table at a casino as James Bond so memorably did in his first print appearance, is an almost perfect inversion of the real picture.

Nevertheless, the archetype has legs. James Bond continued to grow and evolve, even after his creator put away his cigarette holder for the last time. To some extent, this was the product of storytelling expediency. The film adaptations started in the middle of a continuing story arc – for Fleming wrote his novels with a modicum of continuity – and while *Dr. No* was the first to make it to celluloid, the novel was in fact a sequel to *From Russia with Love* (which was filmed second). Thus, various liberties were taken with the plot of the canonical novels right from the start. You can read the novels at length without finding anything of the banter between Bond and M's secretary Moneypenny that is a recurrent theme of the films, for example, and that's before we get into the bizarre deviations of the midperiod Roger Moore movies (notably *The Spy Who Loved Me* and *Moonraker*).

The literary James Bond is a creature of prewar London clubland: upper-crust, snobbish, manipulative and cruel in his relationships with women, with a thinly veiled sadomasochistic streak and a coldly ruthless attitude to his opponents that verges on the psychopathic. Over the years, his cinematic alter ego has acquired the stamina of Superman, learned to defy the laws of physics, ventured into space – both outer and inner – and deflowered more maids than Don Juan. He's also mutated to fit the prejudices and neuroses of the day, dabbling with (gasp!) monogamy, and hanging out with those heroic Afghan *mujahedeen* in the late-'80s AIDS-and-Soviets-era *The Living Daylights*. He's worked under a ball-breaking postfeminist M in *GoldenEye*[2], and even confronted a female arch-villain in *The World Is Not Enough* (an innovation that would surely have Fleming, who formed his views on appropriate behavior for the fairer sex in the 1920s, rolling in his grave). But other aspects of the Bond archetype remain timeless. Fleming was fascinated by

[2] An excellent piece of casting that places Dame Judi Dench in the role, apparently inspired by real-life MI5 head Stella Rimington, who has taken to writing spy thrillers in her retirement.

fast cars, exotic locations, and intricate gadgetry, and all of these traits of the original novels have been amplified and extrapolated in the age of modern special effects.

Just how does James Bond – a "sexist, misogynist dinosaur, a relic of the Cold War," to use the words the scriptwriters on *GoldenEye* so tellingly put into M's mouth – survive in the popular imagination more than fifty years after his literary birth? What does it mean when Mary-Sue stalks the landscape of the imagination, blasting holes in the plot with a Walther PPK (or the P99 Bond upgraded to in *Tomorrow Never Dies*)? If we're going to understand this, perhaps we ought to start by looking at Bond's dark shadow, the Villain.

In Search of Mabuse

Bond is, if you judge him by his work, a nasty fellow and not one you'd choose to lend your car to. In order to make this rough diamond glitter, it is necessary to display him against a velvet backdrop of darkest villainy. If you strip the Bond archetype of the bacchanalia, glamorous locations, and fashion snobbery, you end up with an unappetizingly shallow, cold-blooded executioner – the likes of Adam Hall's Quiller or James Mitchell's Callan, only without the breezy cynicism, or indeed any redeeming features at all. The role of adversary is thus a critical one in sustaining the appeal of the protagonist. Fleming set out to depict a hard-edged contemporary world where the usual black-and-white picture of the prewar thriller had blurred and taken on some of the murky gray-on-gray ambiguity of the Cold War era; Bond was the knight in shining armor, fighting for virtue and the free world against the dragon – be they Mr. Big, Dr. No, Auric Goldfinger, or the looming shadow of Bond's greatest enemy of all, Ernst Stavro Blofeld, Number One of SPECTRE, the Special Executive for Counter-intelligence, Terrorism, Revenge, and Extortion.

It is interesting to note that Blofeld assumed his primacy as Bond's #1 enemy only in the movie canon, Fleming originally invented him while working on the screenplay and novel of *Thunderball*, and used him subsequently in *On Her Majesty's Secret Service* and *You Only Live Twice*. (Prior to these later books, Bond typically tussled with less corporate enemies – Soviet stooges, unregenerate Nazis, and psychotic gangsters.) Blofeld was born out of mere corporate expediency. Rather than demonize the Soviets and reduce their potential audience, the producers of the film *From Russia with Love* appropriated SPECTRE as the adversarial organization. With the success of *Thunderball*, the fourth of the films, Blofeld moved front and center, and acquired a life of his own that far exceeded his prominence in the novels. Arguably, Fleming's death in 1964 freed up the movie series to diverge from their original author's plans; and so Blofeld may be seen as a demon of necessity, conjured up from the vasty deep in order to provide Bond with a worthy adversary.

'Twas not always so. Back at the turn of the twentieth century, around the time that the British spy thriller was gradually cohering out of the mists of the penny dreadful and the literature of suspense (via the works of John Buchan and Erskine Childers – not to mention the tangential contributions of Arthur Conan Doyle, by way of Sherlock Holmes), there was no dualistic vision of the great champion confronting the villainous heart of evil. There was no mighty champion: we were on our own against the masters of night and mist, the great and terrible supercriminals. Professor Moriarty, Holmes's nemesis – the Napoleon of Crime – was but one of these: Fantômas, the 1911 creation of Pierre Souvestre and Marcel Allain, is another. The emperor of crime, Fantômas was a master of disguise and an agent of chaos (not to mention standing astride Paris in black mask, top hat and tails in the posters for the 1913 movie of the same name: an icon of decadent wealth and criminal chaos). Nor was he alone. Guy Boothby's 1890s supervillain Dr. Nikola fits the bill, too, right down to the fluffy lap-cat and the fiendish plans. But perhaps the root of Bond's nemesis can be found in his full-fledged form somewhat later, and somewhat further to the east – in the guise of Dr. Mabuse.

Dr. Mabuse is an archetype and a runaway media success in his own right, famous from five novels and twelve movies. The Doctor was created by author Norbert Jacques, and was developed into one of the most chilling creations of the silent era in 1922 by no less a director than Fritz Lang. Mabuse is a name, but one that nobody in their right mind speaks aloud. He's a master of disguise, naturally, and a rich, well-connected socialite and gambler. (Some social context: gambling at the high-stakes table is not so much an innocuous recreation as an obscenity, in a decade of hyper-inflation and starvation, with crippled war veterans dying of cold on the street corners, as was the case in Weimar Germany.) Mabuse has his fingers in every pie, by way of a syndicate so shadowy and criminal that nobody knows its extent; he's a spider, but the web he weaves is so broad that it looks like the whole of reality to the flies trapped within. He is (in some of the stories) a psychiatrist, skilled in manipulation, and those who hunt him are doomed to become his victims. If Mabuse has a weakness it is that his schemes are over-elaborate and tend to implode messily, usually when his most senior minions rebel, hopelessly late; nevertheless, he is a master of the escape plan, and with his ability to brainwash minions into playing his role, he's a remarkably hard phantom to slay.

It is all too easy to make fun of the likes of Fantômas and Dr. Nikola, and even their modern-day cognates such as Dr. Mabuse and Ernst Stavro Blofeld – for do they not represent such an obsessively concentrated pinnacle of entrepreneurial criminality that, if they really existed, they would instantly be hunted down and arrested by INTERPOL?

Careful consideration will lead one to reconsider this hasty judgment. Criminology, the study of crime and its causes, has a fundamental weak spot: it studies that proportion of the criminal population who are stupid or unlucky enough to get caught. The perfect criminal, should he or she exist, would be the one who is never apprehended – indeed, the one whose crimes may be huge but unnoticed, or indeed miscategorized as not crimes at all because they are so powerful they sway the law in their favor, or so clever they discover an immoral opportunity for criminal enterprise before the legislators notice it. Such forms of criminality may be indistinguishable, at a distance, from lawful business; the criminal a paragon of upper-class virtue, a face-man for *Forbes*.

When the real Napoleons of Crime walk among us today, they do so in the outwardly respectable guise of executives in business suits and thousand-dollar haircuts. The executives of WorldCom and Enron were denizens of a corporate culture so rapacious that any activity, however dubious, could be justified in the name of enhancing the bottom line. They have rightfully been charged, tried, and in some cases jailed for fraud, on a scale that would have been the envy of Mabuse, Blofeld, or their modern successor, Dr. Evil. When you need extra digits on your pocket calculator to compute the sums you are stealing, you're in the big league. Again, when you're able to evade prosecution by the simple expedient of appointing the state prosecutor and the judges – because you're the president of a country (and not just any country, but a member of the rich and powerful G8) – you're certainly not amenable to diagnosis and detection in the same sense as your run-of-the-mill shoplifter or petty delinquent. I'm naming no names (They have intelligence services! Cruise missiles!), but this isn't a hypothetical scenario.

Interview with the Entrepreneur

In an attempt to clarify the mythology surrounding James Bond, I tracked down his old rival to his headquarters in the Ministry of Inward Investment in the breakaway Republic of Transdniestria. Somewhat suspicious at first, Mr. Blofeld relaxed as soon as he realized I was not pursuing him on behalf of the FSB, CIA, or IMF, and kindly agreed to be interviewed for this book. Now at age seventy-two, Blofeld is a cheerful veteran of numerous high-tech start-ups, and not a few multinationals where, as a specialist in international risk management and arbitrage, he applied his unique skills to business expansion. Today he is semi-retired, but has agreed to work in a voluntary capacity as director of the state investment agency.

"It took me a long time to understand the agenda that the British government was pursuing through the covert activities of MI6," he told me over a glass of sweet tea. "Call me naïve, but I really believed – at least at first – that they were honest capitalists, the scoundrels."

Over the course of an hour, Ernst explained to me how he first became aware that the UK was attempting to sabotage his business interests. "It was back in 1960 or thereabouts that they first tried to destroy one of my subsidiaries. Until then I hadn't really had anything to do with them, but I believe one of my rivals in the phosphate mining business at the time put it about that my man on site was some sort of spy, and they sent this Bond fellow – not just to arrest my man or charge him with some trumped-up nonsense, but to kill him." His lips paled with indignation as he contemplated the iniquity of the situation: that agents of the British government might go after an honest businessman for no better reason than an unsubstantiated allegation that he was spying on American missile tests. "I warned Julius to be careful and advised him to put a good lawyer on retainer, but what good are lawyers when the people you're up against send hired killers? Julius brought in security contractors, but this Bond fellow still murdered him in the end. And the British government denies everything, to this day!"

Ernst obviously believes in his own moral rectitude, but I had to ask the obvious questions, just for the record.

"Yes, I was chief executive of SPECTRE for twelve years. But you know, SPECTRE was entirely honest about its activities! We had nothing to hide because what we were doing was actually legal. We've been mercilessly slandered by those rogues from MI6 and their friends in the newspapers, but the fact is, we're no more guilty of criminal activity than any other multinational today: we simply had the misfortune to be foreign and entrepreneurial at a point in time when Whitehall was in the grasp of the communist conspirators Wilson and Callaghan, and their running-dog, so-called 'Conservative' fellow Heath. And we were pilloried because what we were doing was in direct competition with the inefficient state-run enterprises that my good friend Lady Thatcher recognized as mosquitoes battening on the lifeblood of capitalism. That cad Fleming put it about that SPECTRE stands for 'Special Executive for Counter-intelligence, Terrorism, Revenge, and Extortion' – absolute tosh and nonsense! Would a group of criminals really call themselves something that blatant? I'll remind you that SPECTRE is actually a French acronym, as befits a nonprofit charity incorporated in Paris. The name stands for 'Société professionelle et éthique du capital technologique réinvesti par les experts.[3] Venture capitalists specializing in disruptive new technologies, in other words – commercial space travel, nuclear power, antibiotics. Not some kind of half-baked

[3] Literally: "Professional and Ethical Society of Technological Capital Reinvested by Experts."

terrorist organization! But you can imagine the threat we posed to the inefficient state monopolies like the British Aircraft Corporation, the coal mining industry, and Imperial Chemical Industries."

Blofeld paused to sip his tea thoughtfully.

"We were ahead of our time in many ways. We pioneered business methods that later became mainstream – Sir James Goldsmith, Ronald Perelman, Carl Icahn, they all watched us and learned – but by then, the commies were out of power in the West thanks to our friends in the establishment, so they had an easier time of it. No need to hire lots of expensive security and build concrete bunkers on desert islands! And yes, that made us look bad, don't think I'm unaware of it – but you know, you want bunkers and isolated jungle rocket-launch bases? All you have to do is look at Arianespace! It's fine when the government bureaucracies do it, but if an honest businessman tries to build a space launch site, and hires security to keep the press and saboteurs from foreign governments out, it's suddenly a threat to world security!"

He paused for a while. "They put the worst complexion on everything we did. The plastic surgery? Well, we had the clinic, why not let our staff use it, so the surgeons could sharpen their skills between paying customers? It was a perk, nothing more. We did – I admit it – acquire a few companies trading in exotic weapons, nonlethal technologies mostly. And that business with Emilio and the yacht, I admit that looked bad. But did you know, it originally belonged to Adnan Khashoggi or Fahd ibn Saud or someone? Emilio was acting entirely on his own initiative – a loose cannon –and as soon as I heard about the affair I terminated his employment."

I asked Ernst to tell me about Bond.

"Listen, this Bond chap, I want you to understand this: however he's painted in the mass media, the reality is that he's

AFTERWORD 409

a communist stooge, an assassin. Look at the evidence. He works for the state — a socialist state at that. He went to university and worked with those traitors Philby and Burgess, that MacLean fellow — communist spies to a man. He didn't resign his commission when the British government went socialist, like a decent fellow; instead he took assignments to go after entrepreneurs who were a threat to the interests of this socialist government, and he rubbed them out like a Mafia button man. There was no due process of law there, no respect for property rights, no courts, no lawyers — just a 'License to Kill' enemies of the state, loosely defined, who mostly happened to be businessmen working on start-up projects that coincidentally threatened state monopolies. He's a damned commissar. Do you know why Moscow hated him? It's because he'd beaten them at their own racket."

Blofeld was clearly depressed by this recollection, so I tried to change the subject by asking him about his personal management philosophy.

"Well, you know, I tend to use whatever works in day-to-day situations. I'm a pragmatist, really. But I've got a soft spot for modern philosophers, Leo Strauss and Ayn Rand: the rights of the individual. And I've always wanted to remake the world as a better place, which is probably why the establishment dislikes me: I'm a threat to vested interests. Well, they're all descended from men who were threats to vested interests, too, back in the day, only I threaten them with new technologies, while their ancestors mostly did their threatening with a bloody sword and the gallows. I don't believe in initiating force." He laughed self-deprecatingly. "I suppose you could call me naïve."

Trade Goods

When I played back my tape of our discussion, it took me some time to notice that Ernst had carefully steered the conversation away from certain key points I had intended to quiz him about.

One of the most disturbing aspects of the Bond milieu is the prevalence of technologies that are strangely out of place. Belt-buckle grappling hooks with wire spools that can support a man's weight? Laser rifles? These aren't simple extrapolations of existing technology – they go far beyond anything that's achievable with today's engineering tools or materials science. But forget Bond's toys, the products of Q division. From Blofeld's solar-powered orbital laser in *Diamonds Are Forever* to Carver's stealth cruiser in *Tomorrow Never Dies*, we are surrounded by signs that the adversary has got tricks up his sleeve that far outweigh anything Bond's backers can provide. These menacing intrusions of alien superscience – where could they possibly have gotten them from?

The answer can be discerned with little difficulty if one cares to scrutinize the writings of the sage of Providence, Howard Phillips Lovecraft. This scholar – whose path, regrettably, never crossed that of the young Ian Fleming – asserted that our tenancy of this planet is but a recent aberration. Earth has in the past been home for a number of alien species of vast antiquity and incomprehensibly advanced knowledge, and indeed some of them may still linger alongside us – on the high Antarctic plateau, in the frigid oceanic depths, even in strange half-breed colonies off the New England coastline.

If this strikes you as nonsensical, first contemplate your nearest city: How recognizable would it be in a hundred years' time if our entire species silently vanished tomorrow? How recognizable would it be in a thousand years? Would any relics still bear witness to the once-proud towers of New York or Tokyo, a million years hence? Our future – and the future of any once-proud races that bestrode our planet – is that of an oily stain in the shale deposits of deep history. Earth's biosphere and the active tectonic system it dances upon cleans house remorselessly, erasing any structure that is not alive or maintained by the living.

Consider also the extent to which we really occupy the planet we live on. We think of ourselves as the dominant species on Earth — but seventy-five percent of the Earth's entire biomass consists of bacteria and algae that we can't even see with the naked eye. (Bacteria from whose ranks fearsome pathogens periodically emerge, burning like wildfire through our ranks.) Nor do we, in any real sense of the word, occupy the oceans. Certainly our trawlers hunt the bounty of the upper waters. But submarines (of which there are only a few hundred on the entire planet) fumble like blind men through the uppermost half-kilometer of a world-ocean that averages three kilometers in depth, unable to dive beneath their pressure limits to explore the abyssal plains that cover nearly two-thirds of the planetary surface. Finally, the surface (both the suboceanic abyss and the thin skin of dry land we cling tenuously to) is but a thousandth of the depth of the planet itself; we can't even drill through the crust, much less contemplate with any certainty the nature of events unfolding within the hot, dense mantle beneath.

We could be sharing the planet with numerous powerful alien civilizations, denizens of the high-energy condensed-matter realm beneath our feet, and we'd never know it — unless they chose to send emissaries into our biosphere, sprinkling death rays and other trade goods like glass beads before the aboriginal inhabitants, extracting a ghastly price in return for their largesse . . .

A Colder War?

James Bond was a creature of the Cold War: a strange period of shadow-boxing that stretched from late 1945 to the winter of 1991, forty-six years of paranoia, fear, and the creepy sensation that our lives were in thrall to forces beyond our comprehension. It's almost impossible to explain the Cold War to anyone who was born after 1980; the sense of looming doom, the long shadows cast by the two eyeball-to-eyeball superpowers, each possessing vast powers of destruction, ready and able to bring about that destruction on a planetary scale in pursuit of their recondite ideologies. It was, to use the appropriate adjective, a truly Lovecraftian age, dominated by the cold reality that our lives could be interrupted by torment and death at virtually any time; normal existence was conducted in a soap-bubble universe sustained only by our determination to shut out awareness of the true horrors lurking in the darkness outside it, an abyss presided over by chilly alien warriors devoted to death-cult ideologies and dreams of Mutually Assured Destruction. Decades of distance have bought us some relief, thickening the wall of the bubble – memories misting over with the comforting illusion that the Cold War wasn't really as bad as it seemed at the time – but who do we think we're kidding? The Cold War wasn't about us. It was about the Spies, and the Secret Masters, and the Hidden Knowledge.

It's no coincidence that the Cold War was the golden age of spying – the peak of the second-oldest profession, the diggers in the dark, the seekers after unclean knowledge and secret wisdom. Prior to 1939, spying of the international kind rather than the sordid domestic variety (let us pass swiftly over the tawdry Stasi archives of sealed glass jars full of worn underwear, kept as scent cues for the police dogs) was a small scale, largely amateurish concern. With the outbreak of the Second World War, it mushroomed. Faced with employment vacancies, the first response of a growing organization is to recruit close to home. Just like any 1990s dot-com start-up, growing as the founders haul in all their friends and anyone they know who has the right skill set, the 1940s espionage agencies were a boom town into which a well-connected clubbable London playboy would inevitably be sucked – and, moreover, one where he might try his hand and succeed, to everyone's surprise. (In the 1990s he'd end up in marketing, with stock options up to here. *Sic transit gloria techie.*)

When the Second World War gave way to the Doomwatch days and Strangelove nights of the Cold War, it entered a period in which the same clubbable fellow might find himself working in a mature organization, vastly larger and more professional than the half-assed amateurism of the early days. The CIA was born in the shadow of the wartime OSS, and grew into the emblematic Company (traders in secrets, overthrowers of governments), locked in titanic struggle with that other superpowered rival, the KGB (and their less well-known fellows in the GRU).

The age of the traditional sneak-spies with their Minox cameras gave way to the era of the bugging device. With the 1960s came a new emphasis on supplementing human intelligence (HUMINT) with intelligence from electronic sources (ELINT). New agencies – the NSA in the United States, GCHQ in the UK – expanded as the field of "spyless spying" went mainstream, aided by the explosion in computing power made possible by integrated circuits and, later, the microprocessor. As telephony, television, telex, and other technologies began to come online, a torrent of data poured through the wires, a deluge that threatened to drown the agencies in useless noise. Or was it the whispering on the deep-ocean cables? Maybe the chatter served to conceal and disguise the quiet whispering of the hidden oracles, dribbling out strange new concepts that warped the vulnerable primate minds to serve their inscrutable goals. The source of the incredible new technologies that drove the advances of the mid-twentieth century was, perhaps, the whispering of an alien farmer in the ears of his herd . . .

Times change, and the golden age of spying is over. We've delivered the harvest of fear that the secret masters desired, or maybe they've simply lost interest in us for the time being. Time will tell. For now, be content that it's all over: the Cold War was a time of strangely rapid technological progress, but also of claustrophobic fear of destruction at three minutes' notice, of the thermonuclear stars coming and bringing madness and death in their wake. Retreat into your soap-bubble universe, little primate, and give thanks.

From the perspective of the twenty-first century, Bond was a poor archetype for a hero; certainly he couldn't save us from the gibbering horrors of the Cold War, but only cast a shadow beneath their unblinking ground-zero glare. But we found salvation in the end, in the most unlikely place of all: if you turn on the TV you're likely to see one of old Ernst's protégés being held up for praise as an object of emulation. President of Italy, captain of industry or chief executive of Enron – SPECTRE won and it's their world that we live in, the world of the lesser evil.

Charles Stross
Edinburgh, UK
February 2006

GLOSSARY OF ABBREVIATIONS, ACRONYMS, AND ORGANIZATIONS

Abwehr   Foreign Bureau/Defense of the Armed Forces High Command: the German intelligence organization founded in 1921; after WWII, in order to appease the Allies, the organization supposedly focused only on defense, i.e. counterespionage [Germany]

AIVD   General Intelligence and Security Office: the Dutch domestic counterespionage agency [Netherlands]

APT(N)   Atlantic Patrol Task (North): standing Royal Navy patrol in the Caribbean and North Atlantic area [UK]

Black   (Pertaining to an organization or project) Secret and off the record, except to governmental intelligence oversight bodies [All]

Black Chamber   American cryptanalysis agency, officially disbanded in 1929; predecessor to the NSA; nickname for the contemporary

	superblack agency dealing with occult intelligence [US]
CESG	Communications Electronics Security Group: a division within GCHQ [UK]
CIA	Central Intelligence Agency; also known as The Company [US]
The Company	Nickname: see CIA [US]
COBRA	Cabinet Briefing Office Room "A": where the Civil Contingencies Committee meets and is thus often referred to as COBRA; able to invoke Section Two powers under the Civil Contingencies Act (aka Martial Law) [UK]
COTS	Commercial, Off The Shelf: computer kit; a procurement term [US/UK]
DERA	Defense Evaluation and Research Agency, privatized as QinetiQ [UK]
FSB	Federal Security Service, formerly known as KGB [Russia]
Faust Force	Nickname: see GSA [Germany]
GCHQ	Government Communications HQ (UK equivalent of NSA) [UK]
GMDI	Hughes Global Marine Development, Inc. [US]
GRU	Russian Military Intelligence; an intense rivalry existed between the GRU and KGB [Russia]
GSA	Geheime Sicherheit Abteilung: contemporary German domestic occult intelligence agency [Germany]
HMG	Her Majesty's Government [UK]
HUMINT	Human Intelligence: intelligence gathered from human (as opposed to electronic) sources [All]

INTERPOL	International Criminal Police Organization: created in 1923 to assist international criminal police cooperation [All]
KGB	Committee for State Security, principal Soviet intelligence agency; renamed FSB in 1991 after disintegration of the Soviet Union [USSR]
The Laundry	Nickname of the former Department Q of the SOE, dealing with occult intelligence; spun off as a separate black organization in 1945, no publicly known name [UK]
MI5	(originally Military Intelligence Section 5) Security Service, also known as SS, responsible for internal security [UK]
MI6	(originally Military Intelligence Section 6) Secret Intelligence Service, also known as SIS, responsible for external security [UK]
MOD	Ministry of Defense [UK]
NSA	National Security Agency (US equivalent of GCHQ) [US]
Number Ten	10 Downing Street, London: the historic office and home of the British Prime Minister [UK]
ONI	Office of Naval Intelligence [US]
OSS	Office of Strategic Services (US equivalent of SOE), disbanded in 1945, remodeled as CIA [US]
Politburo	Political Bureau: the executive organization for the Communist Party [USSR]
Q Division	Division within The Laundry associated with R&D [UK]
QinetiQ	See DERA [UK]
SAS	Special Air Service: British Army Special Forces [UK]

SBS	Special Boat Service: Royal Marines Special Forces [UK]
SIS	See MI6 [UK]
SOE	Special Operations Executive (UK equivalent of OSS), officially disbanded in 1945; see also The Laundry [UK]
Superblack	(Pertaining to a black organization or black project) Secret and off the record to all, including governmental intelligence oversight bodies [All]
Territorial SAS	Territorial Army, British equivalent of the US National Guard. Territorial SAS, the part-time weekend soldier arm of the SAS, mostly staffed by veterans [UK]
TLA	Three Letter Acronym [All]
Two-One SAS	21 Special Air Service Regiment; also known as Artists' Rifles [UK]

extras

www.orbitbooks.net

extras

about the author

Charles Stross is a full-time science fiction writer and resident of Edinburgh, Scotland. The author of six Hugo-nominated novels and winner of the 2005 and 2010 Hugo awards for best novella ("The Concrete Jungle" and "Palimpsest"), Stross's works have been translated into over twelve languages.

Like many writers, Stross has had a variety of careers, occupations and job-shaped-catastrophes in the past, from pharmacist (he quit after the second police stake-out) to first code monkey on the team of a successful dot-com startup (with brilliant timing he tried to change employer just as the bubble burst). Along the way he collected degrees in Pharmacy and Computer Science, making him the world's first officially qualified cyberpunk writer (just as cyberpunk died).

He's currently working on a variety of novels, including the fifth volume of the Laundry Files, *The Rhesus Chart*. In 2013 he will be Creative in Residence at the UK-wide Centre for Creativity, Regulation, Enterprise and Technology, researching the business models and regulation of industries such as music, film, TV, computer games and publishing.

Find out more about Charles Stross and other Orbit authors by registering for the free monthly newsletter at www.orbitbooks.net.

if you enjoyed
THE JENNIFER MORGUE

look out for

BITTER SEEDS

by

Ian Tregillis

PROLOGUE

23 October 1920
11 kilometers southwest of Weimar, Germany

Murder on the wind: crows and ravens wheeled beneath a heavy sky, like spots of ink splashed across a leaden canvas. They soared over leafless forests, crumbling villages, abandoned fields of barleycorn and wheat. The fields had gone to seed; village chimneys stood dormant and cold. There would be no waste here, no food free for the taking.

And so the ravens moved on.

For years they had watched armies surge across the continent with the ebb and flow of war, waltzing to the music of empire. They had dined on the detritus of warfare, feasted on the warriors themselves. But now the dance was over, the trenches empty, the bones picked clean.

And so the ravens moved on.

They rode a wind redolent of wet leaves and the promise of a cleansing frost. There had been a time when the winds had smelled of bitter almonds and other scents engineered for a different kind of cleansing. Like an illness, the taint of war extended far from the battlefields where those toxic winds had blown.

And so the ravens moved on.

Far below, a spot of motion and color became a beacon on the still and muted landscape. A strawberry roan strained at the harness of a hay wagon. Hay meant farmers; farmers meant food. The ravens spiraled down for a closer look at this wagon and its driver.

The driver tapped the mare with the tip of his whip. She snorted, exhaling great gouts of steam as the wagon wheels squelched through the butterscotch mud of a rutted farm track. The driver's breath steamed, too, in the late afternoon chill as he rubbed his hands together. He shivered. So did the children nestled in the hay behind him. Autumn had descended upon Europe with cold-hearted glee in this first full year after the Great War, threatening still leaner times ahead.

He craned his neck to glance at the children. It would do nobody any good if they succumbed to the cold before he delivered them to the orphanage.

Every bump in the road set the smallest child to coughing. The towheaded boy of five or six years had dull eyes and sunken cheeks that spoke of hunger in the belly, and a wheeze that spoke of dampness in the lungs. He shivered, hacking himself raw each time the wagon thumped over a root or stone. Tufts of hay fluttered down from where he had stuffed his threadbare woolen shirt and trousers for warmth.

The other two children clung to each other under a pile of hay, their bones distinct under hunger-taut skin. But the gypsy blood of some distant relation had infused the siblings with a hint of olive coloring that fended off the pallor that had claimed the sickly boy. The older of the pair, a gangly boy of six or seven, wrapped his arms around his sister, trying vainly to protect her from the chill. The sloe-eyed girl hardly noticed, her dark gaze never wavering from the coughing boy.

The driver turned his attention back to the road. He'd made this journey several times, and the orphans he ferried were much the same from one trip to the next. Quiet. Frightened. Sometimes they wept. But there was something different about the gypsy girl. He shivered again.

The road wove through a dark forest of oak and ash. Acorns crunched beneath the wagon wheels. Gnarled trees grasped at the sky. The boughs creaked in the wind, as though commenting upon the passage of the wagon in some ancient, inhuman language.

The driver nudged his mare into a sharp turn at a crossroads. Soon the trees thinned out and the road skirted the edge of a wide clearing. A whitewashed three-story house and a cluster of smaller buildings on the far side of the clearing suggested the country estate of a wealthy family, or perhaps a prosperous farm untouched by war. Once upon a time, the scions of a moneyed clan had indeed taken their holidays here, but times had changed, and now this place was neither estate nor farm.

A sign suspended on two tall flagpoles arced over the crushed-gravel lane that veered for the house. In precise Gothic lettering painted upon rough-hewn birch wood, it declared that these were the grounds of the Children's Home for Human Enlightenment.

The sign neither mentioned hope nor counseled its abandonment. But in the driver's opinion, it should have.

Months had passed since the farm was given a new life, but the purpose of this place was unclear. Tales told of a flickering electric-blue glow in the windows at night, the pervasive whiff of ozone, muffled screams, and always – always – the loamy shit-smell of freshly turned soil. But the countless rumors did agree on one thing: Herr Doktor von Westarp paid well for healthy children.

And that was enough for the driver in these lean gray years that came tumbling from the Armistice. He had children of his own to feed at home, but the war had produced a bounty of parentless ragamuffins willing to trust anybody who promised a warm meal.

A field came into view behind the house. Row upon row of earthen mounds dotted it, tiny piles of black dirt not much larger than a sack of grain. Off in the distance a tall man in overalls heaped soil upon a new mound. Influenza, it was claimed, had ravaged the foundling home.

Ravens lined the eaves of every building, watching the workman, with inky black eyes. A few settled on the ground nearby. They picked at a mound, tugging at something under the dirt, until the workman chased them off.

The wagon creaked to a halt not far from the house. The mare snorted. The driver climbed down. He lifted the children and set them on their feet as a short balding man emerged from the house. He wore a gentleman's tweeds under the long white coat of a tradesman, wire-rimmed spectacles, and a precisely groomed mustache.

'*Herr Doktor,*' said the driver.

'*Ja,*' said the well-dressed man. He pulled a cream-colored handkerchief from a coat pocket. It turned the color of rust as he wiped his hands clean. He nodded at the children. 'What have you brought me this time?'

'You're still paying, yes?'

The doctor said nothing. He pulled the girl's arms, testing her muscle tone and the resilience of her skin tissues. Unceremoniously and without warning he yanked up her dirt-crusted frock to cup his hand between her legs. Her brother he grabbed roughly by the jaw, pulling his mouth open to peer inside. The youngsters' heads received the closest scrutiny. The doctor traced every contour of their skulls, muttering to himself as he did so.

Finally he looked up at the driver, still prodding and pulling at the new arrivals. 'They look thin. Hungry.'

'Of course they're hungry. But they're healthy. That's what you want, isn't it?'

The adults haggled. The driver saw the girl step behind the doctor to give the towheaded boy a quick shove. He stumbled in the mud. The impact unleashed another volley of coughs and spasms. He rested on all fours, spittle trailing from his lips.

The doctor broke off in midsentence, his head snapping around to watch the boy. 'What is this? That boy is ill. Look! He's weak.'

'It's the weather,' the driver mumbled. 'Makes everyone cough.'

'I'll pay you for the other two, but not this one,' said the doctor. 'I'm not wasting my time on him.' He waved the workman over from the field. The tall man joined the adults and children with long loping strides.

'This one is too ill,' said the doctor. 'Take him.'

The workman put his hand on the sickly child's shoulder and led him away. They disappeared behind a shed.

Money changed hands. The driver checked his horse and wagon for the return trip, eager to be away, but he kept one eye on the girl.

'Come,' said the doctor, beckoning once to the siblings with a hooked finger. He turned for the house. The older boy followed.

His sister stayed behind, her eyes fixed on where the workman and sick boy had disappeared.

Clang. A sharp noise rang out from behind the shed, like the blade of a shovel hitting something hard, followed by the softer *bump-slump* as of a grain sack dropping into soft earth. A storm of black wings slapped the air as a flock of ravens took for the sky.

The gypsy girl hurried to regain her brother. The corner of her mouth twisted up in a private little smile as she took his hand.

The driver thought about that smile all the way home.

Fewer mouths meant more food to go around.

23 October 1920
St. Pancras, London, England

The promise of a cleansing frost extended west, across the Channel, where the ravens of Albion felt it keenly. They knew, with the craftiness of their kind, that the easiest path to food was to steal it from others. So they circled over the city, content to leave the hard work to the scavengers below, animal and human alike.

A group of children moved through the shadows and alleys with direction and purpose, led by a boy in a blue mackintosh. The ravens followed. From their high perches along the eaves of the surrounding houses, they watched the boy in blue lead his companions to the low brick wall around a winter garden. They watched the children shimmy over the wall. And they watched the gardener watching the children through the drapes of a second-story window.

*

His name was John Stephenson, and as a captain in the nascent Royal Flying Corps, he had spent the first several years of the Great War flying over enemy territory with a camera mounted beneath his Bristol F2A. That ended with a burst of Austrian anti-aircraft fire. He crashed in No-Man's Land. After a long, agonizing ride in a horse-drawn ambulance, he awoke in a Red Cross field hospital, mostly intact but minus his left arm.

He'd disregarded the injury and served the Crown by staying with the Corps. Analyzing photographs required eyes and brains, not arms. By war's end, he'd been coordinating the surveillance balloons and reconnaissance flights.

He'd spent years poring over blurry photographs with a jeweler's loupe, studying bird's-eye views of trenches, troop movements, and gun emplacements. But now he watched from above while a half dozen hooligans uprooted the winter rye. He would have flown downstairs and knocked their skulls together, but for the boy in the blue mackintosh. He couldn't have been more than ten years old, but there he was, excoriating the others to respect Stephenson's property even as they ransacked his garden.

Odd little duckling, that one.

This wasn't vandalism at work. It was hunger. But the rye was little more than a ground cover for keeping out winter-hardy weeds. And the beets and carrots hadn't been in the ground long. The scavenging turned ugly.

A girl rooting through the deepest corner of the garden discovered a tomato excluded from the autumn crop because it had fallen and bruised. She beamed at the shriveled half-white mass. The largest boy in the group, a little monster with beady pig-eyes, grabbed her arm with both hands.

'Give it,' he said, wrenching her skin as though wringing out a towel.

She cried out, but didn't let go of her treasure. The other children watched, transfixed in the midst of looting.

'Give it,' repeated the bully. The girl whimpered.

The boy in blue stepped forward. 'Sod off,' he said. 'Let her go.'

'Make me.'

The boy wasn't small, per se, but the bully was much larger. If they tussled, the outcome was inevitable.

The others watched with silent anticipation. The girl cried. Ravens called for blood.

'Fine.' The boy rummaged in the soil along the wall behind a row of winter rye. Several moments passed. 'Here,' he said, regaining his feet. One hand he kept behind his back, but with the other he offered another tomato left over from the autumn crop. It was little more than a bag of mush inside a tough papery skin. Probably a worthy find by the standards of these children. 'You can have this one if you let her alone.'

The bully held out one hand, but didn't release the sniffling girl. A reddish wheal circled her forearm where he'd twisted the flesh. He wiggled his fingers. 'Give it.'

'All right,' said the smaller boy. Then he lobbed the food high overhead.

The bully pushed the girl away and craned his head back, intent on catching his prize.

The first stone caught him in the throat. The second thunked against his ear as he sprawled backwards. He was down and crying before the tomato splattered in the dirt.

The smaller boy had excellent aim. He'd ended the fight before it began.

Bloody hell.

Stephenson expected the thrower to jump the bully, to press the advantage. He'd seen it in the war, the way months of hard living could alloy hunger with fear and anger, making natural the most beastly behavior. But instead the boy turned his back on the bully to check on the girl. The matter, in his mind, was settled.

Not so for the bully. Lying in the dirt, face streaked with tears and snot, he watched the thrower with something shapeless and dark churning in his eyes.

Stephenson had seen this before, too. Rage looked the same in any soul, old or young. He left the window and ran downstairs before his garden became an exhibition hall. The bully had gained his feet when Stephenson opened the door.

One of the children yelled, 'Leg it!'

The children swarmed the low brick wall where they'd entered. Some needed a boost to get over it, including the girl. The boy who had felled the bully stayed behind, pushing the stragglers atop the wall.

Seeing this reinforced Stephenson's initial reaction. There was something special about this boy. He was shrewd, with a profound sense of honor, and a vicious fighter, too. With proper tutelage . . .

Stephenson called out. 'Wait! Not so fast.'

The boy turned. He watched Stephenson approach with an air of bored disinterest. He'd been caught and didn't pretend otherwise.

'What's your name, lad?'

The boy's gaze flickered between Stephenson's eyes and the empty sleeve pinned to his shoulder.

'I'm Stephenson. Captain, in point of fact.' The wind tossed Stephenson's sleeve, waving it like a flag.

The boy considered this. He stuck his chin out, saying, 'Raybould Marsh, sir.'

'You're quite a clever lad, aren't you, Master Marsh?'

'That's what my mum says, sir.'

Stephenson didn't bother to ask after the father. Another casualty of Britain's lost generation, he gauged.

'And why aren't you in school right now?'

Many children had abandoned school during the war, and after, to help support families bereft of fathers and older brothers. The boy wasn't working, yet he wasn't exactly a hooligan, either. And he had a home, by the sound of it, which was likely more than some of his cohorts had.

The boy shrugged. His body language said, *Don't much care for school.* His mouth said, 'What will you do to me?'

'Are you hungry? Getting enough to eat at home?'

The boy shook his head, then nodded.

'What's your mum do?'

'Seamstress.'

'She works hard, I gather.'

The boy nodded again.

'To address your question: Your friends have visited extensive damage upon my plantings, so I'm pressing you into service. Know anything about gardening?'

'No.'

'Might have known not to expect much from my winter garden if you had, eh?'

The boy said nothing.

'Very well, then. Starting tomorrow, you'll get a bob for each day spent replanting. Which you will take home to your hard-working mother.'

'Yes, sir.' The boy sounded glum, but his eyes gleamed.

'We'll have to do something about your attitude toward education, as well.'

'That's what my mum says, sir.'

Stephenson shooed away the ravens picking at the spilled food. They screeched to each other as they rode a cold wind, shadows upon a blackening sky.

23 October 1920
Bestwood-on-Trent, Nottinghamshire, England

Rooks, crows, jackdaws, and ravens scoured the island from south to north on their search for food. And, in the manner of their continental cousins, they were ever-present.

Except for one glade deep in the Midlands, at the heart of the ancestral holdings of the jarls of Æthelred. In some distant epoch, the skin of the world here had peeled back to reveal the great granite bones of the earth, from which spat forth a hot spring: water touched with fire and stone. No ravens had ventured there since before the Norsemen had arrived to cleave the island with their Danelaw.

Time passed. Generations of men came and went, lived and died around the spring. The jarls became earls, then dukes. The Norsemen became Normen, then Britons. They fought Saxons; they fought Saracens; they fought the Kaiser. But the land outlived them all with elemental constancy.

Throughout the centuries, blackbirds shunned the glade and its phantoms. But the great manor downstream of the spring evoked no such reservations. And so they perched on the spires of Bestwood, watching and listening.

'Hell and damnation! Where is that boy?'

Malcolm, the steward of Bestwood, hurried to catch up to the twelfth Duke of Aelred as he banged through the house. Servants fled the stomp of the duke's boots like starlings fleeing a falcon's cry.

The kitchen staff jumped to attention when the duke entered with his majordomo.

'Has William been here?'

Heads shook all around.

'Are you certain? My grandson hasn't been here?'

Mrs. Toomre, Bestwood's head cook, was a whip-thin woman with ashen hair. She stepped forward and curtsied.

'Yes, Your Grace.'

The duke's gaze made a slow tour of the kitchen. A heavy silence fell over the room while veins throbbed at the corners of his jaw, the high-water mark of his anger. He turned on his heels and marched out. Malcolm released the breath he'd been holding. He was determined to prevent madness from claiming another Beauclerk.

'Well? Off you go. Help His Grace.' Mrs. Toomre waved off the rest of her staff. 'Scoot.'

When the room had cleared and the others were out of earshot, she hoisted up the dumbwaiter. She worked slowly so that the pulleys didn't creak. When William's dome of coppery-red hair dawned over the transom, she leaned over and hefted him out with arms made strong by decades of manual labor. The boy was tall for an eight-year-old, taller even than his older brother.

'There you are. None the worse for wear, I hope.' She pulled a peppermint stick from a pocket in her apron. He snatched it.

Malcolm bowed ever so slightly. 'Master William. Still enjoying our game, I trust?'

The boy nodded, smiling around his treat. He smelled like parsnips and old beef tallow from hiding in the dumbwaiter all afternoon.

Mrs. Toomre pulled the steward into a corner. 'We can't keep this up forever,' she whispered. She wrung her hands on her apron, adding, 'What if the duke caught us?'

'We needn't do so forever. Just until dark. His Grace will have to postpone then.'

'But what do we do tomorrow?'

'Tomorrow we prepare a poultice of hobnailed liver for His Grace's hangover, and begin again.'

Mrs. Toomre frowned. But just then the stomping resumed, and with renewed vigor. She pushed William toward Mr. Malcolm. 'Quick!'

He took the boy's hand and pulled him through the larder. Gravel crunched underfoot as they scooted out of the house through the deliverymen's door, headed for the stable, trailing white clouds of breath in the cool air. Malcolm had pressed most of the household staff into aiding the search for William, so the stable was empty. The duke kept his horses here as well as his motor car. The converted stable reeked of petrol and manure.

Mr. Malcolm opened a cabinet. 'In here, young master.'

William, giggling, stepped inside the cabinet as Mr. Malcolm held it open. He wrapped himself in the leather overcoat his grandfather wore when motoring.

'Quiet as a mouse,' the older man whispered, 'as the duke creeps around the house. Isn't that right?'

The child nodded, still giggling. Malcolm felt relieved to see him still enjoying the game. Hiding the boy would become much harder if he were frightened.

'Remember how we play this game?'

'Quiet and still, all the same,' said the boy.

'Good lad.' Malcolm tweaked William's nose with the pad of his thumb and shut the cabinet. A sliver of light shone on the boy's face. The cabinet doors didn't join together properly. 'I'll return to fetch you soon.'

The duke, William's grandfather, had gone on many long expeditions about the grounds with his own son over the years. Grouse hunting, he'd claimed, though he seldom took a gun. The only thing Mr. Malcolm knew for certain was that they'd spent much time in the glade upstream from the house. The same glade where the staff refused to venture, citing visions and noises. Years after the duke's heir – William's father – had produced two sons of his own, he'd taken to spending time in the glade alone. He returned to the manor at all hours, wild-eyed and unkempt, mumbling hoarsely of blood and prices unpaid. This lasted until he went to France and died fighting the Hun.

The duke's grandsons moved to Bestwood soon after. They were too young to remember their father very well, so the move was uneventful. Aubrey, the older son and heir apparent, received the grooming expected of a Peer of the Realm. The duke showed little interest in his younger grandson. And it had stayed that way for several years.

Until two days previously, when he had asked Malcolm to find unting clothes that might fit William. Malcolm didn't know what happened in the glade, or what the duke did there. But he felt honor-bound to protect William from it.

Malcolm left William standing in the cabinet only to find the duke standing in the far doorway, blocking his egress. His Grace had seen everything.

He glared at Malcolm. The majordomo resisted the urge to squirm under the force of that gaze. The silence stretched between them. The duke approached until the two men stood nearly nose to nose.

'Mr. Malcolm,' he said. 'Tell the staff to return to their duties. Then fetch a coat for the boy and retrieve the carpetbag from my study.' His breath, sour with juniper berries, brushed across Malcolm's face. It stung the eyes, made him squint.

Malcolm had no recourse but to do as he was told. The duke had flushed out his grandson by the time he returned bearing a thick dun-colored pullover for William and the duke's paisley carpetbag. Malcolm made brief eye contact with William before taking his leave of the duke.

'I'm sorry,' he mouthed.

William's grandfather took him by the hand. The ridges of the fine white scars arrayed across his palm tickled the soft skin on the back of William's hand.

'Come,' he said. 'It's time you saw the estate.'

'I've already seen the grounds, Papa.'

The old man cuffed the boy on the ear hard enough to make his eyes water. 'No, you haven't.'

They walked around the house, to the brook that gurgled through the gardens. They followed it upstream, crashing through the occasional thicket. Eventually the crenellations and spires of Bestwood disappeared behind a row of hillocks crowned with proud stands of yew and English oak. They traced the brook to a cleft within a lichen-scarred boulder in a small clearing.

Though hemmed about by trees on every side, the glade was quiet and free of birdsong. The screeches and caws of the large black birds that crisscrossed the sky over the estate barely echoed in the distance. William hadn't paid the birds any heed, but now their absence felt strange.

Several bundles of kindling had been piled alongside the boulder. From within the carpetbag the duke produced a canister of matches and a folding pocketknife with a handle fashioned from a segment of deer antler. He built a fire and motioned William to his side.

'Show me your hand, boy.'

William did. His grandfather took it in a solid grip, pulled the boy's arm straight, and sliced William's palm with his pocketknife. William screamed and tried to pull away, but his grandfather didn't release him until the blood trickled down William's wrist to stain the cuff of his pullover. The old man nodded in satisfaction as the hot tickle pulsed along William's hand and dripped to the earth.

William scooted backwards, afraid of what his grandfather might do next. He wanted to go home, back to Mr. Malcolm and Mrs. Toomre, but he was lost and couldn't see through his tears.

His grandfather spoke again. But now he spoke a language that William couldn't understand, more wails and gurgles than words. Inhuman noises from a human vessel.

It lulled the boy into an uneasy stupor, like a fever dream. The fire's warmth dried the tears on his face. A shadow fell across the glade; the world tipped sideways.

And then the fire spoke.